SUPER!

SUPER!

Jennifer Chen

INSOMNIAC PRESS

Library and Archives Canada Cataloguing in Publication

Chen, Jennifer, 1989-, author
Super / Jennifer Chen.

Issued in print and electronic formats.
ISBN 978-1-55483-205-7 (softcover).--ISBN 978-1-55483-209-5 (PDF)

I. Title.

PS8605.H4463S87 2018   C813'.6   C2018-901099-1
                                                C2018-901100-9

The publisher gratefully acknowledges the support of the Canada Council for the
Arts and the Ontario Arts Council.

Printed and bound in Canada
Insomniac Press
520 Princess Avenue, London, Ontario, Canada, N6B 2B8
www.insomniacpress.com

THE CANADA COUNCIL | LE CONSEIL DES ARTS
FOR THE ARTS | DU CANADA
SINCE 1957 | DEPUIS 1957

ONTARIO ARTS COUNCIL
CONSEIL DES ARTS DE L'ONTARIO

For everyone who has ever asked
when they will get to read my book,
thereby subtly
encouraging me to finish it.

Acknowledgements

No person is an island unto themselves, and likewise, no book is the product of just its author. Although my name appears on its cover, Super! is a manifestation of effort by dozens of unseen minds. So, let me take some valuable space to thank the people behind the scenes.

First, I must thank the twist of fate that allowed me to land in the only ever Writer's Craft class hosted by my high school. It was in this classroom that I realized my obsession with creating imaginary worlds and journeys was a valid skill, that it could be honed, and that it could be turned into a lifelong vocation. Without this class, I suspect I would not have pursued writing with the same vigour that ultimately resulted in *Super!*.

Second, many thanks go out to my classmates and professors at UBC for their warm encouragement, harsh critiques, and steadfast advice. Without them, this book would just have been an unpolished mess of scenes at the bottom of my drafts folder. Extra special thanks go out to Maggie de Vries for her insight through the early drafts of Super!, and my editor, Gillian Rodgerson, for flushing out every inconsistency and error that dared show its face.

Third, thank you to my publisher, Insomniac Press, for taking me on and putting it all together, and shout out to Doris, my self-appointed agent, whose excitement over the story helped bring it to the eyes of those who could release it to the world.

Finally, I must mention my friends, who, despite enduring hundreds of pages of rough fiction and hours of plot-or-character-related babble, have somehow managed to always show enthusiasm for my writing. You know who you are.

Table of Contents

Prologue

Tuesday, December 7, 1935.
London, England

The doctors were puzzled. So were the researchers. So were the paranormal investigators. Reporters crowded the room, elbows bumping, fingers wrapped around boxy cameras with silver flash discs. They, too, were puzzled. Even the parents were hushed. All eyes were on the girl.

She was doing it again. She had done it twice before, once while eating dinner and again while skipping to school with her two best friends. If it had only happened once, they could have dismissed it as an accident, but now that it had happened twice, there was no ignoring it. She was shipped to Great Ormond Street Hospital for examination. No one knew what to do with the girl, so they merely watched. They waited for her to make the first move.

The girl's name was Frances E. Shaw, and she was ten years old. She had curly brown hair the colour of fawn's coat, and her cheeks were like rosy peach halves. Now, she was asleep, clutching a worn bunny toy to her chest. Dressed in a lacy white dress, complete with a periwinkle ribbon, she looked like an angel.

She floated exactly two feet off her bed.

It was a *phenomenon*.

A flashbulb went off.

The headline the next day contained five bold question marks.

Part 1

Chapter 1

Attack

Saturday, October 7, 2017
Toronto, Canada

Read About It, our middle school newspaper, lists the Ice Cream Emporium as one of the top ten coolest after-school hangouts. It has cushioned booths, creamy blue-pink-white swirls on the floor and walls, and fifty-four flavours of ice cream that can be mixed and matched any way we want. The Emporium has been our favourite hangout since we found out about it in grade three. Ling Wu, Nuha Bahar, and I, Beata Bell, hang out there at least once a week and do homework assignments. If we are lucky, like we are today, Gweneira Kendricks, my oldest friend, joins us and entertains us with her vivid stories, which makes the afternoon even better.

"And with Frances E. Shaw came the dawn of a new era. The era of Supers. The world would never be the same again." Gwen finishes with a curl of her lips. She leans back into her seat and takes a long sip of her ice cream float. She is dressed in a loose hoodie today, her thick blonde hair wrapped in a bun under a baseball cap. Even in casual wear, she radiates the grace and elegance of a movie star. In the afternoon light, she almost glows. "So, what do you think?"

Ling speaks first. "Excellent execution!" she declares, clapping her hands against the table. Her mango-coconut sundae sits forgotten. "You told that like a real pro. Very dramatic!"

Gwen smiles. "That's high praise coming from you," she says, catching my eye and giving me a quick wink. I can't help but grin back.

Usually, it's all business at the Emporium, getting homework and assignments done. We have a system: Ling handles English, Nuha manages science, and I deal with my best subject, math. If we get done early, we work on side projects. Nuha and I are trying our hand at creating apps, and Ling has dibs on beta tester. But Gwen's presence changes everything. She's two years our senior, and tells a mean story. We have been at the Emporium for nearly two hours, and my algebra sheets still sit untouched. There's no way we'll get to our programming at this pace.

Ling leans forward. Her earrings glint. A pair of big sunglasses sits on her head. Her black jeans match her black tank top, which is accentuated by a honey-coloured silk scarf. "See, that's how you tell the story of your ancestors," she says, with a pointed look at me.

"I'm sorry I'm not as silver-tongued as either of you," I reply, feeling a slight heat creep up my cheeks. "Mom never really talks about great-grandma, so I don't hear much about her. I didn't even know that was how her powers awoke!"

Gwen laughs. Ling rolls her eyes.

"If *I* were the great-granddaughter of the world's first Super, I would tell the story every day," Ling says with a sigh. She leans back. "Oh, to be so renowned."

"We'd never hear the end of it," pipes Nuha. She's the smallest member of our group, and almost the opposite of Ling. Her hair is long, thick, and roped in a braid. She wears a tie-dyed T-shirt and dusty capris. Her only accessory is her round glasses. She sits like she's trying not to take up space. "Probably with unrealistic embellishments too."

"A story so grand needs no embellishment," declares Ling dramatically. "It embellishes itself!"

"That makes no sense!"

"Now, now," says Gwen. "Let's be nice—"

Something buzzes, jolting us all into silence. Gwen closes her mouth midsentence, and a tiny frown appears on her brow. Ling, Nuha, and I blink at her. Gwen rolls up a sleeve, exposing a small pager embedded in her bracelet, where a small orange light flashes. The laid-back atmosphere suddenly dissipates. Without skipping a beat, Gwen rises from the table.

"Excuse me, ladies," she says. Even though her voice is light, I watch her face slip into a professional mask. Her eyes go sharp and serious, and though her movements stay fluid, there's a looseness in them that reminds me of a snake about to strike. "This is important."

We watch Gwen retreat outside to take her call, head bent to speak into her bracelet. I sip my kiwi soda and stare out the window. Gwen holds her wrist to her ear and strides around the corner, out of sight. The sky is blue and there isn't a single person out, not even in the park across the street. Gwen's always on call, even on her days off. I let the bubbles of my soda tickle my tongue and try to swallow my nerves. If Gwen is getting called, it means a mission, and if she's the one they're calling, the incident must be close by. My stomach does a flip-flop. In my mind's eye, I imagine fires. Destruction. Police lights spinning. Just a few months ago, Gwen was called away, and the next thing anyone knew, the city was under attack by a giant robot. *A Gripping Battle between Order and Chaos*, the newspapers declared with glee. We were in lockdown, unable to leave our basements for a day and a night, as the authorities dealt with the threat.

"I have a bad feeling about this," I say, suddenly nervous.

"Really?" Ling is suddenly interested. Her face lights up with curiosity. "Like a regular bad feeling, or a *Bad Feeling*?"

Her voice is conspiratorial. Ling likes to think I have precognition, the power to see the future. She loves superpowers and everything about them. She gets that from her mom, who was the lead investigative reporter for the supernatural division of the local news back in her native China. Every time I get a feeling, she sticks her face close and examines me like a science experiment.

"No, it's just my stomach feels a bit weird." I glance towards the streets. No sign of Gwen. "Maybe we should go home early."

"You always get so nervous when Gwen gets called in for missions," says Ling, stretching easily. "You need to chill. Come on, we're having fun."

I blow bubbles into my soda. I don't feel like having fun anymore. Whenever the city calls someone like Gwen, it means something urgent is going down. It means a threat has popped up and needs to be neutralized *ASAP*. My drink foams until Nuha gently pushes it away. I make a weak grab at it, but she gives me a stern stare and I let it drop. We wait ten minutes, then fifteen. We fidget but don't say much.

"I don't think she's coming back," says Nuha finally.

"Guess not," says Ling with a sigh. For a moment she looks disappointed, but then a lazy smile stretches across her face. "Ah well, it was good while it lasted."

We pack our papers. The daylight has taken on a yellowy tone, a telltale sign it's getting late. The bell atop the door jingles as we leave. I breathe in summer air as we head down the sidewalk. Tall buildings flank the road, interrupted only by a cluster of greenery out in the distance, a lonely city park. Ling is gabbing about the latest tabloid scandals—actors caught kissing in dark corners, with their pants down, getting drunk or high—when I hear whistling. Not the happy sort of whistling but a high, aimed, focussed sound of something very big, falling very fast.

Suddenly, I feel cold all over. I grab the first arm within reach. It's Nuha's. My fingers dig in hard enough to make her yelp. She looks at me in shock. My mouth opens but no sound comes out. Instead, I point at the sky. Ling spins around ahead of us, frowning.

I see it. A dot of darkness. It races towards earth at an astounding speed. It grows from a dot, to a dime, to a sphere the size of a house. The whistling intensifies. I want to cover my ears, but I'm frozen in place. *I'm right*, I think with dread. Whatever incident Gwen needed to attend is near. Very near. Ling must have caught my expression. She peeks over her shoulder, then in one smooth motion, grabs both Nuha and me.

We hit the ground not a moment too soon.

The object smashes into the park, ploughing through trees and heaving dirt into the air. If I weren't already on the ground, the impact would have knocked me over. My teeth clack. Shock ripples through my bones.

I curl into a ball and cover my head. A statue of John A. Macdonald flies through the air like a toy. It clips a building and spins onto the street, knocking over post boxes until it scrapes to a stop by a road sign. I think, *This looks just like a 3-D movie*, with the bouncing debris and the dust cresting everywhere. I think, *This is it. Game over.* Then Ling is on her feet again. Her fingers clamp around my shoulder. She shakes me. My ears ring. Her mouth opens and closes.

Ling leans in and screams, "MOVE!" but she sounds far away.

I look towards the park and see something move in the dust. A monster. No, too stiff. The afternoon light glints off its metal body. A robot.

I yell, "Where's Nu?" but I can't hear myself either. Ling waves behind us. Nuha is on her knees, groping for her glasses. Ling grabs them from the ground and shoves them onto her face. Nuha blinks.

The robotic tentacles flail. The rest of the machine is buried in the dirt. It looks like an upended crab. My stomach tumbles. In the last robot attack, only one unfortunate soul perished, but this time there are no guarantees.

The door to the Emporium bursts open, and the barrel-shaped owner leaps into the street. His cap is lopsided. People stream out of buildings, some fleeing, some filming. Their shoes throw tiny puffs of dust into the air. Ling motions frantically at me and I stumble to my feet. We join the ranks of retreating citizens. The earth vibrates. Behind us, the robot starts to right itself. A great red light sweeps the streets, scanning. I urge my legs to move faster. Ahead, Nu's thick braid bounces along her back.

There is another whistling sound, and I dive to the ground on instinct. I've watched enough action movies to know what an incoming missile sounds like. I see Ling and Nu hit the ground beside me. I cover my neck and head with my hands and wonder if the additional flesh will stop shrapnel from entering my brain. I wonder if I should have been a better person.

In the distance, I see the red-blue flicker of police lights, but they're too far away to do any good. From the corner of my eye, I see the missile streak towards a nearby building. I squeeze my eyes shut and wonder if it'll hurt.

But the explosion never comes.

After a few ragged breaths, I peek upwards. The missile is frozen in mid-air, like a wayward prop. A black jet hovers close by, its sleek body a sword in the sky. The letters L-O-S are printed in bold font on the bottom. My breath snags in my throat. The League of Supers.

The robot screeches.

The jet's hatch opens.

A girl dives from the machine like a falcon. As she passes the missile, she reaches out and brushes it with her bare fingertips. As though in slow motion, I see the missile dissolve. Its shell liquefies. Its wires melt. The remaining parts fall to the ground, harmless as dust, as the liquid metal transforms into a sword in the girl's hand. Without pause, the girl continues to plummet. She spins to an abrupt stop just above the city streets. Her golden locks flare around her. Her emerald-green eyes flash.

Gweneira Kendricks, the Super, no longer wearing her bulky everyday clothes but a sleek, new Supersuit. Lit by the afternoon sun, she strikes a pose, one arm out, hand beckoning, one arm on her hip, legs shoulder width apart. I can't hear the helicopters, but I can see their whirling silhouettes as they struggle to catch up. Her media team. I know they're filming, zooming in from a distance with their hi-def lens, preparing to broadcast the fight to an eager audience. Sponsors' patches blaze on her uniform, bold against the gold-white of her suit.

Gwen spins once more. Her hand brushes against the shaft of a metal telephone pole. The pole dissolves. A dozen swords flare around her, like a fan.

In my daze, I want to shout, *Hi Gwen*, but I know she's too busy to notice me. I watch as she triangulates her swords into a point and dives towards the robot. Her face is as calm and determined as ice water. She seems like a whole other person.

She'll probably get another medal for this.

Chapter 2

Super Testing

Super research has taken great strides in the past few decades. In Frances E. Shaw's time, theories bounced all over the place, and most were false. During World War II, there were dark whispers of human experimentation and alien technology. Some superstitious communities even blamed witchcraft. Luckily, science found an answer: Genetics.

In grade five, I wrote a report on the origin of Supers, a topic that never ceases to fascinate me.

In 1935, an unlikely astronomical event occurred. A comet broke away from the Oort cloud and raced towards the earth. In a freak coincidence—one that debatably saved all of mankind—the moon swung into its path, clipping the massive ball of ice and jarring thousands of pieces from its core. As the main body spun into the oblivion of space, the smaller pieces got caught in the earth's orbit, and slowly descended into the atmosphere, where they burned all colours of the rainbow before dissolving to vapour. Onlookers called it one of the brightest and most beautiful meteor showers on record.

Other than being pleasing to the eye, the pieces held another gift: Radiation. As the debris vaporized, radiation drifted down and penetrated the DNA of people like Frances E. Shaw. In adults, the changes lay dormant, but in children, it was a different story.

That year, as girls and boys approached puberty, reports began flooding in from every continent on earth. Strange occurrences. Impossible powers. *Magic*.

And at the forefront, Frances E. Shaw, the Original Super.

Since then, echoes of the comet reverberate through our population. Some girls and boys approach puberty and, *boom*, gain amazing powers—flight, invisibility, or laser vision. It peaks around fourteen or fifteen for girls, and sixteen or seventeen for boys, and then tapers off in adulthood. Scientists use big words, like *somatotropin* and *endocrine systems* to describe the phenomenon, and labs all over the world still publish hundreds of papers a year on the topic. It's a complex field, involving all sorts of sciences—astronomy, biology, and pedology, just to name a few—but the bottom line is simple: We're growing. Things change. Sometimes explosively.

I got an A on the report.

Of course, not everyone becomes a Super. That's common knowledge. The trait runs in families, but that doesn't mean Super parents always have Super children. For example, even though we both come from Super families, it's Gweneira's face that's currently being projected on our gym wall, not mine.

Today, Gwen is being interviewed by CTV. A gold medal hangs around her shoulders like a pendant. Gwen's bedroom is filled with trophies and ribbons, and keys to various districts of Toronto. She wins so many medals; there are boxes in her basement filled with them. This particular medal's too big, but Gwen makes it work. She looks like a princess with her blue dress and pearly white gloves.

Sir Frederick Banting Public School livestreams her interview as we all watch at assembly. All three hundred students cram into the gymnasium. The teachers stand dewy-eyed beside their classes, except Mr. Uzune, our homeroom teacher, who is nodding off in a corner. I sit cross-legged, sandwiched between Ling and Nuha, our knees overlapping. The air is muggy. I can see dust motes in the beam of the projector.

"This is the third robot octopod appearance in the past few months," says the reporter, eagerly leaning forward in her seat. "Three people killed and several dozen injured. Insurance companies are swamped with claims."

"Yes," replies Gwen with a smooth nod of her head. "If we could have a minute of silence for the poor souls who were injured or killed in the grievous and unjustified attack against our great city, please."

The gym falls silent as students bow their heads. After the attack, my parents took me to the hospital to get checked out. I waited over two hours in the waiting room before a harried doctor gave me a five-minute checkup. I was fine. Only a few nicks and bruises. Nothing serious. But I was lucky. Several people were badly injured, and a few didn't make it. Given that the robot octopod was firing missiles, the city is lucky it didn't lose any more than three lives.

It's all thanks to LOS and its Super children.

"How does it feel to save our city again?" the reporter asks. Her voice echoes. "If not for your quick actions, many more would have undoubtedly been injured. Or worse."

"I am just doing my duty, ma'am," says Gweneira's huge head. She places a hand over her heart. "I am just glad I could stop it before it caused more harm. My heart goes out to the families who lost loved ones in this senseless violence."

She wipes her eyes.

The audience sighs.

"Look at her work that camera," says Ling, with genuine admiration. "Chin up, brave smile, but not wide enough to squish her eyes. Let the medal catch the light. Oh yes, that's perfect! Isn't she wonderful?"

She nudges me and Nuha in the side. We both nod. Yes, she's perfect.

"This is your second medal of honour this year," says the reporter. "How does it feel to receive so many accolades?"

Gweneira's cheeks flush, though she remains composed. "The greatest reward is being useful to the community. It's nice to have my work acknowledged, but this medal really belongs to everyone on my team. I thank everyone for their continued support."

Another collective sigh.

"With the culprits still at large," continues the reporter, "undoubtedly, enemies of the city are watching this broadcast. Do you have anything to say to them?"

Gweneira sighs in a way that conveys both pity and patience. She looks directly into the camera. "It's a free country," she says, calm, "but if you set foot in my city again, I, Gweneira Kendricks, I will put you in a world of pain, as I always have and always will."

There is a moment of silence as her words sink in.

Then she winks.

The gym erupts in applause. Several students raise a giant poster with Gweneira's face on it. Shouts of *we love you* and *bravo* echo through the room. A wave of students stands. I stand alongside and clap until my palms hurt. Gwen is incredible, I tell myself. She's a long-time friend. Maybe even my best friend. I look around at all the adoring faces and press down a swell of jealousy. Yes, I'm proud of her, just like everybody else is. She trains hard, and works hard, and has everything I could ever wish for.

When we return to class after the assembly, a slender woman is standing behind Mr. Uzune. She has the stern expression of a librarian. Her nose is like a bird's beak. My mouth goes dry as the room erupts in excited whispers.

She's an Agent from the League of Supers, or LOS for short. In the brief hubbub after the robot octopod attack, I forgot today was recruitment day. LOS was established in the forties to seek and train Supers. Every year, Sir Frederick Banting Public School, like all other elementary and middle schools, welcomes a team of Agents into its classrooms to seek new talent.

I used to be excited about recruitment day. The first year, I pulled an all-nighter because I was too excited to sleep, but now that I've failed two years straight, I dread it. I take a deep breath as I slide into my chair. Nuha catches my eye and gives me a stern look. *You ok?* I give a small shake of my head and sit on my trembling fingers. I stare at the blank blackboard, hoping to calm the sudden pounding of my heart.

When I get nervous, I like to go over numbers. I'm twelve now. Average girls develop powers at ten. Time is ticking away. I see my mom's face. Her smile, usually patient, now barely conceals worry. At my age, she was already fighting crime, dropping nets on people with her teleportation. I know she wants me to carry on her legacy, to bring pride to our famous lineage. The first year I was tested, she baked a cake to celebrate, expecting me to come back with laser vision, or water manipulation, or super speed, but it never happened. Her disappointment was so intense I could barely look at her for a week afterwards. It was embarrassing. I hear my dad's voice: *Don't worry, sweet pea. You're a late bloomer.* He's always so supportive, which somehow makes it worse. A lump settles in my stomach. I don't want to let them down. I don't want to let myself down either.

Not all children become Supers. Only about one in five kids gets powers, so it's totally normal to fail recruitment, but the trouble is I have it in my blood. Both my parents were Supers. My grandparents were Supers. Worst of all, my great-grandmother was Frances E. Shaw. The Girl Who Floated. Frances Fantastic. The Original Super. The world's most famous, beloved, accomplished, and influential Super. It's rumoured the British military used her name to turn away entire battalions in the Second World War. *Be good, or we'll send in Frances Fantastic.* No one wants to face a girl who can melt tanks with her eyes. Her presence bolstered troop morale. A picture of her on our living room wall shows her posing with the Royal Air Force, a pair of goggles on her head, looking humble and flattered among the grinning men. She made a difference in the world. Ever since I was little, I've wanted to be like her. I don't want to disappoint her spirit.

Already, I can feel eyes on me, some expectant, some full of pity. Whispers bounce around the classroom, none too quiet. Doubts. *Maybe she's not Super at all. How embarrassing would that be? Awkward! Totally embarrassing.* I stare at my desk. Every failed assessment hurts like a stab wound.

Frances, I think, *please let it be this year.* Sometimes, when I'm feeling nervous, I imagine talking to her, even though we never met. I imagine she's perfect, reasonable, and completely proper. Maybe, somewhere, she can hear me.

Mr. Uzune claps for attention. He is pushing thirty, and always wears a long coat, even when it's hot out. He has a small scar along his chin, which is a subject of many rumours— that he fell asleep one day and knocked himself out on a desk, or runs a secret fight club at night. I don't believe any of it. Mr. Uzune is one of the most harmless people I know. He pauses mid-clap to yawn. "Class, pay attention please. Let's give a hearty welcome to Agent Ecru."

Agent Ecru bobs her head in greeting. A few students begin to clap, but she doesn't smile, and the claps die down.

"I'm sure you all know the procedure by now," Mr. Uzune continues. "Agent Ecru will call you over one by one for assessment. In the meantime, I want you to do your work until your name is called. Give her your cooperation, ok?"

I nod mindlessly.

I glance towards Nuha, but she's already engaged with her schoolwork. Ling catches my eye from across the room and gives me a look that's half encouraging, half amused. She's stretched out in her chair, completely relaxed. She doesn't expect to be Super and doesn't want to be. The entire testing process is just a talking point for her, nothing more. No pressure. A happy smile lingers on her face, and for a second, I feel a rush of resentment. Then out of nowhere, she gives me a double thumbs-up. *You got this!*

I bite my lower lip. *What if I don't got this?*

Ling rolls her eyes. *You'll get it.*

I frown. *I'm not sure.*

Ling makes a fist and a determined face that looks a bit constipated. *You got to BELIEVE.*

Agent Ecru motions for the first student, Abathy Algernon, to follow her. I swallow hard, but the lump doesn't go away. I squint at my math, but the numbers mix together. I want to bury my head in my arms and melt into another dimension. You know you have a serious case of nerves if you can't even do what you're good at.

There isn't a rule saying superheroes needed to be beautiful, but they always are anyways.

It's the team, Gwen once said, motioning to her face and body with an elegant sweep of her hands. *They dust your face with HD powder, and spray your hair, and make sure all your makeup is done just right. I just sit and let them do their magic.*

Never mind that she could do actual magic.

Gwen was one of the youngest heroes to get into LOS. The age of qualification is officially twelve, but Gwen's powers—and entertainment value—were not to be denied. She joined at the age of nine. Now, at fourteen, she already has her own trading card and always ranks top three in the *Most Popular Female Supers* polls.

I have known Gwen since forever. Our parents were in LOS together, so technically, we knew each other before we were even born. As babies, Gwen and I sat through play dates and barbeques together. Gwen, with her golden hair and big smile, was like a cherub in the garden. I, with my clumsiness and sensitivity, was more like a finicky ogre.

Gwen got her powers earlier than most. At age eight, she

leapt from the monkey bars and never came down. Levitation. A year later, she flipped a coin into the air and folded it into a metal, origami crane. Metal manipulation. Relatives *aah*ed and looked at me expectantly, but I sat like a lump and never did anything extraordinary. Gwen is a polypower. The rarest of the rare. If one in five of us is a Super, then only one in a hundred Supers is a polypower. That's a zero point zero zero two percent chance. Super rare. But I can't even get one measly power. I'm not anything special.

It's not like I don't try. Every recruitment day, I grind my teeth and concentrate until I feel like my eyeballs are going to pop, but nothing ever happens.

Just relax, Gwen once advised, an elegant hand on my shoulder. *It's like using an arm or a leg. You shouldn't strain.*

But strain I do. I strain until I sweat, but the results are always the same. Goose eggs all across. Zilch. Zero. Nada. No powers whatsoever.

The other kids have a name for my type, the civilian kids of Super parents. They call us *Duds*. All our wiring is in place, but when it's time to blow, we flub instead. Maybe it's a violent comparison. Maybe not. Supers are known for a bit of bang.

It's a gorgeous day outside. The sky is clear. A flock of birds flits through the air. But I don't notice any of it. I only see the back of Agent Ecru's wrinkleless suit as she leads me to the temporary testing station, where all sorts of intimidating contraptions gleam in the sun. My knees jitter so hard I nearly trip half a dozen times. Agent Ecru walks with long, quick strides, like she's trying to catch a bus but considers herself too regal to run. Her face is neutral, but I know she's impatient by the glint in her eye. She motions at an X in the grass. I totter over to it, feeling lightheaded.

"Miss Bell," says Agent Ecru.

"Yes?" My voice comes out high and squeaky.

"Daughter of Tessa and Phil Bell?"

"Yes," I answer quietly. I wait for Agent Ecru to say more, to make mention of my great-grandmother, but she only purses her lips.

"Let's begin with the basics. Have you or have you not experienced anything that could be classified as a superpower?"

"No," I stutter. "I mean, maybe some pre, um, precog—"

"Precognition," says Agent Ecru. A flash of annoyance crosses her face, and I feel a stab of shame. *Breathe*, I remind myself. The Agent reaches into her purse and pulls out a set of cards.

"This will be a simple test," she reassures in a voice that's not reassuring at all. "I'm sure you're familiar with it. You will tell me which card is at the top of the pile. I will then verify the card. You will tell me the subsequent card. We will do this twenty times. Am I clear?"

I mean to say yes, but the small sound that emerges from the back of my throat sounds more like a whimper.

Agent Ecru fixes me with a stern stare. "Begin," she says.

"Eight of hearts!" I blurt.

She lifts the card and looks at it, then puts it away. She motions for me to continue.

"Queen of spades!"

Another look, another wave. Her face betrays nothing. I begin to shake. In the corner of my eye, I see other students with Agents of their own. As I watch, a girl bursts into flames.

Her Agent nods appreciatively. The girl stares at her own hands as though in shock, then begins to laugh and whoop. My mouth drop open.

"Concentrate," snaps Agent Ecru. "Don't allow yourself to get distracted. Next card."

"Seven of—"

The fiery girl extinguishes herself with a quick motion of her hands, but the grass around her is still on fire. Her Agent removes a small aerosol can from his suitcase and snuffs the flames with a thorough spray.

"—of clubs."

The Agent shakes the girl's hand, congratulating her. The girl's smile is so wide it swallows her face.

"Miss Bell!" says Agent Ecru sharply. I snap to attention. My cheeks burn.

"Sorry!" I stare at the cards with intent, determined not to look up again. I reach into my gut. Never in my life have I wanted anything more. Precognition isn't a flashy super-power. I won't be flying beside Gweneira, taking down bad guys, or saving people from burning buildings, but it's better than nothing. "Two of spades! Wait, no. Two of hearts! Wait, do jokers count?"

Agent Ecru peers over her glasses. I shrink back. I can tell by her expression that it is the wrong question to ask.

Chapter 3

A Challenger Appears

I burst into the house and head straight for my room. I flop onto my bed and bury my head in the blankets to avoid meeting the gaze of my idols—famous inventors, Supers, my mom, and especially Frances E. Shaw. Even though her expression is neutral, I can almost see disappointment in her face at times like these.

I messed up, I think in her general direction. I'm in deep trouble now. Recruitment day only happens once a year. I got nothing this year, which means I have to face one more year of scorn and disappointed glances.

"Beata?" my dad calls. I pretend not to hear him. The downstairs TV is on, replaying Gweneira's interview. I hear Dad's footsteps come up the stairs and pause at my door. I hold my breath.

"Bea? Do you want to work on some programming together?" The door muffles his voice.

In our spare time, Dad and I sometimes make little text-adventure games in various languages—JavaScript, Objective-C, Super XCoder—just to practice my skills. I inherited a lot from my dad, including his mousy brown hair and eyes as well as his computer-savvy nature. Dad loves computers, and so do I. Programming is relaxing, and I love seeing my codes come to life. I like knowing I'm at the helm, in control of everything, and that what I put in is what I'll get out. Coding is like math. As long as all my ones and zeroes are in place, it's completely predictable. I know he's trying to draw me out of my shell and make me feel better.

"Maybe later, Dad."

"All right, if you say so." Dad sounds hesitant but pads away anyhow.

I'm grateful he doesn't try to come in. I need time to myself. I breathe deep and listen to the tick-tock of my clock. I count three hundred seconds before I roll over and reach for the Rubik's Cube beside my bed. I scramble it and solve it. *Click, click, click.* Repeat. It makes me feel a little better.

After the cards, Agent Ecru ran me through a dozen tests. She held tools to my eyes, measured my limbs, told me to blow into funny-shaped tubes filled with liquids. She had me run a lap around the track while she stood there with a stopwatch in hand and an expression of mild impatience. When I returned, she thrust a pile of papers in front of me and told me to solve the problems. I think I did ok on that part, but I obviously didn't do super.

I lift my Rubik's Cube and turn it around in the sun. The sides are worn from years of use. I finally lower it and face my idols again. My mom as a Super, all perky and cute. I have her button nose, but it doesn't look as good on me as it does on her. Sir Isaac Newton and his apple. Lady Ada Lovelace, founder of computer science. Beautiful Hedy Lamarr, actress and inventor. Worst of all, several old-timey photos of Frances E. Shaw. My favourite one is on my desk. She must be only fourteen, soaring through the sky with aviator goggles covering her face and the Union Jack splashed across her chest. Her dark hair streams out behind her like a cascade of sepia ink. The date says 1939, the beginning of

World War II. Only two years older than me and already a contributing citizen of her country, out in the skies, defending our freedom. I sigh and cover my face again. I stay like that until the light begins to fade.

I barely manage to drag myself down for dinner, but Mom makes the most delicious mac and cheese. The smell makes my mouth water as I enter the room.

My parents are talking in undertones and don't notice me at the door. My mom's hands flutter urgently around her face as she speaks.

"This is the third year, Phil. I'm afraid—"

"I keep telling you. Relax. What's the worse that can happen? Lots of kids bloom late."

"Do you really believe that? Like really, really? You know what everyone is saying! That she might be a—"

She clears her throat and leans in. I don't hear the word, but I see it in the shape of her mouth. *Dud*. Like it's something to be kept secret. My heart leaps as my face heats up.

"I don't see what the big deal is, Tessa."

My mom straightens. She puts her hands on her hips. "It might not matter to you, but as a direct relative of the Original Super, I have a certain reputation to uphold—"

"You're being too hard on her! You know she has no choice—"

My mom throws up her arms. "I know, I know, it's just that people are going to talk, and you know how the media is—"

When my dad straightens, his back is unusually stiff. He says, louder than necessary, "I don't care what *they* say, Tessa. Beata's *my* superstar, despite it all."

I know I've been spotted. A flicker of guilt passes over Dad's face before he replaces it with a tight smile.

"Hey," he says, turning towards me, arms wide in an exaggerated gesture of welcome. "There she is, my little girl!"

"Hey, Dad," I reply, settling carefully into a chair. *Breathe.*

Mom pushes a bowl to me, and I dig in without another word. She's avoiding my eyes. I hate it when they talk behind my back, but I'm not going to push it. The less I think about my nonexistent powers, the better.

"How are you doing?" asks Mom, sounding strained.

I give her an A-ok sign with my fingers.

"Does your back still hurt from the attack?"

I nod my head. "But just a little," I add quickly. "Don't worry about it. I'll heal."

"You know," says Dad, "you can take it easy. Don't stress yourself too much."

"I know, Dad." I also know he's not only talking about my bruises.

Dinner has never felt so awkward. I spoon pasta into my mouth, feeling like I might cry. Every time I swallow, I imagine pushing down my tears. My parents keep glancing at each other, like they're sending secret messages with their eyes. I concentrate hard on eating and volunteer to do the dishes after. My parents retreat to the living room to watch the evening news.

Pyrokinetic Super Indigo Murphy apprehends the third criminal of her young career, earning ten points for herself and her team. This up-and-coming new star—

I bite my lip. *A busy mind is a happy mind,* Gweneira's voice rings in my head. She always has something smart to say. I focus on the bubbles in the sink, heaving and piling them into peaks. The dishes sit heavily on the bottom.

I hear the news move onto more everyday subjects. The weather, the traffic, and politics. The drone of the broadcast along with the soapy water is almost relaxing. Then the TV makes a harsh, buzzing sound. There is a burst of static, like tearing paper, then cold silence. I hear my parents murmur.

"Mom?" I ask. "Dad? What happened?"

I wipe my hands on my pants and poke my head into the living room. Dad is on his feet, looking quizzical. There is a darkened face on the TV screen. A silhouette stands in the shadows, and my gut churns. The bad feeling is back. Dad clicks the remote, but the TV's unresponsive.

"Hacked," he mutters, and frowns.

"Hello, my lovely Gweneira Kendricks," says a sly, amused voice. My heart pounds. The face on the screen slowly smiles. It's all teeth, like a shark's. "I have a message for you."

The school is abuzz with gossip.

"Did you see?"

"It was a challenge."

"An *official* challenge."

"Are they going to fight?"

"Oh my God, that would be *epic*."

Everywhere I turn, students chatter about the mysterious figure on TV. *Read About It* releases an emergency early edition of their paper. The headline reads: *A SUPER SMACKDOWN IN THE WORKS?! STAY TUNED!!!* Recycled stock photos of Gweneira soaring through the sky, with badly photoshopped explosions in the background, are plastered all over the cover.

"What do you think's going to happen?" asks Ling, starry-eyed. "There hasn't been an official challenge for almost a decade! Who was in the last one? Oh yes, the telekinetic guy, Hitori Yuuma and the supervillain Beamsman. It's too bad we were only babies then, and had no object permanence, let alone exciting memories of the fight. I don't even think Beamsman issued a challenge on television, but I guess things were different back then. He was very bold."

"Who? Beamsman?" I ask.

"No, this new guy," says Ling, jabbing her chin at Nuha's phone. Nuha has downloaded the entire address. We spent some time poring over it on Skype yesterday, trying to figure out who the shadowy figure was, but we're just as clueless as before. He could be anyone. There is no guarantee he is even male. There are enough gadgets out there to disguise his voice. "Not everyone is brave enough to interrupt national TV!"

"Consider me your antithesis," says the voice on Nuha's phone.

Ling makes a noise in her throat. Her eyes shine. "*Antithesis*," she says, savouring the word. "He sounds sophisticated. Am I right or am I right?"

She sighs.

"You sound like you're crushing on this guy," Nuha says. Ling snorts and shakes her head. "I'm not crushing, dummy. I'm just excited. An antithesis. Can you imagine? How *dramatic*!" Ling pretends to swoon. Something about her easy manner makes me grit my teeth.

"This isn't a soap opera, Ling. Gwen could be in real trouble here!" I interject.

Nuha nods in support, her arms crossed.

"Whoa, whoa, what's gotten into you two? No need to snap at me!" Ling bites her thumb. She gets a distant look, but her eyes are still glittering. "Look, we shouldn't be too worried. Just because there's an official challenge doesn't mean anything will come of it. Tons of villains just like to put on airs. I mean, if the threat is serious, LOS would do something."

"Beamsman still managed to get the better of LOS," Nuha pipes up.

"For a little while, maybe," Ling dismisses. She wrinkles her nose. "But they got him in the end. No big losses."

"Hitori Yuuma disappeared after too," says Nuha.

I turn on her. Although my family keeps up with Super news, we don't follow it too closely. I feel a sudden spike of panic.

"*What?* What does that mean?" My voice comes out louder than I intend. A few students glance over, and I duck my head to avoid their gazes.

As though sensing my thoughts, Ling places a hand on my shoulder. "Chill. Hitori retired. That's all."

"No one's seen him since," Nuha continues.

"Because he's an intensely private person," says Ling pointedly. "He's probably having fancy drinks on a beach somewhere. Don't make it sound so suspicious, Nu."

"I'm just stating the facts," says Nuha, but falls silent anyways.

"That was eleven years ago," continues Ling. "A lot has changed over the decade. Every Super works in a team now, and seriously, this is Gwen we're talking about. Has she ever failed anything?"

Some tension leaves my shoulders. "No."

Gwen is perfect in every way. She's good in school and good at sports. Adults and children alike love her. She's elegant and ladylike, yet powerful and efficient. I would be happy with even a third of her talent. When Gwen is on television—which is a lot—my parents like to gush over her latest feat. I don't know if it's because they genuinely love her or because they're excited someone they have known from birth is so tremendously famous, but it makes me feel a little miffed. Like they care more about Gwen than they do about me.

Ling looks proud of herself. "So stop worrying. You'll get wrinkles."

I try to smile at her joke, but I just can't relax. I need to speak to Gwen directly, but she's not in today. She's allowed to skip a lot of classes because of her work. It makes sense, but it also makes contacting her a huge hassle. Instead, I think about Ling's words. She's right. Gwen is good at everything. It's like she was born confident. Besides, she has her powers, her team, and all of LOS to support her. There is no reason to feel uneasy. None at all.

What can you do for her anyways? asks a voice in my head. *Anyone else in your family might have been able to help, but not you. You're the useless one. You would just get in the way.*

I hang my head and sigh. I wish I could do more than just worry, but there aren't many alternatives. In the world of Supers, civilians, or "Civvies" as we are called, are like sparrows among hawks, small and fragile, and needing protection. It drives me crazy, but it's the truth.

I follow Ling and Nuha to class, scuffing my shoes all the way.

I dread recess today. I stick close to the edge of the school-yard, feeling exposed. I don't want people to see plain old me, still not a Super, still a failure. I can see newly discovered Supers all over the playground, with their heads in the air, high-fiving other Supers, looking around as though seeing the world through new eyes. I tuck myself behind Ling and Nuha, hoping no one will ask me how recruitment went.

Even though most kids are Civvies, it's like all I can see are Supers. One group zips around overhead, whooping. Another few compete to see who can throw fire the farthest. A group of Civvies cheers them on. I watch until a teacher charges from the school, waving her arms. *Shoo, shoo! Not on the grass!*

"Incoming," says Nuha.

We duck as the flying Supers zoom overhead. They're a varied group, old and young, experienced and new initiates combined. They pass so close I feel my hair lift.

"Heeeeey, Dud, Dud, Dud!" one of them chants. He reaches down to skim my hair but aims too low and smacks me in the back of the head instead. The blow stings, and I suck in air through my nostrils to compose myself. I didn't even have time to retaliate before they're gone.

Ling makes a rude gesture at their retreating backs. "Yeah, you better run! Or fly! Whatever!" she shouts.

"You ok?" asks Nuha.

"What do they know?" I mutter. I rub the back of my head. I'll probably have a bump there by the end of the day. "Maybe I passed the test this year."

"Ignore them. They're stupid boys," says Ling, a hand on her hip.

Stupid boys with powers, my traitorous mind whispers. My

fingers itch for my Rubik's Cube, but I left it in my backpack. I chew my cheek instead and start counting prime numbers in my head. *Two, three, five, seven.* It's not the same as having my cube, but it helps.

Before long, there's a racket. For a moment, I think there must be another contest between newly recruited Supers, but then a helicopter flutters overhead, so close it barely makes it over the school. I throw my arm up to fend off its downdraft. A swell of excitement bubbles up in the schoolyard. A helicopter that close only means one thing. Nuha, Ling, and I share a quick glance before we hurry towards the entrance of the school.

I see the crowd before I see her—a crush of media, bodyguards, and curious onlookers. Amid it all, a single, familiar figure.

Gweneira marches towards the school, head high, face calm. Gweneira's Agent, an attractive middle-aged woman whose age only shows through the faint crow's feet around her eyes, marches beside her in a prim red suit. Her equally red hair is wrapped in a bun. She carries a clipboard and taps it with a pen, as though late for an appointment. Reporters scramble around Gwen like hens around a feeder pail and poke their lenses into her face. Whenever they get too close for comfort, she smiles at them with pearly white teeth and says, "Excuse me, please." They part like a school of fish encountering a shark.

There are already so many people gathered I can't even get close to her. Instead, I thrust both my arms in the air, wave, and yell, "Gwen!"

My voice is swallowed by a dozen others, but Gwen's head comes up anyways. Her eyes flick over the crowd, and a twinkle appears as she finds us. With all the cameras around, she doesn't give any more than the slightest nod before ascending the steps to the school. The crowd follows her. We let the crowd sweep us up the stairs, through the school doors, and into the hallways.

The recess bell shrills. Almost immediately, the PA dings.

"All students back to your classes," rings the voice of the principal. "Please. Return to your classes. We're all excited for Miss Kendricks, but there is no need to run amok. Anyone not in class in the next five minutes will receive a week's detention. No, I'm not kidding."

A groan echoes through the crowd as students begin to file back to class. I see Gwen turn a corner and head in the opposite direction from my homeroom. I bite my lip and make a decision. I clap Ling and Nuha on the shoulders.

"Don't wait up." Before they can reply, I slide through the crowd, bumping shoulders and treading on toes.

"Beata?" I hear Ling's voice call, but I don't stop.

I crane my neck but don't see Gwen anymore. Her media team has probably shuffled her along. I think about what I would do if someone put a dozen cameras in my face. I wouldn't have Gwen's calm, that's for sure. I'm not good at fighting or standing up to people like she is. I would probably want to hide. The student body thins around me until I am alone in the hallway and a hundred percent late for class.

I sigh deeply and resign myself to a week of detention when a nearby locker pops open.

Quicker than I can yelp, a hand shoots out and grabs my arm. It drags me into the dark. I fight against it, but another hand covers my mouth. The locker door clicks closed.

"It's me," says a cool, soft voice. "Don't bite me, please."

The hand moves and a light appears, a cellphone light. Two familiar green eyes stare at me.

"Gwen?" I ask, incredulous. "How did you get in here?"

Gwen smiles. "Metal, remember?" I notice the locker is more spacious than usual, with enough room for the two of us to stand comfortably. It's probably three or four empty lockers combined. Gwen brushes her fingers against another metal wall. It melts away, revealing another locker, this one with a lunch bag and coat.

"See?" Gwen waves her hand. The pane reappears. "Easy."

"What are you doing here?" I ask, keeping my voice quiet.

Gwen sighs. "I wanted to talk to you. This was the only way to get away from my crew." She leans close and narrows her eyes. I can see the gloss of her lips in the dark. She smells like peach petals. "How do things look from the outside? How are people reacting?"

I think of Ling. "They think this is going to be the next big faceoff."

Gwen nods slowly, like an approving teacher. She doesn't move away. "What do you think?"

"I don't know, Gwen. I don't feel so good about this. I mean, he hacked the entire system—"

"Satellites, actually," says Gwen. "He got all the major broadcasting stations."

"Is he a Super? Gwen, are you going to be ok? What's LOS saying? Who is he, anyways?"

Gwen smiles again. This time, there's the slightest hint of wry on her lips. "My *antithesis*, apparently," she murmurs. "My ticket for higher ratings. People are already eating it up. It's been too long since a good supervillain arrived on the scene, and viewers are hungry. My sponsors are tripping over themselves, throwing money in our direction, trying to get their name in the spotlight. LOS is working on tracking the perpetrator, but all we know is he's a good hacker, or works with someone who is. You don't have to worry, Beata. We have everything under control. If the man wants to dance, we can dance. He won't win."

"Then why are you hiding in a closet?"

"Don't read too much into it. I just wanted to talk."

There is a pause.

"How did recruitment go?" asks Gwen.

I shrug and look away. It's the question I've been avoiding, but it's hard to avoid anything when stuck in a locker. "I don't know, Gwen, I might be a Dud after all."

"Not with your history, you won't. You're Beata Bell, great-granddaughter of the Original Super. It'll come when it comes. And when it does, I'll lobby hard to get you on my team, whatever your power is. It'll be nice to finally have a friend around. My team is already nice as it is, but—" She waves a hand. "Let's just say it's not ideal."

"I wish I could be as certain as you."

"Besides, who's been calling you a Dud?" Gwen asks. Her eyes go hard, but her expression doesn't change. "Is someone bullying you?"

I remember the flying Supers but shake my head quickly. I hear the clop of shoes outside, heavy and organized. I glance at Gwen. She bites her lip lightly.

"Time's up."

"Miss Kendricks?" calls a sharp woman's voice. Gwen's face shows annoyance a moment, so briefly I almost don't catch it. She closes her eyes. When she opens them again, she wears an expression of serenity. She winks at me once and mouths *showtime*, then brushes her fingers against the lockers. I squeeze into a corner to avoid the metal sheet that appears between Gwen and me. The space is suddenly cramped and dark.

I hear Gwen's locker door open.

"Agent Scarlett," says Gweniera's voice, smooth as a calm ocean. "Sorry to keep you waiting."

"Where have you been?" asks Agent Scarlett. Her voice sounds pinched. "You know we have an interview in an hour! We still have to get you to makeup and have the stylists look at your hair too. It's starting to look frazzled. And what were you doing crammed in that locker? You'll put folds in your dress. Good thing no one saw you come out of there. Think of what the gossip magazines would say!"

Her voice disappears into the distance. After it quiets, I count to ten, then push on the locker door. The fluorescent lights nearly blind me, but thankfully, the hallway is empty. I step carefully out of the locker and trot off. I hope Mr. Uzune doesn't notice me slipping in late.

Chapter 4

Super Bluff

When we were small, Gwen and I would pretend to be Supers. We saw it as practice for the future. Since our parents were good friends, we hung out at the Kendricks's suburban home almost every weekend, where we would sling bath towels over our shoulders and tear through the backyard, through the tall oaks and around the cerulean pool, shrieking attack names and bellowing sound effects. For no particular reason, the games always ended with Gwen chasing me, guns blazing, while I dodged her attacks.

"Boom!" she would shout, pointing at me.

"Deflect!" I would scream, waving my hands.

"Zap!"

"Defend!" I would wrap my arms around my head and curl into a ball.

"Pew, pew, pew!" she would finally shout, pointing her finger like a gun.

"*Auuugh!* Not the lasers! Anything but the lasers!"

Then I would fall to the ground and writhe. No one escaped or deflected lasers. They were concentrated beams of destruction, hotter than lava, quicker than a falcon's dive, able to melt through wood, concrete, and metal alike. It was the weapon of the great Frances E. Shaw, the ultimate offensive move.

"Why always lasers?" I asked one day, after we settled down and poured ourselves some cool orange juice.

Gwen shrugged. "They're the best. If you could have any power, wouldn't you want the most powerful one?"

"Aren't you afraid of burning your hands?"

Gwen had a mysterious smile even then. She struck a pose, like a conductor preparing her orchestra. "Don't be silly, Bea. Supers can't hurt themselves with their own powers. That's like throwing a punch and hitting yourself. It doesn't make sense."

"I want to teleport," I said, thinking of Mom. "Think of how easy it would be to get around!"

Gwen wrinkled her nose. "I guess it would be easy to get to school, but it kind of sounds boring, don't you think?"

"Or invisibility. Then I can sneak around without anyone seeing me!"

"What's the point of having powers if no one sees them?"

"My dad had powers no one could see," I said, feeling defensive. "He could talk to computers!"

Gwen smiled calmly. "And that's why he wasn't on the front lines," she said. Her voice was matter-of-fact.

I clamped my mouth shut and pushed down the sudden bubble of anger that rose in my chest. I didn't like how she said that, all dismissive, like my dad wasn't important because he was behind the scenes. I liked Gwen a lot, but sometimes I kind of hated her too. Looking back, it set her apart from other children. She was always so sure. Even before LOS recruited her, even before the fame and the medals, it felt like she was better than everyone else.

Ling calls the cafeteria a *microcosm*, a miniature reflection of the world as a whole.

The student body is broken into groups. Supers occupy all the best seats, the ones closest to the windows and doors. Civvies take up the rest of the space, cramped in the uncomfortable middle benches, or against the walls. There are no groups of Duds. They're too rare to warrant a space, or too awkward to hang out together. Looking around, I hope Ling is wrong. I hope this isn't a *microcosm*. I don't want to deal with this sort of division forever.

I try to hide behind Ling as we find seats, but it's hard to stay invisible when there's as much speculation floating around you as there are around the mysterious supervillains.

"Hey, Bell!" one of the flying boys shouts as I enter. My heart sinks. Dieter Jaeger, from class B3. Dieter and I have been on bad terms almost forever. He's pushy and rude, and goes out of his way to make me uncomfortable. "I have a question. Can I ask a question?"

No. I urge Ling to go faster.

"We're really curious here. We've got a pool going and need you to clarify," Dieter calls, loud enough for the entire cafeteria to hear. "Are you a Dud or not?"

"Yeah, I've got five bucks you are!" one of his lackeys adds.

"I got five bucks you get some dumb power, like empathy!"

There's a peal of laughter as the boys holler, "Feelings! Feelings everywhere!" My cheeks burn. Even empathy is better than nothing. I open my mouth to retaliate, but Nuha catches my eye. She shakes her head a little.

"They just want a reaction," she says.

I bite my cheek and clutch my lunchbox closer. I know Nuha means well, but she doesn't have generations of expectations to live up to. Anger tumbles in my belly. I wonder if it'll emerge as fire, or electricity.

It doesn't.

As we approach a table, a couple of Civvies shuffle over to let us sit. I unzip my lunchbox with more force than necessary. The contents jump out. I grab my apple to stop it from rolling off the table and smack a nearby Civvie with my elbow.

"Ow," she says reproachfully.

"Aren't you tired of not getting good seats?" I ask, suddenly exasperated. The flying boys occupy a good quarter of the room, even though there are only a few of them. They hover and pelt one another with food when the cafeteria monitors aren't looking. The floor is littered with cheese, ham, and bits of bread. I make a face. Gross.

"They're going to be heroes one day," says the girl, looking puzzled. She doesn't seem fazed. "Or even better, celebrities!"

"Yeah, maybe, but they're not very nice."

The girl's eyebrows fly up her face. She leans in until I feel claustrophobic. "Are you *jealous*?" she hisses. Her eyes go soft with pity. "Oh my God, you are! You *are* a Dud!"

Not again. My mouth opens. "I'm not jealous!" I insist, tasting the lie like a sour pit on my tongue. A beat too late, I add, "I'm not a Dud, either!"

I bite into my apple so hard my gums hurt. Across the room, the flying boys' food throwing escalates into a full-on food fight. The cafeteria monitors watch with distaste but don't step in. I roll my eyes internally but empathize with their frustration. It's hard to tell Supers to do anything, especially ones who can float out of reach.

As I take another bite, a shadow zips overhead. A split second later, a stream of soup hits my head. My chair squeals against the floor as I jerk to my feet, gasping. The soup is cold already, but the shock still shoots right through me. Noodles and bits of chicken dribble through my hair.

"I got the Dud!" Dieter whoops, returning to his flock. "Told you I could do it! You owe me a Snickers bar!"

In a burst of frustration, I slap my hands against the table.

"I am *not* a Dud," I thunder in a voice I didn't know I had. The cafeteria quiets. I wipe soup from my eyes. There's a tight lump in my chest. I face a sea of wide, expectant eyes. Everyone holds their breath. I can almost see the headlines now. *Great-granddaughter of the Original FINALLY to reveal powers?! STAY TUNED!!!* Across from me, Ling and Nuha wear twin expressions of surprise.

Panic grips my lungs. Now that I have everyone's attention, I'm frozen. It feels like I'm standing on open tundra—open, with nowhere to hide. Soup soaks into my shirt. The cotton sticks like a second skin.

Ling grins, like it's all a show, *Let 'em have it* but Nuha's brows come down in a deep frown.

A flutter of uncertainty tickles my chest, but I can't sit down now, not with everyone staring. Sitting down would be like admitting defeat. Instead, I stand and shake. Defiantly.

"Yeah, that's right," I say, trying to fuel my words with anger. "I can do things too." I take a deep breath and point at Dieter. "Terrible things!"

Fear flickers across Dieter's face for a split second. Then he sneers. "Yeah? Like what?"

"I—" I search for words. My brain ticks. *Click, click, click.* "I can *curse* people."

There's a bloated pause. Then someone giggles.

"That's not a real thing. That's stupid!" It's Matt Kiel, Dieter's best friend. He giggles like a pixie, which is both weird and creepy, since he's built like a quarterback, which makes him menacing

A gush of real anger floods my chest. I stand up straighter. I've seen enough Supers at work to imitate their movements. I raise my hands. *No lame finger movements*, I remind myself, breathing carefully. Elegant, yet powerful. Think of Gwen. And Frances. What would Frances do? I sweep my hands in Dieter's direction and trace out the first five symbols of the Greek alphabet in quick succession. I'm sure no one recognizes them.

"May thy fortunes wither and thy health be forfeit!" I declare in my most intimidating voice. Dieter actually *flinches* before checking his face and limbs to make sure everything is still in place. Relief rises on his face.

"Nothing happened." He sounds confused.

"Not yet," my breath comes shallow, "but just you wait. It'll strike when you least expect it!"

"You're lying!" He doesn't look so sure now.

"Fine. Don't believe me."

"But don't close your eyes either," adds Ling gleefully.

It might be my imagination, but Dieter pales. His flying entourage gathers around him like a protective barrier.

"Don't worry, she's bluffing."

"Yeah, she's nobody. She wants to be somebody, but she's not."

They hover off.

"See you when your face falls off!" sings Ling.

"*Ling*," hisses Nuha. Ling leans back in her chair, giggling. She gives Nuha her best innocent face. Nuha turns her attention on me, rises from her chair, and takes my elbow. I'm mortified. What's wrong with me? I don't usually lie. My cheeks burn as though someone's rubbed chili peppers on them.

"Let's get you a new shirt," Nuha says. "You can have my gym clothes."

I can feel noodles slithering down my back. I shudder and let Nu lead me out of the cafeteria. Ling stuffs the rest of her sandwich into her mouth before following us out.

"Just for the record, you *don't* have any powers, right?" Ling asks in the hallway.

I shake my head. "I panicked. I made it all up."

Stupid! With all the witnesses in the cafeteria, word will get out. Gossip magazines will pick it up. Then maybe the more serious ones, too. I'm the great-granddaughter of the Original Super. My mom always tells me that I have to be more careful because I'm related to someone famous. I can't give the media any reason to spin wild stories about our family and ruin our reputation. *Do you want to sully Frances's name?* she asks, hands on her hips. *Well?*

I don't! I shout in my head. I really don't. I imagine Frances E. Shaw's face on my wall. She's a hero. I can't disappoint her. If word gets out, the entire school will find out I lied, and I'll be a laughing stock. *Read About It* will publish an article. *A FAMILY'S HEARTBREAK: ORIGINAL SUPER LINE BROKEN. BEATA BELL, CERTIFIED DUD.* There will be editorials and interviews and embarrassing photos. Dieter's jeering face looms in my mind's eye.

"Maybe I can change schools," I say, squeezing out a painful smile.

"Running won't help," Nuha says.

I wince. I know. I bury my face in my hands just as Ling slings an arm around my shoulders.

"It's not so bad being a Civvie," she says breezily. "We don't have to worry about fighting robot octopods... We don't have to get up at three a.m. to chase down robbers. If we're lucky, we even get to be rescued by cute boys."

I manage a weak laugh, but there's no joy in it. She's right, but she's also wrong. A Dud is different from a Civvie. A Dud is a letdown. That's way worse than normal. *The strong must protect the weak*, Gwen's voice whispers in my head. Except I don't want to be protected. I want to be useful.

Chapter 5

Challenge Accepted

LOS announces Gwen's media response far in advance. Friday afternoon, 4:30 p.m. The news reminds us every half hour. *Remember folks, three more hours until the LIVE broadcast from in front of City Hall, where Gweneira Kendricks is expected to host a press conference—*

"I don't understand," I say, already feeling butterflies. The halls are abuzz with talk about attending the conference, seeing the renowned Gweneria Kendricks speak live, as though they didn't hear her speak enough when she attends classes. "Why would they broadcast from City Hall? It's so risky."

"With LOS around, there is no such thing as risk," says Ling, examining her nails. "You would have to be pretty stupid to attack them straight on. Besides, they want to show they're not worried."

"If LOS needs to show everyone they're not worried, doesn't it mean they're secretly worried? What if they lob a robot octopod straight into the square?"

Ling raises a single eyebrow but doesn't speak. She has been practicing the expression all day, claiming it looks sophisticated.

No one gets much work done in class. Even the teachers are distracted. I even overhear a debate between two teachers about whether the event will be better live or on TV. Mr. Uzune attempts to teach Canadian geography, but the class is too excited to talk about anything other than the upcoming conference. Mr. Uzune does his best to stay on topic, but it's an uphill battle.

"Can anyone tell me the capital of Nova Scotia? Yes, Miss Flores?"

"Will you be going to the conference at City Hall later?"

Mr. Uzune sighs. "I suppose I will. Now, let's get back on track. Yes, Mr. Ortiz?"

"Who do you think is going to win?"

"As always, I am on the side of justice. Now, if we can just get back to geography, please."

The clock slowly ticks towards the end of the day. *Remember folks,* echoes the PA, on cue, every half hour. The atmosphere is charged with anticipation.

When the bell finally rings, the school empties so quickly it might as well have been evacuated. It's not a cold day, but it's not warm either. Ling drags us down the street after school, camera bouncing off her chest, chatting about getting good seats and good pictures.

We arrive at City Hall more than an hour early, but there's already a crowd. The overcast sky makes Nathan Phillips Square look especially dull. City Hall reaches into the sky, grey on grey. The only dots of colour are the food trucks that line the streets, eager to profit off the hungry spectators. It smells like fried sausages and greasy fries. Ling elbows her way through the adults. I duck my head and drop *sorrys* and *excuse mes* in her wake.

At least no one will recognize me here. After my outburst in the cafeteria, my classmates sidestep me in the hallways and follow me with suspicious eyes, as though I might go crazy and curse everyone. Yesterday, I ate my lunch in the classroom to avoid their stares—Mr.Uzune was nice enough to let me stay. During recess, I feel like a spring wound too tight.

Every time I spot a suit, my throat seizes up. What if LOS finds out I lied about having powers? Will they send another Agent to test me? I don't think I can handle another round of rejections. Will they appear at home in front of my parents?

"Not the best of stages," Ling grumps, waving at the set up. "Look at all those exposed metal bars. They couldn't have boxed those up in some pretty plywood or something?"

"It's very open," I agree.

Ling glances over at me. "You're still worried?"

"No," I lie, not wanting to draw her ridicule. "I'm just saying."

I tell myself LOS knows what they're doing. They've been around for more than seventy years, prevented dozens of wars in a dozen different countries, brought crime rates down to a historic low, and never failed before. Even so, the lonely podium standing before City Hall seems dangerously bare. It's not that I want to worry; I just can't help it.

Despite Ling's best efforts, we don't get great seats. Press photographers and their big cameras already occupy the closer spots. Even though I know it's a letdown for Ling, I'm relieved I'm further away from the reporters. I didn't want them recognizing me and pulling me over for impromptu statements. Luckily, tall screens have been erected all over the square so people who don't have good seats can watch from afar. Ling pouts and grouses but doesn't push any further.

I pull out my cellphone and hand it to her. In the past few months, Nuha and I have been furiously perfecting the Sound

Isolator app we invented. She puts together the gadgets—in this case, a tiny but powerful microphone that isn't any bigger than a person's thumbnail—and I program the software to isolate certain sound frequencies while excluding others. When installed, it lets someone's cellphone pinpoint and zoom in on sounds, a useful feature for up-and-coming journalists like Ling who can't afford expensive equipment yet. The interface blinks. Ling's face lights up when she sees it.

"It's not finished yet," I say, "but it might help you hear."

"Consider this a beta run," adds Nuha.

"No time like now to try it out then," chirps Ling cheerfully, all shadows of her former frustration dispelled. She aims the cellphone towards the podium.

"You can't lock on until there's someone speaking," I remind her. "I put in some new codes to help it auto-equalize so you don't have to manually refine the sounds in case you're in a hurry, but I don't know if it'll work at this distance."

"Looks like we'll just have to wait." Ling carefully removes a hair tie from her pocket and secures my phone to her camera.

"I'll give it share capacities soon," I add. "So you can zoom in on a performance, or an important speech, and I can hear it on my end, even if I'm kilometres away."

"That way, you guys can help me eavesdrop on conversations!" Ling says. Her eyes gleam with excitement. "Thanks, guys, you're the best! I'll definitely get a good scoop this way."

"Er," says Nuha, "that's not exactly what we had in mind—"

Ling wraps her in a tight hug, cutting off her words. Nuha

shoots me a look over Ling's shoulder, like, *Can you believe this girl?* I make a face. Ling is just being Ling.

A thin wind chills my neck. I look back at the lectern and swallow thickly. "How did the last challenge start? Beamsman didn't have a broadcast."

"Nope," says Ling, fiddling with her zoom lens. "He just started blasting."

"Whoever the Counter-League is, I hope they don't start blasting stuff."

"They're supervillains. Of course there's going to be blasting." Ling breathes deep. A breeze lifts her dark hair, and in the shadows, she looks almost contemplative, but when it settles, her smile is back. "There's going to be blasting on both sides."

I wonder how she stays so calm, whether it's confidence, or stupidity, or something else altogether. "How did they bring Beamsman down eleven years ago?"

Ling tries to raise one eyebrow again but gives up halfway and raises both of them instead. "For someone who comes from a Super household, you sure don't know a lot about Super history." She leans forward. "Do you have data on your phone?"

"Yeah."

"Cool." Ling connects to the Internet and navigates to UTube, a video-sharing site. With a few quick swipes, she brings up some shaky footage. "Watch."

It's the middle of a November night. The trees are bare and the roads are wet. The video is shot from a bird's-eye view, and it's a little fuzzy in the rain. Suddenly, a bolt of bright red slices through the neighbourhood, searing the ground. It happens so quickly I wince.

"Beamsman's on a rampage, carving up suburban neighbourhoods with his powers. Hitori Yuuma is hot on his tail." Ling points to a small figure in white rushing down the road, then at another small figure entering the screen in pursuit. He has black hair and a red cape. It's soggy and flops against his back. He pauses at an intersection, as though to check for oncoming traffic, then darts across the road in a dead run.

"No one can get close to Beamsman except Hitori Yuuma," says Ling. "No one has his sort of range or versatility. Also, he's a telekinetic. Majorly cool."

I watch as they tear down the streets. Hitori leaps forward and makes a motion with his hands. Nearby cars levitate from the ground. He sweeps his arms forward, and the cars crash towards Beamsman, spilling glass all over the streets. Beamsman has gone mad, blasting in every direction. Hitori's chucking whatever he can at him, trying to stop him.

Someone—possibly the cameraman—whispers a faint expletive, and I second his awe. My heart races as I watch the two tiny Supers weave through the roads. It's like watching a sci-fi movie, except completely real. And frightening. A laser beam smashes through the front of a nearby house, cutting through it like butter. It hits the house behind it, and another, and another, tapering off only at the fifth one. The cameraman swears out loud. I want to look away, but fascination compels me.

Lasers, just like Frances. There's old footage of Frances E. Shaw in battle too, but it's much grainier. Whenever she used her powers, it registered as a flash of light so brilliant the cameras couldn't handle it. Lasers are terrifying to watch.

"You know, almost a dozen people died in that fight," Nuha says. "It was nighttime, and people were sleeping.

Beamsman went psycho so fast they didn't have time to evacuate the neighbourhood."

I swallow hard and nod. The Beamsman versus Hitori Yuuma fight was a Code Red. That meant the threat presented an immediate danger to the people of the city, and it meant massive evacuations.

Onscreen, Beamsman fires a laser in Hitori's direction. Hitori flings his arm upwards, and asphalt peels from the road. It curls up to form a shield. The laser smashes into it. Immediately, the asphalt begins to glow and melt. Hitori replenishes his shields as they're liquefied, grabbing more asphalt and melding it in, rebuilding as quickly as they're destroyed. *Nothing can stop lasers*, my mind whispers. I shiver.

Beamsman stops shooting and turns to run. Hitori takes a moment to recover before pursuing him. They end up in a train yard.

"Here it comes," says Ling with a wide grin. "The finale. The last hurrah."

Hitori's telekinesis is strong enough to lift entire railroad cars, so that's what he does. Even from far away, I can see him yelling as the oil tanks begin to rotate above them. A battle cry maybe? Or is he trying to negotiate? Beamsman stands among the containers. He's yelling back. Hitori's body language relays anger. It's a standoff. I hold my breath, even though I know how it ends.

Beamsman looks tired, dripping with water, his shoulders slumped. He begins to raise his hands, as though to surrender. Without warning, he jerks to the side. A feint! Hitori drops his hands. The two oil tanks fall and crash to the ground.

"Boom," whispers Ling as the video lights up so bright

that everything goes white for a second. The commotion is so loud it blows out the recording equipment, and everything goes silent. "Witnesses say the explosion could be heard over five kilometres away."

I watch the silent video. When the camera recovers, everything's on fire. I can't see either fighter in the smoke. An unpleasant feeling settles in my stomach. Even though there were no onscreen deaths, the knowledge that people died makes my gut churn.

"Where's Hitori?" I ask, my voice thick with panic. "I can't see him."

"He has telekinesis. He's obviously barricaded himself behind a shield somewhere." Ling flicks off the video. She grips my shoulder. "Calm down; it's a happy ending. He won a lot of accolades for taking Beamsman down."

"I wonder what they said to each other in the end."

"No one knows. It's a mystery." Ling waggles her fingers. "Probably something like, *Vile villain, you'll go no further! Taste my inflammable rage!*"

"No way."

"Yes way."

"Why would Beamsman feint like that?" I wonder out loud. "It seems sort of pointless. Hitori pretty much had him cornered."

Ling laughs shortly. "Are you trying to find logic in a Super battle, Bea? Oh, you're priceless. Who knows what he was thinking? He was crazy."

It's getting close to speech time. People press around us, arriving in buses, in taxis, and on foot. Their murmurs become a din. I begin to feel claustrophobic in the sea of bodies.

"By the time LOS arrived, the entire train yard was on fire." Ling's eyes glitter as she speaks. "They had water-based Supers to spray the place down, and wind-based Supers to blow away the smoke, but it took the entire night to tame the flames. Early in the morning, just as the sun peeked over the horizon, they found a body."

"Beamsman?" I ask.

"Of course it's Beamsman," says Ling impatiently. "You know how the story ends!"

"Hitori disappears forever," I murmur.

"No," Ling says, hard, "he *retires*. Big difference."

As the minutes tick down, the crowd swells. Compared to the brightness of the video, City Hall looks more boring than ever. It's so lacklustre it's almost comforting. I decide I prefer boring to *everything on fire*.

Someone behind me bumps my back and I stumble. Maybe I'm woozy from watching the video, but my toe catches on the foot of another spectator, and I pitch forward. My arms shoot out to stop my fall, and I plough into the man in front of me. It's a bad chain reaction. The man falls forward, knocking another man, who knocks into yet another one. There's a clatter of equipment as the person I bumped hits the ground. I see one camera lens roll into the forest of feet. I catch myself and step back, hands on my mouth.

"I'm so sorry!" I yelp. "I'm so, so sorry! Are you ok?"

Half-hunched, I duck through legs to help him retrieve his escaped equipment. The man—a teenager, now that I look closer—picks himself up and waves a hand. He's gangly with a maroon hoodie and baggy pants. At least three cameras are attached to his body, two around his neck, and a smaller one wrapped around his wrist.

"I've been through worse," he says.

I hand him back one of his lens. It's dented.

"I'm sorry," I say again, weakly. He shakes his head and lifts a hand in a sign of peace. I scuff the ground with a shoe. An awkward silence settles around us. I contemplate whether it would be more or less awkward to run away. I peek at him from my peripheral vision.

"So," I pipe up, "you're a photographer?"

"Yes."

"Oh."

More silence. I open my mouth, then close it, then think of something else to say.

"Which paper do you work for?"

"None, really. I'm more of a freelancer. I have an independent blog where I write articles about Supers, Super culture, and mass media influence. I'm here to gather information and observe the proceedings," he says.

I shrink further into myself. It sounds important. I look over at Ling and Nuha. Ling raises her eyebrows at me, undoubtedly enjoying the show. A spark of annoyance lights in my chest. *Thanks, Ling.* Nuha wears a deadpan expression.

"What are you here for?"

"I-I'm here 'cause I'm friends with Gweneira," I blurt, trying to fill the silence. I can't stop myself. If my cheeks get any hotter, people around me will suspect me of being feverish. As soon as the words leave my mouth, I know I've made a mistake. Anyone associated with Gwen will get attention, and attention is the last thing I want right now. "But don't tell anyone," I add quickly. "I mean, not that it's a secret or anything, but—you know. I don't really want the reporters to notice I'm here."

He turns to look at me, curious. "Are you three *all* friends with Miss Kendricks?"

"Yes," says Ling, puffing out her chest. "We hang out on a regular basis."

"Is that right?"

"It's true," Ling says. "You don't believe us? We go to the same school."

"Of course I believe you," says the stranger, holding up his hands in defence. "Never said I didn't. I'm Alexander, by the way."

I take his hand weakly, still feeling mortified. It's weird to shake hands with someone. It makes me feel too adult. Once we're done with greetings, he takes a step back and regards us all with something like amusement. "Well, well, well, it's not every day I get to meet Miss Kendricks's personal friends. What is she like in real life? Is she nice?"

"She's cool," I say. *Nice going with the adjectives, Beata*, my mind hisses.

"Way glamorous," says Ling.

"Have you seen her manipulate metal up close and personal?"

Ling shrugs. "A couple of times. Ask Beata. She's her *best* friend."

Alexander looks towards me. "Beata *Bell*? Descendent of the great Original Super?"

I shrink a little and nod. I've never been good at talking to strangers. It makes me all shifty inside. I wonder if he's going to try to get statements or ask me how it feels to be descendent of Frances E. Shaw. Instead, he just says, "Wow, no pressure, huh?"

"What?"

"I always figured it must be hard being related to famous people. Correct me if I'm wrong."

"It's a little hard," I say, suddenly feeling a spurt of warmth pass over me.

"Don't worry. I won't ask you what it's like being related to *the* France E. Shaw. I'm sure you're tired of that by now. The question is cliché anyways. Is it true you guys hang out all the time? I can't imagine someone like Gweneira Kendricks just hanging out, but I suppose all Supers have lives outside of upholding justice, huh?"

"Sometimes she flies me around," I say. "She can make origami cranes out of sheets of metal."

"She's that good?"

"Y-yeah, I guess. I mean, she's one of the most popular Supers of our generation, and she's always getting called away on missions, so she must be good. One of the best, probably."

"Of course," says Alexander with an awkward smile. "How silly of me to ask. And the rest of you, I didn't quite catch your names."

"Ling," says Ling, holding out a hand to shake, "and the quiet one is Nuha. I work for the school newspaper, *Read About It*. Hey, this might be forward, but can I check out your cameras? What sort of lenses are you using? What specs?"

I'm glad for Ling's distraction. I take the chance to shuffle to the side as the two discuss camera technicalities and shooting strategies.

"Nerds," says Nuha, almost fondly.

I nod, relieved at the respite.

We wait. In the crowd, I feel terribly short. I can barely see the stadium between the people. All I see are backs and shoulders. I listen to Ling's easy chatter with Alexander, and wonder at her confidence. I could never strike up a conversation so easily.

"The Canon Super Rebel 500? I hear that has a problem with subject tracking." Ling brandishes her own lens. It's big and heavy. I bet it weighs as much as her lunchbox. Maybe more.

"Yes, slightly, but with better resolution than the Nikon Super 980."

"Not enough for the naked eye to see."

"You'll see the differences in Photoshop."

"Guys," Nu's voice finally chimes in softly. The crowd heaves. Ling and I both turn to the street, where an LOS limo has pulled up by the sidewalk. Reporters swarm the car. The flashing of cameras is so intense it hurts my eyes even though I'm far away.

Agent Scarlett steps from the limo first. Her mouth is pressed into a thin line. She carries her clipboard. As Gwen exits, a reverent silence settles over the crowd. The reporters step back to give her room as though choreographed.

Gwen sparkles as she emerges. Her fitted turquoise gown stretches to her knees before flaring out like a koi's tail. Her neck glitters with golden necklaces. As usual, she has long white gloves. Gwen's metal manipulation is triggered by touch. Even though her control is exceptional, she wears the gloves just in case.

In case I fall asleep in the limo and accidentally dematerialize a door, she once told me. *It's happened before. It's not nearly as funny as it sounds.* Her voice had gone serious after that. *You can never be too vigilant.*

As she turns to face the reporters, her hair catches the wind and billows out in soft waves. The clicks of camera shutters sound like mechanical applause.

"Just like a shampoo commercial," Ling says in delight. "You can't plan moments like that! Isn't she something?"

"She certainly is," murmurs Alexander. He tweaks his camera settings. "Excuse me, ladies, but I have to get closer. Nice meeting you all."

He slips into the crowd. I resist the urge to call out another apology for denting his lens.

Gweneira projects cool confidence, with her nose raised imperiously and a smile that's both calm and sharp. A pile of microphones lies before her. Recording devices are hastily taped to the podium's sides. Agent Scarlett steps up first to summarize the situation and make a statement on LOS's behalf. Her words float over me. As she speaks, the crowd's excitement swells. Ling and Gwen are right. People love the rivalry. They don't see it as dangerous. They see it as entertainment. The thought makes my stomach turn. A few members of the audience are even dressed up as Gwen, with white-gold costumes and blonde wigs. *It's like a sports competition.* I wonder how many people are watching the broadcast right now. Millions, probably.

"The League of Supers has handled greater threats than a few anonymous hackers," Agent Scarlett finishes, "and I assure you, the League will undoubtedly prevail in this matter."

"Miss Gweneira, does this mean you'll be accepting the challenge?" a reporter from CNN asks.

Gwen flashes her teeth at him.

"Naturally," she says.

The rabble of noisy reporters jostl for position.

"Miss Gweneira, are you nervous at all?"

"Let me tell you, Paul," says Gweneira, addressing the reporter. "There are people out there who should be nervous, but none of them are standing before you."

Nuha nudges my arm. She holds up her smartphone. A Tweeter page is open on the screen. A list of short blurbs, the thoughts of people all over the city, occupies the page.

"Barely five minutes," says Nuha, "and the top five trending hashtags have to do with the broadcast."

"Of course," scoffs Ling. "This is going to be the biggest television event of the decade!"

At the lectern, Gweneira smiles at a joke. She looks perfectly relaxed, but I know better. Her eyes skim over the crowd, observing, analyzing, processing. I wonder if she'll see me if I wave, but I restrain myself. I don't want to be a distraction.

"If they are serious," Gwen says in response to a question I didn't catch, "they will show themselves. Only cowards and weaklings hide behind technology, in the shadows, like rats, afraid of light. I say bring it on." She pauses dramatically and turns to stare into a camera. "I'm ready. Are you?"

For a moment, there's just silence. At first I think the reporters are lost for words, but then I see the focus in Gwen's face. The tiniest frown appears on her forehead.

I notice it. A strange shadow falls over the stadium.

There is just enough time for the hairs on my neck to rise before Gweneira leaps backwards. She shoves Agent Scarlett behind her with one hand and rips the glove off her other with her teeth. In one smooth motion she sweeps her bare hands across the podium. It dissolves into a stream of formless metal, along with all the microphones. The speakers let out a piercing whine. I clap my hands over my ears.

Gweneira moves faster than I can follow. She whips

around, hands in motion, spinning a shield around herself and Agent Scarlett just as an I-beam slams into them. The sound of metal hitting metal crashes like a thunderclap. Gwen's shield dents but holds. For a moment, the I-beam is balanced, like a circus performer, before it leans and starts to fall. Shrieks sound as it crashes to the ground, cracking concrete and sending up a cloud of dust.

I'm rocked by the impact, but I am far enough away not to get hurt. "Oh my God!" The yell bursts from me before I can control it. My voice is one of many. Several other people are struggling to get back on their feet. "What's happening?"

I can no longer see the stage. I only see dark shapes running, scrambling—and lying still on the ground. *People are hurt. Or worse.* Ling grabs my hand. Her grip is tight, and it takes me a moment to realize she didn't grab my hand out of fear, but excitement. Her black hair is dusted with greyish powder but her eyes are bright. She nods towards the sky, where a dark humanoid shape races into the distance. A moment later, a turquoise blur shoots from the dust, rising like a vengeful comet. Suddenly, LOS officers are everywhere, waving signs and shouting for calm.

My relief is quickly overshadowed as Ling darts after Gwen's retreating shape, camera in hand. I try to grab her, but she's too quick. Instead, Nuha and I exchange a look.

I raise my eyebrows. *What do we do?*

Nuha rolls her eyes. *She's crazy.* But then she jerks her head in Ling's direction. *But we can't leave her.*

I press my lips until they hurt, and I nod solemnly. The things I do for friendship. Before the LOS agents can properly seal off the scene, we take off after our friend, darting through bodies and kicking up dust.

Chapter 6

A Fight in the Skies

There's no way to describe what a Super battle is like to someone who's never seen one. Exciting, yes. Scary, yes. But also out of this world. Not in an awesome way, but in a completely, totally, weirdly alien way. It's like entering the Twilight Zone. Watching a human being fly in person is different from watching a human being fly on TV. Something in us tells us it shouldn't be possible, that our eyes are fooling us. Somehow, even though I have been around Supers all my life, seeing their powers in person always makes reality seem unreal. Like I've stepped into an action film. Like I'm in a dream.

Gwen is fast. She flies with the same determination as a bullet, arms to her sides, spine stick straight. Her turquoise dress flaps around her with such vicious energy that I'm surprised it doesn't tear right off. The assailant barely keeps ahead of her. He's dressed in grey to blend in with the sky. Gwen ducks low to sweep her hand against a skyscraper. I see the shimmer of blue sparks as she materializes her telltale swords. Like a ruthless hawk, she dives towards the mystery figure. He spins out of the way.

Ling has her lens pointed towards the sky. How she runs and shoots at the same time is a mystery to me. I'll never have that much coordination. Ling does sixty sit-ups and push-ups every morning, then jogs around the neighbourhood, even in winter. *To chase after those hot stories* she claims. She knows downtown Toronto like the back of her hand.

Gwen's attacker twists away from her and dodges between the buildings. His monochrome outfit is obvious against the darkened glass of the skyscrapers. Gwen chases after him. Her swords scrape against the buildings. It's too far to hear, but I can imagine metal shrieking against glass. They leave a trail of falling shrapnel in their wake.

"Ling," I shout, "it's not safe!"

"This is premium material!" she shouts back. "Imagine the scoop! I'll make senior editor for sure!"

Ling needs to get her priorities in order. I think it's unfair to be both fashionable and so good at sports. Ling is an excellent long-distance runner and has been asked to join Sir Frederick Banting's track team for two years straight. She has always refused, claiming media as her one true love.

I keep a close eye on the battle. I can hear the whir of media helicopters as they give chase and the wail of sirens as EMS responds to the crisis.

Gwen and her attacker dip through the city, spiral upwards, and fall back towards the ground as though dancing. The two weave between buildings so quickly I feel like I'll pull a neck muscle if my head swivels any faster. Ling is ahead of us, her long strides eating up ground. My legs burn, and my lungs hurt. I'm wary of falling glass and debris. Gwen's assailant veers to the right. Gwen throws one of her swords at him, cutting him off. It crashes to the ground, spearing a bus shelter. Glass spills all over the street.

I'm getting out of breath. How long until LOS's Super teams arrive on the scene? They must be powering up their jets by now. All around us, people stream from their offices, their eyes to the sky. The streets fill with the clicking of cameras. The media is going to have a field day tomorrow, sifting through all the photos sent in from everyday witnesses.

"Isn't this exciting?" I hear a woman gab as I dash past.

That's one way to put it.

I want to tell people to run. To get out from under the battle. Don't they understand the danger? It's not a baseball game. My mom's always telling me stories of Supers getting hurt during their missions, and if Supers can get hurt, what chance do Civvies have? I spot Ling weaving between office workers as she chases the Supers. I curse and wish I could slap a tracker on her. *There's an app in that*, my mind whispers, and I tuck the idea away for future reference.

"Ling! You'll get hurt!" Nuha echoes my sentiment.

At first it seems Ling doesn't hear her, but her steps slow just a bit.

"Maybe," she calls back.

"Then let's get where it's safe!"

"You can get somewhere safe if you want to," Ling calls back. "I won't stop you."

"That's not the point!"

"I have to," she says with sudden vehemence. She turns to us, and I can see determination in her eyes. "This could be my Big Scoop!"

Nuha and I share another glance. We know Ling's family history. Back in China, both her parents were journalists. Her mother was a relatively famous news investigator. One of the youngest ever. Ling loved to watch her mother on television. She wanted to be just like her. Then they decided to emigrate to Canada. For an even better life, they claimed.

That's when the trouble began. They had studied English in

university, but they weren't fluent. They tried to secure jobs, but they couldn't. Instead, they did menial things, babysat for richer people, cleaned their houses, tidied their bedrooms, and finally scrounged enough to open a small stir-fry place in Chinatown. They never reported another story again.

To Ling, this is the embodiment of injustice.

I'm fluent in English, she told me once. *I'm gutsy and capable. I'm educated. One day, I'll rocket to the moon!*

Ling is determined to elevate her family back into the good life. Her Big Scoop is her Holy Grail, and she chases it like a knight on a quest. As though the Queen herself ordered it.

Up above, the mysterious figure rockets for a construction zone. Gwen puts on a spurt of speed. As she passes into the skeleton of a rising skyscraper, she skims her fingers along the I-beams. Strips peel from the foundation, and spin into liquid around her. She forms half a dozen swords.

Magnificent, my mind betrays me. I wonder what it's like to be so glorious. It's probably something I'll never experience.

"Let's help her," Nuha says breathlessly beside me. Nuha isn't the most athletic person in the world. I can see her limbs drooping. Colour dots her cheeks.

At first I think she means Gwen.

Impossible, my mind chimes. Neither of us has the capacity to help Gwen. We're both Civvies, grounded and forever watching.

But then I realize she means Ling. Nuha has her phone out. She sets it to camera, points it at the sky, and zooms in. Two blurry figures race across its screen, like a couple of dark comets. She makes a frustrated clicking sound with her tongue.

I follow suit.

"At least this way we'll have a better chance of getting a good shot and getting out of here," Nuha says. Glass crashes in the distance. We both wince. "It really is quite dangerous."

As though to emphasize her words, the skeletal skyscraper begins to lean. Loud *ping*s reach my ears. Screws popping. The metal structure groans. Gasps rise from spectators around us as the skyscraper crumbles under its own weight, kicking up a cloud of dust in its wake.

I hope no one is under it.

Nuha and I take off down the road.

Whup, whup, whup.

Finally, the helicopters are on their way! In front of us, Ling hurdles a concrete bench. She lands with the slightest of stumbles and ploughs on.

A part of me wishes the helicopters would arrive faster. The faster help arrives, the faster we can get out of here. I'm dreadfully aware of how squishy I am compared to a block of concrete.

Ling stops so suddenly I nearly smash into her back.

"What?" I gasp. "What is it?"

"I know where they're going," she says, eyes fixed on the two Supers. "Gwen is herding him towards LOS headquarters."

"The Toronto Islands?"

"She's smart. She knows she can't contain him forever, so she's directing him right into LOS's hands. It's her base. Her team is there. I see animals do this all the time on *National Geographic*! A group of wild dogs will chase an antelope right into the jaws of their friends. Then everyone eats." Ling turns to me, her eyes gleaming. "Let's take a shortcut. Come on, I know a way!"

She runs straight for a fenced-off university residence and begins to climb.

"*Ling*," I hiss, and motion at a big sign that says *NO TRES-PASSING*. "We can't do that!"

"It'll be fine," comes her muffled voice. She hops over the top like a monkey. "Come on, Bea! Come on, Nu! It's easy. Just think of it as a jungle gym."

I sigh deeply and shove my phone into my pocket. I take the bars with both hands. It's sticky. *Uugh*. Ling will do anything for her Big Scoop. A part of me admires her dedication. A larger part of me wonders if she's crazy.

"It'll cut our time down by half. If we do this right, we can get right under them!"

"That's exactly where I *don't* want to be," I groan. I'm not fit like Ling, but I manage to topple over the fence.

On the other side, Ling dances from one foot to the other, filled with boundless energy. Before Nuha can even cross over, she's is already scurrying through the lawns.

I race after her, breathing hard. I spot a security camera staring in my direction. I drop my chin and hide my face.

It doesn't take long to cross the residence grounds. On the other side, Ling jumps another fence. She lands on the sidewalk and jaywalks across a busy road. I groan again and follow her. She darts into a narrow alley. Her sneakers splash in questionable puddles of grimy brown and grey. It smells like rotting garbage. I nearly lose sight of Ling twice as she takes a few unexpected turns.

I can't wait to get started on that tracking app.

When we break out of the alley, we're in front of the Royal Ontario Museum. Its crystal entrance towers above us like a glass meteorite, half embedded in concrete, half reaching for the sky. Ling hunkers down by a corner to adjust her camera lens. Her cheeks are pink with triumph. I peer up. Two dots bob through the air.

Somehow, we're in front of Gwen and her combatant. I double over and suck air into my lungs.

"Am I good, or am I good?" Ling crows, grinning.

I grin back even though I don't want to. Her enthusiasm is infectious.

Nuha joins us a moment later, breathing harder than either of us. She flops onto the concrete, mindless of appearance, and brushes her hair from her face.

"Hate—you—" she manages to say between gasps.

Ling just laughs.

"Here they come," I warn. The two dots grow larger. One of them is carrying something long and dark. I pull out my camera.

Gwen has an I-beam ready. I marvel at her ability to float something so large and heavy. She once told me that once the metal is under her control, it loses its weight. It's how she can handle so much of it at once. A car feels like a laundry basket. An I-beam probably feels like a classroom desk, or nightstand. Apparently having metal manipulation *and* levitation allows her to levitate metals as a bonus. Had she only one power or another, she wouldn't be nearly as striking. It's this mix-and-match effect that makes most polypowers so versatile—and powerful.

"Marvellous," breathes Ling, camera to the sky. A little red dot blinks from the corner of her machine. Recording live. Her mouth is open in awe. "Fantastic. What a shot!"

Gwen swings the I-beam down at her opponent as though it were a golf club. Somehow, she makes the cumbersome motion seem elegant. Her opponent swerves out of the way. I can see the drag of the I-beam buffet him. He wobbles in its wake.

They're right above us now. I grab my cellphone and snap away. I can't make out any features on the mysterious figure or determine if he's the same one that's making threats on television. He doesn't seem so menacing when he's in the air and tiny. Gwen chucks the I-beam at him once more.

It makes a beeline for him.

I hold my breath.

It's a beautiful throw. I can almost see the trajectory of the beam, the shallow inverse parabola it makes as it soars through the air. I can sense it before it collides.

It's going to be a direct hit.

I see the I-beam smash into the figure. I feel a stab of horror and elation. She got him! Gwen prevails!

But then something strange happens.

Cracks appear along the slab of metal. Mere hairlines.

With a sharp *crack*, the slab of metal snaps into pieces. Uncontrolled, they plummet towards the earth, like dark, sharp meteors. I hear myself shout in alarm.

Gwen pauses. Her body language is shocked. She dives towards the earth, her arms outstretched.

She touches the first shard, grabs onto it. It dissolves into a liquid stream of metal. She touches the second.

But she's not fast enough. There are too many pieces.

The metal is bigger close up. Much bigger.

A shard smashes into the Royal Ontario Museum. The crystal lobby shatters. Screams erupt around me. Nuha dives to the ground as glass fills the air. She covers her head. All around me, people scramble for cover.

The glass twists in midair. Pieces as small as splinters. Pieces as large as my torso. Sunlight illuminates them from above, and they glow as though on fire. I see it all in slow motion. Like giant translucent scales, descending.

I throw up my hands.

Glass crashes around me. A violent jangling fills the air.

There's a terrible pressure along my side, like someone has sucker-punched me in the ribs. My hands fly up to defend them, but they meet something sharp and hard. A long glass shard sticking from my shirt. I touch it experimentally. *Oh.*

Time stops. My mind reels.

I've been stabbed.

Then the pain hits. It's hard to breathe. I want to hunch over, but my mind screams at me to stay still. I watch as a slow red blossom spreads along my side, hands useless. I'm cold all over, except for the red-hot fire burning into my side. The pain makes my knees shake.

Ling's camera slip from her fingers. Her face is pale.

I hear Nuha scream for help. Her voice sounds small and remote. The world begins to tilt. My legs buckle. *I can't die like this*, I think. I'm an only child. If I go, my bloodline ends. It's important I stay alive. The last thing I see is a dark shape spiralling towards me from above.

I black out.

Part 2

Chapter 7

Evening the Odds

Not all is sunshine and lollipops in the world of Supers, or so my dad likes to remind me. Only a select few Supers are as famous as Gwen. Even then, there are risks.

During one of her earlier expeditions, a robber shot Gwen in the chest. All Supersuits are bulletproof, but it didn't stop the impact from cracking three of her ribs. In the hospital, I insisted that I would develop healing powers so I could help her feel better faster. I couldn't imagine anyone who would shoot at a ten-year-old. Gwen only looked at me sadly. *No power can alter organic matter outside your own body*, she reminded me gently. *That's why no one can bring back the dead or cure terrible diseases*. I kicked a bedpost in frustration. Gwen patted my arm. *If you think this is bad*, she said, gesturing slowly at her bandages, *you should see the other guy*.

Ten-year-old Gwen, knocked off balance like a backhanded ragdoll, had dematerialized a nearby fire hydrant, crumpled it into a ball, and smashed it into the robber in retaliation. It knocked him flat, breaking six of his ribs. Officials took him to ER before they took him to detention. Gwen was praised for her spirit, for staying conscious, and for carrying out her duty despite her pain. *BRAVEST LITTLE SUPER IN THE WEST*, the headlines claimed. The photograph in the paper that day showed her clutching her side, beside the broken hydrant, under an umbrella of water, a knife-thin smile plastered on her face.

It's pretty common for Supers to be hospitalized after a mission. Most of the time it's just a check-up; LOS wants to make sure their Supers are always in good fighting condition. But sometimes it's because something has gone wrong.

My head is groggy. The blankets around me are too hot. I want to kick them off, but my limbs are heavy as sandbags.

I can hear the scuff of footsteps outside my door, and quiet, serious voices. They've drugged me, I'm sure. An ache pulses through my right side with every heartbeat. I count fifty beats before cracking my eyes open just a little. It's night, and the hospital lights are dimmed. My mouth tastes like plaster.

For a moment, I can't remember what happened. Then pain shoots across my side, and it all rushes back.

I groan. I suppose if being a Super has one downside, it would be frequent injuries.

I wonder how many times Frances E. Shaw got hurt, how many times they had to stitch her up and mop her up. I remember her face in photos, all smooth and calm, like a statue. But photos can be altered, and there's always makeup. I wonder whether she had scars anywhere. I wonder about my mom, who took part in her fair share of dangerous missions but always recalls her Super days with fond nostalgia.

I close my eyes again and will myself to sleep. I ignore the pain in my side and concentrate on the quiet whoosh of the ventilator instead, matching my breathing to its easy rhythm. *1…2…3.* The smell of disinfectant is unpleasant, but I eventually manage to nod off.

I'm tossed from my sleep by loud voices. Some female, some male. All urgent. I blink blearily at the ceiling. Shadows bustle to and fro behind the frosted glass window of my hospital room's door.

"We're just curious, ma'am. You must understand, the great-granddaughter of the Original Super—"

"Surely you can at least give us her condition!"

"The public is hungry for information! Will Miss Bell be all right?"

A stern male voice rings out. "Hospital regulations state that there are not to be any visitors until Miss Bell recovers her health. Her family has requested that you respect their privacy at this time. Now I'll kindly ask you all to back away."

"Just one question, doctor!"

Of course. It's the reporters. It seems they always show up at the most embarrassing times. I don't want to be photographed, drugged up, injured, and *helpless*. I don't think they're interested in my well-being anyways. They're only making a big deal of my injuries because of my lineage. It's embarrassing. The great-granddaughter of the Original Super can't even protect herself from falling glass. I pull my covers over my head and wait for the reporters to leave.

"Just tell us her condition, doctor! Millions are wondering—"

There's a haggard sigh. "Miss Bell is currently in stable condition. Now, please—"

"What are her injuries like? How long until she's released from hospital? What is your opinion on the state of public Super battles? Doctor? Why won't you answer our questions?"

There's a sudden hush, as though someone has thrown a

blanket over the crowd, followed by a collective murmur of surprise and a smatter of camera flashes. A light, commanding voice speaks.

"I wish to see Miss Bell, please."

My ears perk up. I peek out from under the covers.

"Again, visiting hours have not yet begun," says the exasperated doctor. "Please wait—"

"I don't care. I want to see her."

"I assure you, it's better to let Miss Bell rest—"

"Don't you know who I am? I'm—"

"Miss Kendricks, we are all very aware of who you are. Yet policy must be observed—"

My door bursts open with enough force to bounce off the wall. I nearly topple off my bed. Camera flashes light up the room for a split second. Their brightness makes my head hurt. I see the poor doctor's back as he barricades the entrance, arms waving as though to shoo away flies. Gwen sweeps through my door, eyes bright, and the door slams, leaving the reporters scrambling outside. The pain in my side flares up again, and I assume a fetal position, wincing. Gwen pushes the doctor aside and rushes over.

"Gwen," I say. My voice sounds all thick and gooey. *Guueenn.* It's like I've forgotten how to talk.

"Beata, how are you feeling? Are you ok? Are you in pain? Do you need any medication? I can tell them to bring you painkillers. What about water? Are you thirsty? Hungry?"

I begin to lift my right hand, but even small motions hurt.

"I'm ok," I try to say, but it comes out weedy and pale.

Gwen looks the roughest I've ever seen her. The tips of her hair are tangled, and her make-up hasn't been refreshed.

"This is my fault," Gwen says, straightening and running

a hand through her hair. It's a graceful yet uneven motion.

I shake my head. "No." *Nuuhhn*.

Her eyes flash. "Of course it's my fault! I'm a Super. It's my job to protect the weak! How can I call myself a Super if I can't even protect my best friend?"

I feel a tinge of annoyance. *Weak*. Right. I'm one of the weak ones, without the ability to protect myself. I have to be shielded from harm, like a babe. Gwen paces the room. She's changed from her turquoise gown into a simpler white summer dress. It shows off her smooth shoulders. She chews on her lip, looking frustrated.

"They're treating me good," I reassure her, swallowing hard to get the words out right.

"They better be," she replies a little too fast. I can't help but be taken aback. Gwen doesn't lose composure, but there is something frayed about her movements. I don't like seeing her like this, so I try to change the subject.

"Did you get him?" I ask. My voice cracks a little.

Gwen pulls up a chair and perches in it, barely sitting at all. Her face darkens. "No. I lost him. But don't worry, he won't get far. LOS is on his trail, and I'll personally make sure he pays for his actions."

"Did you get a good look at him?"

"A teenager. Maybe around my age. Male. Curly black hair. I didn't get a good look at his face. He had a mask."

"Like a real supervillain." I smile weakly, but Gwen's face remains stony. "He attacked LOS in front of the whole world," I continue quietly. "He's bold. And he's a Super."

"A polypower," corrects Gwen. Now that we're talking about more technical things, she seems calmer. I breathe lightly so as to not inflame my injury.

"I hit him with an I-beam, to give him a taste of his own medicine," said Gwen.

"I saw." I replay the scene in my head. *Glorious*. "He survived being hit with an I-beam?"

"No, he shattered it, remember? I don't think that can count as being hit."

Right. My mind is still foggy from the drugs. I cycle through a list of powers in my head. It's like looking through molasses. My thoughts are stiff. "Imperviousness?"

"No." Gwen pauses and looks contemplative.

I watch her retreat from her body, become distant and quiet.

"I think he's the same as me," she finally says, green eyes glittering. "I think he has metal manipulation."

I let her words sink in. A polypower just like Gwen. Evenly matched. The thought is both terrifying and exhilarating. I begin to shake. What are the chances? Improbable. Nearly impossible, even. Pain stitches my side, and I try to calm myself. Getting nervous now will only hurt me. "Do you know him then?"

Gwen's head comes up. She frowns. "Know him? Of course not. Why would I?"

"LOS keeps track of all Supers, right? Aren't polypowers like you rare?"

"One in a hundred Supers are polypowers," Gwen recites.

"So shouldn't LOS know who he is? How many polypowers can fly? I mean, they go to school every year to scout new talent. They have a database."

Gwen shrugs. "I don't keep very good track of other polypowers," she admits. "I let LOS admin deal with the numbers. I haven't met many others, let alone got to know them. We get together once a year for an international connections retreat, but other than that, we keep to ourselves. Besides, he's a villain. That means he probably keeps underground and engages in unsavoury tasks. He could have erased his file."

"He seemed pretty well trained for someone with no access to LOS," I reason. All Supers receive training from LOS. Without proper training, I doubt he would have been able to keep up with someone as skilled as Gwen.

"Well, he works with the Counter-League. There might be a bunch of them, training in secret. Who knows what these criminals do in their spare time?"

She's getting defensive. I can see it in her face. A small part of me, a tiny, shameful part, thinks, *This is payback for calling me weak*, but I feel bad almost immediately.

"So, what will you do now?" I ask.

The ventilator breathes a slow exhalation. Gwen's jaw tightens.

"Bad behaviour deserves to be punished," she says simply, and I'm not sure she's talking to me anymore. It's more of a declaration than a reply. "He's made his move. Now, it's my turn. Next time, he won't escape. I'll nail him to a wall if I have to."

She laughs a little. Not a joyous laugh. A low laugh that sounds more eager than happy. It startles me. She looks a little crazed with the fluorescent lights bringing out the white of her eyes, and the tips of her hair tangled and tinged with dust. I swallow hard, suddenly feeling more uneasy than ever.

They keep me in the hospital for another day, then release me back home. The nurses insist on rolling me out in a wheelchair, despite my protests. Other patients stare as I head through the lobby. I have apparently gained some fame during my stay.

"Are you sure there are no reporters?" I ask for the umpteenth time. I didn't want the world to see me squat like a lame duck, getting pushed around by other people. It would be lower than low. Famed descendent of the great Original Super, unable to even stand properly. I think I see my nurse roll her eyes.

"There will not be any reporters. We will allow you to exit through a private entrance, away from the main roads."

My wheelchair has a squeaky wheel. It echoes in the hallways, turning heads all the way. I focus ahead, trying not to lose my cool. I only start to relax once we turn away from the main lobby and head down a smaller corridor. A few minutes in, we run into a familiar face, and I motion for the nurse to stop.

"Mr. Uzune," I gasp. "Um, hello!"

He startles as though jolted from a dream. A shock of white bandages are wrapped around his wrist. "Oh, Miss Bell. How are you doing?"

I wonder if he knows about my injury. He must. My parents must have told him why I am absent. Even though I know he has a life outside of school, it's always weird seeing him outside the classroom. "Better now, sir. The doctors say my stitches are healing up nicely."

"Good, good," he says, bobbing his head like a pigeon. I remember overhearing his plans to head to City Hall for the live conference, and a jolt of worry shoots through me.

"Were you hurt in the attack?" It bothers me to think someone I know was hurt by debris, especially someone nice like Mr. Uzune.

"Just a little," he says, pinching his index finger and thumb together with his good hand to make a small gap. "I tripped and got cut by some glass. It wasn't bad, certainly not compared to what you went though."

"Well…" I pause. I can feel my heart rate begin to spike. I'm not good at small talk. I have no idea how to end a conversation without seeming rude. "I'm glad you're ok."

"And I you, Miss Bell. I will see you in class soon." He smiles kindly at me. "I have given all your homework sheets to Miss Bahar. Make sure you complete as much as you can so you don't fall behind, ok?"

As my nurse wheels me past him, I give a small wave, which he returns. Before long, we roll up to a locked, private door, where she helps me into my coat before pushing me though. The fresh air washes over me, and I breathe deeply. After days of antiseptic, the smell of grass is amazing. I squint against the sun. I want to run out and sing, but a mild stab of pain in my side derails the thought. Instead, I spot my parents' Prius waiting against the sidewalk.

I grin so hard my face hurts.

At home, my parents fuss over me like hens. I'm ordered to rest for at least a week while my wound heals. No vigorous exercise. Lots of fluids. I'm lucky. I have all my limbs, and all my organs escaped unscathed. According to the news, at least three people were crushed by falling concrete, and a dozen are in hospital with serious injuries. *Thankfully, no important political personnel were injured*, says the evening news scrolling across the bottom of the TV screen. Given the size of the attack, I'm surprised so few people perished.

"We have LOS to thank," my mom says. "It's their quick response that saved lives."

"They're very efficient, aren't they?" I say, reading the scrolling sentences at the bottom of the screen. *Cleanup underway at Nathan Phillips Square. Funeral for the victims to be held on Tuesday.* Praise for LOS's heroic actions abounds. I think of Gwen, soaring through the sky, and her mysterious challenger. *Masked villain still at large: LOS investigates.*

I bite my tongue. Still? It's been more than a week now.

"For an organization so efficient, is it weird that they can't find the guy?"

My mom looks over at me, her bright eyes contemplative. She puts a hand on my head. "Don't worry. Trust in LOS. Gwen's probably patrolling the city right now, looking for him. She's really quite wonderful. She'll find him and bring him to justice. You'll see."

Her expression takes on a dreamy look. It's a look I'm familiar with, proud and nostalgic, as though she's watching an especially good school play. It happens a lot when Gwen is mentioned. Every time she adopts that look I feel a pang of longing. She never looks at me like that.

"Oh, to be young again," she says with a sigh.

My mom and dad spend a couple of days fending off reporters. Mom even makes an appearance on CP24, our local news channel, to reassure everyone that I'm ok and to talk about the danger of Super battles. Dad was opposed, saying it would only make them hungrier for more interviews, but Mom overrode him. *The best way to get rid of reporters*, she reasoned, *is to give them what they want.* Still confined to my house, I watch her on television as she slips back into her old Super persona, all hair flips and coy glances.

"Risks are always present," she tells the eager host, smiling slyly at the camera. "All Supers accept that fact, and everyone else around them should as well. Really, how else are you going to stop a supervillain? They have no code of honour. Do they spare civilians? No. So we fight them wherever we can. Supers try to be discreet, but people are going to get hurt along the way. That's just how things are."

She tosses her hair. Her green earrings sparkle in the incandescent light. She bought them just for the broadcast.

"Sometimes I think she misses being on television," Dad says with a slight shake of his head. "Even after all this time."

He seems put out, but I don't blame her. Television makes people glamorous. If I had the spotlight, I'd hate to give it up too. My mom on television looks brighter, more beautiful, and more elegant than ever. On television, she seems more like her younger self, exuberant and brimming with energy. Nothing like what she's like at home. I think of Gwen and the adulation she receives. A pang of jealousy rises in my stomach, and I press it down with difficulty. Why couldn't I be seen in that sort of light? Useful and admired, rather than all banged up.

Dad makes me chicken noodle soup, which I eat carefully so as not to aggravate my side. It's good to be back in my own room, in my own blankets, and among my old posters, even though it's a bit hard facing Frances E. Shaw's calm gaze after getting injured. I'm sure she got injured once in a while too but only while doing heroic things, like saving people or fighting off the enemy. Not standing around as a bystander.

Hey, Frances, I think at her shyly. As usual, she doesn't reply.

On a Friday afternoon, Ling and Nuha visit, bearing get-well cards, treats, and homework. Ling throws herself at me. I'm afraid she'll land on me, but she holds back at the last moment and folds her hands instead.

"Are you angry with me?" Ling asks, more bashful than I've ever seen her.

"No," I say, and am somewhat surprised to mean it. She wasn't the one who rained glass on me, after all. "It was a freak accident."

She opens her mouth as though to say more but doesn't. She just shakes her head. Apologies don't come easy to Ling, but I know she's sorry.

"What did I miss?" I ask. "How's school?"

"People send their best wishes," Nuha says, moving to sit cross-legged in my chair.

I raise an eyebrow. "Do they really?"

"Well, most of them." Nuha shrugs. "It's not every day a classmate is hit by shrapnel and gets so many cool stitches. You're kind of famous now. I mean, more famous than before."

I'm not sure how I feel about that. Being famous for getting hurt. It's not exactly the brand I'm looking for. My glum must have shown, because Nuha drops the newest volume of *Popular Mechanics for Kids* in front of me to cheer me up.

"There's an article about apps in here," she says, flipping the pages with a practiced hand. "An entire two-page spread about Objective-C versus Super XCoder!"

"No contest. Super XCoder is more powerful."

"I don't know, Bea. Objective's upgrades look pretty sweet."

We chat about programming, which bores Ling, and have a snack of cheese and crackers. Programming is completely predictable. You get out what you put in. There are no unexpected side effects—at least, none that can't be fixed with a bit of tweaking. I give Ling the latest version of our Sound Isolator app, which seems to pique her interest. She scrambles downstairs and out onto the sidewalk to test it on random passers-by.

"What sort of interface do we want to give the Sound Isolator?" Nuha asks. We can see Ling from my bedroom window, doing her best to look nonchalant as she aims the Sound Isolator at total strangers. "I'm thinking something easy to work with. Simple."

"One big button. Hit to record. Hit again to stop."

Nuha nods. "Let's make it orange."

"Why orange?"

"I don't know. It seems like a cheerful colour." Nuha plays with her braid. She has on a loose green T-shirt with a yellow patterned hem today. Her shorts are bright red. She clashes so hard it's difficult to look directly at her.

Suddenly, there's a terrible noise from outside, a sharp shrieking, like fingernails across a chalkboard. Nuha and I both yelp. Nuha leaps to the window, and I follow awkwardly behind. Ling has her palms clamped over her ears. My cellphone is on the ground. She must have dropped it.

"What happened?" demands Nuha.

Ling makes an exaggerated shrug from below. She cups her mouth. "I just hit playback!" She turns to look at me, her eyes incredulous. "I swear!"

The front door opens and my dad rushes out. He still has an apron on.

"Is everyone ok?"

"We're good, Mr. Bell! We're good!" Ling says, a little too loud. I don't blame her. She just got an earful of that awful sound. "We're just playing with the Sound Isolator. It must be glitching or something. Yes, I'm sure it's ok. Sorry again! Please, go back to your scones. They smell really good, by the way! Sorry, neighbourhood!" She waves at the curious bystanders and takes a bow, as though on stage. Once our audience is pacified, she picks up my phone from the ground and scampers back in. Her footsteps reverberate all the way up the stairs. Inside my room, she drops my phone on my bed as though it might bite her.

"It nearly busted my eardrums!"

"I swear it's not supposed to do that. Let me take a look at the coding again." I pick up the phone and connect it to my computer. I pull up Super XCoder and begin to scroll through lines of programming. "Did you record anything?"

"A conversation between a lovely lady and her dignified poodle, yes. It was something about not dropping turds in inappropriate places—"

"The app must not be saving right." I frown hard at the screen. I'm good at programming apps. It's my *thing*. It bothers me that it malfunctioned so badly. "It must be replaying the last conversation it recorded before I made any adjustments."

Or in this case, the horrible screech of metal hitting metal during the City Hall incident. My hand goes to my side. The memory of the glass shard entering my flesh still makes me flinch. I can feel the rough outline of my bandages under my shirt. I quickly distract myself by searching for errors. "The app isn't recording correctly, or not saving sounds correctly, or it's just not recalling correctly."

"Whatever it is, I'm not touching it again until I'm guaranteed the safety of my hearing." Ling pats her ears.

"I have no idea what went wrong. Sorry, Ling."

"This is what beta testing is for," says Nuha reasonably. She peeks over my shoulder. "I don't see any immediate red flags, and the program doesn't notice anything wrong."

"It's probably an extra bracket somewhere," I say unhappily. "I'll have to go through manually and check every statement." Numbers and letters crawl across my screen like tiny ants. Then out of nowhere, I yawn. Since my injury, I tire quickly.

Nuha's face softens.

"Go to sleep, Bea," she says. "We'll work on this later."

"No, I can keep going."

"Bea," Nuha says again, looking stern.

Usually, I would not relent, but I can feel sleep sneaking up on me like a shadow. "Ok, fine. Your place next time?"

"My place. I'll text you." She nudges Ling. "Come on. Let's give Bea some time to rest."

Ling shoots me another look as she leaves, eyebrows raised. *We're good?*

I give her a thumbs-up. *We're good.*

Once they're gone, I tuck myself into bed and do my math sheets to relax. The doctors still have me on painkillers, so the throbbing in my side isn't debilitating, but it still makes it hard to write. Even math is harder than usual. The doctor said healing might interrupt my ability to think for a few days. Apparently my body needs energy to reknit, so it diverts energy from my brain. As I reach to turn the pages of my textbook, an extra strong pang stabs up my side, and my pencil rolls into the crack between my wall and mattress.

I curse and carefully roll from bed to fetch the pencil.

There, I spot an old album. It's my Super card collection. When Gwen got her own card, she gave me a signed one for free. I spent a few years attempting to complete the collection, but stopped when I couldn't take looking at happy Super faces anymore. Some younger than me. All of them radiant.

I brush away my bitterness and pull out the album. My cards are arranged by date. The first, granted posthumously, is Frances E. Shaw. My great-grandmother. The card people took a sepia photograph of her and filled in the colours. Burnt brown hair. Periwinkle eyes. Her card is special. It's holographic. I flip the pages absently.

Hitori Yuuma. He's short for his age. In his photograph, he looks somewhat bewildered, as though just shaken from bed.

My mom, Tessa. She looked even more like a pixie when she was younger, with big eyes and round cheeks. She must have been only ten or eleven when the picture was taken.

My dad doesn't have a card. His skills weren't interesting enough to be broadcast, so he didn't get merchandise.

Then I notice something. A few lines below my mom's card there's a picture of a boy with curly red hair and a smatter of freckles. Powers: lasers. Name: Charley X. Beamsman.

I pause. Beamsman. *As* in *the* Beamsman? The supervillain?

I check his active dates.

They overlap with Hitori Yuuma's.

I suck in a breath. It *is* him. I scan his face and remember the footage of his last moments. On his card, he's giving an uncertain smile. It's hard to imagine a kid like him going bad, using his powers to harm people, hunted down and blown up in an explosion. It's weird staring at his photograph. Like looking into the face of a ghost.

It takes effort to get down the stairs thanks to my burning side. My parents gave me a buzzer to press whenever I needed anything, but I hate the thought of bothering them. Only my dad is home this evening. Mom is at a charity event at the local soup kitchen. She goes every week, saying it makes her feel like she's still making a difference now that her powers have faded. When I peek into the living room, my dad springs to his feet.

"Bea. What happened to the buzzer?" He strides over, ready to lend a hand.

"I'm ok. Besides, the doctor said I should move around a bit anyways. It'll help me heal."

"Not this early in the game." He helps me to the couch. "What are you doing down here? You should be resting."

I sit on the couch and show him Charley X. Beamsman's card. "I never knew Beamsman was a part of LOS."

Dad sits down beside me. He does this gingerly, as though afraid his weight would disturb me. "Charley X. Beamsman, yes. I remember him. He joined LOS a few years after I officially left, so we didn't interact, but I did meet him once."

"You *met* Beamsman?" Now that I think about it, my dad isn't that much older than Beamsman and Hitori Yuuma.

"Well…" Dad looks abashed. "Let's not say I knew him. I did pass him in the hallways once when I was visiting LOS HQ for private business. I said, 'Hello,' and he said, 'Cheers,' in sort of a quiet way. Did you know he had a Scottish accent? Not many people do. I remember being sort of star-struck. I was twenty-two, and he was only twelve, but he had already accomplished so much more."

He pauses, eyes floating over the card in my hand. "It's hard to believe the same kid went on to kill so many people."

The silence that settles over us is subdued. Dad is still looking at the card, but I know he's not really seeing it. He's asking the same question in his head as I am in mine.

"Why did he go bad?"

I think about Gwen and her team. *Let's just say it's not ideal*, she told me once. LOS politics, perhaps? Someone vying for her leadership position? Personal grudges between Supers? It bothers me to think that someone close to her could snap at any moment. "Did he just not get along with people?"

Dad's brow pinches. It's a sign that he's considering his words carefully. "No one really knows why anyone goes rogue," he says finally, "whether it be external pressures, or even internal ones. No one truly knows but the person themselves, but I've known people who have cracked under the pressure of serving the public. And I've known people who have quit."

He says this without judgement, only sadness.

"How many Supers become supervillains?" I ask, dreading the answer. Gwen said she didn't recognize her challenger. But she also didn't get a look at his face. There's still a chance he could be someone close to her. Dad looks at me carefully and for a good ten seconds.

"I honestly don't know," he says at last.

It's neither the answer I wanted nor dreaded. It's barely an answer at all. Maybe I'm a pessimist, or a worrywart, or naturally neurotic, but it makes my stomach turn.

Chapter 8

A Bad Day

I had thought my absence from school would make people forget about my outburst, especially given my recent injuries, but I was wrong. My appearance in the news only makes me stand out more. It doesn't help that a small tabloid, *Super Juicy*, has published a short article titled *THE BRIGHT FUTURE OF THE BELLS*, with a blurb about me developing the ability to "curse" people. My mood is stormy even before I walk through the front doors. I had spotted the article at a local convenience store as I walked to school and wanted to buy every single copy, just to get it off the stands.

As I enter Sir Frederick Banting, I am greeted in the hallway by a recording device.

"Miss Beata Bell!" declares a junior reporter on *Read About It*. Her hair is tied in a tight ponytail. Her glasses are so large they reflect my whole face. My hand jumps to my side, as though to protect it. "How does it feel to *finally* develop powers?" She draws out the word *finally*. "And have you contacted LOS yet?"

It takes me a second to get over the shock and spit out my response: "What're you talking about?"

Passing students glance sideways at me. It's like they're trying to avoid staring outright. A trail of whispers circles through the hall. I want to shrink into myself. I hate the feeling of eyes on me, watching, judging.

"And what are your thoughts on changing other people's karma when you can't change your own?" the girl presses with a tilt of her head. She motions carelessly at my side. "It must be frustrating, huh? Do you think with enough practice you'll be able to curse yourself for the better?"

Her bluntness isn't surprising—many news reporters are blunt—but it *is* off-putting. I take a step back. "You're mistaken. I'm not a Super."

"Well, duh." She rolls her eyes. "You're not registered with LOS yet."

"No, you're not getting it. I don't actually have powers."

"That's not what *Super Juicy* says."

I'm starting to get annoyed. I try to push past her, but she blocks my way. "Well, they're wrong, ok? You think *Super Juicy* knows more about me than I do?"

"Whoa, no need to get snippy there. I'm just asking questions. It's a part of my job, you know."

"Get out of the way. I have class to get to." I try to step around her, but she darts in front of me again. I almost knock my teeth on her recording device. "Excuse me, *please*."

Finally, I outmanoeuvre her.

"Are you relieved?" the girl calls after me. "It took long enough for you to develop. *Way* later than the other girls. Were you worried you might never get powers? Can you imagine if you never did? It would be a total scandal! Do you think you have what it takes to fight crime? How will you best apply your powers? Are you and Gwen going to work together on the same team? Will you have a cool team name?"

There's no reasoning with her, so I shove past her and duck my head. The girl crows after me, waving her arms. People slide out of the way as I approach, as though I have a force field around me. I think of how Gwen parts crowds and wonder if this is what it feels like to be famous and powerful. I hope not. It doesn't feel good at all.

It feels lonely.

Even students who were neutral to me seemed to be avoiding me now. I wonder how deep the rumours run, and bite the inside of my cheek. I don't want to be famous for cursing people. I want to be famous like Frances E. Shaw, or Gwen. I want to be loved and admired. Not feared. I hurry to my classroom early to get away from all the silence.

Mr. Uzune is writing math equations on the board. I check for bandages, but his hand seems fully healed. I wave at him as I take my seat, and he nods back. I fiddle with my Rubik's Cube and wait for my friends to arrive.

Ling is annoyingly helpful today. The first thing she does is shunt her desk next to mine—a noisy movement that Mr. Uzune either allows or doesn't notice—so she can remove my textbooks and pencil case from my bag and arrange them on my desk. She even tries to flip the pages as Mr. Uzune begins to teach. She sticks to my side so closely I want to tell her to lay off. I'm hurt, but I'm ok. She doesn't need to baby me.

I finally push her away when she attempts to hand-feed me my animal crackers during recess. "Ling, stop. It's embarrassing."

She looks at me with a calculating expression. There's doubt in there, and stubbornness. I hold her gaze.

"You don't owe me anything," I say with finality. For a second, I think Ling's going to fight me, to insist on being my caretaker, but then she tosses her hair.

"Fine," she says, attempting to sound nonchalant, "but if you *do* need anything, you have to tell me."

"I will," I reply, relieved.

We take it easy during recess. Nuha has brought some old Pogs she found lying in her basement, and we ogle at the weird images. From the corner of my eye, I see Dieter and his flying cronies hogging the jungle gyms. A flash of white catches my eye. His right arm is bandaged up to the elbow. He flies with a certain caution, fewer brash movements and more hesitation. He keeps his injured arm close. I nudge Ling.

"What happened to Dieter?"

"It's your curse, finally taken hold!" says Ling with a cackle, and I'm glad to see her usual bravado is back, but Nuha quiets her with a disapproving look. She turns to me, serious.

"Dieter had an accident with a Bunsen burner the other day," she explains. "Something was wrong with the gas. It exploded when he turned it on."

"We could hear him howling all the way from homeroom," adds Ling.

"He went to the hospital," said Nuha, quieter. She stares at me pointedly.

Suddenly, all the wary glances make sense. I cursed Dieter in the cafeteria. In front of everyone. And now he's hurt. I know it's just a series of bad coincidences, but something in me tingles unpleasantly. People can take coincidences the wrong way. There's even a scientific term for it: *Apophenia*, or seeing patterns where none actually exist.

"You know I didn't actually curse him, right?" I glance from Nuha to Ling. A small, desperate note sneaks into my voice, and I clear my throat. "I don't curse people. You guys know that. I panicked and lied. That's all."

I'm not a bad person, I want to say, but I don't want to sound desperate.

"We know," says Nuha soothingly, "but not everyone knows."

"Yeah, *Super Juicy* has really been pressing the crazy angle. I think they refer to you as 'dangerously unstable' at least twice." Ling's shoulders heave as she sighs. "It's shoddy writing, but people will read anything these days."

"Is that why people have been avoiding me?" I ask, incredulous.

I cast my eyes over the playground at two Supers juggling fireballs in one corner, and the dozen Civvies squeezed into a four square game in another. A light breeze touches my neck, and I shiver. Dieter and I were never on good terms. He loves to remind me of my lack of powers, messing up my hair and dropping things on my head. I want to feel glee over his injury, but I can't. It looks like it hurts. The Bunsen burner must have had faulty wiring, or a loose screw. It could have been anything except a curse.

Yet a small part of me wants to claim responsibility.

Because it would mean I have powers.

It would mean I'm a Super after all.

As soon as the thought crosses my mind, I feel terrible. No, it's wrong. Supers aren't supposed to hurt people. Supers are revered, like Gwen. Not dreaded.

I'm sure Frances E. Shaw wouldn't threaten anyone with her powers. She would be disappointed to know her great-granddaughter is using her powers to bully people even though I don't even have powers to begin with! Gwen's words haunt me. *The strong protect the weak.* It's my greatest wish to be a Super, but I wonder if I have what it takes. Supers are brave, and generous, and composed. I don't feel very brave or generous right now.

I hug myself.

"Bea?" asks Nuha, observant as ever.

"It's nothing," I say, a little too fast. "I'm going to go to the bathroom."

Nuha frowns but doesn't follow me. In my haste, I almost bowl over a third-grader emerging from a stall. She squeals and falls backwards.

"Sorry!" I blurt. "Are you ok?"

She starts to nod but halts when she sees my face. She squeaks a quick apology and scrambles out the door.

"Wait!" I grab for her but miss. Pain stabs my side in protest, and I bite my cheek.

She's afraid of me. I slowly shift into a stall and lock the door. The pain in my side throbs. I check for bleeding, but my stitches are holding ok. It's a small relief in what's starting to feel like a very long day.

I bring my lunchbox to homeroom and knock on the door. There's no response, so I poke my head in to take a look. Mr. Uzune dozes at his desk, half-graded homework papers sprawled across his desk.

"Mr. Uzune?" I ask.

"I'm awake!" His head comes up so fast he knocks his papers off the table. Student reports and newspaper clippings flutter to the ground at my feet. I bend over to pick them up. *LOS: New Recruit Report* stares at me from the top of the pile. I rip my gaze away from the title. It's like everything is trying to remind me of my nonexistent powers.

Mr. Uzune looks about blearily before patting the desk for his glasses. "Oh, Miss Bell. Hello. How is your injury?"

"Not bad," I mutter, and pass him his papers.

"It's healing up nicely?"

"Pretty nicely."

"Good." He piles his papers into a messy heap at the corner of his desk. "So how can I help you today? Do you have questions about class?"

"No," I mutter, and pass him the papers. "I was actually wondering if I could eat in here today."

Mr. Uzune frowns. "Again? Shouldn't you be out with your friends?"

"I just need some room to think." I hope he doesn't ask too many questions. Mr. Uzune is a nice teacher. I like him a lot. Even though he gives a lot of homework, he never gets angry or shouts when we don't finish it or hand it in. He just looks sad, which is, in a strange way, even worse.

"Is something going on, Miss Bell?"

"No! It's not like I'm being bullied or anything."

Smooth, my mind chimes nastily. My cheeks burn. Mr. Uzune seems harmless enough, but he can surprise you with sharp observations. The last thing I want now is more questions. I want to curl up and forget all of today.

Mr. Uzune studies me.

I hold my breath.

"Are the reporters harassing you again?" he asks, leaning in as though to share a secret.

"No, nothing like that." I don't think the girl for *Read About It* counts as an actual reporter. Last time reporters came to interview me, Mr. Uzune hid me in the teacher's lounge until they went away. It was really nice of him.

"All right then, you can stay for lunch as long as you're sure you want to." He shuffles his papers and puts them into his desk. "It might be nice to have some company."

I sit down. Not too far and not too close. I don't want to invite conversation, or give the impression I'm snubbing him. It's a careful balance. I unpack my lunch, a simple baloney sandwich with a banana and a cup of yogurt. I notice Dad has snuck me a small chocolate bar too. Mom usually doesn't let me eat sweets.

As I bite into my sandwich, Mr. Uzune's eyes settle on me for a second more before he goes back to his marking. When someone looks at me like that, it always makes me twitchy. It's like they can see right through me. Like they know exactly what is going on. I make myself small and munch my sandwich in silence.

I make a decision. I should apologize to Dieter, or if not apologize, at least check if he's ok. It's the right thing to do. We can have a civilized chat and clear things up like mature people. I spend the afternoon going over scenarios in my head. Should I approach him in private or bring Ling and Nuha along for support? He's always with his friends, which is intimidating, but if I bring my own friends, it might look like I'm trying to gang up on him. Now that everyone thinks I'm a Super who uses her powers for petty vengeance, I'm really self-conscious.

I spend most of last period counting prime numbers in my head and breathing carefully, but I'm distracted by the pain in my side.

Be brave, I tell myself. *You can do this.*

After class, I dodge Ling and Nuha and head to the exit. My palms are sweaty. I want to hide under a rock, but I urge myself on. Misunderstandings need to be fixed. I plan to wait for Dieter on the sidewalk, but once I get there, I chicken out and dodge behind a tree instead. I spot Ling and Nuha in the distance. They must be looking for me. I feel bad for leaving them out of the loop, but I have to do this for my conscience's sake. My cellphone buzzes in my back pocket, and I turn the ring tone to silent. Then I feel even worse. They're probably worried. Dieter is late, and I crouch behind the trunk until most students have gone home.

Finally, I see Dieter float down the sidewalk, and feel a spurt of annoyance that he uses his Super powers for such everyday tasks. Powers are supposed to be used for the greater good, not so you can be lazy.

You're supposed to be clearing things up, my brain reminds me. *Not hiding behind a tree, judging.*

I suck up a breath and step out from behind the trunk. I lift a hand in greeting.

"Hey."

Dieter actually loses control for a moment and lands on his butt. A flash of pain passes through his face as he clutches his injured arm closer.

"You!" he shouts. "Stay away from me!"

Panic spikes. I edge forward, palms out, as though approaching an injured dog. "We should talk."

"No. Haven't you done enough? Stay away, you witch!" He looks angry now, struggling to get to his feet with the help of only one arm. His cheeks are pink with effort. He looks like an upturned turtle, with his backpack weighing him down and his limbs flailing.

"Come on, let me help."

He kicks at me and I jump away. The motion sends a spasm of pain through my side. I bite my cheek and double over.

For a moment, we're both panting, slowed down by our injuries.

"Dieter," I say, using my most adult voice, the sort of voice my dad uses when he wants to be reasonable. "I think we had a misunderstanding. I'm not—"

Something bounces off my head. It stings and I flinch. An acorn tumbles to the concrete and rolls away. A breath of air tickles my neck as a shadowy figure dives from the sky. I scramble backwards to avoid getting hit.

"Scram, witch!" Within the blink of an eye, one of Dieter's friends hovers between us. Matt Kiel. Rumour has it he broke his nose in a fight with a high-schooler, and it never set right. He has a handful of acorns. He heaves them all at me. I cover my face as the nuts splash across my arms and chest. "No one wants you around!"

The hatred in his voice makes me take a step back. More shadows fall across the ground. Dieter's friends are catching up. They circle above, like sharks around an injured seal. My mouth feels dry. Maybe it was a mistake to come alone. I take another step back.

"I don't want trouble, guys," I say, trying to sound calm. My voice comes out in a squeak.

"Yeah, sure," drawls one of the flying Supers from above.

"I'm serious!"

"Let's get her!"

A pine cone clatters from above and lands at my feet.

Dieter has finally gotten up. He takes a couple of skips back before floating upwards. He doesn't take his eyes off me. Another pine cone drops onto my head.

I scoot for cover. "Stop! I just want to talk!"

"Burn the witch!" they begin to chant. "Burn the witch!"

Acorns, pine cones, and sticks rain down. I swat away the first few, but they become too thick to repel. My shouts fall on deaf ears as they advance, sneering and hooting. I turn around to run, but it's hard to outrun flying Supers with an injury. They trail after me, grabbing more ammo. I push my legs faster, but I'm afraid of ripping my stitches. Whenever Dieter's gang has harassed me in the past, there has always been a sense of restraint. Now, I'm not so sure. I'm afraid they'll actually hurt me. Something heavy thunks down in front of me and I balk. It's a rock. My heart leaps into my throat. They're serious this time.

I think I hear Dieter say, "Guys," but it's distant and very quiet. I try to heave my backpack over my head for protection, but my side can't handle it. Pain spasms through my chest. I gasp for air. It hurts so much. A small, traitorous part of me wishes Gwen were here. She could turn back the boys with a flick of her hand. She could keep me safe.

But Gwen's not here. It's just me. Alone.

Something slices past my head and nicks my ear. I lift a hand to cover it and feel wetness there. I stare as a broken piece of brick skids across the road. I'm bleeding, I think, surprised. They're trying to kill me. Fear and shock course through me like a river.

Then…a hot tide of anger.

"A curse on all of you!" I yell, adrenaline kicking in. "Misfortune on your families! You'll pay for this. I hope you all get burned!"

The flying Supers draw back for a moment, as though buffeted by the wind. Doubt crosses their faces.

"She can't get all of us!" one of them shouts.

They rush at me again. I scream and swing out my backpack, missing by a mile. A stabbing pain shoots up my side, and my breath hitches. Tears spring to my eyes. The boys veer away. I clutch my backpack like a shield. If I'm going down, I'm going to go down fighting. My mind is on hyperdrive. What can I do? I'm one Dud against half a dozen Supers. I need some sort of area attack, something to distract them all at once.

My hand drops to my pocket, and I grab my cellphone. My fingers are shaking, but I manage to pull it out. Quickly, I enter my passcode and activate the Sound Isolator app. *Please work*, I pray, as I layer the sounds and max the volume.

The flying Supers dive at me once more. I throw my cellphone to the ground and cover my ears. I watch in slow motion as the boys draw closer.

I hear the app initiate. The last sound recorded, the sound of an I-beam slamming into Gwen's shield, the angry screech of metal against metal, ripples through the air. At full blast, the sound pierces through me like a spear. The Supers falter, surprised by the abrasive noise. One stumbles to the ground and clutches his ears. I take my cue, drop my backpack, and run. My stitches must be all torn up, but I don't care.

I scramble down the street. What was I thinking? Of course Dieter wasn't going to listen to reason. I should have left it alone. This is what I get for trying to be reasonable. The hairs on my neck prickle as a shadow passes over me.

I bolt around the corner and nearly crash headlong into another person. I see a flash of black hair and the reflective glint of a camera lens. Before I can tumble to the ground, an arm grabs me and holds me upright. A loud, commanding voice rings out.

"*What* is going on here?"

It's like someone pressed a pause button.

The flying Supers lift their heads in unison. Their faces are little boy faces, confused now that a witness has entered the scene. I notice curious neighbours peeking out from windows.

Alexander stands with an expression like thunder. He takes a step forward, more imperious now that he's not scrambling for a camera lens. He seems tall, and dangerous.

"Disturbing the neighbourhood, assaulting a young lady: Is this the proper behaviour for a group of young Supers?" Alexander asks quietly. "What would your parents think? What would LOS say? They arrest hooligans like you. Do you know what LOS does with Supers who abuse their powers?"

"She started it," retorts Matt, but his protests sound young and weak. People are emerging from their houses, summoned by the ungodly wail of my app.

"Shame on you all for attacking an injured girl," dismisses Alexander. "You low-lifes better scram before I decide to report you to the authorities. Take it from me, LOS doesn't take well to deviants like you."

"What do you know?" shouts another flying Super. "You're just some high-schooler!"

"I know more than you, you snot-nosed—" Alexander uses an expletive. Shock washes over the Super's face. "Now go home, all of you!"

Matt attempts to be manly by spitting on the ground, but it's more air than phlegm. "Fine." He jumps into the air, but stumbles and lands back on the ground. His face goes red. He tries again and finally gets a good levitation going. "Let's get out of here, guys. She's not worth it!"

One by one, the flying Supers lift into the sky. They rub their ears and wear dour expressions. I'm shocked by how small and defeated they appear, and angry at how easily they were deterred. By another person. Always by another person. Again, I'm the useless one, always waiting for my knight.

"Beata, right? Are you ok?" asks Alexander once they're gone. He shuffles about in his pocket and brings out a fresh Subway napkin. "Here."

I wipe at my face furiously. I didn't even realize I was crying. How embarrassing! Blubbering like a baby.

"Thanks," I say. The word comes out bitter. I hope I don't sound unappreciative. "What are *you* doing here?"

"I live around here. Heard the racket and came out to see what was happening," he says. He points at my ear. "We should probably sterilize that."

With the threat gone, he's just a teenage blogger again. He tucks his hands into his pockets. Now that his role as protector is over, he doesn't seem to know how to proceed. "How's your side?"

My hand moves to my ribs. I can tell it's going to hurt later, but right now, I'm too stunned to feel anything. I reach up and pinch my ear. My fingers come away pinkish. "I'm good," I reassure. "It's just a scratch."

"Are you sure you shouldn't visit the hospital just to check?"

"No," I say quickly. "I don't need that. I've spent way too

long in the hospital anyways."

"I heard about what happened. It was in the news. I'm sorry about your injuries."

I shrug. "It's not your fault."

"I got lucky at City Hall," he says. "I was pretty close. Given the damage, I'm surprised most people got away ok. Except that one poor guy who got crushed by concrete. And you, of course, with the glass and all. Not that I want to re-hash bad memories or anything."

An awkward silence descends and I scuff the ground. I don't really want to talk to Alexander, but I don't want to seem rude either, especially after he intervened the way he did.

"Do they always pick on you like that?" he asks. If anything, this question makes me more uncomfortable. He crouches to bring himself down to my level, but ends up shorter than me. It feels awkward to be looking down at someone who is clearly taller. I take a step back and hug my arms around myself.

"Not when Gwen is around." I laugh, but it's forced and wheezy. Of course, when Gwen is around, no one dares touch me, or Ling, or Nuha. When Gwen's around, we're sacred. No one wants to be on her bad side. For a split second, I feel a twinge of hatred towards her. Good ol' reliable Gwen. What would we *ever* do without Her Highness and her perfect hair and perfect skin and perfect personality? How would we ever survive without her guiding light? She watches over me. Watches over us all.

Like a benevolent goddess.

It's infuriating.

"Have you told anyone? Does your teacher know?"

I almost roll my eyes. Why is he being so concerned anyways? I just want to crawl away, go home, and immerse myself in some programming. I imagine ones and zeroes. *Click, click, click.* Simple and mechanic and soothing.

"Are you meeting up with friends?"

"Why do you care?" I snap. His concern grinds into me like a rusty cog. I rub at my eyes, which I know are going red with irritation. "I'm just some useless kid you met at a news conference. I'm nobody. I can't even fend off my own bullies. Why should you waste your time with me? Don't you have some impressive social blogging to do? Just leave me alone and live your life."

Alexander breathes out slowly. I think he's going to protest and butt in, like an adult, but instead he just stands. "Ok," he says. "If that's what you want."

In a few long strides, he moves down the block. I can't help but stumble after him for a few steps. When he reaches my fallen cellphone, he scoops it up in one easy move. He looks it over, and I'm suddenly self-conscious about my app. What would he say? It's not complete yet.

"Is this what made that horrible sound?"

"Yeah. It's not really refined yet." I scuff the ground, watching him from the corner of my eye.

"You know," he says, tossing and catching the phone a few times. "This is pretty clever. How does it work? It's a sound recorder of some sort?"

I nod wordlessly. "It's a specialized app. It can zoom in and isolate sounds using a tiny microphone add-on. At least it's supposed to. When it's done, it'll be able to stream what it records to other phones, like your friends' phones, or your parents' phones. But that part's not programmed yet. Ling wants to be a famous journalist. Me and Nu made this to help her hear speeches from further away."

"Huh," says Alexander. "Not all kids can build their own app. I'd say that's a special skill."

He grins then, a wide grin that looks a little sharky, but not unpleasant. His eyes crinkle around the sides as he offers me my cellphone.

"Why are you being so nice to me?" I ask weakly, taking the phone in both hands. I tuck it in my pocket. "I don't understand."

"I had a little sister," says Alexander. "I mean, *have*. She's still alive. I don't know why I'm using past tense." He rolls his eyes, but I can tell he's nervous by the way he huddles into himself. "I don't see her much because she's sick. But you kind of remind me of her."

"I'm sorry," I say, because I can't think of anything else to say.

"Don't worry. It's not your fault. She's always asking if I'm ok and telling me to take care of myself. As though *I'm* the one that needs to take care of myself." He shakes his head as though in disbelief. "She tries to be helpful, even though she should just be relaxing. It's frustrating. I'm supposed to be her big brother. She could lean on me a little, you know?"

He's trying to make a point, I know.

"So anyhow, no one can blame her for not being able to go out and run a marathon, or get straight As, or save the world. You need to know that too, I think. All anyone can ever ask is for you to do the best with what you have. You're trying your hardest. That's all that should matter. Sorry if I sound cheesy or anything. But it's true."

I nod.

"And anyone who says otherwise, well"—he offers me a wayward smile—"they're real assbutts."

I can't help it. I snort a little. "That's not a real word."

Alexander's smile returns. "So, do you need someone to walk you home?"

I think about what my parents would say if a high-schooler walked me home. Nothing good, probably. Plus, as former Supers, they don't really want strangers hanging around—in case they alert the media or take unsolicited photographs of our private lives.

"No thanks," I say. "I live pretty close. I can manage."

I let my words hang and then bid Alexander farewell. He shakes my hand again, which seems way too formal for a casual parting, and tells me very seriously to be careful and take care of myself. It's all a bit ridiculous, but it makes me smile. As I walk home under the dying autumn leaves, I feel somewhat better despite myself.

Chapter 9

Rest and Recovery

I throw myself into my Sound Isolator app. It needs a name. Something snazzy yet descriptive. I want it to be good. I want people to look at it and say, *Gee, that's a clever name for an app.* Alexander's words whirl in my head, and I decide he's right. Building apps *isn't* something typical middle schoolers do. The realization makes me want to build even better apps than before.

Nuha and I started building apps almost two years ago. Today is what we call a "down" day, where we lay off troubleshooting and talk about easy stuff, like which colours to use and how big the fonts should be. Today, we're brainstorming names. It's the first thing a person will see about our app, so I want it to be perfect.

"Listen In?" I propose to Nuha over the phone. I sit on my bed, fiddling with my Rubik's Cube. I must have scrambled and reassembled it a dozen times already. "It has a nice ring. If you say it really fast, it sounds like *listenin'*. Funny, right?" I giggle.

Nuha makes a small sound on the other end, something between a snort and a hiccup. "You're feeling better, I noticed."

I do feel better. Working on the app distracts me from the pain in my side and the scorn in the schoolyard. The Sound Isolator is coming along nicely. For the last few days, I have been fiddling with its programming in Super XCoder.

"Forget the name for a sec," says Nuha. "How did the testing go?"

"Pretty good. It's better than before." I tried testing it on a robin this morning. Its song came through loud and clear, but I need to test it on conversations, where there are more random sounds and extra noises. When I tried playing back the recording—with precautionary earmuffs on—there was no sign of horrible metal shrieking.

"We should make it so that it can isolate quiet sounds amidst really loud ones," says Nuha. I can imagine her now, in her pink and brown teddy bear pajamas, amid her huge hamster plushies, braiding and unbraiding her hair with the phone on speaker nearby. Programming is the only thing Nuha really gets into, besides engineering. "Like, it should be able to recognize the flutter of a pigeon's wing in a storm."

"You're kidding."

"No," says Nuha, sounding absolutely serious. "Why would I be?"

I swallow. "I'm not sure I'm that good."

"We want to eventually profit off this app, right?" asks Nuha. "We need to release it to the public one day, so we need to make it the best product possible. It has to be competitive. We're not working on this for fun, are we?"

It's just like Nuha to be forward-thinking and businesslike. Even though she's quiet, she's more ambitious than any of us. Her family established Bahar Industries in the seventies and are well known for their technogadgets. Nuha inherited the Bahar family's telltale steadiness and quiet spirit.

I shake my head, then realize she can't see me. "No," I say out loud. "We're not just doing it for fun." Then I pause. "But it should still be fun along the way."

"Right," says Nuha, picking up on my point. "Let's do the best we can for now and worry about the rest later. How far away can it pick up sound now?"

Last time I checked, it was able to isolate sounds very clearly from across a room, but I wanted to give it a bit more distance than that. "I'm not sure. I have to test it some more."

"Give it to Ling," says Nuha. "She gets out more than us."

"Speaking of Ling," I say, thinking of my new app idea. "What do you think about this?"

I tell Nuha about my new idea. A tracker app. Nuha listens intently.

"It's been done before," she finally says. "Like that app out there that lets you keep track of where your friends are so you can avoid them."

"Oh." I deflate a little. I really thought I had something there.

"But," says Nuha, "it could work if we made it broader. Think of everything in the world that can be tracked! Not just friends like Ling, but everything else that moves."

There's a silence on Nuha's end. Silence means she's thinking.

"Like Supers! A Super Tracker app. People are always Super-watching. They'll want to know where to go if a Super is in town. Do you think it might be too obsessive?"

"Like anything about Supers isn't obsessive," I say with a scoff. The bitterness in my voice surprises me. Naturally, the Supers take precedence over normal people. Did I want people to obsess over me? I wonder.

"Now the real questions is how we track Supers without actually planting a chip on them," says Nuha. She sounds like she's frowning. "'Cause I don't think too many of them will agree to having one on them at all times."

"Tap into social media," I say immediately. Pictures, posts, and discussions about Supers happen all the time on the Internet. All we have to do is take all the information and compress it into a couple of lines: *Gweneira Kendricks, last seen at 43°64'26"N, 79°38'71"W, a.k.a. the CN Tower. Quick, go get your autographs!* Boom. The Super Tracker app. Simple.

"Can we get access to so many databases?"

"No, but we don't need to."

My brain is on fire. I sit up straight. This is where I'm in my element.

"All we need is some clever programming. A—a search engine of sorts! It'll skim over all the public information in, say, the last few days, searching for keywords, like a Super's name. Once it gathers that information, it can run analytics on it—see which location is mentioned most often or most recently alongside their name. Then it can display it in one, short message. That way, people don't have to scroll through pages and pages of Tweeter just to locate that one piece of information."

"Clever," says Nuha. "Also, totally doable."

"Tap into Super culture."

"Give people more of what they want," replies Nuha. "That's smart, Bea. That's real smart."

My parents would love it. They would love having a newsfeed of their favourite Supers. Then they can keep track of Gwen and celebrate with her parents whenever she completes another mission. I should be happy—it really is a good idea—but I can't help but feel a little annoyed too. It's not like Supers need any more glam, but everything seems to revolve around them, even when there are billions of others on earth. My parents sometimes mention the one percent, the very rich people who seem to control everything. I wonder if famous Supers can be considered another sort of one percent.

"I mean, the app should work on Civvies too," I say quickly. "It's not all going to be about Supers. If you're on the Internet, it can track your destinations. I suppose there should be an option for people to block their names from the app too. Just to be fair."

"Yeah, but no one's interested in Civvies. The app will never fly if we advertise it as a Civvie tracker," says Nuha bluntly. It hurts when she says it like that, all matter-of-fact. My excitement ebbs. Why shouldn't people be interested in Civvies? Are they less worthy of attention just because they can't shoot lasers out of their eyes? I think of all the famous Civvies in the world, all the inventors and scientists on posters in my room. Surely *some* people are interested in them.

"Still," I begin, "it should include Civvies."

"I suppose people might be interested in Civvie celebrities," says Nuha slowly. "Movie stars and such."

"It'll literally be able to search for anyone in the world, as long as they have an Internet footprint. It doesn't have to be *just* about Supers." It bugs me a little that Civvies are included as a second thought. Like an add-on rather than a feature.

"Won't that slow the app down? Too much information to sift through? Not enough filters?"

"Don't worry," I say stubbornly. "I'll make it work."

"We can make the interface real simple," continues Nuha. She's getting into it. Her voice always gets breathy when she's excited. "Everyone's looking to streamline these days. We can have one search bar for the Super's name and several filter tabs. Users can arrange the info by most recent sighting, most popular sighting, and so on and so forth!"

"Uh-huh," I say, nodding into the phone, but my enthusiasm is gone, like clamshells washed away by a high tide.

I listen to Nuha speak, and wish I could feel as eager as she sounds. A spectrum of fame and importance opens up in my mind's eye. If Supers get all the good attention and Civvies are mostly ignored, then do Duds get all the bad attention? There's no such thing as bad publicity, or so the entertainment industry likes to say, but there is such a thing as publicity that's bad for you. Maybe, in some small way, it's better to be overlooked than scorned.

Still, it didn't make it hurt any less.

When I go down for breakfast the next morning, a magazine is waiting for me on the counter. *BEATA BELL, TERROR OF THE SCHOOLYARD* is stamped on the front page. Underneath it, in smaller font, a subtitle: *The Great-Granddaughter of the Prestigious Original Super Hits Her Rebellious Years?!* There's a photo of my yearbook picture from last year, photoshopped to look grainy and suspicious. My face heats up. I make a lunge for the magazine but someone beats me to it. The magazine zips into the air, out of my reach.

My dad dangles the magazine out over his head. My mom stands by his side, looking stern. I take a step back.

"What's this I hear about you cursing other kids?" my dad asks in a reasonable voice.

My cheeks are definitely burning now. I spot the author's name in the corner. L.C. Kiel. Matt's dad and a journalist for a semi-popular tabloid, *Superwatch*, a magazine dedicated specifically to Superstar gazing. Anger rises in my gut. That tattletale! Running to his dad with his tail between his legs. I manage to read the first sentence of the publication. *Beata F. Bell, the great-granddaughter of the esteemed Original Super, terrorized a small, peaceful neighbourhood yesterday by loudly threatening to "curse" the entire establishment. The late bloomer, who until recently showed no sign of Super powers, was—*

"Beata Bell," my mom snaps, her voice louder than usual. I flinch. "Have you been *pretending* to have powers?"

I hang my head. "I didn't mean to!"

"Have you been threatening other kids with these pretend powers?"

"It's not like that! They were bullying me! Not the other way around."

Mom's rebuke stings, but it's Dad's sad expression that gets me most. I hate it when he stares at me like that. Not with anger but with a sort of pity. I look everywhere except at his face.

"The first rule of Super training is to use your powers responsibly!" my mom lectures. She's not a tall woman, but she can be scary when she needs to be. Her entire face is screwed up in anger. "Do you know how embarrassing this is? Not only are you pretending to be something you're not; you're perpetuating a bad image! You're the great-granddaughter of a famous and well-respected Super. I'll ask you not to sully her reputation with scandals. What do you think will happen if you go around acting like a teenage wannabe?

There will be reporters at the door, asking questions! And I'll be the one who will have to deal with them. Again!"

My head comes up. Anger flares in my chest at the publication, at Matt Kiel, and at my mom. It's not fair that I'm being blamed for defending myself. I don't talk to my parents about my school problems a lot. It's humiliating, and I don't want to be a bother, but it would be nice to at least have the benefit of the doubt.

"You don't seem to mind so much," I mutter.

"Excuse me, young lady?" My mom's mouth drops open. She takes a more aggressive stance, looming over me. It reminds me of her former official Super pose, hands on her hips, leaning forward—only this time there's no pixie grin and mischievous wink.

In my peripheral vision, I see my dad shake his head. *Sorry, Dad*, but I'm too bothered to stop.

"I said you don't seem to mind so much. I've seen you on television. You play it up! You're always running to the media whenever you have the chance! How can you tell me not to perpetuate an image when you're doing it too?"

"That's different."

"How?"

"When you grow up, you'll understand the difference between playing a role and lying."

"You're worried about being a Dud," my dad intervenes, hands up. "We know. But you can't just go about saying irresponsible things. Ok, Bea?"

"Gweneira understands," my mom pushes. "She's a good kid. She would never lie like that. Why can't you be more like her?"

It's like a slap to the face.

"That's not fair," I say. "You're always comparing me to Gwen. I'm sorry you had to get stuck with me instead of her, that I'm not famous and useful and good and beautiful like she is."

My mom's expression remains stony. The fact that she doesn't look offended or shocked is even worse than if she just got angrier. My eyes flood with tears. I turn around and race for my room. My stitches twinge, and pain webs across my side.

"Beata!" my dad calls, only to be violently shushed by my mom.

"You're grounded, young lady," she calls after me.

Who grounds an injured person? I know the family name is important, but aren't I important too? I stop running as soon as I'm out of sight. My side can't handle it. I push down a lump in my stomach. Yes, I am a disappointment. It's true. I'm disappointed in myself too. But she could have at least denied it. She didn't have to look at me like that, as though I had read her mind.

I fume. I sit at my computer desk, arms crossed, steam rising from the top of my head—or so I imagine. Super XCoder is open in front of me, but I can't concentrate. After a few minutes of trying to program the Super Tracker app, I give up and reach for my Rubik's Cube instead. *Click, click, click, clickclickclick.* I work it so fast that it slips from my hands and clatters to the floor. It rolls all the way under my desk and comes to rest in a tangle of computer wires.

There's a soft knock on my door.

"You're not grounded, Bea. I'm overturning the ruling."

I sigh. "Not now, Dad."

"Come on, let's talk about this."

Except I don't want to talk about it. I want to grab my Rubik's Cube and get lost in meaningless movements. I want to drown myself in code.

"I'm glad you aren't Gwen," my dad says through the door. "Otherwise who would I make text adventures with?"

There's a pause.

"I'm coming in, Bea."

I turn my chair around and try to stare at my screen. I hear my dad close the door behind him and sit on my bed. For a while, he's silent. "You know, Bea, if you're having difficulties in school, you can tell us. Everyone has trouble once in a while. There's nothing to be ashamed of."

I groan. "You have no idea."

"Sure I do. Do you think it was easy for me, marrying into the family of the great France E. Shaw? I never felt like I was good enough either, and your grandpa never let me forget it."

I didn't know my grandparents for long, but I remember being a little afraid of Grandpa. He had the same face as Frances E. Shaw and the same calm stare. He didn't smile much, especially not at my dad. "You got over it eventually."

"Well…" He shrugs. "Sometimes I'm not so sure about that."

There's an awkward silence. Then he clears his throat.

"Point being, Bea, the shadow of Frances E. Shaw has a long reach. Yes, it means that we have to be a little more careful in public. Yes, it means people will write mean things about our smallest mistakes. Yes, it means sometimes feeling inferior. You can't help it, being associated."

"So I'm just supposed to suck it up and deal with it?"

"That's not what I mean, and you know it. I know you weren't trying to cause trouble. You're a good girl. But I want you to be a bit more careful. Being even a little famous means we always have a spotlight on us. It might not be as big as Gwen's spotlight, but it's still there, and you know how the media can be. Your mom and I just want you to be safe."

"It's not like I lied on purpose. It was the only way to get them to leave me alone." I glare at my computer screen. "You can't get Supers to do anything unless you outpower them."

"Have you told your teachers about your troubles?"

"Mr. Uzune wouldn't be able to do anything anyways. He's just a Civvie. Supers don't have to listen to him if they don't want to." I cross my arms. "None of this would happen if I had powers."

My dad sighs. "Being a Super doesn't solve everything."

I know he's going to launch into a speech about how being Super isn't great. I've heard it numerous times over the years, and more so recently. The life of a Super isn't always TV interviews and big endorsements, he says. There's a lot of glamour, sure, but only for a select few. A lot of Supers work behind the scenes, or don't get hired at LOS at all. Look at the no ranks and D-ranks. They can't really do much with their powers, so they're never found on the field. He worked in IT for LOS. He doesn't even have a collectible card.

"I admit, I might be a little bitter about it. Still, after all these years. Trust me, having the powers, being admired, having fans chant your name on the streets, then having it snatched away in adulthood—it can be rough. Look at your mom. The famous teleporter. Loved by the masses. She pretty much grew up on television. After so long, giving it up is like giving up air. Seeing her on television, all bubbly and witty, sometimes makes me wonder…" He trails off, but I think I hear him murmur *which Tessa is real*.

Another silence. Some anger towards my mom ebbs. I know what it's like to want something, but to want it *back*— like missing a favourite toy, or a best friend who moved away. I think of Gwen, how we used to spend weekends together, swimming, going to amusement parks, hitting baseballs in the park together. It's nostalgic.

"Still," I say at last. "It would be nice to at least have *some* sort of power."

My dad doesn't deny it. Instead, he says, "You can never disappoint me, Beata."

"Thanks, I guess."

I peek under my desk to check on my Rubik's Cube, then slide my chair back so I can crawl under and get it. I spend a little extra time, pretending to untangle it from cords. Maybe I can never disappoint him, but I can still disappoint Mom, our family, and Frances E. Shaw. And, worst of all, I can still disappoint myself.

One of the perks of being bigwigs in the technology industry is that other companies are constantly trying to please you. As a Bahar, Nuha obtains the new PlayStation 7x Pro all-inclusive, 360-degree immersive, virtual reality gaming system a full week before it releases to the public. She gets gadgets sent to her residence on a weekly basis, but none are better than the state-of-the-art gaming systems.

"My place after school," she demands before class has even ended, slapping down a copy of *CrashDasher 4.0*. "We're racing Mecha-Lamborghinis."

"*Mecha*-Lambos?" I groan. Nuha is a quiet girl, but get a PlayStation console within her sights and she becomes as fired up as an Olympian in the semi-finals. "No, Nu, we have homework!"

"That can wait," she says, glowing. "Research comes first!"

"Er, I'm not sure racing Mecha-Lambos counts as research."

"It counts as a certain *type* of research." Nuha's nostrils flare. There's no refusing her now. "As a member of the proud Bahar household, it is my duty to beta test new technologies before they become available in stores!

"Besides"—she leans in so close I can feel her breath in my nose—"*Gwen is coming*."

"What?" I snap to attention, nearly pulling my side.

"I texted her last night. She can make it today. Not to school, of course—she has a hospital event to attend, some sort of ribbon-cutting ceremony—but she says she'll have a few hours free between three and seven. It'll be fun. There's nothing better than an evening of virtual carnage and aggression."

I'm not usually big on video games, but this changes everything. Gwen is coming. Excitement and nerves thrum through me.

"So, you in?" Nuha asks, eyes bright.

I give her a solid nod. "I'm in."

Nuha grins—an expression I rarely see on her—and squeezes my shoulder gently. Then she flits off, almost skipping. It's like early Christmas for her. I sit back and try to concentrate on my history textbook. It doesn't work. I get to see Gwen again. I haven't seen her since I was hospitalized, and she seems busier than ever. It's a treat whenever we get to hang out. *Maybe*, my mind chimes optimistically, *it'll be just like old times*.

Nuha's basement is a giant entertainment centre. It's wide and tall enough to toss a football through. The floors are solid mahogany. The walls are soft beige, with warm coffee tones. Silky yellow lights line the walls. There's a grand piano sitting in one corner, a standing microphone, and a karaoke machine. In the middle, there's a foosball table, a Ping-Pong table, and a pool table. There's also a bar, which we're strictly prohibited from. As cool as everything is, the star of the show is a television so large it covers the entire wall. It's surrounded by leather sofas.

We settle into the sofas as Nuha hurriedly plugs in an assortment of wires. She never lets us touch her precious gaming systems, so Ling and I are reduced to making ourselves comfortable. Ling says something about celebrities, but I only half listen. I keep looking towards the windows and doors.

It's not long before Gwen arrives. She enters through the back basement door so as to not draw attention to herself. Today, she wears a fashionable jean jacket with a long black skirt and a knit beanie. Her gorgeous hair is bundled in a messy knot on her head. She carries an eco-friendly bag.

"Gwen!" Ling and I chorus as she steps into the room.

"I brought snacks!" she sings. She tosses her bag unceremoniously on the sofa. A pile of snacks pours out—LOS-brand cookies and chips. Rock candies that fizzle in your mouth. Chocolate wafers with LOS insignias pressed into them.

"You're the best, Gwen!" Ling declares, falling on the snacks. "Mind if I take some home for Yue?"

Ling's little sister is barely five. Ling spoils her terribly.

Gwen waves a hand. "As you will."

I'm almost afraid to approach her. Last time I saw her, I was groggy and in the hospital. LOS still has no leads on her mysterious challenger, and I am not sure how Gwen would react if I mentioned it. *Badly*, my mind chimes. The entire debacle must frustrate and enrage her. Thankfully, the Counter-League hasn't made any public challenges recently. I scan Gwen's face for hints of stress, but she hides it well.

Nuha darts out of the room and clambers back with an armful of equipment—controllers and headsets. She jams one onto my head. The world goes blank for a moment. Then it powers up. The room returns, with glowing numbers and specs along the edges.

"Whoa," I exclaim.

"Isn't it *incredible*?" asks Nuha's voice. "Technology is *incredible*. Everything is wireless. Wait till I turn on the game. You're going to love it."

I hear Ling yelp. Nuha must have jammed a headset on her too. Then laughter from Gwen. Nuha dances back, excitement swirling in her eyes. She puts on her own headset.

"Everyone ready?"

"Um," I say, but Nuha's not listening. She flicks on the PlayStation.

I'm transported into another world. I'm no longer in Nuha's elegant basement. I'm on a freeway. I'm at the wheel of an expensive luxury machine. It's like sitting in the head of a Transformer, one part humanoid robot, one part race car. I can hear the engine purr. I turn my head. We're in Paris. The roads are cobbled, and the Eiffel tower shines in the distance.

Kkzzzt, buzzes my headset. *Nuha to Bea. How is it?*

"How do you work this thing?" I ask out loud. I can feel my vocal cords working, but I can barely hear my own voice. Instead, it's caught by the headset's microphones and relayed in a digital fashion.

It's all simulation, Bea. Just project yourself onto the mecha. Be the mecha.

I reach out my arms. To my surprise, my Mecha-Lambo glides forward. I shift my arms back, and the vehicle glides backwards. I give it an experimental turn. It moves smooth as butter.

Gas on the right. Brakes on the left, for those of you who CAN'T HANDLE THE SPEED.

I can't help but giggle. Nuha's a completely different person when she's playing video games. She can trash-talk with the best of them. Despite myself, I'm getting pumped up.

How do you switch models? Ling's voice asks. *I got a Mecha-Toyota.*

Looks like you'll have to deal.

Aww.

All right, peeps. Enough talk. Let's roll!

Onscreen, a sleek black Mecha-Lambo rockets down the street, its hull so dark it seems to absorb light. Nuha cackles as she takes a sharp turn, bowling over a trashcan. Napkins and fruit rinds fly onto the street. The simulation is so real that I can almost taste her dust.

I press on the gas and feel the breath leave my lungs. It's so real. Paris streets zoom by me. Stunned tourists stare and snap pictures as I breeze by them. I forget I'm in a basement. I'm driving. I'm racing.

It's exhilarating.

A green Mecha-Viper pulls up beside me. I peek over and

see Gwen flash her teeth at me. She makes a jerking motion towards Ling's dinky Toyota and mouths *watch this*. She twists the wheel with such violence I'm afraid it might fly off. Her machine rams into Ling's.

You BUTT! Ling howls as she spins off a cliff.

All's fair in love and war, Gwen breathes. She winks at me, then presses the gas and zips forward. *See you at the finish.*

I let out a breathy laugh and lean on the gas. I can see Nuha's vehicle in the distance, skimming along the ground like a hunting beast. I urge mine faster.

Turns out I'm a good driver. Or at least as good a driver as the simulation allows. I veer down the twisted streets without a single incident. I project my mind down the street, anticipate sharp turns and predict movements. Credit my excellent spatial sense. Or my comfort with virtual worlds. Or my ability to understand and break down programs in a snap. In a few minutes, I'm almost neck and neck with Nuha, and lengths ahead of Gwen. I can hear Ling whooping in the background. I edge my car forward. Nuha yanks her wheel and cuts me off. I bite back a yell. Nuha stomps on her brake. I jerk my wheel and feel myself go into a spin.

Auuugh. A wall races to meet me. My heart thunders. I throw up my arms and cover my face. I hear the collision but don't feel anything.

Right, a simulation.

Nuha comes in first, with Gwen close behind.

"You're good," Nuha compliments after the round ends. She pulls off her headset. Her thick brown hair is ruffled. "Not many experienced racers can keep up with me, and you're just a newbie."

"Thanks," I say, flushing with pleasure.

I must have gotten too excited. My bladder aches uncomfortably. I excuse myself to go to the bathroom. After the exhilaration of the game, Nuha's bathroom feels incredibly serene. It smells like chamomile.

As I emerge, Gwen meets me in the hall. I hear echoes of Nuha thrashing Ling in *CrashDasher* from beyond. Gwen's eyes seem to glow under the dim lighting. It might be my imagination, but the circles under her eyes are darker than ever. She's shed her jean jacket. Underneath, she wears a black, sleeveless turtleneck. It makes her look very adult.

"How is your injury?" she asks with a serious expression.

My hand touches my side.

"The stitches are coming out on Saturday," I tell her.

"How many?"

"What?"

"How many stitches did you get?"

"Twenty-four," I say hesitantly, "but don't worry, the doctors said—"

"Twenty-four too many," Gwen mutters. Her eyes go distant. I remember how frazzled she looked sitting in my hospital room, and I'm suddenly filled with the need to reassure her.

"The wound wasn't very deep," I say, "and there was no damage to any important organs. The doctors said it was a good wound overall. Very clean. Mostly, they just had to stop the bleeding and let my muscles and skin heal. It's the perfect example of a flesh wound." I flash her a smile.

I had hoped my joke would soothe things over, but Gwen's stormy expression doesn't clear.

"I read the *Superwatch* article."

I squirm. "Yeah, I'm still not a Super yet. The article lied."

Gwen sighs. "I know. Cursing isn't registered as an established power in LOS's eyes. I checked the list."

"Sorry, Gwen. You probably got all excited, thinking I finally got powers."

"It's ok. I know you probably have your reasons for pretending." She suddenly gets serious. "I hear you're having a hard time with some Super boys at school. It's appalling. Supers aren't supposed to use their powers for intimidation. Tell me their names, and I'll deal with them for you."

"I really don't—"

"Think of it as my way of making it up to you, for being too busy to hang out."

"You don't owe me—"

"Is it that Jaeger boy?" Gwen's eyes sparkle. "He's training with LOS, you know. A C-rank. Barely anything at all! I can deal with him there. Give him a hard time. Next time he needs a sparring partner, I can volunteer and knock him around a bit."

So much for Supers not using their powers for intimidation, I think. If Gwen steps in to handle my bullies, I'll be the laughing stock of the school. If Frances E. Shaw could handle entire armies, why can't I handle schoolyard enemies?

"I can handle Dieter." The words come out more forceful than I intended. Gwen looks at me, her mouth open. "Don't." I stumble. *Don't baby me.* "Don't go out of your way."

"It's not out of my way, Bea. As a Super and a good friend, it's my responsibility to—"

It's suddenly too much. I open my mouth and words flood out.

"I don't want to hear it, Gwen! Whatever you're going to say, whatever quotable, just—*don't*. Super this and Super that. I don't need it, ok? I can take care of Dieter on my own. You think I'm helpless. You think everyone who's not a Super is helpless, but we're not! We can do things too! I'm tired of you treating me like a child!"

I regret my words almost as soon as they leave my mouth. This is the first time I've seen Gwen in ages, and I throw a temper tantrum! Surprise flits across Gwen's face. Then pain. Then something hard enters her eyes.

"You *are* a child," she says, drawing herself up.

I refuse to bend. "So are you," I retort.

"I'm just trying to help."

"You should focus on your own problems. Like dealing with the Counter-League."

I hit a sore spot. Gwen's eyes flash. "Well, excuse me for taking time out of my busy life to check on you."

"I didn't ask you to check on me, Gwen."

"You can at least be appreciative."

"Why? Every time you're around, I just get more useless by comparison. I already have a lot of pressure, Gwen. I don't need you around to make me seem like more of a loser."

She opens her mouth as though to say something but closes it again. I can see her barely biting back words.

"Let's just get back to the others," I mutter.

Gwen nods curtly.

The walk back to the theatre room is one of the most awkward I've ever experienced. Anger radiates off Gwen like an aura. As we step out of the hallway, Gwen's wristwatch beeps. Ling and Nuha glance over. Gwen's face is impassive as she checks it.

"Code Orange, guys. I have to go." Code Orange means imminent danger to the public. Small areas of the city evacuated.

"Of course you do," I say. "You're always saving the world."

My voice comes out bitter.

"A Super's duties are never done. Not when there are villains on the loose." Gwen refuses to meet my eye, but the primness of her voice betrays her irritation. "Looks like I'm off to make valuable contributions to the city again."

I bite my cheek. I hate it when she has a point. I hate it when she's right. I hate it most when she gets all uppity with me. Sure, she has a job to do, but she doesn't have to be so condescending about it. Sure, I don't catch criminals for a living, but it isn't my fault. If I had powers like her, I would be out every single day, kicking bad-guy butt.

"An entire city to watch," I say flippantly. "How will they ever get along without you?"

"They can't," Gwen says easily.

"Wow, arrogant much?"

"It's not arrogant if it's true."

"I'm sure the police department does *something*."

"They help," Gwen says, her voice light, "a bit."

Nuha and Ling exchange a quick glance, but neither speaks.

"I'll see you guys later," Gwen continues, tight-lipped. There's a little bit of colour on her cheeks. "When I'm done with my obligations, we can go to the Ice Cream Emporium and take a good, long rest. Until then, take it easy. You have that luxury, so take advantage of it. I don't."

"Yeah, fame is a real struggle," I say sarcastically. "I bet it's hard having all those fans."

Gwen's stare is hard. "You have no idea," she says quietly.

I open my mouth to retort, but something in her voice stops

me. A doubtful feeling strikes me in the gut. Gwen is so good at occupying the spotlight that I never really considered whether she likes it or not. I imagine having reporters hound me every day, having to be polite, kind, and perfect. I certainly couldn't handle it, but I always assumed she could.

Gwen shrugs on her jean jacket and picks up her eco-friendly bag. I notice a sliver of white in there. Her Supersuit. She brought it with her. A flash of annoyance pushes out my doubt. Why did she even bother to come if she knew she was going to get called away? It's an unreasonable thought. As a famous Super, of course she would be on call. Still, it makes me feel small. As though I were a side project. A hobby that can be ditched at any time.

"We'll watch you on TV," calls Ling cheerfully, with a too-wide grin. "What channel?"

"Any," says Gwen, more airily than normal, as though she's trying to keep her voice carefree and casual. "I'll be on all of them, as usual."

I bite my tongue.

She doesn't look at me as she leaves, only waves in our general direction. She steps outside. I can already hear the whir of the LOS helicopter coming to pick her up.

Chapter 10

Car Chases and Other Exciting Business

This is how Supers are ranked. No rank is the lowest grade. It means your powers barely manifest at all. No-rank Supers aren't *really* Supers. They're kids who can change the colour of their eyes at will or grow hair at an accelerated rate. D is the second lowest grade. Like Dad. Most empaths are D-rank. C-rank is where most Supers with physical powers are, like those who can stretch their bodies like rubber, or run faster than normal, or lift heavy objects. It's also where most flying Supers are. They can do things Civvies can't, but they're not very volatile, and they aren't very dangerous on their own. If a flying Super decides to go bad, LOS can chase them down in a helicopter and arrest them, even without the help of another Super. B-rank is where things get interesting. That's where fire throwers, and wind generators, and earth movers are. Their powers are harder to control, more dangerous, and, more importantly, have a longer range. LOS can stop B-rank Supers, but it usually takes specialized equipment, like fireproof jackets or riot gear. A-rank has even more firepower. Lasers are A-rank. Not only are they longer-ranged and more difficult to control; they're also hard to stop without the help of other Supers. Gwen is A-rank, and so were Hitori and Beamsman.

Then there's a special rank. A+. It's an exclusive rank. I only know of one Super ranked A+. Frances E. Shaw. I wonder briefly what it would have been like if she'd decided to go on a rampage. It would have been terrifying, I imagine. A flying Super with the power to burn through fighter jets, melt ships, and blast through walls from a distance. Good thing she never strayed to the dark side. If she could stop armies, who could stop her?

Personality is also a factor. A really shy Super with a powerful gift probably wouldn't be as effective as a really brave Super with a less powerful gift. LOS tests each Super before assigning them a rank, and Supers can always jump ranks if they really want to. Take Mom, for example. She started in C-rank, but she worked hard and used her teleportation resourcefully. She proved herself, and LOS eventually upped her to B-rank.

It reminds me a little of school, but it's a danger scale rather than a smartness scale.

As soon as Gwen is out of sight, Nuha unplugs her PlayStation 7x Pro system and flips on the television. Ling tears open a few chocolate bars and samples the flavours, but there's a tension in the room. I'm embarrassed. I hate throwing temper tantrums. Whenever I do it, I can see my mom's face and her big, disapproving eyes. *You're being childish, Beata.*

I squirm. Somehow, the silence makes things worse.

The incident Gwen was summoned for is already on all the news channels. A violent bank robbery in progress. Three banks hit, and a fourth currently being held up. Two armed men with rifles and pistols, poking their weapons at terrified cashiers.

Code Orange, the second highest of all the warnings. Only Code Red ranks higher.

"The financial centres are in lockdown!" declares a Serious Announcer. "Downtown offices have been told to keep their doors locked and for their employees to stay away from all windows. Those who are on the streets are being told to evacuate—we're being told LOS has deployed Super teams! Could this be the work of the Counter-League? Or is it completely unassociated? Stayed tuned!"

As an A-rank Super, Gwen attends most of the highest risk missions. Dangerous Supers to oversee dangerous crimes. It makes sense.

"So," Ling drawls, stretching. "Are you going to tell us what that was all about?"

"*Ling*," hisses Nuha, eyes flickering to me. Her face says *respect her privacy*.

"No, it's all right. We just had a disagreement." I sigh deeply, feeling the air pass through my lungs.

"You two almost never disagree."

Out loud, my mind whispers. There are plenty of times I've disagreed with Gwen but not many times I've voiced it in public. Did that make me a coward?

"Sometimes," I say carefully, "she treats me like I'm five."

"You and Gwen have been friends a long time," says Ling easily. "She probably thinks of you as a little sister. No one wants their kid siblings to get hurt, even if they are annoying sometimes. If Yue got hurt, I'd freak out too."

I drop my head to hide my shame—and my annoyance. Ling makes a lot of sense—maybe too much sense. It makes me feel young and unreasonable. *Some friend Ling is*, my mind grumbles. She's supposed to be on my side.

"*And here she comes*," roars the announcer. "Miss Gweneira Kendricks, flying from the east! Her team is not far behind her!"

Gwen streaks onto the screen, all fury and lustre. She pulls up, poses for the cameras, then hovers over the streets. Other members of her team scramble about on the ground while she floats above, sunlight shining off her iridescent white outfit, like a beacon of justice. Coils of chain are wrapped around her arms. They dangle around her like squid tentacles. She wears a headset. It's painted white to match her outfit. Even though I'm angry with her, I can't help up suck a breath in. She's perfect, as always.

Suddenly, she tilts her head and speaks quickly into her headset. On the ground, her team bursts into action.

"They've spotted them!" roars the TV announcer, so excited I can imagine the spit flying from his mouth. "The getaway car appears to be at the corner of Bay and King—*no*, Bay and Adelaide! Oh, they know they've been spotted! They're on the move—*and the Supers are rushing in to pincer them*—"

Ling pops a chip bag in excitement. Its contents spill over Nuha's couch and onto the ground. No one seems to notice. Onscreen, the camera cuts to one of Gwen's teammates, a tall girl in an emerald-silver Supersuit, her hair bundled into a tight, high ponytail. The TV flashes her card. Steeple Morrison. Age – 15. Rank – B. Power – Energy barriers.

As Ling crunches potato chips, Nuha nudges my side.

The camera zooms in on another one of Gwen's teammates. Khevan Gupta, the newbie. The boy's stats come up. Age – 12. Rank – B. Power – Energy blasts.

"Beata," she hisses. "Test the Super Tracker app!"

I nod and pull out my cellphone. Even though I don't feel great, and my stomach rolls like a rough ocean tide, I can't deny that an exciting news report is a great time to beta test. Nuha and I have barely had any sleep in the past few days writing up and troubleshooting the code for our Super Tracker app. At first I was resentful, creating yet another program that can promote Super obsession, but as the days ticked by, I got more involved. It felt good to be coding. I want to resent the app, but I can't. It's hard to hate something you created.

Besides, it might take my mind off things.

Gwen speaks into her headset again. It's impossible to know what she's saying unless you can read lips.

"It looks like Steeple Morrison is poised to strike! We can only predict she will be setting up a barrier along Queen while the others catch up!"

Shh, I think at the reporter. What if the robbers are listening? It's dangerous.

"I don't get why they have to give us a play-by-play like that," I protest. "We can see what's happening onscreen."

"It's more exciting this way," says Ling. "Supers don't have anything to worry about anyways."

As I feared, the getaway car pulls a tight U-turn and heads in the opposite direction instead. The reporter gasps, appalled. Gwen changes her trajectory and arcs in a new direction. The chains around her sparkle. She makes a quick motion. They dissolve and reform into something that looks like wings. She shoots forward, faster than before.

"She's using her powers to stabilize her flight," says Nuha. "Good girl."

I turn on the Super Tracker app. A pale blue screen pops

up along with a white search bar. *Subject?* asks the search bar. I type Gweneira's name. The loading screen appears, a bluish circle that spins and spins. I wait.

Gwen dives towards the getaway car. She shoots out a perfectly positioned hand, fingers stretching. Her liquefied metal wings reform into chains weighed down by anchors. They smash towards the vehicle, which swerves to avoid them. The anchors slam into the ground, upending asphalt. Gwen makes a disappointed motion with her lips, but it's so quick and slight that only those close to her would recognize her frustration. She flicks her wrist, and the anchors dissolve in sparkles of blue. They lift back into the air as though they weighed nothing, and default into long chains.

My Super Tracker app loads. Nuha leans over and nearly breathes down my neck in an effort to see. It's not perfect. We don't have the search and categorization options set up yet, so the screen is filled with lines of news gathered from Internet outlets all over the world.

> GweneiraKendricks on site over financial district! Robbers on the run! #CityTV
>
> I'd hate to get hit by that anchor. #GoGwenGo
>
> Bets are up 6 to 1 that GweneiraKendricks gets the final takedown. Odds 8 to 1 that Steeple Morrison claims an assist. #BetsBetsBets
>
> WE LOVE YOU GWEN! KICK THEIR @$$! (((o(^-^)o))) #GoGwenGo

More official news fills the page too, short articles by CP24 and CTV, written in haste by on-scene reporters and released online through their smartphones. *Gweneira*

Kendricks, hero of the sky, has the criminals running. I turn my screen to show Nuha, who nods in approval.

"It's something. At least we're able to pull information from the Net."

I nod. "Now, the tricky part. Condensing it."

Onscreen, Gweneira leaps into the air again. I'm amazed by her grace, even in situations of high tension. She veers around, tossing a chain out to hook around a billboard. She tugs, using the anchor to swing herself around, increasing speed all the way. My breath hitches. It's a reckless move. She flings herself through an alleyway, bursting out in front of the escaping car and stops so hard I cringe. Chains shoot forward towards the vehicle, becoming swords, cutting into its hull. The car jerks and flips onto its side. The robbers inside flail. Once the vehicle stops rolling, the doors fly open and two men spill onto the sidewalk.

Ling almost squeals with excitement. Even calm, quiet Nuha seems to vibrate with energy.

"This should be it, folks! *This is the finish.* The robbers are in disarray!" shrieks the announcer. "They are running like headless chickens!"

Gwen dives, scattering them. Her chains clang and jingle. One hit could kill a robber, and Supers aren't supposed to kill unless it's absolutely necessary. Her chains smash through newspaper boxes and nearby streetlights. A shower of sparks rains down on the street. One robber falls to the ground, cowering.

"Stop!" he shouts. "I give up! I'll give the money back! Stop!"

"Coward," mutters Ling unhappily. I have a feeling she wanted a longer car chase.

The robber looks right at the camera, which zooms in until I can see the whites of his eyes. "I didn't sign up for this!" he shouts. Gwen lands in front of him, so close he's forced to stumble back. Her metal swords shine in the sun. "This wasn't in the contract! You never told me I'd be facing *Gweneira Kendricks.*"

"Whom do you think he's talking to?" asks Ling, her eyes gleaming. "It sounds like he's a part of some criminal ring or something."

"The Counter-League?" I mutter. Maybe they need money for their terrorist activities. Still, something seems weird. Robbing banks is such a—*normal* crime.

"Looks like it's ten points for the revered Steel Angel!" shouts the announcer. "The chase is over almost as soon as it began!"

Every time a Super is directly responsible for successfully ending a mission, they are awarded ten points. The points system is purely for fun. It's not like they get any more perks than usual, but it does go on their Super card, and they get bragging rights. *It's an ego thing*, said Gwen once, brushing it off as though it were nothing. She has one of the highest point-to-mission ratios to date. Assisting in ending a successful mission gets you five points, and being on a team that successfully completes a mission gets you one.

"And here are the rest of her team!" sings the announcer. "Tardy to the party, but better late than never!"

Two more faces flash across the screen.

Terrell Lewis. Age – 16. Rank – C. Power – Super strength.

Laire Flannery. Age – 13. Rank – C. Power – Precognition.

The robber takes a step backwards, awed by the sheer firepower of five eminent Supers.

"Don't move!" Gwen commands, narrowing her eyes. Two long beams hover dangerously at her arms. The robber raises his hands into the air.

"I'm innocent!" shouts the robber. "I was paid to do this! I swear!"

"By who?"

"I don't know—someone in a suit! I don't know his name! He said if I did this I wouldn't get hurt, and I'd get paid twice as much as I stole. He said I could trust him!"

Ling, Nuha, and I exchange looks. Ling rolls her eyes, as though to say *a likely story*, but I'm not so sure. I watch with growing uneasiness as the robber gets more frantic. Robbing a bank is a really stupid thing to do with LOS protecting the city. They would need to be desperate.

Or coerced. Or blackmailed.

"Is it the *Counter-League*?" Gwen snarls. I'm taken aback by her poison. Even in the midst of danger, Gwen is usually composed and serene. I wonder, briefly, whether our fight has anything to do with her impatience. "Tell me! Who are your employers? What are their names?"

The robber lets out a crazed laugh. "I *told* you. I don't know!"

"You're lying!"

"No! You think I *wanted* this?" The robber waves his arms around, motioning at the broken glass and flickering street lights. He begins to stumble to his feet, hands out as though to prove he is weaponless.

"Don't *move*, stupid," Ling mutters, just as Gwen leaps forward, a blur of white and gold. In a motion that looks like a pirouette, she smacks the robber across the midsection with one of her beams. I can hear the breath leave his lungs—and bones cracking. The robber's eyes bulge as he's lifted into the air. He hits the ground and rolls several metres. The announcer gasps audibly. Gwen stands for a moment, her chest pumping up and down, a fierce snarl on her face.

"Let this be a warning to you," Gwen breathes. "You *and* your criminal employers. You do the crime, and I *will* find you. I will not rest until I bring you to justice. If we weren't around, our city would overrun with garbage like you. It's why we work so hard. It's why *I* work so hard."

The announcer is silent. Stunned.

I'm stunned too. Ling and Nuha's mouths hang open.

Then slowly, like the rising dawn, realization blossoms over Gwen's face. She looks surprised for a moment. Her metal beams *clang* to the ground, kicking up dust.

She frowns as though deep in thought. The frown doesn't leave her face even as LOS paramedics rush to surround the fallen criminal. Nor does it shift when her teammates rush over, wide-eyed. It's only when the media floods the scene that Gweneira moves. She gazes around, as though coming out of a dream. Without saying a word, she brushes past her teammates, strides through the crowd, and climbs into an LOS vehicle. Behind her, paramedics load the injured robber onto a bright orange stretcher. Overhead, helicopters shine a floodlight on his prone body. I wonder, for an icy second, if he's dead. Then I wonder why I should care. Gwen is right. He's a criminal, trying to leech off honest citizens. A degenerate. Did he really believe feigning ignorance would help him?

But deep down, I can't help but wonder. The Counter-League has never used a middleman before. It would be so easy to blame the Counter-League, so why did the robber play dumb? Maybe he *is* dumb. Or crazy. Or maybe he's loyal to the Counter-League somehow, defending the higher-ups—

I shake my head.

No use brainstorming theories. I should follow Occam's razor and assume the easiest explanation has the highest chance of being right—that the robber is desperate and trying to deflect responsibility. Besides, if the Counter-League can afford robot octopods and can hack into satellites without blinking an eye, then they're well-funded already. They wouldn't need to rob a bank. Plus, they like grabbing attention and causing a scene, so it wouldn't make sense for them to swear their goons to secrecy.

The uneasy feeling remains. If the robber is telling the truth, then there is another organization out there causing trouble for the city—and for the Supers.

Tweeter is clogged with statements about the robbery.

Robber identified as Thurston Payton. In critical condition following emergency surgery after scuffle with #GwenKendricks. #CBC

How much force is too much? Join justice specialist Mandy Weber@6pm for an exclusive interview!

Criminal Thurston Payton, diagnosed with schizophrenia by two court lawyers. Unable to tell reality from fiction. #CityTV #GwenKendricks

Even though most people agree that criminals need to be

stopped, there are rumours of a lawsuit against LOS. LOS has some of the best lawyers in the world, so it's unlikely the case will fly, but it leaves a bad fog in my mind anyhow. Supers are good guys, and it's not like they started it, so why are some people so angry with them? Mom scoffs when activists against Super brutality call for an inquiry into the robber's broken ribs and psychological trauma. A small group gathers in front of City Hall to picket and chant. A teary-eyed woman, claiming to be Payton's sister, recalls a tragic story about how he was a good person, but fell on some bad times and buried himself in debt. "He didn't deserve to get hurt," she wails. "He's my brother."

"When I was with LOS," Mom says over a bowl of cereal, "there was none of this hoopla. Criminals are criminals. They choose the life they live. If you do the crime, prepare for payback. I once broke a criminal's shoulder when I dropped a cindercone on him. No media backlash at all! He was someone's brother too, but he was also a criminal."

"Settle down, honey," says Dad, patting her on the back. "Things were different back then."

Mom rolls her eyes. "Pacifist. You can't do this job without hurting people."

"This job? Tessa, you're an artist now. The job's not yours anymore."

"I still feel somewhat responsible." Mom's mouth sets in a hard line. She shoots me a pointed look, as though I'm supposed to agree with her. "Listen, Beata, when you become a Super, don't be afraid to do your duty. You can't baby criminals."

I just nod solemnly. It appeases her.

I use the flood of media output to improve our Super

Tracker app. I feel a little guilty using Gwen's bad publicity to hone a program, but it's too good an opportunity to miss. I work late into the night, scrolling through symbols on Super XCoder, trying to get all the configurations right. It's tough work. There's a lot of information on the Web, and there's a real danger of overloading the app. I crash it half a dozen times using Gwen's name. It's frustrating but also sort of fun.

"I'm going to need a bigger processor," I mutter to myself after the seventh crash. Like the ones they use at LOS. I replay the robbery scene in my head. It's amazing that LOS had all the streets evacuated before the criminals even fled. Like they could predict everything, see every flight route beforehand, anticipate every fight. Their algorithms must be crazy complicated, and their processors incredibly powerful. Supercomputers, probably.

When my systems come back online, I find myself using three screens: mine, and Dad's laptop, *and* my phone's. Out of curiosity, I delete Gwen's name and enter my own. A flood of headlines appear, most with question marks, most wondering when I'll get powers. I bite my lower lip and snuff the search. Bad idea. I go back to Gwen's name. The flow of code is soothing, and I soon lose track of time. I let the brackets, periods, and if-then statements flow over me.

"What do you think of the Payton lawsuit?"

Nuha looks up from her book, brown eyes calculating. "It'll never go through."

"Is that right?" I lean back in my chair and sigh deeply. Today is sweater weather. The air carries the bite of winter. The last mission was a disaster for Gwen. Paparazzi hounded her, trying to find the least flattering photo. There were panels on the responsibilities of a Super, discussing the boundaries between law enforcement and law brutality. I've made a habit to avoid the news, but it's hard to stay completely away when your app depends on following it.

"That'll never succeed. LOS is too powerful to sue. Their lawyers are too good. They're doing some powerful PR though."

"I guess that's good."

"That no organization can sue LOS?" Nuha glances over her book once more. The move makes her look like a stern librarian. Her thick braid is curled around her shoulder. She wears a moss-green headband and a navy shawl that's more suited for someone three times her age. "That LOS monopolizes all the good lawyers for themselves?"

"Well, when you put it that way…" I trail off. Sometimes, talking with Nuha makes me feel stupid. She knows all the big words, like *monopolize*, and sometimes speaks like she's already an adult—a habit from her business-minded parents.

"What do you think of what he said?" I ask at last. "About being paid by someone else? Crazy, right?"

Nuha puts down her book. "Sounds like a tall tale. People will say all kinds of things to avoid responsibility."

"Hmm," I say. She's right, of course. Nuha is about as smart as three of me, maybe more. Talking to her always helps settle the doubts in my mind.

In this day and age, making an announcement on the Internet can reach more people, but nothing really beats the drama of television. Ling, Nuha, and I are piled in Nuha's basement once more, watching *Celebrity Jeopardy*. Nuha and I like to shout out the answers, while Ling fawns over the fashions. This time, the broadcast interrupts right at 8 p.m., right at prime time.

The screen goes mosaic for a moment, and the image of the news channel's sleek headquarters is blurred by squares. Then the picture fuzzes up. I hear something in the background. When I recognize what it is, my hairs stand up. It's laughter. The room, jovial and light before, turns silent in a second.

The screen blurs once more. The news channel comes on for a split second, but the sound and image are both jumpy. Ling has gone still, her eyes wide. My blood feels cold. Nuha has her hand around Ling's wrist, and is gripping tightly, but neither seems to notice. I know exactly what's happening. Someone is forcing their way onto the airwaves. It's the Counter-League.

The screen flickers once more, and laughter echoes through Nuha's sound system. It's oily and smooth, and devoid of all humour. I don't like it one bit. It gives me the shivers, but I'm not surprised when the mysterious figure appears onscreen once more, silhouetted against a darkish backlight, face hidden. I cringe when he begins to speak.

"I watched your last escapade, Miss Kendricks, and I must say I'm disappointed." The figure's face is hidden, but I can hear the amusement dripping in his voice. "Looks like little Miss Perfect is slipping. Hitting that poor Payton fellow! What a fiasco! Didn't LOS teach you? Supers *protect* people, not break their bones. What's making you so angry? Don't tell me our little exchanges have you all flustered."

Vile, I think. What a *vile* person. A real bully.

"You're weak, Gweneira Kendricks," says the mysterious figure, pointing towards the screen. "You're not fit to be my nemesis. Do you know why?"

The figure pauses dramatically. I lean forward. I didn't mean to, but the TV has an odd power over me. I want to reach through the screen, grab the figure, and yell in his face to leave us alone.

"You don't own your purpose. You obey LOS's orders without thinking. You fight, but you don't fight from the heart. You fight for LOS's silly chivalrous ideals, but have no clue as to what they mean. Protect the weak? Pah! If the weak are always protected, how will they ever grow strong? Maybe the weak don't deserve to be protected. What have they ever done for you? That Payton fellow was a dirty criminal. He'll rob you blind if you turn your back. Why *shouldn't* you break his bones? Think about it, Miss Kendricks. You're a follower, not a leader. You're not a hero. You're an attack dog. LOS says jump and you ask how high.

"And that makes you weak. You have no conviction. But I do. I think for myself. I act for myself. I fight for myself. You're a dog, domesticated and tame. I'm a wolf, slave to no one. I'll show you the truth about LOS and its oppressive ways. I'll prove to you the difference between us. You can't protect your friends, but I can hurt them. I can take them away from you. Consider this a promise, Miss Kendricks."

The television flickers once more, and the shadow of Gwen's face appears for a split second. The two channels fight for airtime, but the mysterious figure prevails.

"Catch me if you can. Stop me if you can. I look forward to it."

The TV flickers again, and this time, LOS takes control,

and Gwen's face appears onscreen, perfect and serious. I blink.

That was fast, I mouth at Ling.

Ling nods in agreement.

Every hair on Gwen's head is combed and ready. She looks like a model. Her television team must be superb. An emerald necklace sparkles around her neck. I wonder how many people it takes to prepare her so quickly.

"Citizens of the city, rest assured," Gwen declares. "LOS is ready to address all Counter-League's threats. Cowardly attempts at intimidation only strengthen our resolve to protect the city and its inhabitants. If the Counter-League thinks they can win through unsavoury and unlawful actions, they should think again. LOS will always stand against terror and injustice. We will find those who seek to do harm, and we will punish them. That is a promise." Gweneira brushes her hair behind her ear so casually, so perfectly, that I can't imagine her feeling anything but calm and confident. Her gaze is steady. I'm filled with a fierce pride.

"You challenge me to find you. I accept. You challenge me to stop you. I will. You look forward to it. As do I. I look forward to the end of your mad ways and your blatant disregard for public safety. I won't rest until the streets are safe. That is my pledge as a Super and a keeper of the law. You call me weak, but you are the one who is alone."

The edges of her mouth turn downwards, and a dangerous glint enters her eye.

"And let's not forget, dogs kill wolves. If you so much as lay a finger on my friends, I, Gweneira Kendricks, will personally end you. Consider that *my* promi—" Her lips curl up into a snarl, and the broadcast cuts suddenly, as though someone pulled a plug. I sit with my mouth open. It's the closest I've seen Gwen get to breaking her composure on air.

A breath is released in the room, and we're free to move again. "Logically, it's the middle book of Dante's *Divine Comedy*," says Alex Trebek. The quiet doesn't last long though. The TV flickers once more and the large face of a news anchor fills the screen.

"We interrupt the current broadcast with some *exciting* news. A nail-biting day for Toronto's Super community! Never before have we seen such a quick exchange of challenges. The question now is what will happen next? And just how is Miss Kendricks handling the pressure? She seemed frazzled to me. Did she seem frazzled to you, Jean?"

"Indeed, John. Tune in at six for our special panel discussion. Social media. How does the advancement of technology change the classic Super challenge?"

"Wow," says Ling in admiration.

"Wow," says Nuha, quieter, with a hint of worry.

"Were we just threatened?" asks Ling, puffing up like an offended bird.

"I believe we were," Nuha says.

"Good luck." Ling snorts and rolls her eyes. "Gwen will smack him flat. Isn't that right, Bea? They don't stand a chance against her."

I get up and leave the room. I hear Ling call my name in confusion, but I ignore her. It takes me a moment to realize I'm biting my nails. As I remove my fingers from my mouth, I wonder why I feel so unsettled.

It's nearly midnight when Ling calls me. I'm about to drop

off when my cellphone buzzes me awake. From the other end comes what appears to be a tribal chant.

"Beata, Beata, *Beata–*"

I stifle a loud yawn. "Ling? It's—" I check the clock. "Past bedtime."

"Exciting news!" declares Ling. If I didn't know better, I'd think I was listening to a radio broadcast. "I was sifting through the photos I took of Gwen's fight with that Counter-League—" She calls him a bad name.

"*Ling.*"

"What?" She does her best to sound innocent. "I call it like it is. Anyway, I found something interesting. See, I didn't actually get a scoop for *Read About It* because other news outlets got better photos than me, and the newspaper decided to use *those* instead of the work of one of their own hard-working, self-sacrificing reporters."

I clear my throat.

"Right, so I managed to find a frame that shows something pretty interesting."

"And you have to tell me *now*? It's a school night."

"I know, I know, but wait till you hear what I found," says Ling, breathless. I can't help it. I'm beginning to catch her enthusiasm. I sit up in bed. "There's this photo that shows his face! I had to zoom in on Photoshop, but it's definitely a face! For just a second, his mask slipped off. I mean, it's not a full face, but it's a good portion of it. I called Nuha, but her phone goes straight to voice mail. It says, "Stop calling me so late, Ling. Go to bed, you insufferable night owl." I think she programmed her phone to block me after a certain time. I sent the picture to you. I'm thinking of releasing it to the media. What do you think?"

I roll from bed and pull myself to the computer. I try not to make too much noise, since I'm supposed to be asleep and healing. Almost through habit, my fingers trace the stitches on my side. I pop open my laptop and wait for the start screen to load. My heart is pounding.

"Are you sure no other media outlet has a picture of this guy?" I ask, making my voice small. If Ling really has an exclusive picture, this is the perfect chance to be useful, to actually help out. "There were helicopters everywhere!"

"They didn't have our angle," says Ling, sounding smug. "There are some things you see better when you're a lowly Civvie with a heart of steel and a state-of-the-art telescopic lens."

"You know what this means, Ling?"

"Fame? Fortune? I bet someone's willing to pay a bundle for this picture."

"No, it means we can help LOS counter the Counter-League!"

"That too, if that's your thing."

"*Ling.*" A thrum of excitement shivers through me. "We can end the Counter-League! Us. Civvies. Help take down a supervillain organization."

"It's big news, I know." Ling finally sounds serious. "I'm stumped on what to do. It's not even that clear of a photo. It was a lucky shot. I tried to reduce the noise, but it's still blurry. There's only so many touch-ups I can make before people will accuse me of tampering. Maybe I can write a press release."

My laptop finally loads, and I quickly check my email. Ling, in typical Ling fashion, has named the file OMGWUT.jpg. I download the file.

"What about your parents?" I breathe, feeling the need to

speak softly. "They used to be reporters, right? They'll know what to do. Maybe you should give the picture to them."

"Back in China, maybe," says Ling with a short bark. "Now they're just regular chow mein makers, feeding the masses instead of informing them."

"But this can get them back into the loop, right?" I swallow as the file finishes downloading. I take a deep breath before clicking it. "I mean, if it's a big enough scoop—"

I stop. The picture loads onto my screen. Ling is right. It's still pixilated but not badly enough to make it unrecognizable. There are a few blurs here and there, but she did a good job cleaning it up. My jaw goes slack.

"Beata?" asks Ling's voice. It sounds far away.

I recognize the face. It wasn't even a week ago that I saw that black, curly hair.

"*Hellooo*?" Ling chimes.

The phone slips from my hand and lands in my sheets with a soft *frump*.

It's Alexander.

Chapter 11

Reporting at LOS Headquarters

Looking back, Charley Beamsman was an ideal supervillain. He wreaked havoc, but he did it openly and with gusto. He never had hidden motives or used sneaky tactics. Whenever Hitori was on the field, they met head on, like jousters, facing off in the street. He didn't make dirty shots, like taking citizens hostage or razing innocent neighbourhoods. He was a villain, but there was a certain sort of honour in how he fought.

Nowadays, it's different.

I don't sleep much. My side aches more than ever. I even snuck an extra Advil from the bathroom to ease the pain, but the medicine doesn't seem to make a difference.

Stupid. My mind is on fire. It's Alexander. Alexander is the mysterious figure on television, threatening us all. I bury my head in my arms to stop myself from whimpering. *Frances, what do I do now?*

I told him we were Gwen's friends! I didn't know that he was a bad guy, but it didn't matter. I remember the Counter-League threats. We're targets now, me, Ling, and Nuha.

He knows where I go to school.

Does he really live around Sir Frederick Banting, or was he planning on doing bad things that day? Maybe he was stalking me. The thought makes me shiver. Maybe he's stalking me *right now*. I pull the covers over my head.

I should tell my parents. Or maybe I should go straight to the authorities. My parents wouldn't know what to do. They aren't Supers anymore. They won't be able to protect me if Alexander decides to come for me. Telling them would just make them worry.

I pull up Gwen's number on my phone. Gwen would be able to fight off Alexander if he decided to attack. For sure.

Or would she?

My finger pauses over the call button.

Could she even win against him in a one-on-one? Alexander is older than Gwen. He probably has more experience. If he's not a part of LOS, that means he mastered his powers all on his own. That makes him a genius. Or at least a very quick learner. My fingers go cold. I've never doubted Gwen before, but Gwen's never fought another polypower seriously before, let alone one with the same powers as her. I feel horrible for having such doubts. I should believe in my friends.

Except I don't, not completely anyway.

I stare at the photo glumly.

It's impossible. A part of me doesn't want to believe Alexander is the mysterious leader of the Counter-League. He was so nice. He didn't look down on me or dismiss me as Gwen's less famous sidekick. He didn't seem like a threat, with his big cameras and weirdly polite way of saying goodbye. He fought off Dieter's gang and cheered me up. Maybe there's a good reason he's with the Counter-League. A story always has two sides, right? I feel like I owe him at least a chance to explain himself.

But my thoughts turn dark again. What if he was being nice to me to make me drop my guard? Maybe he was manipulating information out of me, Gwen's best friend, to get an advantage over her? Didn't I already give him an advantage by mentioning we were close? I stifle a groan. I feel like I'm about to throw up. Why didn't I just keep my mouth closed?

What would Frances E. Shaw do?

It's a stupid question. I'm not Frances E. Shaw. I'm not a Super. I don't have incredible powers, or fame, or the backing of wealthy corporations to support my every action. Besides, Frances E. Shaw wouldn't have to do anything, because LOS would have a plan.

I need to go to LOS.

A chorus of birds greets the rising sun. I watch the sky go from dusky black to monochrome grey. I decide to skip school and head straight for LOS headquarters down at the Toronto Islands. To prepare, I print out Ling's picture, fold it, and tuck it in my backpack. Then I lie in bed and recite prime numbers until I hear my parents' footsteps as they rise and prepare breakfast.

I gingerly make my way downstairs. The Advil has softened the pain in my side, but my stomach still churns. As I pace into the kitchen, I imagine Alexander bursting through the roof, metal whirling everywhere, and kidnapping everyone. A cool sweat breaks out on my body.

"Morning," my mom sings, sliding a bowl of Choco Puffs in front of me.

I grunt in response. She raises her eyebrows a bit, like she wants to ask me something but lets it slide.

It's hard not to say anything over breakfast. I poke my cereal without eating it and do my best not to look glum.

"You're not even touching your food today," says my dad. "Not hungry?"

"No," I say, pulling a brave face. I slurp at my cereal without much enthusiasm. The cold milk sets in my stomach and makes it grumble. "I guess I'm just nervous about getting my stitches out in a few days."

"Oh, it's nothing," says my mom. "I've had stitches taken out about half a dozen times." She pushes back her hairline and points at a faint scar there. "They don't hurt as much coming out as going in. We used to have a saying back in my Super days. You're not a real Super until you have a scar. Just try to relax and let the doctors do their work."

I nod at her words. I neglect to mention I'm not a Super at all.

I almost never skip school. The last time I did so was when Gwen was awarded her first medal. I snuck out during last period and went to watch her ceremony in person. I was caught and got detention for a week. My parents grounded me for another week. They said I should have asked their permission. They would have granted it in a snap. I was completely embarrassed.

When I leave, I bring the biggest pair of sunglasses I can find. I don't want to be stopped by reporters or curious bystanders. I try to walk with confidence so no one questions where a middle-school girl is going alone. I take a bus that smells like stale coffee and air conditioning down to Harbourfront. The swaying motions make me a little nauseous, so I calm myself by playing with my Rubik's Cube. *Click, click, click.* I practice breathing slowly, like they do in yoga, and keep my mind blank until the vehicle wobbles to a stop.

LOS headquarters is so large it's visible from most of downtown. It's a tall, pyramidal building with a strong steel finish that shines in the light. LOS headquarters is almost taller than CN Tower from base to tip, and it comes with its own aircraft launchpad and marina. At night, it's lit with roaming floodlights. It's the biggest feature in Toronto, and it attracts tourists from all over the world. The building looms like a mountain face.

It's sunny today; a refreshing breeze blows off Lake Ontario, and the water sparkles. Toronto's Harbourfront didn't used to be this nice, according to my parents, but since LOS purchased the islands, they've cleaned it up. Now I can look through the water and see the aquatic plants waving lazily from the bottom. Birds frequent the docks—cocky seagulls, nervous sparrows, and strutting pigeons.

The bus pulls to a stop by a pale, man-made bridge that connects Harbourfront and the island. I get off and board one of the dozen free shuttle buses that move people to and from LOS headquarters. Chattering tourists snap pictures and wave brochures as we cross the lake. One nearly jostles me out of my seat with his oversized bag. I bite my tongue and refrain from saying anything. It's a short ride across the bridge. We roll under a large sign. LEAGUE OF SUPERS HEAD-QUARTERS, it says, and underneath, in slightly smaller letters, FOR JUSTICE AND FREEDOM.

It's like entering a different world. LOS employees wear white uniform, with a golden, winged shield stitched across their breast. There are Supers everywhere, floating documents back and forth, pushing heavy equipment, and taking super-fast jogs around the building. A lump gathers in my throat as I watch them. I want to be out there. Even if I'm just washing windows, I want to be among the Supers, working, in my own way, to keep the city safe. I make myself look away.

The shuttle bus rolls to a stop with a slight jerk, and I trundle off. The LOS building is overwhelming up close. As I enter through two giant glass doors, a blast of chilly air caresses my face. The ceiling is high and arched, and tall plants encircle the reception area. Other than the splashes of green, the place is clean, minimalistic. I wonder how much polishing needs to be done every day to keep the building so glossy. There are people everywhere, and serious receptionists sitting at desks. They all have stern expressions and perfectly groomed hair.

"Agent Olive to B3, Agent Olive to B3. Your team awaits on training field four," booms the PA system. It echoes but not unpleasantly.

I feel out of place in my dingy grey T-shirt and equally grey pants. Looking up, I feel dizzy. I'm a speck in a big, empty space. I don't know where to put my feet or who to ask for help. Alexander's picture is folded up in my backpack. It feels like a thousand bricks on my back. My mouth is dry.

A group of Supers brushes past me, following their Agent, a tall man dressed in navy blue. One Super shoulders me as she passes by. I stumble and almost lose my sunglasses.

"Watch it, Civvie," I hear her mutter, and I swallow a burst of anger. I guess the Super/Civvie gap is the same everywhere.

I take a few deep breaths to calm myself before approaching a reception desk. There's a line. The sun streaming through the tall glass windows feels hot on my neck, and I'm glad I have my sunglasses. It's almost unbearably bright without them. I settle down and visualize my Super Tracker app to pass the time. I imagine the changes I have to make to the code before it can go live.

"Could the owner of the vehicle with licence plate BAPD 808 please report to the front desk," booms the PA. It's a busy system. Every few minutes, there's another call for some group to please move somewhere, or for someone to please report to some area. Attendants at desks monitor LiveMaps systems, making sure everything in the building, from air conditioning to electrical inputs, runs smoothly.

The woman in front of me wears too much perfume, and the stench of honey and vanilla nearly chokes me. Behind me, there is a man in his mid-forties, a little chubby, talking quickly on a Bluetooth headset. When I get to the desk, I have to look up at the receptionist. Even the employees in LOS are big.

"Yes? How can I help you?" he asks, leaning over to get a better angle on me. His heavy eyebrows give him an especially sombre expression.

"Hi, my name is Beata Bell," I say. I'm not sure why I feel compelled to reveal my identity, but I do.

The receptionist raises an eyebrow, unimpressed.

"You know, the daughter of Tessa and Phil Bell?"

"Yes," he says, stoic as a statue. "How can I help you?"

"I have some important information, but I don't know who to talk to."

"If you have information or concerns about crime in the city, it's best to call the LOS hotline," says the receptionist. He sounds bored.

"But I think I have evidence about"—I pause and lower my voice—"the Counter-League." Even though I whisper the name, I feel like I've shouted it. I glance around at the people behind me, but they stare back with restless eyes. "I-I think I better show it to someone in person."

"Do you have an appointment, Miss Bell?"

I blink. "What? No. I just got here."

"All meetings require a prior appointment. Would you like to make an appointment today?"

"Sure, of course. The soonest one please."

"The next open slot is in a week."

"*What?*" My voice echoes and I feel my cheeks go hot. "That's too late! This is really important!"

"If you have an emergency, please call the LOS hotline or your local authorities," says the receptionist, not showing a single sign of worry. His calmness is starting to creep me out.

"I already told you; I need to speak to someone ASAP. Isn't there a sooner slot? Is there someone I can speak to right now? Or even sometime today? I can wait a few hours."

"If you have immediate concerns that are not emergency related, please take a ticket at the consultation desk and speak to one of our representatives." He waves a hand at the room behind him. I can see rows of chairs and a large red sign. It says B132 in neon orange. Almost all the seats are full.

"Ok, and how long will that take?"

"Depends on the number of inquiries."

I sigh deeply. "You know, this is really important."

"LOS headquarters is a busy establishment, young lady," he says. I'm sure he's being condescending, even though his face is perfectly impassive. "You will have to wait, just like everyone else."

I slide away, shooting him a venomous glare. He's not fazed in the slightest. I slink my way into the inquiry room and print myself a ticket. B344. I stare at it in disbelief. Three hundred forty-four minus one hundred thirty-two is two hundred twelve. There are two hundred twelve inquiries ahead of me. I take the seat nearest to the door. It's cold, hard, and sends shivers up my spine.

The numbers tick by slowly. People slowly get up, slowly saunter into private booths, and slowly re-emerge. For a while, I occupy myself by watching some Super children training outside. They're sparring with one another. Fire, water, bursts of air rush across the courtyard. They're supervised by a stern Agent in orange. It looks dangerous but also like a lot of fun. Way more fun than waiting for a consultation, anyhow. I close my eyes and will the numbers to pass faster, but when I open them again, only two sessions have gone by.

At this rate, it'll take forever.

I get up. It's not every day that I get to visit LOS headquarters. Even though I begged my parents when I was younger, they were reluctant to take me. *Too much nostalgia*, my mom always said. If I have to wait, I might as well explore. A group of flying Supers zooms past the window, drawing *ooh*s and *aah*s from the seated crowd. I leave the room.

The neon sign says B147. If I'm lucky, I'll meet with a consultant by the time school ends, but I don't want to get home too late or it'll be suspicious. By this time, the principal has probably called about my absence. I want to reach our answering machine before my parents get home so I can erase the message, but at this rate, I won't have the chance. As I gaze around the hallway, bustling with tour groups and Super teams and important-looking bystanders, I feel a thrum of annoyance. I skipped school to be here, and they won't even see me! I bet Supers don't deal with this. I bet Frances E. Shaw could skip all the lines she wanted. Gwen too.

I stride down the hall, towards quieter areas of the building.

In the past, LOS headquarters was just one building, but now it's several buildings connected by tunnels and bridges. The main building, the biggest one, is where most of the boring administrative stuff happens—meetings, consultations, business deals. The side buildings include training facilities and bunks for Super exchange students. They also have classes here. *It's important to maintain our academics*, Gwen had told me once, in an uppity way that I find irritating. *Just because we're Supers doesn't mean we can slack off in other areas.* When I asked why she didn't just take school at LOS headquarters, she said something about maintaining contact with the average person.

Average person, I think with a snort. Not everyone can be Miss Perfect. Not everyone is a Super. Not everyone can show up on test days and get an A+.

The main lobby is the only place tourists are allowed to take photographs, and they do enthusiastically. Their clicking cameras sound like scorpion pincers. As I make my way towards the side halls, portraits of famous former Supers and well-established LOS Agents greet me. There are newspaper clippings framed in gold recounting the highest moments in LOS history: The end of World War II, the Canadian Super Peacekeepers in Vietnam, Korea, the Middle East. The pictures get progressively clearer and more colourful. The hallways get smaller the further I go. It's like making my way into an anthill.

Finally, I come to a hallway where there are mostly closed

doors. An office section for administrators and paper pushers, perhaps. Even though the wall on one side is still made of glass, and frames an expansive view of Lake Ontario, it feels snugger. I find a white leather couch along the windows and sit down. It's nearly 11 a.m. I've been here almost two hours and haven't accomplished anything.

I open Mobile Super XCoder and access my programs on my personal cloud. There's a draft of my Super Tracker app, waiting to be tested, and my nearly finalized Sound Isolator app. I pull out the latter and skim over the code one more time. The hallway is quiet. It's a good chance to test my app's range. I run the app and leave my phone on the couch. Then I scurry down the hallway, count ten steps, and call, "Test!" I repeat this until I'm almost at the end of the hallway.

Just when I turn to go back, I hear voices, and a large group of Supers turns into the hallway, led by a wide, rectangular-shaped man with a bristly moustache. I can tell by their casual, or "civilian," clothes that they're newly initiated Supers—no assigned uniform yet. As they pass by the couch, a spike of panic rushes through me. My phone! I dart back towards it.

Somehow, I always feel awkward around Supers who are not Gwen. As I dive into the group of new initiates, I wonder what made them so special and deserving. Did they work harder than me? Were they better people than me? I reach for my phone, stepping on one Super's foot.

"Ergh!" he yelps, more out of surprise than pain. I mutter an apology and wriggle through their bodies, hands out-stretched. Noises of annoyance trail me. One girl turns green on contact and shoots me a withering glare, but I only have eyes for my phone. I breathe a sigh as my fingers close around its smooth case.

Someone bumps into my back.

"Hey!"

"Sorry!"

The girl behind me rubs her nose. "You can't just stop and turn around in the middle of nowhere. Keep moving!"

"Sorry," I repeat, "but I'm not really—"

"Come on, we're falling behind!" She pushes against me. I resist, but her prods are insistent. Finally, I relent. The swarm of new initiates creates a wave. I'm swept along with them, the narrow hallway a curse rather than a blessing. The Agent, "Taupe" says his name tag, unlocks a door near the end of the hallway and ushers us in.

"Quickly, folks," he says, sounding both chipper and tense, his meaty hands palming the air. "We were supposed to be there ten minutes ago."

"Sorry," I call as I pass him, trying to turn back once again, "but I need to get back."

"Whatever you've forgotten will be brought to your temporary dorms. Be at ease. You're a part of LOS now. Now *vite*. Hurry, hurry!"

"But I'm not supposed to be here!"

"Cold feet, huh?" Agent Taupe says amicably. "Don't worry about it. It'll pass."

They think I'm a Super, I realize with a jolt. I'm around the right age. I suppose it's not hard to be mistaken as a new initiate. I pause a moment longer, but Agent Taupe only raises his eyebrows and waves harder. I bite my tongue and pass through the door. The resulting hallway is similar to the last. In fact, I can't really tell the difference at all. We keep walking. A part of me is horrified that I'm trespassing. Another part of me, a bigger part, is excited. I'm going to get a tour of the building *and* I'm going against the rules! It's oddly stimulating.

"Where are we going?" I whisper to the girl that bumped into me.

She shoots me a look that asks, *Are you stupid?*

"To get our uniforms fitted, duh. Didn't you listen to Taupe's speech at all?"

"Uh," I say, "no."

She rolls her eyes. "So what's your power anyway? Do you have laser vision or something?"

She wriggles her fingers at my sunglasses.

I curse people, my mind chimes bitterly. Only my parents' reproach stops me from blurting it out. Instead, I make an unintelligible grunt.

Luckily, the girl doesn't seem interested. "I can see through walls and stuff," she offers before I can come up with a reasonable answer. She points towards a blank wall. "That room there has a meeting going on. There's a bunch of Agents watching videos and looking very serious. That other room has a guy napping at his desk. The room beside it has two people—"

"I don't think you're supposed to be spying on people like that," I say, shocked at her blatant misuse of her power.

She rolls her eyes at me.

"What are you? My mom or something? I'm not ashamed of my power."

"That's not what I mean—"

"Settle down, children!" Agent Taupe has stopped in front of a large elevator. "This will take you to the upper levels. The elevator holds only fifteen people at once, so we'll have to split into two groups. I'll come up with the second group. I'll ask you kindly to wait for me in the lobby above."

I'm crammed into the elevator with fourteen Supers. As the doors slide closed—almost nipping my knee—a bust of excited whispers arise.

"I hope I get to choose my colours!"

"I want a cape!"

"No you don't, stupid, you'll get caught on something!"

"Ok, then I want cool shades."

"That's even stupider!"

"Hey," says the girl beside me, staring into my face. I realize a moment too late that my sunglasses have slipped down my nose during the rush, exposing most of my face. "Who are you anyways? You look kind of familiar." She leans over to the boy next to her. "Hey, doesn't she look familiar?"

"I dunno. Sort of?"

"Were you on TV or something?" The girl peers into my face. I try to turn away, but it's difficult to move when you're pressed in the midst of a group of bodies. "You kind of look like that Bell girl. What's her name? You know, the Dud."

"Beatrice, I think," says the boy behind me.

I squirm. The elevator travels both vertically and horizontally through the massive building, but it moves so smoothly that I almost don't notice it.

"Wasn't she hurt in a Counter-League attack? I heard about it on the news."

"Pfft! Civvie problems."

Actually, I think, *plenty of Supers get hurt too*, but the group dissolves into a clamour of Civvie-bashing, and I'm afraid speaking up might draw their ridicule. I stand still and hope the heat in my face doesn't show too badly.

By the time the elevator doors open, I want nothing more than to get away. As the press of bodies moves into the lobby, I dart between two larger boys and slip into the nearest hallway I can find. I half-run, half-stumble through the halls until I can no longer hear the voices of the new initiates. I don't think I have ever been more uncomfortable in my life. My hand goes to my side and traces the stitches there. My other hand is still tightly around my phone.

The upper floors are padded with fine beige carpet the texture of a well-knit sweater. The walls are warmer. I realize with some trepidation that I don't know where I am anymore. Did I turn right or left at the intersection? All the hallways look the same.

But then a burst of red catches my attention. I spot Agent Scarlett turn a corner. *Lucky break!* Her hair is in her standard bun, and her heels are silent on the carpet. I lift a hand to wave at her, but she doesn't see me.

"Agent Scarlett!"

She pauses and gazes around in confusion.

"Over here! It's me! It's Beata Bell!"

She turns around, a smooth motion that seems carefully coordinated. At first, I think she frowns, but then a considerate, patient look appears on her face.

"Oh, Miss Bell," she states. My stomach does a tumble. Every time I see an LOS Agent, I remember the times I've failed the Super exams. "This is a restricted area. Agents and Super initiates only. How did you ever find yourself here?"

"I'm sorry," I say, scuffing the floor. "I got swept up here."

An idea occurs to me. "Agent Scarlett, are you busy?"

She raises an eyebrow and motions at the clipboard tucked

under her arm. "I do have appointments to attend, yes. Is there something the matter, Miss Bell?"

I straighten my back and attempt to look important. *Imagine you're reporting for duty.* "I know you're busy, ma'am, but I have some important information for you regarding the Counter-League."

Agent Scarlett's face goes smooth. "Of course. Your input is welcome. Shall we speak somewhere more private?"

I nod wordlessly, surprised she accepted so easily. After the unrelenting receptionist, I didn't expect to get an audience with only a few sentences. Agent Scarlett walks very fast. I have to trot to keep up with her.

Agent Scarlett leads me down more hallways until we hit a door with her name embossed in gold. She swipes her ID card. The door swooshes open. *Welcome, Agent Scarlett*, says a soothing computer voice.

"Welcome to my office, Miss Bell," says Agent Scarlett.

"Um, it's very nice," I say. Her desk is made of rich, reddish wood, and there's a large motivational poster on the wall with the picture of a submerged iceberg. POTENTIAL: *Look past the exterior, and see that there is so much more within. Then decide to unleash that potential to the fullest. –Lincoln Patz.* She motions at a chair by her desk, which I take. It's surprisingly soft, even though it looks stylish and stiff.

"So." Agent Scarlett has her business face on. "What is this I hear about Counter-League evidence? We take tips about the Counter-League very seriously around here."

I take a deep breath and tell her about the photos Ling took at City Hall, about meeting Alexander and chasing Gwen down the streets of Toronto. She's a good listener, nodding and making encouraging noises when I pause. Her eyes glitter with sympathy when I motion at my side, and she makes short *tsk, tsk* sounds with her tongue. I pull the grainy photo from my backpack, conscious of how wrinkled and low quality it looks compared to everything around it. It sits like trash on her elegant tabletop.

Agent Scarlett takes the photo with the tips of her fingers and looks closer. I hold my breath. The office is silent. No doubt it's soundproof. I search for the comforting, steady tick of a clock, but there's no clock to be found.

Finally, Agent Scarlett nods. "Well, Miss Bell, this is an excellent effort on your part, and I must thank you on behalf of LOS for taking the time to bring this to our attention." She pauses and sighs. It's a small sound, almost pleasant. "But as you must know, this photo is not of—excelsior—quality."

I hang my head. "I know."

Agent Scarlett shakes her head. "I'm afraid we can't act on this scant evidence alone. It would not be right to act against a citizen of the city before there is unimpeachable proof that he is a part of the Counter-League. It's a serious accusation."

I start to get up. "But—"

She holds up a hand, and I swallow my words with difficulty. A part of me knew it would be an uphill fight, but I thought speaking with Agent Scarlett would at least give me leverage. Frustration rises in me once more. It would be different if Gwen presented the photo. Gwen could give the world a photo of Bigfoot, and they would add Bigfoot to the list of endangered animals and advocate his protection. Everything Gwen says is gold.

"Miss Bell, I understand that you're worried, but we must address the situation objectively." I bite my cheek, glum.

She's using the tone my parents take when I'm throwing a temper tantrum. It's patient and gentle, but also painfully reasonable.

"LOS is actively working to track down members of the Counter-League. The City Hall debacle was a mistake, a huge media sensation, and a failure by LOS to protect its citizens. Rest assured, we won't let a group of terrorists get under us again."

"You could maybe investigate?" I ask weakly.

"We keep good track of polypowers all over the world. In the heat of battle, things aren't always as they seem. You say he dematerialized metal, but did you *see* him dematerialize it?"

"Gwen did," I say, sounding petulant to my own ears. "She told me he's like her!"

"Gweneira Kendricks has made clear to me what she saw in battle," says Agent Scarlett, "but without solid proof, we can't move forward. We can't arrest anyone on a hunch. Do you understand, Miss Bell? Can you imagine how embarrassing it would be for LOS to detain him and learn that he is completely innocent? The last thing LOS needs right now is more public outcry."

"So you *know* he's a polypower."

"It's not a matter of knowing. It's a matter of proof."

"So you *know*. You *know* he's dangerous, and powerful, and probably could cause lots of damage."

"We do not know definitively."

"You're going to wait and let this guy attack the city again just to get more definitive evidence?" I sputter. "That's—that's *stupid*."

"Miss Bell, calm down."

"I *am* calm!"

"Miss Bell." Agent Scarlett fixes me with a stern stare. I have to bite my lip to stop myself from ranting on. I miss Ling and Nuha. Maybe I should have brought them for moral support. Plus, they're both better at arguing. Ling would be able to convince Agent Scarlett to take action. Ling is articulate and confident. I'm not. Even Nuha can argue me under the table if she wants to. I just don't have a combative personality. I run away from conflict. When I'm silent for long enough, Agent Scarlett speaks again.

"Don't worry. Believe in LOS."

I'm surprised at how calm she is. For a second, I see Gwen sitting in her place, her gloved hands folded in a perfectly ladylike fashion, her face like a statue's, her shining hair falling in waves over her shoulders. Boldness rises in me.

"I'm surprised LOS doesn't have him on record," I say. It's easier imagining I'm arguing with Gwen than Agent Scarlett. "The Counter-League polypower, I mean. Whether he has metal manipulation or not, he definitely has two powers. Otherwise, that I-beam would have ended him for good. I checked the LOS database. There isn't a polypower listed who can fly *and* deflect entire I-beams. Gwen is really powerful. She's one of Toronto's greatest heroes. Yet this guy could match her. Isn't it kind of sloppy to have a powerful polypower running around for this long and not notice him?"

"We do not force Supers to register with LOS," says Agent Scarlett. She crosses her arms in a motion that says, *I'm being patient.* "It's just *highly* recommended. If a polypower chooses not to enter the organization, we respect their decision."

I stare at the floor, the perfectly even kinks in the carpet. Everyone could be in danger! My friends, Gweneira, my parents, even members of LOS if Alexander causes more commotion. I know it's him. Even with the low quality of the photo, I know it's him. It makes me sick to think I took comfort from his words, but even Beamsman seemed like a perfectly nice person—until he went crazy. Agent Scarlett's room is very quiet. I can hear my own blood pulsing through my ears.

"Miss Bell," Agent Scarlett says at last, quieter than before. "Do you not believe in LOS?"

Her question catches me off guard. *Careful*, whispers my mind. I cross my arms in response and consider her question. Even though the room is cool, I'm overheating. My stomach is upset and my side hurts. "I thought I did, but now I'm not so sure."

Agent Scarlett smiles. She's a pretty lady, with her refined features and perfectly straight teeth, but there's something sharp about her too. She reminds me of a hunting hound.

"Doubt is an ugly emotion," she says, and I frown. Am I being criticized? I'm not sure how to respond. "It's poisonous, you know. It builds and builds, and eventually blinds you to even the most obvious truths."

"Ok?" I say, confused. Agent Scarlett rearranges a few papers on her desk. Her movements are prim and proper, and I'm reminded of Gwen again.

"Tell me, Miss Bell, are you satisfied with the way things are now?"

"I don't know."

"Do you want to change the world?"

"Of course I do!"

"You are part of a very prestigious, very successful line of Supers, and I value your input, since you clearly are a clever child." Agent Scarlett leans forward. "So I have a proposition for you. What would you say to working for us?"

I blink. Did I just get a job offer? My frustration scatters in a spurt of surprise.

"Of course, we couldn't pay you." Agent Scarlett twirls a hand. "Legalities and whatnot. But LOS can always use clever people like you. Clearly, you're worried about the welfare of your friends, family, and the city."

"I am," I say with a slow nod.

"I invite you to volunteer your time." Agent Scarlett reaches into her desk. She removes a stack of cards primly and holds one out. It's a business card printed on paper so luxurious it's almost velvety. "The school board requires students to do forty hours of volunteer work before graduation anyhow. This is a good opportunity to progress your academics *and* contribute to your city."

I take the business card warily and finger its rounded edges. A winged shield is printed on the back. On the other side, it says: *Agent Scarlett: LOS*. Her office phone number, cell number, and email are listed underneath.

This is your chance to contribute, my mind whispers. *To work in the same field as Gwen.*

Agent Scarlett leans back in her ergonomic chair. "It's a small time commitment for a good cause. If you ever see anything suspicious, call or email me directly. With luck and enough help, we might stop the Counter-League yet."

"Yes," I say, trying to keep my voice neutral. Report personally to one of LOS's most notable Agents? I'm still half angry with Agent Scarlett, but I can't deny it's a good opportunity. *There's no shame in working behind the scenes*, my dad's voice echoes in my head. If I'm not out in the streets, apprehending criminals, I can at least work behind the scenes, investigating. "I'll consider it, maybe."

"I hope you understand why we can't move with your evidence." Agent Scarlett watches me carefully. "I hope you won't let resentment blur your judgement."

A small swell of embarrassment overcomes me. It's like she read my mind.

I tuck Agent Scarlett's business card in my pocket with determination, and she nods at me approvingly.

"If there is anything else I can do to help ease your worries, be sure to tell me," she continues. "Would you like undercover LOS Agents at your home? We can safeguard your family until this Counter-League business is dealt with."

After Supers like my parents retire, they are given homes according to their performance during their careers. Dad didn't rank high, but Mom was successful enough to ensure a nice middle-class house in the suburbs. The locations of Super residences are all private. Supers, especially famous ones, sometimes make enemies over the years, or worse, intense fans, and LOS doesn't want outsiders learning their whereabouts. Of course, if retired Supers want to announce their location—and some do, missing the fame and cameras—they are free to do so. As far as I know, Mom and Dad aren't big on giving away our address, and I'm always careful when inviting friends over.

Also, the thought of having Supers around our private home makes me squirm. I don't need kids my age or younger, accomplishing more than me, reminding me constantly of what I failed to become. I shake my head.

"Thanks but no thanks."

"Well, then." Agent Scarlett fixes her red frames. "Thank you for bringing us this information." She smiles like she's posing for the camera. "We'll be keeping the photos, of course. As evidence. And naturally, as a potential associate with LOS, I ask you to operate with discretion."

I nod.

"Would you like an escort back home?"

"No, thanks." I know my way back home, and I have more than enough bus tickets.

"Take care then, and be careful out there. I'll walk you down to the lobby. Luckily, it's on the way to my next appointment." Agent Scarlett taps her clipboard, which hasn't left her arm the entire time. Together, we navigate the labyrinthine halls of LOS's upper floors and take the elevator back to the main lobby. I shoot a glare at the stoic receptionist as I pass and make a show of tossing my consultation ticket into the recycling bin, but I don't think he notices. As I step through the gliding doors of the entrance and into open air, I feel infused with renewed purpose.

Chapter 12

Investigation Time

The shuttle back is emptier than the shuttle over. There aren't any tourists to knock into my legs and snap pictures. I'm glad. I need some quiet to think. As the LOS's hyper-white, hyper-clean colour scheme fades and the world falls back into the bold greens and browns of autumn, it's like awakening from a dream. LOS headquarters is so different from the rest of the city that I wonder if they're a part of the same realm at all. Supers on one side, Civvies on the other, and a long, white bridge in between. High-end gadgets and fancy chairs versus toddling buses and IKEA furniture.

A busy mind is a happy mind, Gwen's voice chimes in my head. She's right. Now that I'm supposed to keep a lookout for suspicious behaviour, I am hypervigilant. My eyes skim over fellow commuters. Everyone has big bags these days. It would not be hard to conceal something dangerous. I pull out Agent Scarlett's personal business card and gaze at it. In the daylight, the paper is almost shiny—like a pearl. I tuck it into my wallet for safekeeping. I pull out my phone to check the time: 2:15 p.m. I can still get home and race to the answering machine. Hopefully, my parents haven't come home early from work. I have one text from Nuha.

Bea, we missed u in school 2day. I heard from Ling. We shud probs talk. Also, I have ur homework sheets.

It sounds like Ling's told Nuha all about Alexander. With

some luck, Nuha will have convinced Ling not to post it all over the Net in excitement. I'm sure Alexander won't appreciate us busting his cover, especially after he put so much effort into hiding his face on television.

Then I notice an orange light blinking in the corner of my phone.

Oh, right. I forgot to turn off the Sound Isolator app when I grabbed my phone from the couch. I swipe to bring up the app and hit "end record." The orange light goes away. I fish a pair of earbuds out of my pocket and plug them in.

It's a beautiful day. The clouds are perfect whipped cream dollops in the sky. The trees are waving gently in the slight breeze. I wonder what Frances E. Shaw would say about my working for LOS. I might not be out kicking butt in the streets and posing for photo shoots, but I can at least work from the shadows, constantly watching, like a sentinel. Somehow, it feels mysterious and heroic in its own way. I'll help people without their knowing and catch criminals without expecting medals. And aren't Supers supposed to be selfless anyways? What's more selfless than doing things for others without getting anything in return? After all this time, I can finally be somewhat useful.

I set the Sound Isolator app to playback and close my eyes.

"Sound Isolator test," my voice says, loud and clear. I wait. Even my footsteps sound crisp and smooth. So far, so good. "Test," my voice sounds, further away.

I listen to the recording as the bus lumbers down the street. The Sound Isolator plays back my voice. Each time, it gets a little quieter but never loses its clarity. Delight surges through me. It's working almost perfectly! Finally, I hear the new initiates walk in. Their footsteps echo, and the Sound Isolator jumps from person to person, catching snippets of conversations. It feels wrong to be listening to other people talk without their knowing, but some of it is so interesting I can't stop.

"All my friends are Civvies," says a morose-sounding girl. "I don't want them to hate me."

"For being a Super?"

"Yeah, and now that I'm not going to see them every day, what if they forget about me?"

Someone in the background laughs a little too loudly, and the Sound Isolator jumps to them.

"I don't know. It's weird, I guess. Sometimes I wake up and my pajamas have scorch marks. Then I gotta get new ones. My mom's pretty pissed, but it's not like I can help it."

The Sound Isolator jumps to the voice of Agent Taupe telling everyone to stay together and hurry up. Then my own voice come into the mix, louder than the rest, apologizing. The app records static as I stuff my phone into my pocket. For the next few minutes, the sound of rustling fabric muffles all conversation.

Then, through the noise, a couple of quiet voices. They aren't children's voices but solemn adult ones. I can barely hear them over the more immediate chatter of new initiates, but whatever they're saying sounds serious.

"—propaganda—credibility—tabloids mostly, but even small rumours can spiral—rebel underground groups with Super members—undermining LOS."

A scramble of sounds. More rustling. The sound of someone giggling before I can clearly make out the adult voices again.

"—saying we haven't caught them?"

"Teams of—deployed—understandable discretion required to stop a total—public opinion. There is no need to spread—in the streets of the city. People's—LOS must remain intact. We need to initiate—capture the rebels, especially their leader, quietly—"

The app jumps to the sound of footsteps again, and I almost curse. The girl I bumped into begins inquiring about my powers. For the next few seconds, our conversation blocks out all other voices. I squeeze my phone.

One clear sentence emerges from the chaos. "Do we know who the rebel leader is?"

"We do indeed. Ladies and gentlemen, please remain seated. The name I am going to release will be shocking and familiar to all of you."

Murmurs and more rustling. In the excitement, the name is lost in the din. I bite my lip in frustration. It's not right to pry into other people's business, but I'm rapt, drawn in like a leaf to an eddy. Instead of a name, I hear an outcry.

"Impossible—how can it—he's *dead*!"

"No, Agent Ecru, he is most definitely *alive*, and—ruckus. You understand—gravity of the situation—"

The conversation fades from the record, overtaken by the sound of excited new initiates. I exhale slowly and frown hard. When did this conversation happen? *That room there has a meeting going on*, the newly initiated girl at LOS headquarters had told me. Did my Sound Isolator manage to listen in on conversations that even I didn't catch with my own ears? I gaze at my phone in wonder. Even though it's still a bit jumpy, the Sound Isolator works better than I ever anticipated. A spurt of pride rushes through me, followed closely by a rush of panic.

But what is this talk about rebels undermining LOS? I'm

suddenly self-conscious. I have a very private conversation in my hands. It feels wrong to have it leave LOS walls. My stomach clenches, and my thumb hovers over the erase button. *It's probably nothing*, I tell myself. LOS has meetings all the time. They handle the nation's top security threats, from international tensions to neighbourhood drug busts. A small group of rebels in a big city like Toronto isn't a big deal.

Still, it's weird thinking LOS needs to have behind-the-scenes talks. On television and in real life, they're always perfect, planned, and orderly. Every disaster is handled with minimal lives lost. Even the robot octopod attacks don't faze them. LOS always comes out on top. Always. Their teams are so well trained that their missions might as well be choreographed. It's still a mystery to me how they manage to clean up so effectively, but I imagine they have all sorts of advanced technology that no one else can afford. I wonder what crime fighting was like before Frances E. Shaw developed powers, what it would be like if all the world had were police officers and tasers. A robot octopod attack without LOS would probably leave thousands dead.

I shudder at the thought.

The bus rumbles to a stop at my transfer station. I turn off my app and shove my phone in my pocket as I hop off. The bus chugs off with a puff of hot wind, and my mood dips as I spot Dieter waiting at the stop. I walk fast, hoping to bypass him, but he spots me and his face curls into a sneer. For a second, I think he's going to confront me about skipping school, but then common sense kicks in and I relax. Dieter wouldn't care whether or not I skipped school.

"Bey-ah-ta Bell," he calls, almost singsong. It sounds like a taunt.

"What?" I ask, bracing for confrontation.

Instead of attacking, Dieter looks nervous. His arm isn't bandaged anymore, but he still holds it close to his body. He sighs and scuffs the ground with his sneaker. "Hey, man, don't look at me like that. I just wanted to talk. Like decent people. We got off on the wrong foot, I think."

"You mean *you're* always a jerk." I'm surprised by the aggression in my voice. It's been a hard day. "*I* was perfectly decent to begin with."

He raises his hands as I glare at him. "Fair," he says, "but don't you think this has gone far enough already?"

I know he's rehearsed this. His words are like something that would come out of my parents' mouths when they're disappointed about something. I narrow my eyes at him, and he assumes an innocent face. The silence stretches out. In the end, he breaks eye contact first.

"What do you want, Dieter?" I ask, exasperated. "I have better things to do than talk to you."

"I want you to take your curse off me," he says, looking equally exasperated.

I feel a pang of annoyance. *Not this again.* Dieter must have caught my expression, because his voice goes desperate.

"Oh, come on!" He's almost pleading. "Ever since you cursed me in the cafeteria, bad things have been happening. Not only the arm"—he proffers his bandage-free arm like a slab of meat—"although that was the worst of it, but also everyday things. Nothing is going right. I had a pop quiz last week and I failed. It was in social science, Bell. I'm the bomb at social science. Then, flying formations for LOS, I almost electrocuted myself on a power line. For no good reason. It wasn't even windy! I lose things. I trip over things. I bang my knees against every coffee table I see. Call off the curse, Bell. You win, ok?"

"I can't do that, Dieter," I say. There's no curse in the first place, but before I can give him an explanation, he throws up his hands.

"What do you want me to do, Bell?" he asks, cheeks growing pink. "You want payback? I'll give you money. I'll be your servant for a week. What do I have to do?"

"Nothing," I say, aghast that he thinks I'm the sort of person to extort others. "I—"

My words catch in my throat. We are about three blocks from Sir Frederick Banting and four blocks from my house. The streets are lined with modest semi-detached homes and townhouses, shaded by towering oaks. Across the road, a door opens, revealing a tall figure in black. I take a step back automatically. The figure fiddles with some keys and walks down the stairs in a telltale teenage slouch. He doesn't have his camera equipment today. Alexander.

My mouth goes dry and my knees feel weak. The hairs on my neck and arms stand up. *At least he didn't lie about living close by*, my mind twitters glumly. I fight the urge to dive behind a shrub. It stuns me to think he's a polypower, the same as Gwen. It's hard to imagine he's dangerous, with his tired gait and slumped shoulders, except I know he is. I want to run, but I don't. Running would make me obvious, and he might give chase. I can't possibly outrun a flying Super. I turn to Dieter instead.

"Look, I'll make you a deal."

If Dieter were a dog, his ears would have perked up. "Shoot," he says.

"Carry me into the air."

Dieter frowns. "What?"

"You heard me. Carry me into the air. The higher the better."

"But why?"

"*Just do it, ok?*"

Alexander heads down the sidewalk, drawing closer to the bus stop. My heart doubles its pace. I grab Dieter's arm, which he yanks out of my grip in confusion. My mind races. Would Alexander try something suspicious? There are no bystanders around. He could easily get rid of Dieter if he tried. And then what? Would he try to kidnap me and use me against LOS? Against Gwen? I grab Dieter's arm again and dig my fingers in.

"Ow! Cut your nails, woman!"

"Dieter!" I glare at him. "I'll *double* the curse. I swear!"

Finally, he relents. "Fine. Be weird. I'll piggyback you."

I jump on him and he stumbles. Grumbling under his breath, he wraps his arms around my legs and takes a few hops before gliding upwards. I watch the houses and trees pull away from me and swallow my nerves. I'm not afraid of heights—when Gwen first got her powers of flight, she used to carry me way up into the air, much to my delight and the panic of our parents—but I *am* afraid of being noticed.

"Higher," I urge Dieter. He cranes his neck to shoot me a dirty look. I stare back at him, eyebrows raised to say, *What are you waiting for?* Cool wind brushes my face as we ascend. My fingers already feel numb, but I don't care. Alexander is below me, a dark speck against the sidewalk. I don't think he's spotted us. Now, he walks with purpose, as though he knows where he's going.

I point. "Follow that man."

"What? That's creepy. You stalking him or something?"

"Yeah, I'm totally stalking him. Now go! But don't get too close. I don't want him seeing me. Keep behind him if you can."

"Just so you know, you're being totally crazy right now." Dieter glides in Alexander's general direction.

"How fast can you fly?"

Dieter makes a face. "I don't know. Never really timed myself. Why do you ask?"

"In case we need to make a getaway."

"You're seriously creeping me out now, Bell. What the hell is going on here? Is this guy dangerous or something?"

"It's a secret. Confidential business. Do you want that curse lifted or not? Hurry now, he's getting away!"

I fiddle for my phone. It's harder to get a grip with one hand, but I manage. I flick on the Sound Isolator app and direct it in Alexander's direction. The app glows, triangulating, and locks on. I listen with bated breath. Only footsteps. So far.

From a distance, it's hard to imagine him as a supervillain. He looks like a normal high-schooler. We follow him for nearly ten minutes. He walks fast, his long legs eating up space. Once in a while, he stops to glance around, as though checking for witnesses. His phone rings, and I nearly fall off Dieter's back.

"Watch it, Bell!"

"Shh!" I concentrate. My cellphone's battery is dangerously low. I have never tested the Sound Isolator app for more than a few minutes at a time, and I've certainly never left it running for an entire afternoon. I need to make every second count. If I can get incriminating evidence, maybe LOS will finally make an arrest.

Then glory will be yours, my mind crows. I shake my head to clear it. *I'm not doing this for glory*, I tell myself. *I'm doing it because it's the right thing to do*. Because Counter-League criminals need to be put away.

"Uh-huh," Alexander says below. It's an effort to hear him over the sound of the wind. He sounds unenthusiastic. A long pause. "I'm not thrilled about the idea, you see." A shorter pause. "Of course I understand. It's just that—" He turns around on the sidewalk so quickly Dieter has to put on a spurt of speed to veer out of his line of vision. I bite back a yelp and lock my arms around Dieter's neck. He makes a choking noise.

Alexander sounds flustered. "Yes. No! Yes, I'll have it done."

He hangs up.

I bite my tongue in frustration. That wasn't incriminating at all! In the movies, it's easy to plant a bug on someone and get evidence off it. It seems real life is nowhere as convenient. Alexander could be talking about a school project for all I know.

Down below, Alexander turns around again. Dieter makes another wide swerve to stay out of sight. He's beginning to breathe hard, and I'm beginning to feel bad for him.

"Bell," he gasps. "Lose some weight. What are you? Like two hundred pounds?"

My sympathy vanishes like mist in the sunlight.

"Maybe you just need to work out more," I snipe.

"Can you at least tell me *why* you're so into this guy?"

"I told you. Confidential business."

"Just to let you know—I might have to—land soon."

Dieter huffs like the big bad wolf. "Unless you want to fall out of the sky. I mean, if you do, go ahead—I don't have any objections or anything—don't get me wrong."

Something catches my eye. A dark shape sitting in the hidden intersection of a small roadway. I narrow my eyes. It's a sleek black car, nothing like the ones I see driving on the streets. It's so dark it seems to absorb light, and it reminds me of the vehicles LOS uses to pick up Gwen, except it doesn't have any of LOS's symbols. Or a license plate. My skin prickles. Definitely suspicious. I check Alexander's trajectory. If he keeps going, he will pass right by it. My breath hitches. Maybe this is my second chance to record something incriminating.

"Bell," Dieter groans. "I'm serious."

He's beginning to shake now, struggling to stay aloft. A part of me is afraid he might actually drop out of the sky. Another part of me is disdainful. *Nothing like Gwen*, my mind chimes. Gwen's flight is smooth and steady. She could carry me forever.

"Fine," I snap. "Land behind the fence there. The one with all the bushes."

"That's private property!"

"It's the only place where we won't be seen!"

Dieter sighs long and deep. We begin a shaky descent. Dieter dips several times, struggling to stay aloft. I hang on tight, just in case.

We land inelegantly, all limbs and awkwardness. Dieter collapses to his knees as I tumble off his back. Almost without pause, I scramble to my feet and press myself against the fence. The cool wood digs into my nose and cheeks, but I don't care. I fiddle with my phone and point the Sound

Isolator app between the cracks. Then I wait. Behind me, Dieter gulps big breaths of air.

"Remember, stay out of view!" I hiss at him.

"I know, I know." He mumbles something. I catch the word *stupid*, but I'm too excited to care. My entire body is vibrating with energy.

Alexander walks as though he's cold, with his hands in his pockets. A cool sweat breaks out on my brow as he draws closer to the dark vehicle. Will he pause? Or will he pass it by? As far as I'm concerned, an unlicensed car is suspicious activity, whether it's Counter-League related or not. I wonder how quickly I can switch from my Sound Isolator app to my phone's camera. I want solid proof this time. Undeniable proof. For a minute, Alexander just walks. It looks like he might pass the car after all, and my stomach drops in disappointment.

Then out of nowhere, he speaks.

"You're following me again. You should leave me alone."

I jump in the bushes. For a split second, I think I've been caught, even though I'm hidden from view and too far away to see with the naked eye. Still, it feels like he's staring right at me.

But someone else answers Alexander from the shadows. "With all due respect, Alexander, I will *not* leave you alone."

"I don't need a babysitter."

I frown. A partner? The driver of the car, perhaps? He doesn't have an especially diabolical voice, more calm than anything. I can't help but think it's a little familiar. I glance back at Dieter, who has settled on the ground, cross-legged. I consider asking him to fly back up and take a peek at who-ever is in the bushes, but he might just fly off and leave me stranded. The man in the shadows speaks again.

"We can work together. I'll help you, if you'll listen."

"I don't need your help."

"What nonsensical plan are you enacting this time?"

Alexander looks angry. "You don't need to know. My mission is my own. No one appointed you to watch over me. In fact, things might work out better if you just butted out altogether. It would be safer for everyone that way."

"I have experience with these things. No one will catch us. All we have to do is keep under LOS's radar."

"I'm done listening to you. I won't participate in your nonsensical vengeance plan, Hitori."

Hitori? My mind whirls. My knees hurt, but I'm too engaged to move. There must be more than one Hitori in the world, but only one comes to mind right now. Hitori Yuuma, the disappeared Super. *Retired*, Ling's voice hisses in my head. I remember Ling's clip. The explosion. The fires. The smoke. Could anyone survive chaos like that? *He was one of the world's only telekinetics.* Supers don't usually get to retire early, but a Super of *his* status could probably do whatever he wanted. I remember the conversation I recorded in LOS, the gasps of surprise upon learning the identity of the rebel leader, the one that everyone assumed was dead. Could they have been talking about—I swallow—Hitori?

"Vengeance plan?" the mysterious speaker doesn't sound angry, only sad. "Don't lie to yourself, Alexander. You know very well that—"

The Sound Isolator sputters. *No, no, no, no!* I twist the earbuds, but nothing else comes through. My phone is dead; the screen is dark and empty. I curse under my breath and press my face against the fence. Alexander is still speaking, but I have no way of hearing him. His body language conveys frustration, all jerky arm movements. I want to chuck my phone at the ground. I can't believe it failed at this critical time!

The sky takes on a late afternoon hue, and the clouds are stained flaxen. Dieter seems to have recovered his breath, and I motion for him to come over. He rolls his eyes, but does so.

Do you have your phone on you? I mouth. My voice is stuck in my throat, and I'm afraid of talking out loud even though I know I'm too far away to be heard. Dieter shoots me a quizzical look.

I lift my own phone and gesticulate at it clumsily. *Phone. You know, phone.*

He holds up a finger to stop me and rummages through his pockets. From them emerges an old Nokia phone, chunky as a brick, with no data functions whatsoever. An old-school gadget with a number pad and primitive camera functions. I sigh and shoot him a disbelieving look. Luck is working against me. Of all the children in Sir Frederick Banting, I happen to pick the one with no smartphone, no cloud functions, and no app compatibility. Dieter just shrugs. I peek back through the fence.

No Alexander.

A spike of panic lances through my chest. My head swivels as I check the skies above me, almost expecting him to swoop down like a bird of prey. Clouds. Setting sun. No Alexander. I breathe deep and start counting primaries. *1...3...5...7...* After a minute or so, I check the roads again. He's gone, and so is the mysterious black car. I've missed them.

I lean against the fence and swear silently. Urgency makes me tremble. If Dieter and I flew out now, would we be able to spot the black car?

And Hitori. Surely it can't be Hitori Yuuma. Why would he ever work against LOS? Alexander's voice echoes in my head. *Nonsensical vengeance plan.* I bite my thumb. Something big is happening. I can feel it in my gut, churning. A tiny part of me wants to call Ling and brag. I *knew* something was off about Hitori's so-called retirement. Why wouldn't he contact anybody afterwards? Why couldn't the reporters find him? Most people don't avoid society altogether after retirement. I replay Hitori Yuuma's final battle with Beamsman in my head. It's the last known recording of him, but Gwen always has follow-up interviews and television appearances after every dangerous mission. Why didn't Hitori? It's like he disappeared right after the fight.

"Dieter," I say. "We have to fly."

"Aw, man, again? Can't we just walk?"

"Are you a coward, Dieter?"

"What? No!"

"Perfect. I need you to do something dangerous for me." I stare him straight in the eye to relay my seriousness. It works, because he listens without interruption. Once I'm done my explanation, I scan his face for signs of nervousness. He eyes me up and down. I don't break eye contact.

"You owe me an explanation," he says finally. "I don't know what you're playing at, Beata Bell, but you're not joking around."

"I promise I'll tell you if you do this for me."

Dieter's face is grim. "Deal," he says, holding out a hand. I slap mine into his in a firm, damp handshake. "Don't blame me if you get airsick."

"Please," I say, grinning widely. I'm sure I have a crazy glint in my eye. "I'm the great-granddaughter of Frances E. Shaw, treasure of the Royal Air Force. I've flown with Gweneira Kendricks, the Steel Angel. I'm sure I can handle it."

We climb into the sky. As the sun lowers towards the horizon, long shadows crawl over the ground. Dieter pants and shakes, but I have my arms locked around his neck. They're starting to get sore from holding on so tight, but I don't dare relax.

"Are—you—sure?" Dieter asks for the umpteenth time. I grit my teeth. It's windy, and my hair blows into my eyes. "What—if you—fall off?"

"You just better make sure I don't." My heart pounds like a bass drum. Every beat makes me body pulse. I suck in air through my mouth and try not to look down. Despite my earlier bravado, I'm nervous about flying *this* high.

Finally, we pan out. The houses are so small they look like Lego blocks. I scan the roads for the mysterious black car, but I don't see it anywhere. Fine, I didn't expect it to still be around anyways. I only hope the stranger in the shadows hasn't gone too far. I pause to swallow my nerves. This is how Frances E. Shaw must have seen the world: tiny, distant, and surreal.

"Remember," I call, "the point is to gather enough speed so that whoever is in the bushes doesn't get a good look at us."

Instead of replying, Dieter gives a thumbs-up. For a second, we hang there, suspended.

Then we dive.

It's like being on a roller coaster but much scarier. The horizon tilts as we plummet. The wind stings my eyes as we pick up speed. I want to close them, but I know I can't. My hand is in a death grip around Dieter's old Nokia. The ground rushes up to meet us, and Dieter's hair tickles my nose. My own hair tugs against my temples so hard it almost hurts. I bite back a yell as we plunge towards the road.

Dieter grunts as he tilts. I can see our descent stretch out, like a steep parabola. Houses and trees zip past us. My fingers are numb, but as we glide down the street, I lock my left arm around Dieter's neck and hold up his phone with my right. As we zoom past the spot where Alexander stood, I take a series of burst photos. Even though our flight is too shaky for me to see clearly, I hear someone jump backwards with a surprised yelp. *Success!*

"Go!" I hiss. "Go, go, go!"

I don't know if Dieter hears me, but he puts on a spurt of speed anyhow. We rocket towards the sky again, pulling away from the road and into the open air. I risk a glance behind me as the ground drops away. My stomach drops with it. Dieter banks over the trees, wobbling. Nausea dizzies my head, but I shake it away. Dieter bobs once more, struggling for height, before finally dipping towards the ground. I hold my breath. He grunts in an effort to rise again but doesn't manage it. The ground rushes up to meet us.

I make an executive decision. Before we crash, I let go. I'm maybe three metres above the grass—close enough to the ground not to suffer any major damage if I'm lucky. A stabbing pain erupts in my side as I twist in mid-air to get away from Dieter. For a second, it's like I'm floating. My clothes flap around me. *This is what it feels like to be a flying Super.* Then gravity kicks in. I tuck my arms and legs into a defensive position. A team of professional jiu-jitsu trainers taught our gym class how to break-fall once. My body reacts almost automatically. I cover my head and neck and hit the ground. Leaves burst up around me. The ground and sky blurs. Sticks and debris poke at my body as I tumble. Finally, I roll to a stop, Dieter's phone clutched to my chest.

It takes me a few minutes to gather my breath.

"Bell?" echoes a voice from far away. "Bell? Are you dead?"

My chest heaves as I breathe. The sky is above me, fiery and darkening. I can't help it. I giggle breathlessly. My side hurts, but I take it as a good sign. I'm still alive.

"We did it!" I gasp, pushing myself up and hunching over Dieter's phone. Twenty-four photos in total. It looks promising. I flip through them. Most are blurry, showing nothing but foliage and asphalt. Then a figure caught in mid-step. He is stepping out of the coverage of the trees. He's older, maybe in his thirties, but not that much taller than Alexander. He wears a thick brown coat and a darker brown scarf. On his head is an equally brown hat, balanced over frazzled black hair.

My jubilation slips away as my body goes cold. Dieter's phone slips from my fingers. It hits the ground and thumps onto its side.

"No way," I mutter. "No. Freaking. Way."

"What is it?" Dieter peeks over my shoulder. I turn my head so fast my hair whips him across the eyes. He jerks back, cursing under his breath.

"Dieter, do you know where Nuha lives?"

"No, why would I?"

"Fine, that's ok. I'll give directions. We need to get there right away." Urgency slips into my voice. I try to sound calm, but I'm shaken up inside. I struggle to my feet. "Like right now. *Right now.*"

Chapter 13

Emergency Meeting

Nuha's house is easy to find for two reasons. First, it's built on a hill, so it peeks above the neighbourhood like a gallant, geometric sentry. Second, it's huge—bigger than all the other houses in the area. Nuha says her parents had their house built in a middle-class neighbourhood to stay in touch with the common people. She says this sarcastically, with a slight shrug that indicates she doesn't believe the strategy worked. Nuha's parents are always at business meetings in other countries, or fancy parties where they meet the VIPs of other companies. Nuha herself was raised by a series of nannies.

I get Dieter to land in front of the gates to the Bahar residence. I don't want Nuha's security freaking out over a Super hopping the fence. The Bahars are quirky, and I'm not one hundred percent sure they don't have experimental anti-intruder technology aimed at the perimeter.

It feels good to be back on solid ground. My knees feel like jelly after the flight. They shake, but I press forward despite their weakness. Dieter is in much worse shape. As soon as his feet touch the ground, he doubles over. I wonder if he's going to throw up. I buzz Nuha's number.

"Helloooo?" sounds Ling's voice. "You have reached the Bahar residence. How can I help yoouu?"

"Hi, Ling. I'm glad you're here too. It's me." I wave at the security cameras.

"Oh, hey, Bea, just one second." There's a shuffling noise, followed by a beep. "Ok, everything is a go. Is that Dieter with you?"

"Yeah."

"Ew, why? Is he coming in?"

In the background, I hear Nuha say, "Be nice, Ling."

I glance at Dieter. I owe him an explanation, and I plan on keeping my word. Even though I don't like him, I don't like the thought of dragging him into something dangerous either. Besides, a small part of me admits I don't want him running back to school and blabbing about my unexplained behaviour. The last thing I need is to have *Read About It* write an article about my "mad adventures."

"Yeah," I say reluctantly. "It's better if he does."

"Okey-dokey, then," sings Ling's voice.

The gates slide open. It's a psychological thing, but I feel a little better when I step onto private property.

Nuha opens the door. She's wearing a rusty-orange hoodie and carrying an iPad open to Google Maps. Ling is behind her, phone in hand, a beta version of our Super Tracker app on its screen. I can see the blue text of Tweeter scrolling across it.

"Glad you could make it," says Ling, "but why the baggage?"

She juts her chin out at Dieter, who opens his mouth as though to retort but gives up speaking to gasp instead. Ling sounds more sarcastic than angry, but I interrupt before they can start arguing.

"Guys, I have something important to show you."

The solemnity in my voice must have reached them, because everyone goes serious at once. Even Ling, whose smile is a permanent feature, grows quiet. Nuha studies me.

"You look rough," she says softly. "Both of you." She points at my side. "You're bleeding, Bea."

"What?" I look down. Dark spots stain my sweatshirt. *Shoot.* I must have torn some of my stitches in the fall. "Oh, it's not so bad. It hardly hurts anymore."

Nuha beckons us in and shuts the door. *Click*, goes the lock, and I feel a little more secure—just a little. I open my mouth to speak, but Nuha quiets me with a steady hand.

"Wait. Let's go to the basement."

Dieter's head twists as he takes in Nuha's impressive house. The floors are polished to a shine. As we walk, a small robot spider skitters across the floor, a red light blinking on its head. A mechanical glider soars overhead, flapping lazily. Usually, I would be fascinated, but today, heaviness dampens my curiosity. My head is jumbled. I replay the conversation the Sound Isolator recorded at LOS headquarters. I think about Hitori Yuuma and about the picture on Dieter's phone. My stomach is still queasy from the flight. I distract myself by watching Nuha's braid swing as she walks. We walk down the shining hallway and take a spiral staircase down.

When we reach Nuha's basement, I sit down gingerly. Nuha scampers off to grab some disinfectant and bandages to patch up my side. Once everyone is settled, I take a deep breath to steady my nerves.

"I suppose I should start with that picture Ling sent this morning," I begin. I relay the story of my visit to LOS headquarters, the covert recording on the Sound Isolator app, the conversation in the streets, and the wild escape with Dieter. When I finish, my mouth feels dry, and the atmosphere is thick with tension. I play the recording for Nuha and Ling, who lean in as though it's a suspenseful drama. I watch their faces for signs of distress. They're both stony. Finally, I show them the picture. Recognition registers in their eyes. Ling's mouth actually falls open. We gape in silence. Anxiety crackles around us like electricity.

"We all know who this is," I say quietly.

"It's Mr. Uzune," says Ling, scanning the photo. She touches the screen in disbelief.

Ling's confirmation is like a splash of cold water. I swallow. A small part of me hoped I was wrong. It *is* Mr. Uzune. I thought the mysterious speaker in the bushes sounded familiar. Now I know why. I listen to it every weekday as it explains geography, history, and English. I understand why I felt so uneasy behind that fence. In retrospect, it explains a lot.

He was at Gwen's conference at City Hall. I ran into him in the hospital afterwards. I remember his bandaged arm. Was it all a sham? Was he really hurt, or was he snooping for information? I remember the report on his desk. *LOS: New Recruit Report*. Why would a homeroom teacher have a copy of something like that? Now, to top it off, he's speaking with a member of the Counter-League.

Frances, I've stumbled across a real doozy, I think glumly. What would she do? Fly in and confront both persons face to face, probably. There's so much a Super can do that a Civvie can't. If I could melt faces with lasers, I wouldn't be afraid of confrontation either. I wouldn't need to be discreet. I wouldn't be hiding in Nuha's basement like a rat or a cockroach, too afraid to face the big, wide world. I wouldn't be afraid of anything.

"He's conspiring with the Counter-League?" asks Nuha,

wide-eyed. "Why?"

She wears a dismayed expression. We all like Mr. Uzune. I remember eating lunch with him, but I'm not sure how to feel about it now.

"I don't know for sure if he's a conspirator," I say miserably, "but I know he's involved."

"He's a Civvie by his age. If Alexander really wanted him out of the way, Mr. Uzune wouldn't be able to stand up to him," reasons Nuha. "That makes him suspicious at the very least. What sort of Civvie has power over Supers?"

I finger Agent Scarlett's card in my pocket. "People with power," I answer. "People who know things."

"If he's the disappeared Super," Ling breathes. Despite the tension, I can see excitement building in her. "He's intimidating enough to give most people pause."

"Hang on, slow down. *You* always said Hitori Yuuma retired," I say, eyeing her carefully.

Ling breathes a short laugh. More a huff of air than anything. "You caught me. So I withheld my opinion on the subject. You're always so nervous, Bea, especially now that Gwen is involved in a Super rivalry. I don't want you stressing out. Yes, he disappeared. Yes, it's weird. But that doesn't mean he's *not* retired on some tropical island."

"Doesn't mean he *is* either," I mutter, feeling a pang of resentment.

"Wait, wait, wait," Dieter interrupts, his hands in the air. He's still a little red around the cheeks. "You're saying Mr. Uzune is actually Hitori Yuuma? *The* Hitori Yuuma? Badass Extraordinaire? This is Mr. Uzune we're talking about. The flop who can't even stay awake in class?"

Despite myself, I feel a flare of anger. "Well, he's obviously not a flop if he's orchestrated a rebel group against LOS."

"You really expect me to believe he's Hitori Yuuma returned?" Dieter's face is disdainful. "You're crazier than I thought, Bell. Your spying gadget is definitely malfunctioning."

"It is *not*. Besides, we used *your* brick phone."

"What do you think he means by a vengeance plan?" Nuha interjects. "Let's say Mr. Uzune *is* Hitori Yuuma. Let's assume he didn't retire—" She shoots a look at Ling, who stares at the wall impassively. "If he *did* run away somehow, that would explain his sudden disappearance from public life. Let's say everyone assumed him to be dead, but he actually formed a rebel group under everyone's noses. That would explain the conversation you recorded at LOS. My question remains: *Why* would he want revenge?"

"Maybe he snapped under the pressure," Dieter offers, "or inhaled too many fumes and went nuts."

"You seem to be pretty hung up on this insane thing," I say, a little snide. "What's up, Dieter?"

"Believe it or not, all Supers are not as flawless as your precious Miss Kendricks," Dieter retorts with more venom than I expected. "Your family is full of famous Supers, so you don't know anything about what it's like to be rank D or C. It's hard, you know. Some people *do* go nuts. Your family's full of laser-shooters and teleporters. My family is full of D-ranked *empaths*. LOS doesn't pay for our house or give us benefits. LOS doesn't cover my mom's depression or send her cheques when she's unemployed. You're surrounded by stardom. You have no idea what it's like on the outside."

I give a bitter laugh. "Yeah, I have no idea at all. I guess living in my family's shadow isn't hard at all, especially with you dropping food on my head!"

"I was jealous, ok?" Dieter blurts, and flushes from neck to forehead. "You don't even have to do anything to live well. You can live off your name. You didn't have to curse me for it!"

"Guys!" Nuha claps her hands on the coffee table, her eyes blazing. Dieter and I jump at the sharp noise. It's so violent I almost expect the wood to crack. "Let's not forget the subject at hand." She glares at us both, as though challenging us to retort. "You can bicker later, but we have serious problems right now."

I look down at my shoes, the warmth of shame creeping up my face. Nuha is right. Even though I'm angry at Dieter, there are bigger things to worry about. I compose myself in silence, my lips pursed, and give Dieter a withering look, which he either doesn't notice or ignores.

"Does anyone want tea?" asks Nuha primly, breaking the silence. Without waiting for an answer, she trots away to put a kettle on the stove. Once she's gone, I turn to Ling.

"What do you think?"

"I think it's a great scoop," she replies.

"*Ling—*"

"I'm serious." She stares at me until I squirm. I hate it when she looks so stern. I'm too used to her easy-going nature. "I'm not sure if I believe any of this, that our homeroom teacher is the famous Hitori Yuuma, or that he's plotting revenge against LOS, or that he leads some sort of rebel group. It doesn't make sense to me. Why would one of LOS's most respected and famous Supers run away? What beef does he have against the organization? They gave him everything, training, education, money, fame. But don't get me wrong, Bea, it's a great story."

I'm hurt. "You don't believe me."

Ling shrugs. "Let's just say it's a little shocking."

"I heard them speaking, Ling. You heard the recording too!"

"I heard people talking, sure, but I'm not sure it's related. It's not a reporter's duty to connect the dots. We only tell the facts as they are."

"I know we're missing something. I can feel it in my gut." Even as I speak, a flash of doubt passes through my mind. Maybe it's not connected. Maybe I'm just being paranoid. Maybe LOS really was just having a meeting about a small uprising in the city. Maybe it was a different Hitori. Maybe he just so happened to look like our homeroom teacher—and have the same coat, and same face.

No. I calm myself. I'm positive something is wrong. A gut feeling isn't very objective, but I can't help but worry.

"There's got to be more," I say. "My dad says a lot of work goes on behind the scenes. Like icebergs. There's a bit that everyone sees but a whole lot under the water."

Nuha returns with a bamboo tray of steaming teacups. She places one in front of each of us. The smell of fresh, flowery tea calms me just a tad. Nuha sits once more, cross-legged, closes her eyes, and breathes deep as though meditating. Once she opens them, she adjusts her glasses.

"Ok, let's clear our heads and start from the beginning with the facts. What do we know for sure?"

"Alexander attacked City Hall and fought Gwen," I recite. "He's a polypower. He's a part of the Counter-League, which may or may not consist of more than one person."

"The Counter-League threatened Gwen's friends," Ling continues.

"We're Gwen's friends," Nuha adds.

"So we're all in danger," says Dieter with a sneer. "Whoop-de-doo. Good going, guys. Weren't you people taught anything about privacy?"

"You're not Gwen's friend, so," —Ling waves a hand in dismissal—"you can leave. No one's forcing you to stay."

"No," counters Nuha. She hands Ling a second cup of tea, which Ling accepts and chugs down, seemingly without feeling its heat. "Dieter can't leave because it would be irresponsible, especially now that he knows everything."

"What?" Dieter says. "I won't blab."

"But your friends might," I mutter under my breath, thinking of Matt Kiel. Even now, I'm mortified I ended up in a gossip magazine.

"As for the unconfirmed: Our homeroom teacher may or may not be a bad guy," Ling continues, ticking off points on her finger. "Hitori Yuuma might be coming out of retirement. Hitori Yuuma might be Mr. Uzune. Mr. Uzune might be evil. We're just not sure."

"What we need to determine is our next course of action," says Nuha, calm as a windless lake.

She waves nonchalantly at the tea—*help yourselves*—curls up, and picks up a nearby notebook. Nuha likes to take notes while planning. She says it helps keep her thoughts straight. "Beata's already gone to LOS, but they refuse to move without more evidence. The evidence we do have is shaky at best, but we can't just stay silent and wait either."

"What if we did a news release?" Ling asks. "You know, get the story out? Purposefully cause some ruckus and paranoia? LOS would have to react, right? They're supposed to serve and protect us. They'll want to calm down the commotion. I still have the photo on my memory card. Even if we don't go to legit news sites, we can contact tabloids."

I wince at the word *tabloids*. When I was younger, I used to sneak tabloids off my mom's dresser all the time. Mom had them ordered to keep up with the new and exciting Super world. I used to pore over the glossy photos and gasp at scandals. Back then, it was tons of fun, just stories on a piece of paper, rather than the lives and feelings of actual people. Now that I know what it's like to be featured in one, I have less than savoury thoughts about them.

"No, it's too risky," says Dieter out of the blue. Ling's head comes up and her eyes narrow.

"What do you mean?"

"If this Alexander guy really is part of the Counter-League, then letting him know we're onto him is the worst thing to do." Dieter runs his hand through his hair and takes a breath. I understand how he feels, contradicting Ling in her field of mastery. She can be intimidating when she stares like that, like she can slice right to your soul. "If he knows you know, then he'll come after you, and soon. I've seen enough movies to know it'll just drive him into action."

Even though I don't want to admit it, Dieter has a point, and I know Ling recognizes it by the way she stays silent.

Nuha glances around and jots something down in her notebook.

"Ok, option two: Go to our parents. Ask for help."

"I really don't want to pull my parents into this," I groan. I'm supposed to be making them proud, not getting in more trouble. I can see my mom's face, filled with disappointment as she places her hands on her hips and rolls her eyes. *Not again.* I don't want her thinking I'm just an annoying, useless kid who can't even solve her own problems. It's bad enough I don't have powers.

"But the option is still there," says Nuha. "Especially for you and Dieter. Your parents were Supers. They have connections with LOS. You can probably get LOS protection if you tell them you're worried about the Counter-League threats."

"Oh, LOS doesn't bother with *my* parents." Dieter rolls his eyes. "No one would care if they disappeared."

I feel like someone's punched me. "Wouldn't *you* care?"

"They're not the greatest parents," he says, shrugging.

"How can you say that about your own *parents*?" I hiss.

"Did you miss the bit about my mom being super depressed? Oh, and my dad's not that much better. He's always blowing our money on some stupid plan to get on television, get famous, and get rich. FYI, it's not happening. Plus, it's true. Only really famous Supers get LOS's attention. Most are ignored. Like Civvies."

"My parents are lowly cooks," says Ling airily. "Maybe they could pull up their *professional* media experience from China to help, but we've already decided going to the media was a *bad idea*."

I have the feeling she's bitter.

"Nevertheless, they should know what's going on," says Nuha with a definitive air. She chews on her lower lip and spins her pen. "Ok, option three, we tell Gwen. It's her challenge, her opponent, her rivalry."

I release an unintentional grumble, and all heads turn towards me. It's like having a spotlight shine on your face: intimidating. I shrink into my chair. Memories of our fight flood my mind. I know Gwen best. If I call her for help, she'll come, even if she's angry with me. She'll fly over because she's a Super, because she's Good and Just, and everything a perfect hero should be. But all I can see is the weird glint in her eye when she barged into my hospital room, and the way she snapped at the Payton fellow. My stomach turns uneasily.

"Gwen's—" I can't help but think she'll do something stupid and brave. She might charge after the Counter-League all on her own. "She's—she hasn't been in top form lately."

Plus, if we call Gwen, she'll just kick some butt and get another medal. *This is your chance*, my mind whispers. *This is your mission*. Agent Scarlett asked me to help. Not Gwen. I try to keep my face smooth and calm. Is it selfish to want to fix things myself?

"Yeah, she's been messing up," agrees Dieter.

Ling glares at him. She opens her mouth, but I stop her with a shake of my head.

"If we tell her, I have a feeling she might," I mumble, feeling a flush of guilt at my greedy thoughts, "you know, get reckless and hurt herself."

"Yeah, isn't she kind of going mental?" goads Dieter.

"I swear to God I'll punch you out," retorts Ling.

"Should we tell her anyway?" asks Nuha.

I don't know why everyone is looking at me, as though it's my call. I don't like feeling so much responsibility on my shoulders. It makes me squirm.

I imagine Gwen, surrounded by media, being coached by Agent Scarlett, getting groomed by her hairdressers, being prepped by her stylists, moving from conference to conference, cutting ribbons, engaging talk shows, training with her team, flying in missions and protecting the city. She hardly ever comes to school anymore, even though her grades are top-notch. I'm sure she shows up once in a while just to bring Sir Frederick Banting some excitement. I tell myself I'm doing this for her so she can get some rest, so she has one less thing to worry about.

I shake my head. "I don't think so. Not if we can end this ourselves. Not before we get more proof, and quickly."

"Yes, yes, but the question is *how*," says Ling.

I think hard. "We have school tomorrow," I say. A hardness settles in me. I place a hand over my wallet, where Agent Scarlett's card is nestled. "I have an idea. Nuha, Ling, do you have the latest version of the Sound Isolator app installed?"

The two nod.

"Ok." I lean forward. "Here's what we're going to do."

Chapter 14

Baiting the Lion Trap

I find Mr. Uzune napping at his desk again. I think back to all the times I've caught him sleeping outside of class time, like he's always exhausted. *Which he would be if he's teaching full-time* and *running an underground rebel group.* Currently, he looks peaceful, snoring over a pile of textbooks, a strand of hair flapping against his nostril. For a second, I allow myself to imagine that everything is ok. Mr. Uzune is just my homeroom teacher. He has nothing to do with the Counter-League. Life is normal, and no crazy villains are after us. Gwen is going to catch some criminals and hang out with us at the Ice Cream Emporium afterwards.

But I shake myself out of my daydream. Supervillains can be deceptive. I can't let my doubts slow my actions.

I try to imagine Hitori Yuuma all grown up. I can't really see the resemblance in Mr. Uzune, but a decade can do a lot to a person. Hitori always had his hair cut short, looking almost military. Mr. Uzune's is floppy and unkempt, as though he forgot how to use a comb. Hitori's nose wasn't crooked either, and he didn't have a scar on his chin.

I sit down at my desk and wait for class to start. Today, we begin with history: WWII, which means at least forty minutes of staring at slides of Frances E. Shaw on a projector. She looks amazing in every photo, even ones where she has soot and scorch marks all over her Supersuit. *Hello*, I imagine saying to her. I notice she's not very tall, not even as tall as my mom, barely five foot two.

"Miss Shaw is best known for her participation at Normandy," Mr. Uzune says, yawning discreetly in the dark. He had woken up minutes before the start of class. "As we all know, the battle was pivotal in determining the Allies' eventual victory."

A few classmates turn towards me to shoot me knowing looks, as though we shared a secret together, as though to say. *Hey, there's your ancestor up there.* They do it every time Frances E. Shaw is mentioned and it never fails to make me self-conscious. I keep my head straight and focus on Frances E. Shaw's flickering face.

I am about to do something very risky, Frances, I think.

The projector clicks, and my great-grandmother's face looks straight at the camera. It must be right after a battle, because the background is covered with fire—and bodies. A shiver travels up my spine.

I mean, not as risky as fighting a war, of course, I correct. Her eyes are fixed on the camera. On me. I hold her gaze for as long as I can. *But it's going to be pretty tough anyways.*

Click. Another picture. In it, Frances E. Shaw is balanced in mid-air. Twin beams of white-hot light shoot from her eyes. They shear through a line of tanks. I can barely make out her shape amid the chaos, but I can make out her power. She's absolutely magnificent. My stomach tumbles. How can I ever compare? How can anyone?

A depressing thought slips into my head. Maybe I'm not meant to compare. Frances E. Shaw could be the crowning moment in our family history, the very crest of the wave, the top one percent, a shining outlier. Maybe the rest of us, my grandparents, my parents, and me, can only be dull in comparison.

"Of course, the Axis powers had discovered their own Supers by now," says Mr. Uzune. "There was a scramble to train them up, but they were too fresh, too young, and without real experience. None had the firepower of Miss Shaw in the first place, and LOS was far better funded than their counterparts in Japan and Germany."

The clock ticks towards recess. With a determined heart, I reach into my desk and turn my phone on. I swipe the screen to bring up the Sound Isolator app. I glance over at Ling and Nuha. Both nod. I gaze once more on Frances E. Shaw's small, indomitable form. *Wish me luck*, I think at her photograph. *I'll need it.*

I practice my most unhappy face. I could never make myself cry on cue, like some of the better actors out there, but I can still look pretty miserable. I prep myself outside the door to homeroom, squashing up my face and rubbing my eyes to make them seem red. When I feel properly dishevelled, I take a few deep breaths and shove into the classroom.

"Mr. Uzune!" The door slams against the wall with a *bang*.

He jumps up, knocking his chair over. "*WHOA*—what? Miss Bell, what's wrong?"

I note with some interest that his first reaction upon being surprised is to drop into a karate stance. A typical teacher reaction? I'm not so sure. I rub my face.

"It's Nuha, Mr. Uzune! We went to the park and climbed some trees. I know it's out of bounds, but it was my idea 'cause I wanted to get away from the bullies. It's all my fault!"

Mr. Uzune looks alarmed now. "Slow down, Miss Bell. What's happened?"

"She fell out of a tree! We were just having fun, but she's hurt pretty bad. I think she broke a leg! Please hurry!"

I rush out of the classroom. I don't check to see if he's following me. I just keep running. I'm afraid if I turn around, he'll see the deception on my face.

The park is empty.

I get there first, only a little out of breath. I can hear Mr. Uzune's footsteps as he follows me. I glance towards the trees, where Ling and Nuha are hiding, their own Sound Isolators pointing in our direction.

"Where is she?" Mr. Uzune is breathing hard. He pivots on his heel, checking all directions. "Where is Miss Bahar?"

A familiar spike of panic grips my chest, but I push it down. "She's not here, Hitori."

There's a pause. Mr. Uzune's response is confused. "Excuse me?"

"You heard me. I know who you are. You're Hitori Yuuma, the disappeared Super, the one who fought in the last great Super rivalry, hiding away as a teacher." I keep my back to him, speaking into empty space. My heart thunders. I keep my ears trained on his every sound, in case he decides to rush me from behind. I don't want to face him, lest he sees the tremble in my chin and the uncertainty in my eyes. I force my voice to stay steady. "I don't know why you retreated from public life. I don't know why you decided to work in conjunction with the Counter-League, but I know who you are."

Silence.

I hope Nuha, Ling, and Dieter are recording. Just in case—I swallow hard—I don't make it out safely. In case something goes wrong. At least my friends will have a copy of the conversation to hand to LOS. A stiff breeze kicks up loose leaves. I can still hear the faint panting of Mr. Uzune behind me.

"Is this a game, Miss Bell?" He still sounds confused.

"Don't play dumb with me. You look just like you did when you were young. I'm not sure why I never saw it. I must be blind or something." I swivel around and flash his old Super card. I chuck it at him, even though it hurts to see a premium collector's item land in the damp grass.

Mr. Uzune takes a step back. I watch his face for signs of recognition, but there's only surprise. When he lifts his head, his expression is disapproving.

"Is Miss Bahar truly ok? This is a highly inappropriate prank, Miss Bell. I expected better of you."

So did everyone else, my mind whispers with a slight, sad chuckle. I chase away the resentment by pressing replay on my phone. The Sound Isolator app kicks into gear. Alexander's voice rings out through the park, loud and clear. I hold it up.

"You're following me again. You should leave me alone."

Mr. Uzune's voice replies, equally clear.

I raise my eyebrows in what I hope is a calm and elegant fashion. *Think Gwen.* "This is undoubtedly your voice, Mr. Uzune. My app can confirm that your voice matches one hundred percent with a certain disappeared Super's."

I hold up my phone screen. There's a picture of Mr. Uzune's yearbook picture side by side with a picture of him in the shadows. Underneath, written in large, bold font, are the words CONFIRMED MATCH. IDENTITY: HITORI YUUMA.

It's a lie. A bluff. The Sound Isolator app can do no such thing, but Mr. Uzune doesn't need to know that. Nuha whipped up the picture in less than half an hour and programmed it to show whenever I play the sound clip. I just hope my computer gobbledygook is too new tech for Mr. Uzune to understand. If I've learned anything from my cafeteria incident, it's that people will eat up lies as long as there is a reasonable chance they might be true. I make my eyes steely and hold my breath.

Mr. Uzune is silent. My recorded message plays itself to its end. I stare at Mr. Uzune's face. Scientists say body language is four times more telling than speech. I scan him for signs of surprise, doubt, anger.

"That's a unique application you have there," Mr. Uzune finally says, not betraying a thing, "but I am not sure what you are playing at. I must say I don't appreciate being tricked like this." A sad expression overcomes his face, the same one he wears when I don't hand in my homework on time. I feel another wave of doubt cross my mind. *Stray strong*, I urge myself.

Mr. Uzune continues, "I suppose the important thing is that Miss Bahar is all right. I do not like handing out detentions, but I feel like this might warrant one. Or two."

"Don't distract from the topic at hand, Hitori," I snap. I'm not actually angry—more terrified—but I can't show weakness. Frances E. Shaw never showed weakness, and neither will I. I think of my mom when she gets upset. Hands on her hips. Mouth upturned. Button nose wrinkled just the slightest. "Admit it, you've been in hiding all this time, plotting with the Counter-League. What has LOS ever done to you? I'm curious. What could make the world's greatest hero run and hide like a coward?"

Mr. Uzune's mouth hangs open. Then out of the blue, he lets out a chuckle.

"So it really was you." He sounds tired. "I thought I recognized your hair, but you were gone before I could call out. I was going to warn you that flying recklessly is dangerous." He sighs and shakes his head. "But whatever you heard, whatever you thought you heard—you're mistaken. I was speaking to the young man, yes, but it had nothing to do with the Counter-League."

"Aha, so you *are* the person in the picture!"

"Yes," admits Mr. Uzune. "Yes, I traversed that particular stretch of road and ran into that young man completely by coincidence. He was convinced I was Hitori Yuuma too. You'll have noticed we bear a certain resemblance. Mr. Yuuma was very famous, and I'm afraid some of his fans have some, er, interesting conspiracy theories."

My hairs prickle. He's lying. He didn't run into Alexander by accident at all. Now that he's admitted he's the person in the shadows, I *know* he's lying. He was waiting. I saw him. It was no coincidence he ran into Alexander. If I had any doubts about my homeroom teacher, they are dispelled. He's suspicious to the nth degree. My heart leaps. My mind kicks into action.

"Alexander isn't a fan," I counter, breathing lightly. "Alexander's a part of the Counter-League. I went and spoke to LOS the day I skipped class. They've already confirmed his allegiance to the dark side." It's another lie, but what harm can it do now? Sometimes, lies must be told to expose bigger lies. Right? Still, telling a lie makes my stomach turn, and it takes all my effort not to falter. "Why were you speaking to someone who is working against LOS?"

"You have a good imagination, Miss Bell." Mr. Uzune presses his lips together. He begins to turn around. "But let me assure you, I'm just a middle school teacher. I know nothing of LOS or the Counter-League. Now let's stop this nonsense and get back to the classroom, where—"

"If you move, Hitori, I'll have Gwen rain her swords down on you!"

"What?"

"Yeah,"—I puff out my chest—"that's right. She's in the sky right now, listening to our every word. You can't see her, but she can see you. You don't believe me? Just try moving. She won't have trouble cutting down a supervillain like you. You know what she did to Payton."

Mr. Uzune eyes me suspiciously. I can see doubt in his hunched shoulders and slack jaw. I have his attention, but I honestly don't know what I can do if he calls my bluff. Gwen's not in the sky at all. A part of me wishes she were, to make the threat real, but a larger part is thrilled I am managing it all without her intervention. *Maybe Duds aren't useless after all.*

Mr. Uzune doesn't move.

"And don't you dare call up your allies," I add, spurred by a terrified excitement. I bring up my phone. "I have our conversations recorded on my cloud, easily accessed by all my friends. Even if you kill us all, the recorded message will automatically post to my social media accounts if I don't enter a special password every hour. You'll be caught within a day."

Another bluff. I'm on a roll today.

"I'm sorry, Miss Bell, but I really don't have anything to

hide. I know it's exciting to imagine, but I don't have a secret identity. I'm not running from LOS, and I'm certainly not involved in any villainy. So, please, stop this lunacy."

"So you don't mind if I send this evidence to LOS?" I ask innocently. I wave my phone. Mr. Uzune's face remains a careful balance of clueless and calm. "Ok, then. I'll do it right now."

"Trust me. LOS would not be interested in mundane information about me."

"Well, the return of the disappeared Hitori Yuuma is a great story. I figure LOS would be the first to welcome you back. I'll just email them and tell them the good news." I lift my phone and snap a picture of Mr. Uzune. I make sure the flash goes off, for added effect. He twitches. Then I make a show out of pulling Agent Scarlett's card out of my pocket.

"This won't take more than five seconds. If what you're saying is true, Agent Scarlett will be able to sort it out. Attaching sound file. Done. Attaching photographs. Done. Entering Agent Scarlett's personal email address. Lady in red at LOS dot com. Done. Sending file—"

"Wait."

My breath hitches in my chest. I glance up.

"It's not what you think, Miss Bell. I'm not working for the Counter-League."

I raise an eyebrow. My finger hovers over the "send" button.

Mr. Uzune runs his fingers through his hair. He sighs deeply and tucks his hands in his pockets. There's a glint in his eye when he looks up, a little like frustration and a little like amusement. "How did you get Agent Scarlett's email?"

"I'm friends with Gwen," I explain simply. Even though

Agent Scarlett didn't tell me explicitly to keep my involvement in the investigation a secret, I don't want to let him to know I'm working with her. It's better to play it safe. "So naturally, I have contact with her Agent too."

"It's rare for an Agent to give their contact information to someone other than their close clients."

"Not everyone is the great-granddaughter of the Original Super," I say, hating myself for using my family lineage as a shield.

"Don't send my information to Agent Scarlett."

"Maybe if you told me the reason you want revenge against LOS, I'll back off."

"I don't want revenge against LOS."

"I don't believe you."

Mr. Uzune holds up his hands. "You win, Miss Bell. What reason do I have to lie?" He offers a shaky grin. "To think my cover would be blown by a twelve-year-old with her technogadgets. You're a smart girl. You and your friends are all smart girls. I don't know how in blazes you managed to get Agent Scarlett's information, or how you're able to develop such technologies at such a young age. Truly, this generation terrifies me, but I'm willing to bargain with you. I'll answer your questions as long as you don't hit send."

For a moment, I'm speechless. It's happening. I hope my friends—and Dieter—are getting all this. *Yes*, my mind chimes. This is my break. This is how I catch a supervillain. *No*, a small voice echoes. I had hoped, in a small, optimistic way, that Mr. Uzune would be innocent. My knees feel weak. I will them not to shake too hard.

"So talk," I say, trying to sound tough. A small waver in my voice escapes anyways.

Mr. Uzune sighs. "I'm not Alexander's ally, if that's what you think. I was trying to stop him."

"But I heard you say you'd help him!"

"Help him get *away* from the criminal life," Mr. Uzune says forcibly. "I told him we can work together to keep him hidden from the Counter-League. Do you think the Counter-League lets go of its members easily? We were in negotiations for his safety, and he was, rightfully, nervous. I wanted to reassure him. After all, I happen to be very *good* at staying hidden."

"What about the rebels? You're their leader, are you not, Hitori?"

"My ragtag team? No. Perhaps we seem like a rebel organization to LOS. After all, we work in close proximity to Counter-League members. We just don't work *with* them. There's a fine distinction. Think of us as a therapy group for Supers gone wrong. We get them away from their demons and help them recover somewhere safe."

I never expected my plan to work so well. I had hoped, of course, but I expected to prove myself wrong. Now that I'm right about Mr. Uzune, I have no idea what to do. I can imagine Ling in the bushes, her mouth wide open, listening to our every word. I can imagine Nuha, carefully jotting evidence in her notebook. I can even imagine Dieter, trying not to fall out of the sky in surprise. It's like the world has ground to a stop. I'm frozen in my tracks. *I'm not prepared for this*. My body is still, but my mind races at a thousand clicks an hour—*clickclickclickclick*—looking for a solution, a way forward.

"If you're actually countering the Counter-League, why don't you want me telling LOS?" I ask cautiously. "If you're innocent, why are you afraid? You're on the same side, right?"

"Sometimes, things work better without the LOS brand. LOS is very official, Miss Bell. Sometimes, discretion is better. If Alexander is a part of the Counter-League and thinks I'm working with LOS, what are the chances he'll believe anything I say? What are the chances he'd deal with me at all? It's far better to be a neutral party."

He has a point, I admit unhappily.

Mr. Uzune sighs wearily. "You're right on another front, Miss Bell. The return of Hitori Yuuma is a great story. One that can't be ignored. It'll cause a ruckus. How quickly do you think the rumours would spread? The fewer people who know the better I can operate."

"And you *don't* want to get vengeance on LOS?"

"No. That's one young man's unfortunate misconstruction of my intentions. Why would I want revenge on LOS? I used to work for them."

"So why are you always around when Super incidents happen? That's suspicious, you know."

"I'm trying my best to stop them from happening, Miss Bell. Not the other way around."

"Why did you disappear in the first place?" I continue, sounding smaller with every word I speak. "You still have tons of fans. Everyone is curious about you. It doesn't seem fair to just vanish like that."

Mr. Uzune shrugs. He looks frumpier than ever. "I just got tired, I guess, of all the fighting and press conferences. I'm an introvert at heart, Miss Bell. I get antsy around cameras. And all the pressure. I'm not a patient person. I just couldn't be perfect all the time."

My face is heating up, and I know it shows. Ling's always telling me to chill out, and now I've gone and made a fool of myself. My gut roils, and I press it down with force. It's hard to breathe.

"So you're *sure* you're not a villain?" I ask plaintively.

"I'm not a villain, Miss Bell," Mr. Uzune says gently. "Can I move now?"

"Oh, yeah, I'll—call Gwen off." *As though I could command her in the first place*, I think. It's too embarrassing to admit she's not actually there, so I keep up the facade and make some fake motions at my phone, just to make it seem legit. Mr. Uzune—*Hitori*, my mind reminds me faintly—picks up his card from the grass. He brushes it off. The expression on his face is unreadable.

"Are you happy? Satisfied?" he inquires, not unkindly.

Of course I'm not. I feel terrible. I misjudged. I want to dig a hole and bury myself. I lower my phone and take a deep breath. "I-I had no idea."

Mr. Uzune shrugs. "It was an honest mistake. I can see how it could seem suspicious from your end, especially with your nerves running ragged. The Counter-League made a menacing threat towards you and your friends. I'm surprised LOS hasn't assigned you personal guards yet. It seems sloppy of them."

"I-It's ok, really. I don't need guards." I don't think I can handle Supers around me twenty-four seven anyways. I look down at my phone. I pause.

"Oh no," I whisper.

"What's wrong?"

My face burns like never before. How could I have been so careless? With trepidation and horror, I turn my phone to face Mr. Uzune. *Hitori*, my mind reminds me again. "I'm sorry," I stutter. "I must have gotten excited and hit it by accident. I didn't mean to—"

MESSAGE SENT, says my phone.

Mr. Uzune goes very still. A distant look washes over his face. I brace myself, wondering if he'll yell at me for being stupid. Instead, he gazes down the street. The wind rustles his dark hair, and suddenly, he looks nostalgic and very alone.

"I need to leave," he mutters. I have a feeling he didn't mean to say it out loud.

As though in a trance, he begins to walk.

"Wait, why?" I take a step forward. "So LOS knows. So what? I'm sure they'll keep your secret if you ask them to! You're famous! Wait, stop!"

He doesn't.

"Don't chase me, Miss Bell," he says, glancing over his shoulder. There's a desperate crack to his voice and a dangerous light in his eye. "Don't make me stop you."

The next moment happens so suddenly I almost can't believe my eyes. A cricket bat floats behind Mr. Uzune. It lifts into the air, wobbling, before crashing down onto the back of his head. He makes a noise, like a hiccup of surprise, and crashes to the ground. I stare at his prone body, then up at the cricket bat. Nuha is suddenly there, her mouth pursed in a grimace, hands wrapped so tightly around the bat her knuckles are numb.

For a moment, none of us move. Even the air's gone still, as though holding its breath. Not a single sound penetrates the park. I meet Nuha's eyes.

"Oh my God," she chants, leaping from one toe to the other. The spell is broken. Her eyes are wider than I've ever seen. "Oh my God, I just knocked out our teacher! In the middle of the street! What if there are cameras around? I'll get in so much trouble!"

"*Nuha*, what did you do?" I groan. "He's not with the Counter-League!"

"I panicked! The Sound Isolator killed my phone, so I couldn't hear the last little bit. I thought he was going to get away, so I hit him—wait, what did you say?"

"He's not the bad guy!"

"*What?*"

She drops the bat and stares at her hands like she can't believe it. I can't believe it either.

"You brought a cricket bat?" I ask, waving a hand at it. "A *cricket bat*?"

"Just as a precaution! I didn't intend to use it!"

Ling crashes from the bushes, leaves stuck to her hair.

"Nice shot, Nu!"

"I didn't mean it!"

"An excelsior shot nonetheless. I can see the headlines: *Local Girl Knocks Out Famed Super*."

A shadow drops from above. Dieter. He has Ling's camera. Since he doesn't have a smartphone of his own, I asked him to take pictures instead.

"Wow, Bahar, you've got a good arm."

Nuha looks up at us, her face pale. "Do you think he's still alive? He has to be alive, right?" She falls to her knees beside Mr. Uzune, flustered. Her hands flap at her sides, like she wants to check for vitals but is too afraid of touching him. "Does he look like he's breathing? I can't tell! *I can't tell!*"

"Whoa." Ling drops down and rubs Nuha's shoulders. "Chill out; relax. He's still breathing. See? You can see the grass moving where his nose is."

"I'm going to be suspended so bad!" groans Nuha. She rubs her eyes. "My parents are going to *kill* me if they hear about this!" She stares at Mr. Uzune and asks in a small voice, "Are you *sure* he's alive?"

Ling pokes him in the side of the head. "He still feels warm."

"It takes *hours* for a body to cool down, you dolt!" snaps Nuha. She slaps Ling's hand aside and presses two fingers to Mr. Uzune's neck. She waits. Finally, she nods. "Ok, ok, he's alive. I don't think I broke anything important, either. I think we're good."

She closes her eyes and breathes deeply. *One*, *two*, *three*, then stands again, her face grim.

"H-how?" I sputter. "You weren't there, and suddenly you were!"

"I never told you guys," Nuha says, her tone more settled. There's only a small hitch to her breath. "I didn't think there was any need. Especially with you, Beata. I know how much you wanted to be a Super, with your lineage and all, it was all to be expected. So when you *didn't* develop powers this year, and *I* did, well, I thought it would be better to keep it a secret."

I try to swallow my surprise. "*You're* a Super?"

Nuha nods and makes a shushing motion. Her eyes flicker back and forth, as though to check for listeners. "Yes, but LOS doesn't know, ok?"

"What do you mean LOS doesn't know?" Ling asks. "LOS knows everything."

"They didn't know about Alexander," I retort. "Or Mr. Uzu—Hitori."

"My power isn't really noticeable, so I didn't bother to register," says Nuha. "No, don't protest. It's literally not noticeable. I'm not even sure when it developed. Sometimes, I kind of just fade from people's perspectives and become almost invisible. If they aren't looking for me, I can get away with walking right under their noses without drawing attention. I've experimented a little, sneaking into the teachers' lounge, and museum exhibits after closing. Even into LOS headquarters once, though I got out of there pretty fast. There's no telling what sort of security they have there."

"You have invisibility," I say. I feel like I am watching myself from a long distance away. Nuha is a Super. Nuha, whose family has no history of Super blood, is a Super. Nuha, who is already rich and smart, is a Super. Jealousy rages through me, hot like a bolt of lightning. It's not fair. Nuha doesn't care about being a Super, but *I* do. So why does *she* get to live my dream?

"No, not really," says Nuha, eyes wide. "If you know I'm here, then I can't become invisible. If I make a noise or draw attention to myself, I can't become invisible. I tiptoed out of the bushes and none of you noticed me because you didn't expect me to be there, but as soon as I—" she pauses and swallows, "—bashed Mr. Uzune, you saw me. It's not like I can just disappear on command. Think of it as a passive ability."

"That doesn't make sense," says Ling. "If that's a thing, why don't we know about it?"

"Because you can't know about something that disappears when you know about it," I snap.

"LOS can't test for my ability because—well, it stops working if anyone pays attention," explains Nuha. "Like, if I could fly only when no one was looking. No one would ever know, because to know I could fly, someone would need to *see* me fly, and if they're looking, I won't be able to do it."

"That's so convoluted," groans Ling. She nudges Hitori with a toe. "What do we do now? Tie him up or something? If he doesn't show up at school, people will come looking."

"I can't believe you're a Super!" I say, my voice high. Everyone is becoming a Super except me.

Nuha looks at me with woeful brown eyes. "Sorry, Bea."

"No," I say, pushing my poisonous feelings aside. "Congratulations. It's great, really."

I'm sure she can sense the lie in my voice. It's a credit to her character that she doesn't say anything. She only looks down at Hitori's unconscious form and purses her mouth.

"He's not a part of the Counter-League," I say glumly, "but at least we know who he is."

Nuha blanches further as the realization dawns.

"I knocked out Hitori Yuuma," she says in a small voice. "Do you think I'll get arrested?"

"I don't think so," I say, just as Dieter says, "Naw, you're underage."

"We have to do something, guys," Nuha says. "Recess is over soon and people will *know*. This is *such* a mess."

"Anyone have any smelling salts?" Dieter asks loudly.

Ling shoots him a scathing glare.

"Why would we have smelling salts?"

"I don't know. Why does Bahar have a cricket bat? You guys are nuts!"

"Let's just get him somewhere covered," I interrupt. I don't want anyone accidentally walking by and seeing the four of us gathered around an unconscious adult. I didn't want tomorrow's headlines to read: *LOCAL GIRLS MURDER IN-*

NOCENT TEACHER.

They make it look easy in movies, but it's tough to drag an unconscious body. Ling grabs his arms. Nuha and I take his legs. We tug and push but barely move him a metre before we stop. He's so limp, and I worry about hurting him more. What if I tug wrong and he ends up in a wheelchair? *LOCAL GIRL PARALYZES INNOCENT TEACHER* is almost as bad. We try once more, and move only another metre before we stop, panting. Dieter rolls his eyes. He shoos us aside and grabs Hitori under the arms. He lifts him a couple inches off the ground. Ling and I grab his legs again so he's fully airborne.

Not three seconds after we get momentum, I get a really bad feeling. I pause and nearly upset the entire operation. Shouts of annoyance emerge from both Dieter and Ling, but I ignore them. The hairs on my neck stand up like tiny guards. *Someone is watching me.* I look around, but the park is empty. Almost by instinct, I look towards the sky instead.

"Bea?" asks Nuha, watching me with big eyes.

My arm muscles begin to shake.

There's a rush of air. My bangs blow into my face. I hear Ling yelp as she drops Hitori. I stumble to my knees as his weight bears down on me. Dieter lets go as a dark form dives from the sky. I jump up and spin around, trying to follow its movements, but end up dizzying myself.

A voice speaks. "Well, well, well, this certainly makes my job easier."

There's a breath of air at my ear. I leap around.

No, whispers my mind. I can see all my nightmares coming true. *No, no, not now. Why now?*

Alexander floats just a few centimetres above the grass, his face a solemn mask. It's strange seeing a Super without a

LOS outfit. He's dressed as I last saw him, in dark clothes and sneakers.

"Hello again, Miss Bell."

I make a strangled noise.

"Am I correct to assume you know who I am? Who I truly am?"

I slowly rise to my feet and nod. Alexander sighs deeply.

"I suspected as much," he murmurs. He draws himself up to his full height. "I suppose I have to thank you for taking out that bothersome man." Alexander makes a motion towards Hitori. "So thank you. Undoubtedly, he would have given me an entire spiel about being Good and Honourable, and other such nonsense."

He has the audacity to bow.

"So, you're the Counter-League guy?" asks Dieter, trying to sound tough. He's floating too but with less expertise than Alexander. He bobs up and down like a duck on water. He holds out his fists and makes mock boxing motions. "Y-you don't seem so tough."

"Don't hurt yourself, kid," says Alexander, deadpan.

"As a Super of LOS, and a sworn protector of the innocent—"

"You'll strike me down in the name of justice?" Alexander finishes for him. "Yes, we all know the speech. I'll ask you politely to get out of the way. Then perhaps I won't have to hurt you."

He makes a swiping motion, quick and aggressive, nothing at all like Gwen's smooth, elegant lines. A reddish streak of light runs down his arm. When it disappears, there's a thin sword in his hand. He must have had metal hidden somewhere on his body. *As a contingency*, Gwen's voice whispers in my head. She once showed me the hidden metal bands and jewellery that she wore against her skin—just in case.

Dieter pales and wobbles, but he doesn't back down. *There's a fine line between brave and stupid*, I think grimly, and sometimes, it's really hard to tell which is which. "Nevertheless, I—"

"Don't be a hero, Dieter!" I hear Nuha hiss. She grabs the hem of his pants and gives a yank. Dieter yelps and tumbles to the ground. Her eyes flick to her cricket bat.

"Curse him, Bell!" calls Dieter. "Make him pay!"

Alexander turns to me with an amused expression. "Curse?"

Usually, I would be embarrassed, but my discomfort seems unimportant compared to the situation at hand. My mind is in full salvage mode. There's no time to be self-conscious. Right now, the important thing is getting to safety.

"You're here to kidnap us, right?" I ask, breathing lightly.

"Aren't we direct today?" says Alexander in a leisurely fashion only those with great power can afford. "But *kidnap* is a harsh word. Let's say I'm here to borrow you. If all goes right, I'll return you before long."

I bite my tongue. A sliver of hate pierces through my panic. How dare he be so calm?

"You want to hold one of Gwen's friends against her, right?" I say instead, taking in a shaky breath and staring Alexander in the eye. "Well, *I'm* Gwen's best friend."

My mind is in turmoil. *What are you doing?*

Being a hero. Saving my friends. Getting in trouble.

It's for the best.

"Ling and Nuha are secondary friends, and Dieter's just some random passerby," I continue. "I'm Gwen's primary friend. If you want the most impact, you need to kidnap me."

"That's the plan," says Alexander easily.

"So I'm willing to cut you a deal. I go with you quietly and peacefully, and you leave the rest of them alone."

"That deal really doesn't hold any water. I could kidnap all four of you."

"I highly doubt it." I frown and think hard. I need to stay one step ahead of him. *Half the battle is in the mind*, Gwen once told me. "You have the power of flight, but you can't carry all of us at once. Otherwise, you'll risk crashing, and believe me, we'll *flail* and make your job harder."

"We'll scream too," adds Nuha, eyeing me carefully. I can see the gears in her mind grinding. She knows what I'm doing. "We'll wake the entire city. Leave a trail for people to follow. People will call the authorities. They'll take pictures. They'll find you."

"And we'll bite," I add. I keep my gaze on Alexander. It's hard, but I manage. "It'll hurt a lot. Dieter will pull in the opposite direction and mess up your balance midair. Do you really want that?"

Alexander solemnly considers his options. "Alternatively, I suppose I could kill a few of you," he says, shooting me a wry smile.

My heart rate spikes. "We'll run in different directions. Do you think you can get all of us before we attract attention?"

Alexander inclines his head as though to say *touché*.

"You want infamy, huh?" pipes in Ling. "How's this for a headline? *Counter-League Kidnaps Frances E. Shaw's Great-granddaughter.* That's what the Counter-League wants, right? More publicity? Well, this is your big chance to really shake up the news world. Kidnapping Beata makes the most sense."

Alexander actually cracks a smile. "You're actually encouraging me to take your friend? Friendship sure has changed from when I was in middle school."

"It's a win-win for both parties, Alexander," I say evenly. "Take it or leave it."

Silence falls over us. My heart pounds so hard I'm afraid I might faint. I work on keeping my face and body language neutral.

Finally, Alexander laughs. It's different from what I expected. It's not an evil cackle or a megalomaniac guffaw. He sounds like any other person in the schoolyard. It's a small, genuine snort. He recovers quickly.

"Fine. Deal." He floats forward. As a group, we shrink back. He frowns. "Oh, right. The sword." With another swiping motion, it disappears. It vanishes so quickly I don't catch where all the metal has gone. "One more clause, if I may."

"Shoot," I squeak.

"None of you may follow me." He looks directly at Dieter, who hasn't bothered to get off the ground. "If I spot any of you following me, I drop Miss Bell, understand? And you don't want me dropping Miss Bell. Trust me."

All three nod.

"So, let's roll," I say, turning to Alexander. I hope my fear doesn't show through my bravado. "How are we going to do this?"

Alexander doesn't respond. He simply makes a quick motion with his arms. Metal slithers through the air and wraps around my middle like a sling. I pull back out of instinct, but it constricts around my chest and stomach, holding me fast.

"Too tight?" he asks.

"Does it matter?" I gasp. Nevertheless, the bonds loosen

slightly. Not enough to allow me any wriggle room but enough so that the metal doesn't dig into my flesh. Alexander gives the metal a tug. I find myself airborne, slung like a bag of groceries.

"Any last words, Miss Bell?"

I think.

"Remember, everyone, don't follow me," I say at last. "I mean it. I don't want to be dropped. And keep working on Project SIA. I want it to be finished when LOS rescues me."

I look into their eyes. *Please, please get the hint.* I scan Nuha's face. Nuha is one of the smartest people I know. If anyone could get hints, she could.

Finally, after an excruciatingly long wait, she nods. Once. I can see that she's fighting back tears.

"Ok," I breathe. It's a small relief, but it's something. "I'm ready."

With a jerk of the metal ribbons, Alexander rockets towards the sky. My stomach plummets as the ground falls away. *I'm not ready*, my mind screams, but I hold it back. We ascend at an alarming rate, so quick I can barely breathe. The park becomes smaller and smaller, until it's just a green square among other squares. With another jerk, we're flying across the city.

Towards the Counter-League base.

Chapter 15

Into the Lion's Den

Alexander is a much better flier than Dieter.

"Comfortable?" he asks, as though I could be comfortable swinging from a thin metal cable.

"What do you care?" I hiss back, wriggling.

"I'm not a monster," he replies.

"Liar."

"Let's not argue semantics."

I have a feeling he's still amused, and a new wave of hatred washes over me. What I would do to get my powers right now. What I would give to burst into flames. To burn him to a crisp. Or to electrocute him with my mind.

"What's Project SIA?" he asks, almost casually.

"Nothing," I retort, proud that I manage to sound petulant rather than terrified. "It's a new app we're working on."

"Hmm," says Alexander. "I did say you were clever with those. What does it do?"

"I'm not telling *you*."

"I'm just trying to make conversation." He almost sounds hurt.

"You chose a funny time to make conversation then."

My eyes water from the air slapping my face. Or maybe I'm so scared I'm crying a little. A fresh wave of upset washes over me. "Why are you trying to destroy LOS?" I ask. "You know it can't be done. Once they find you they'll kill you. You think

Gwen's the only Super they have? You might be powerful, but they have *hundreds*—no, *thousands*—of Supers ready to fight you. You're lucky they're allowing you to fight one-on-one with Gwen right now. Otherwise you'd be fried meat."

"I know," says Alexander, perfectly serious.

"What?"

"I know," says Alexander again. "If they were serious, LOS could take me out in an instant."

"Why are you fighting if you know you can't win?" I ask fiercely. "That's stupid."

"Sometimes it's worth fighting a battle even if you can't win."

"I don't get it."

"Don't worry about it. You have bigger things to worry about."

I bite my tongue. He's right. I switch tactics.

"What are you going to do with me? You can't hurt me or Gwen will hunt you down. You don't know Gwen, but I do. She'll smack you down like a volleyball. You think she's tough now; you haven't seen her angry."

"She's scary when she's angry, huh?"

I hate how conversational he sounds, like we're sitting in a café rather than flying above a city. The cold wind makes it hard for me to pronounce words properly. My lips are stiff.

"Scarier than you. More powerful too, I bet."

"We'll see," says Alexander. He's so calm I just want to rip out his hair, just to see a reaction.

As Lake Ontario comes into view, a sheet of iron beyond the geometric city, Alexander motions at me with his chin.

"I'm going to pass you a blindfold. Take it and blindfold yourself."

"What if I don't?"

"I'll drop you. It's a long way down, Miss Bell. Do you know what happens to the human body when it's dropped from this height? Onto concrete, no less. And there's no guarantee it'll be concrete you hit. You might hit a pole. Or a wire. You'd be cut in half."

I can't help it. I begin to cry for real. I don't want to be hurt, and I hate how helpless I am. I grab the blindfold and loop it sloppily around my face. It's a long, dark scarf. I note with some surprise that it's cashmere soft. At least it won't scratch me.

"Tie it well," Alexander says.

I wrap it around tighter, cursing him out in my head.

"There, all better?" My voice comes out thick and Jell-O-y. I hate it.

There's a moment of silence.

"Hello?" I ask.

"All better," says Alexander, sounding satisfied. I have the feeling he checked my handiwork, even though I'm not sure how. My stomach drops as he veers in mid-air. I hold my breath to stop the cold air from burning my nostrils. Carefully, very carefully, I tuck my hands into my jacket like I am cold and make myself shiver a few times for legitimacy. As I do so, I tickle the face of my phone and make a few quick swipes. It's hard working blind. I don't know if I'm successful, but I need to try. I'm familiar enough with my phone's interface to work it even when I can't see it. Muscle memory is a powerful thing. I discreetly pull my phone from my pocket and snap a photo of the ground below. I tag it #Beata. Then I press at the screen until my phone gives a small vibration, indicating I've uploaded the photo to the Internet. I do this over and over and over again. I pray that it's working, that I'm not accidentally taking pictures of my hand.

Flying blindfolded gives me vertigo, but the last thing I want is to barf. I'm already feeling heavy with nausea. My mind remembers an assortment of hostage movies. When a child disappears, the first twenty-four hours are the most important, they say.

I hate that I just called myself a *child*.

Frances E. Shaw would never have been kidnapped. Gwen either. I wonder how long it'll take for people to find me. I wonder if Ling and Nuha have gone for help yet, and whether it even matters. *They can't save you if they can't find you*, my mind reasons. I snap another picture of the landscape below. Alexander makes another unannounced dip, and I bite my cheeks to stop from hurling. My phone almost slips from my pocket, and I clamp down on it like my life depends on it.

Which it might.

The air rushes past my head, and I know we're diving. When we were younger, Gwen would sometimes take me for flights, just for fun. It feels the same as it did back then, except faster and with more intent. I wonder if Supers ever crash in mid-flight. Suddenly, there's a *whoomp*, and the sound around us closes in as though squeezed from all sides. The air warms up and takes on a metallic tang. We've entered a tunnel. I try to keep track of directions and form a mini-map in my head. *Right, left, descend, left, descend, right, left—*

I lose track. After a few quick turns—jerks that almost give me whiplash—I hear the swoosh of a hydraulic door. I'm dumped unceremoniously on my bottom.

"Ouch," I snap. It's the only sound I can make. My body

feels battered, and my skin stings. It's like a thousand tiny needles have dragged their points across my arms and face.

"You can take off your blindfold," says Alexander's voice. He doesn't sound out of breath at all.

I hook my fingers under the cloth, but my sweat makes it stick to my face. It takes some wriggling before I finally slide it off. It's dark. I blink furiously but see only shadows. For a moment, all that I know is the sound of my breathing. Then excruciatingly slowly, my vision returns. I'm sitting in a cylindrical cell. The walls are steel and so is the floor. It's cold and dark, with only a few lights near the ceiling so dim that their brightness hardly seems to touch the floor. There isn't even a chair.

"Where am I?" I demand.

"You don't need to know," says Alexander calmly. I can see his outline, but I can't get a good look at his face. He holds out a hand, and I stare at it like it's poisonous. "Empty your pockets, please."

I hesitate before handing over my cellphone. He takes it without bothering to look at it. A part of me is relieved he didn't smash it.

"Do you have anything else on you?"

"No."

"You better be telling the truth, Miss Bell."

"It's the truth, *Mr. Supervillain.* How long are you keeping me here?"

"You'll get fed, if that's what you're worried about."

I grind my teeth. As though I would be worried about dinner after a kidnapping. Just how stupid does he think I am? "I'm cold," I complain. I'm not really, but at the moment, I want to make Alexander's life harder.

"That's unfortunate," he replies shortly. It's like a slap to the face. I can't believe I ever thought he was nice!

"This place sure is unimpressive for a supervillain's lair," I say, hoping to goad him. Angry people are careless. They talk, and the more information I can wring from him the better. "Where are the fancy machines? Where are the creepy sidekicks and weird mascots? Where are the robot octopods?"

Alexander doesn't speak. I half hope, half fear I've angered him. But then his silhouette slumps a little and he lets out a breath. It's not an angry sigh, or even an annoyed one. It's tired, and my anger ebbs a bit. "It's going to be a long few days. Try to make yourself comfortable, Miss Bell."

Fat chance. As though anyone could be comfortable in a prison. I glare at him. "You'll pay for this."

"Uh-huh," he replies, unimpressed. When he turns to leave, a spike of panic jolts through my chest. Despite my bravado, it terrifies me to be alone in a dark metal cell. A hatch in the ceiling slides open with a sigh, and he lifts from the ground. Even though I've seen Gwen do it a hundred times, it'll always be uncanny. It's as though gravity has suddenly quit. He floats until his curly hair almost brushes against the ceiling.

"Don't do this," I plead. "Would your sister be proud? You're her big bro. You're supposed to be her hero!"

For a second, I think Alexander flinches, but when I look closely, his gaze is cold.

"Don't try to guilt-trip me," he says, disdain poisoning his voice. "It won't work."

Then he shoots through the door and disappears. The hatch slides closed so tight it barely leaves an outline.

Darkness. I can barely see my hands out in front of me in the meagre light.

I slump against the wall. The coldness of the metal seeps through the back of my jacket. The only sound in the room is the blood thundering through my ears. I sit on my fingers to stop them from trembling.

I'm alone.

Chapter 16

Captive

It's hard to keep track of time when you're stuck in a cell. At first, I try to count. I don't even bother with prime numbers. I count seconds, hoping to pass time quicker or count myself to sleep. I gave up after hitting three thousand. *Three thousand divided by sixty is fifty.* Only fifty minutes have passed. Alexander's right. It's going to be a long wait.

I imagine the outside world. By now, my school will have called my house, wondering where I am. My parents will call my cell, but I won't pick up. They'll start to worry. My mom will try to stay calm while my dad frets. She will hope that I'm just playing hooky and that I'll eventually call.

But I won't. Any time now, the police will show up at their door with bad news. Ling and Nuha will have spread the word. A kidnapping. In broad daylight. By the Counter-League. It'll be their worst fear. Before they can panic, they'll be taken to a station for questioning. An investigator, along with a LOS representative, will probe them with questions about me, my last movements, and their own alibis. It'll feel surreal. Like a dream. Like how I feel now.

I feel leaden with guilt, like I might throw up. I've really done it now.

I wonder if my photos uploaded. They're my only hope. Taking photos was all I could do, being dragged across the sky like a sack of potatoes. Without a trail, I'll have no chance of being rescued. The authorities can search high and low, but they'll only be guessing at my location.

I curl up and try not to shiver.

Please, I beg the universe, *please let it be enough*.

Somehow, despite my misery, I slip into an uneasy sleep.

I jolt awake. What time is it now? The cold floor didn't do any favours to my body. There's a kink in my neck that's blossoming into a headache, and the stitches in my side ache fiercely. The soreness penetrates right to my bones. A click sounds above, and I sit up so suddenly I dizzy myself. The hatch on the ceiling swooshes open, and voices echo above. Angry ones. I hold my breath and listen.

"You had a choice! You didn't have to take this route!" A clipped voice, with the slightest hint of an accent.

"This is for the best."

"Is it really? Think about it, Alexander. What is this worth?"

"It's worth enough."

The voices get closer.

"They're blackmailing you."

"I prefer to see it as a trade."

"Call it what you will, it's not right; You don't like this any more than I do. Don't do it. You still have a choice. You can still back out of it."

"To what end? I have to consider the consequences. It's not personal. Not really. Try not to land on your head."

A shape drops through the hatch and hits the floor. It yelps loudly. I bolt up, nearly giving myself whiplash. Black hair. Brown jacket.

"*Hitori?*" I cry in disbelief. He seems stunned by the fall. I scuttle to him. "Are you ok?"

"*Neurgh,*" he groans. "I'm getting too old for this."

He rolls over, sits up, and touches the back of his head. I remember Nuha striking him there and squirm a little. He checks his limbs and ribs. No breaks. When he's done, he sits and gazes around as though he doesn't know what to do next.

"So he chose their side," Hitori finally says with a wistful sigh. Then he turns to me. "What a pity. Oh, Miss Bell. How wonderful. I was hoping they would put us in the same cell. It appears I've overstepped my boundaries and become an obstacle at last."

"They got you, too?"

"It's not hard to 'get' an unconscious man."

I hang my head. "Sorry."

"No, it's ok. I've gone through worse." He motions towards the scar on his chin. "Living a double life is hard. I don't recommend it to anyone. You lose a lot of sleep, for one."

I'm not sure if he's trying to be funny.

"I may have overestimated myself." He glances up at the hatch and makes a *hrumph*ing noise. I don't think he's speaking to me anymore. "Clever design. Too tall to reach. Counter-League has really upped its game since I was here."

I sit back on my heels. "Is LOS coming for us? Do they know we're here?"

Did my photos make it?

Hitori studies me carefully. The lighting's still dim, so he can't make out much, but I feel like I'm being examined nonetheless, like an interesting specimen. "No, LOS doesn't know we're here. They're well aware that you have been kidnapped though. Your friends made sure of that. They went straight to the authorities."

"My parents?"

"They know as well."

"They must be so worried!"

"They trust that LOS will get their daughter back," Hitori says with a chuckle. "Your kidnapping is causing quite the ruckus, Miss Bell. As the great-granddaughter of Frances E. Shaw—"

"Oh, I know," I interrupt, deflating. Shame seeps into me. "The media must be having a ball right now. How exciting for them! A descendent of the Original Super, fallen victim to a supervillain. After all the villains Frances E. Shaw took out in her career, her descendants have failed to impress. I'm a Dud and a disappointment. I'm a letdown to the Bell name. What a shame!"

I speak in a monotone. Hitori sighs deeply. It's a sound filled with weariness.

"Miss Bell, you're being too hard on yourself," he says at last. I try not to roll my eyes. I've heard it all. "No one chooses to be a Super, a Civvie, or a Dud. It's left up to the genetic lottery. You should know it's out of your hands."

"That doesn't change the fact that I can't blast through these walls." I give the nearest one a nudge with my toe. "Frances would have melted her way out, and no one would have gotten in her way. Even Gwen—she could rip through these walls like paper. What can I do? I can sit here and wait for someone to rescue me. My only role is to be a liability."

"Being a Super has its downfalls," says Hitori. "Trust me. It looks glamorous, but it's a lot of work. And it means the end of your childhood. You're still free to spend your weekends at the park, or at a pool, or hanging out with your friends. Supers don't get that luxury."

What would you know? I want to say. My head is murky with dark thoughts. *You had fame and fortune once. You have no idea what it's like not to have it at all.* I bet tons of kids would trade their boring weekend lives to fly around the city, saving people.

Still, I think about Gwen. She's always getting called away on missions. She doesn't have time to go picnicking or barbecuing with her family. She once told me that she doesn't sleep well either. *I've learned to power nap where I can*, her voice echoes. *I don't see my family much.* A thoughtful look, and a confession, *I don't think I even miss them anymore.* I remember how her parents attended her first few news conferences with beaming, proud faces but stopped after it became a near weekly event. The last time I saw them in a family photo, Gwen looked all splendid and mighty in a sparkling white gown. Her parents stood a little behind her, hands clasped, as though they weren't sure if they were allowed near such brightness.

I feel a stab of pity for her, then I remember all the times she's appeared on television, all the famous people she's gotten to shake hands with, all the admiration and love she receives. She is making a difference in the world. A real difference. Her name will go in history books. My pity fades.

"That's what my dad always says!" I argue, frustrated once more. "Oh, it's not that great to be famous and useful and beautiful! It's what Civvies say to make other Civvies feel better about themselves. You can't honestly think it's better being a Civvie. If I had powers, I would actually be useful. All I do is mess up. I thought I could be useful and help LOS catch a

Counter-League villain, and now we're both locked in here!"

Hitori regards me with an even gaze. Then he sighs again, gets up, and begins to circle the cell. He brushes his fingers against the walls, knocks lightly on them, and presses his ear against them. Curiosity replaces my woe.

"What are you doing?"

"Checking things out." *Tap, tap, tap.* "All walls have weaknesses."

"Even if you find a weak spot, what are you going to do?" I ask stubbornly. "Dig out with your hands? We're just regular people. We don't have special powers."

"There was a time, Miss Bell, when Supers didn't exist." Hitori doesn't pause in his search. His voice carries well in the rounded cell. He's using his Teacher Voice, one that says *there's a lesson to be learned here.* "Before your great-grandmother, the world was a regular, boring place, filled with Civvies. Except they were just called 'people' back then. Even back then, people were doing extraordinary things. There were jailbreaks and inventions and miracles. People getting trapped under ice and coming back to life after they'd been frozen for hours. People getting hit by lightning repeatedly and surviving. Even after the rise of Supers, regular ol' joes were defying the odds. So I'm going to try my best, Miss Bell, even if the odds are against me."

Something stirs in me. I think of all the mathematicians and programmers posted on my wall, how I used to idolize them almost as much as I idolized Frances E. Shaw. I've never thought I was a sucker for inspirational speeches, but something about the way Hitori speaks gets to me. I feel a tinge of shame at my outburst. I stand. At the very least, it's something to do.

I begin to knock on the walls as well.

Tap, tap, tap. Nothing. *Tap, tap, tap.* More nothing.

It's a boring business. We slink against the walls, crouching to check the bottom of the cell and standing on tiptoe to check the top. Without a clock to keep track of time, it feels like we do this forever. I never thought I could be so bored trapped with someone so famous, but you learn something new every day. Maybe it's because I still think of him as my teacher—as surreal as that is—or maybe it's because of his casual manner, but Hitori Yuuma is far more normal than I ever thought possible. *Tap, tap, tap—*

Thunk.

I pause. I try again.

Thunk.

"Hitori!" I hiss. He comes over and double-checks. Sure enough, the wall makes a hollow noise.

"It's thin here," he says. "Well done, Miss Bell!" He squints and inspects the area. "I feel a slight groove. Yes, there's another hatch here but even better hidden than the one above. How mysterious. I wonder what it does." He pries at it with his fingers, but nothing happens. "Whatever it is, this is where we want to blast if we want to get out of here."

Despite myself, I begin to feel better. It's not much, but maybe there's hope after all.

I try to sleep, but my thoughts are jumbled. I flash back to my parents, to my childhood, to my early school days. The memories circle like ravenous sharks, preying upon my conscience. A memory: Me throwing a temper tantrum when I didn't get a Skylander figure for Christmas. Another memory:

Me sulking because I failed my first Super examination. Another memory: Me whining to my dad that it's not fair. Why does Gwen get to go to LOS early? She'll be too far ahead of me!

My memories cycle to my friends. The first time I met Ling, I didn't like her. Loud, bossy, sarcastic. She walked the hallways with no shame, her giant DSLR camera flashing in people's faces. *I'm going to be famous*, she told us all. *The Wus will rise again.* She marched up to me and pointed a microphone in my face. *The famous Beata Bell, great-granddaughter of the acclaimed, Original Super. What does it feel like to be born with such relevancy?* I admit now that perhaps I didn't like her because she embodied the very personality I wanted. Carefree, bold, and gregarious.

The first time I met Nuha, I didn't like her either. She trounced me in the Science Fair. Her robotic, flying duster took the wind out of my badly coded text adventure game. I'm not an especially intelligent person, but I pride myself on being techy. Plus, it was the first bit of coding I did alone— and I was proud of it. Meeting the future heir of Bahar Tech made me feel like a turd stuck to someone's boot. Nuha was smart, in a matter-of-fact way, and blunt too. I thought she was arrogant, and cold, just like her fancy toys. Only after we grew close did I realize she was neither arrogant nor cold. Nuha simply *was*.

It feels good to admit these things.

Across the cell, Hitori is asleep. His light snores echo. How he manages to sleep in such a tense situation boggles my mind, but I suppose he's more tired than I am. I roll over and try to find a comfortable position, but it's futile. My arms and legs go numb if I don't move them every few minutes.

I think of Gwen, a memory as vivid as though it's happening in front of me.

Gwen and I are throwing a Frisbee around in the local park. It's great fun. I can throw any which way, and Gwen zooms off to catch it. Gwen has her big sunglasses on, a big hoodie, and some baggy jeans. Her giveaway golden hair is tucked under her hood. To hide her identity, she even walks different, with more of a slump.

As we hike around a corner, we come across a group of boys gathered in a circle. Two stand in the middle, crouched in fighting stances. Enough scuffles happened at Sir Frederick Banting for me to recognize the atmosphere. Thick with anticipation and electricity.

"Let's move on," I say nervously.

"Let's," agrees Gwen with a wrinkle of her perfect nose.

Then one of the boys, one of the fighters, begins to sparkle.

Suddenly, Gwen has her Super demeanour back. She stands up straight and throws out her chest. Before I can speak, she lifts from the ground and descends in the middle of the crowd.

"*Excuse me*, please," she enunciates. "Stand down, everyone."

I hang back, unsure of what to do.

"Back off, girlie," yells the sparkling boy, "if you know what's good for you!"

I can hear the lustre in Gwen's voice as she discards her big sunglasses. "I am no ordinary girl, *boy*. I am Gweneira Kendricks, defender of justice." She throws back her hood. Her blonde coils unravel from her hat and tumble down her back in golden waves. Even in casual wear, she looks regal.

The crowd breaks out in whispers, some awed, some panicked.

The one and only Gweneira Kendricks.

Gweneira makes a quick motion with her hands. A thin chain erupts from her sleeve and encircles the sparkling boy's wrist. She tilts her head and smiles pityingly. Then she yanks him forward so hard he falls onto his knees.

"*What* were you doing?" she asks, pleasantly enough, though the rage in her voice bristles just under her skin. I can see fire in her eyes so hot it could light matches. Her shadow falls over the sparkling boy, who juts a finger at his opponent, a lankier boy with a twitchy eye.

"He stole my lunch money! I was just getting it back!"

Gwen makes a tutting noise with her tongue. "As a Super, it is your responsibility to use your powers with discretion. Turning a hand against a Civvie is downright shameful. Like kicking a puppy. There's something unclean about hurting something so helpless." She leans in and lowers her voice. "A quick lesson in honour, from me to you. *You leave the Civvies out of it.* If you want a fight, I'll gladly be your opponent."

Her chain slithers back. Gwen makes a snapping motion with her fingers. The tip of her chain becomes an arrowhead. The crowd takes a simultaneous step back, expanding the circle.

The sparkling boy raises his hands. "I wasn't going to hurt him! Look, all I can do is this!"

He braces himself and begins to glow. "I swear! I don't want to fight you! I'm sorry, your highness! Your greatness!"

Gwen is uncompromising. She flicks her chain forward. The arrowhead drifts towards the boy's eye.

My heart leaps into my mouth.

"Gwen," I say. "Stop, please."

She doesn't. The look on her face is one of stony resolution. The arrowhead floats closer.

"*Gwen, you're scaring me.*"

Clink.

The arrowhead falls to the ground as though severed, and Gwen's head swivels towards me. I stare back with wide eyes. Her expression is one of surprise and confusion. She doesn't understand. She doesn't see that *she* is kicking a puppy. She's an A-rank Super, and he's barely anything. The power difference is monumental, but she doesn't see it. She lowers her hands.

The boy books it. As he brushes past me, I see him fighting tears. The others watch him go, their faces frozen in shock. It's impossible to tell which side is which now. Gwen's presence has dissolved their differences. Even the lanky, twitchy boy looks uncomfortable. Job done, Gwen tosses her head and returns to me.

"You know I was just giving him a scare, right?" Gwen asks after we share an uncomfortable silence. "Boys need that sometimes. A good, honest scare. You know I would have never hurt him, right?"

I nod wordlessly. I nod even though I'm not entirely sure.

Hitori snorts, jostling me back to reality. I think long and hard about the memory. I'm not sure what brought it on, but it has me feeling cold all over again. I told Alexander that Gwen is scarier than he is. I wasn't kidding. I just hope I'm right about her being more powerful too.

I blink in and out of sleep. I keep counting. There are three thousand six hundred seconds per hour. I hit that number at least three times, but the cell remains dim. It's dull business, and I'm not doing it right. Little spikes of panic keep thrusting into my rhythm, causing me to falter, but mostly it keeps my mind occupied. It's harder for despair to seep in when my head is filled with numbers.

Finally, just as I am beginning to doze off again, the side hatch slides open. I jump to my feet as a pair of serving trays slide in. Mystery solved. The hatch must lead to a kitchen of sorts. The trays are covered in plastic wrap so thick I can barely see the food.

Hitori sleeps curled up on himself. I pick up a tray and unwrap it.

It's a meagre meal consisting of apple slices, a piece of toast—charred in one corner, barely buttered—scrambled eggs, and a small yogurt—prune flavoured. It's hardly a feast, but I'm hungry, so I pop an apple slice into my mouth. It's mushy, like it's been sitting on the counter for days.

It must be around dinnertime—or is it already morning?—which means I've been down here for at least half a day now. How long does it normally take to rescue a kidnapped person? I imagine helicopters roaming overhead, their rotating blades cutting through the air, diligent searchers with binoculars, scanning the streets like hunting birds. I imagine Ling and Nuha darting to news stations, giving comments and witness statements, getting Dieter to drop pamphlets from the sky. I imagine Gwen raging through the air, like a missile on a mission. Worse, I imagine my parents unable to do anything but wait and believe.

It's hard being cut off from the rest of the world.

I eat my meal slowly. Then I get up and do a few jumping jacks. *Thunk, thunk, thunk*, go my feet on the ground. Hitori sleeps through all of it. I wonder how the class is getting on without him.

Finally, I hear a hissing noise. A slow, smooth *whir* vibrates through the cell. I duck and poke Hitori urgently in the shoulder.

"Something's happening. Wake up!"

He rolls over.

"*Mmm*, five more minutes."

"No, sir, you can't sleep anymore."

More clicks and whirs echo through the room. I shake Hitori. If Alexander is coming back—or *worse*—I would feel better with a conscious adult around. Hitori swipes at my hand, groaning.

I take drastic action. I pinch him in the thigh.

"*Eep!*" He bolts up straight.

"Sorry," I breathe.

Lines appear on the roof. The metal breaks into five very even, very smooth pieces and begin to retreat.

Finally awake, Hitori gives a whistle of appreciation as the ceiling begins to spin. It rotates like a camera aperture, slowly, until the roof is fully open. Intense white lights flood the room. I cover my eyes. When I recover, a single silhouette stands above us, balanced at the edge of the cell.

It takes me many moments to recognize her.

It's Agent Scarlett.

I leap to my feet. "Agent Scarlett! I'm glad to see you! Has help arrived?"

"I'm afraid not." It's not Agent Scarlett who speaks but Hitori. I turn to him. His expression is sombre and wary. He speaks again, louder. "I hoped to never meet you again, but I suppose circumstances dictated otherwise. Hello, Joanna."

Agent Scarlett smiles—no, grins. Her teeth are so perfectly neat they seem chiselled from marble.

"So you're the source poisoning young Alexander's mind." She gives a little laugh. "So you've finally come out of hiding, Hitori Yuuma, once great telekinetic. You've finally returned home."

She turns to me. "Thank you, Miss Bell. You've been most useful. I would have never found Hitori if it weren't for your informative and timely email." I see Hitori's photo flash on her phone. "Imagine my surprise when you sent me information on good ol' Hitori's whereabouts. What luck! Believe me, you've done us a great favour."

I stare up at her. "You know Alexander?"

"Know him? Oh, my girl, let's just say we have a special understanding." Agent Scarlett's grin widens. "You could even call us business partners."

Click, goes my mind.

Suddenly, I don't feel so good.

Part 3

Chapter 17

Super Revelations

Once, my dad said something interesting.

"Super broadcasts have gotten really dramatic these days."

"So has *The Bachelor*," retorted my mom.

"You know it's all scripted, right?" asked my dad. He raised his eyebrows.

My mom dismissed him with a shrug.

"Who cares? So is everything else on television."

I was younger then. To me, it sounded like a tremendous declaration.

I study Agent Scarlett. She doesn't look any different from before. Red, professional blazer. Hair tied in a strict bun. Only now she wears a self-satisfied air, like a fox that just cornered a fat rabbit. It's an unnerving expression.

"How the great have fallen," says Agent Scarlett. The way she says it—with a mixture of pity and condescension—makes it sound oily and mean. "And right into my hands too," she crows. "The acclaimed Hitori Yuuma, one of the world's only telekinetics, celebrated hero and all-round crowd-pleaser. What a shocker! What an absolutely juicy story. This is turning out to be a most *excellent* day."

"Yes, I remember how much you liked your *stories*." Hitori hisses out the last word like it leaves a bad taste in his mouth. "You would trade the world for a story."

"Let me tell you, I was worried about Alexander," Agent Scarlett says airily. From above, she looks like a hawk, perched and waiting. "I wasn't sure he could do it. You gave him some serious doubts, but I prevailed in the end, as I always have. This will be my greatest hit yet."

I want to say something, to ask questions, but I hold my tongue. Sometimes it's best to let information sink in. It's the same with programming. If there's a hitch, you take a step back and clear your mind. Then when you're refreshed, you take a new crack at it. Everything makes sense—eventually. I let my mind put two and two together. If Alexander is a part of the Counter-League, and Agent Scarlett is working with him, then—I narrow my eyes.

"What are you doing in the Counter-League base, Agent Scarlett?" I ask, craning my neck to look at her.

"Oh, Miss Bell," says Agent Scarlett. Her eyes fill with pity. "So innocent. I'm sure all will be clear soon."

"You're betraying LOS," I say, convinced. A flare of anger rises in my chest. I take a step forward. "I can't believe it! You're a villain, too! What about Gwen? What about all the other Supers?"

"One question at a time, Miss Bell." Agent Scarlett waves a hand. An assistant scurries from the shadows and plops a rolled newspaper into it before disappearing into the background again. Agent Scarlett shakes the roll out with gusto. "Listen to these headlines. *Counter-League keeps promises. Gweneira Kendricks makes threats.* Right on the front page of the *Toronto Star. The End for the Bells?! Prestigious Super Family Meets Match.* Oh, that's juicy. What a way to intertwine history. How the great fall indeed."

I'm outraged. "You're using me!"

Agent Scarlett ignores my outburst and continues, picking through headlines as though plucking ripe berries.

"Oh ho, and here's an eye-catcher. *Gweneira Kendricks, Hero or Hostile?!*" Agent Scarlett makes a tutting noise with her tongue. "Poor child. I told her to keep her cool. But this is even better."

"*Hostile?*" I blurt. How can she sound so calm about Gwen losing her cool? Isn't Gwen her best client? "Gwen's not a *hostile*. She's Toronto's greatest hero!"

"Did you not hear? Oh, of course not. You're in a cell." Agent Scarlett finally looks at me. "What a good friend Miss Kendricks is. She's worried sick about her wee Beata Bell. Her little sidekick that never was. She never gave up hope, you know. She used to get so excited talking about how you two would make a dynamic duo. She's tearing up the city looking for you, acting rashly, defying orders, trying to find members of the Counter-League to interrogate. It's a shame. Right after the debacle with the Payton lawsuit too."

My mouth drops open, but no sound comes out. Gwen is looking for me. I don't know whether to be relieved or mortified.

"I see you're still up to your old games," says Hitori. "Do you ever get your fill, Joanna?"

"Supers are so predictable," Agent Scarlett says with a laugh. "All the heroics go to their heads. I suppose we're lucky children are so malleable. It makes them easy to control."

I'm beginning to feel cold. My head swirls. It's clear Agent Scarlett isn't willing to give up information, so I look towards Hitori instead. "She's a part of the Counter-League too?"

"Have you ever noticed," starts Hitori, in a quieter voice, "how everything in the Super world seems so perfect?"

I think about all the incidents where Supers saved the day right on time. All the amazing motivational speeches. My mind jumps to Gwen's quick exchange with the Counter-League right after the Payton incident. Yes, I did think it was an unusually prepared response. So did Ling and Nuha. Something hard and cold swirls in my stomach. I feel light-headed. My gut is bracing me for something big. Something ominous.

"The robot octopod attacks always result in minimal deaths. Supers always save the day. The media is always at the right place for the most sensational report," Hitori continues.

"There's millions of dollars in property damage," I add, thinking, "but they usually hit parks, abandoned buildings, and—" I think back to the attack on City Hall. "Unfinished construction projects."

"The streets are always evacuated on time. LOS always seems to know exactly where to go. They never have false reports. They always respond in a timely manner. They always corner off exactly the number of blocks they need to successfully apprehend the bad guys. Everything is streamlined."

I think of the Payton case, how empty the streets were before the car chase as though someone had cleared up a space especially for the action.

"Either LOS is incredibly lucky, every single time, or—" Hitori prompts.

"They know what's going to happen," I mutter. Everything is always perfect. *Too* perfect. It feels like the ground beneath me is tilting. Suddenly, a whole new perspective opens up before my eyes, and I shake my head to clear it. I always credited LOS's predictive success to their technology, even though I've never seen their supercomputers, or even heard anyone talk about them. Dad never mentioned them either, even though he used to work in IT. I assumed LOS had the technology because they were able to get results, but what if they were able to get results because they already knew what was going to happen? *I've made an assumption error.*

Hitori turns to me. "Think, Miss Bell. If you were the Counter-League, hell-bent on causing havoc, what would you do? How would you maximize damage and embarrass LOS?"

It scares me how easily the answer comes.

"Chuck a robot octopod into the heart of downtown during rush hour, or at the Rogers Centre during a Jays game, or at the CN Tower."

"The robot octopods are high-tech, mechanical war machines—" Hitori says, staring at me intently.

"So how are the attacks so clean?" I finish, eyes wide. I turn to Agent Scarlett, who watches us with barely concealed amusement. "And if LOS is able to predict these attacks, why don't they stop them? If they have such powerful foresight, why can't they do something as simple as track down members of the Counter-League? Robot octopods aren't easy to hide. They're huge! Polypowers aren't discreet. They're a big deal too!"

"It's a discrepancy," Hitori says softly. "You're a smart girl. You've always felt something was off, didn't you?"

Click. Something falls into place in my mind. It reverberates in my skull, exceedingly loud.

"It's a conspiracy," I gasp. "Everything is planned!"

I gaze, wide-eyed, at Agent Scarlett and Hitori. *Tell me I'm wrong.*

"You're right, Miss Bell. It *is* a conspiracy," says Hitori bitterly. "There is no Counter-League. It's all LOS's doing. Just LOS creating and promoting their own stories. The world is their stage, and we're all suckers."

I feel like I've been put through a huge pasta machine. The cell seems blurred and unreal. Agent Scarlett's silhouette is fuzzy from the bright floodlights. My ears ring. I am light-headed, and my stomach is a clenched knot.

"Why didn't you tell me earlier?" I take a step towards Hitori, aghast. "You knew all along, didn't you? Why didn't you say anything when I accused you of being a part of the Counter-League?"

"I wanted to save your feelings. I know you look up to LOS. Most people do. I couldn't bear to tell you, and I'm a coward for it. I apologize."

"So everything my parents did, everything my grandparents did, and everything my great-grandma did was a *sham*?" I can't imagine someone like Frances E. Shaw falling for such tricks. Or my parents. Especially not my dad.

The look in Hitori's eyes is a mixture of sadness and pity. "No, not all of it. Once upon a time there was a need for LOS. Supers won wars, after all. LOS served a noble purpose in the world. They policed the streets, took down gangsters and mobsters, and stifled crime. Make no mistake about it. The world became safer. No ordinary folks could stand up to Supers. How are ordinary people supposed to prevail against children who can move trucks with their minds?"

He shakes his head and shrugs.

"But with crime all but eradicated in the last few decades,

LOS lost its purpose. What does an organization do when demand for its members dries up? Government funding lessened. It takes a lot of money to train Super children and to pay for their facilities. Never mind the thousands of employees. LOS needed money. More than what they could get from the government. And that's when some dastardly minds got together and hatched a master plan."

"Oh please," simpers Agent Scarlett. She rolls her eyes. "Don't use words like *dastardly*. It's embarrassing."

Hitori glares at her. "If public funding has dried up, why not move to private funding? Why not ask businesses for money? Why not ask the public for donations? Super culture is fascinating and exciting, so why not make it even more entertaining? Supers were loaned to parades and celebrations. They did flybys and circus acts. But that wasn't enough. So why not broadcast reality shows? Sell merchandise. Make them compete. Profit off them."

"Poor, delusional Hitori. You always were a pessimistic one. Now, if you're finished, let me explain how things really are." Agent Scarlett looks towards me. Her gaze is piercing. "Listen to me, Miss Beata Bell. A world filled with bored Super children is not something anyone can risk. Bored children cause havoc. They light fires and join gangs. Bored children who can move trucks with their minds, well, that's just asking for trouble. Children need to be trained, kept busy, and given a purpose. Otherwise, chaos will reign. Can you imagine a world where every Super were free to do what they wished? How quickly do you think they'd exploit their powers for selfish gains? LOS needs funding, it's true, and lots of it. The government can only give so much before taxpayers start grousing. Politicians have their own games to play, after all. So what are we supposed to do? Cut back? Shut down? No! We do as everyone else does. We use our minds and smarts to survive and thrive."

I think about LOS's pristine headquarters, so large it spans the Toronto Islands. I remember the fresh potted plants and stoic receptionists in fancy pressed suits. I think of the clean floors, so polished you could see your own reflection, and the shuttle buses that run, sans fee, from the city to the Islands. Thrive indeed.

Yet, *she's not wrong*, breathes my mind. Didn't I think the same of Dieter and his bully friends? No one can control a Super, especially not Civvies. No one but LOS, that is.

"Long ago, LOS was a reputable organization, dedicated to good causes." Hitori stands taller. His voice gets more commanding. He glares at Agent Scarlett, and for a second, I can see a glimmer of his former Super self. "Now, it's a cesspool of celebrity and gossip. You would sell your soul to stay afloat another season. What happened to defending justice? What happened to protecting the weak?"

"Someone sounds sour. Is that any way to treat your former employer?" Agent Scarlett examines her nails, the very image of boredom. She glances down at us with one perfect eyebrow raised. "Is this how you repay us, Hitori?"

"I owe you nothing."

I watch the scene with growing dread. The disappeared Super. The one who fought in the last official challenge. Versus Agent Scarlett, Gwen's mentor and high-ranking official of LOS. I feel like an intruder, a bug listening to their argument. They face one another like two bulls about to lock horns, and me, caught in the middle, an unfortunate rabbit. I try to swallow, but my throat's closed up. I keep thinking of

Frances E. Shaw, and my grandparents, and my parents as children, fighting for what they believed was justice and freedom, sweating and working for entertainment instead. It makes my skin crawl.

But then I picture the world without LOS, a world where all Supers did what they wanted—torched houses and bullied Civvies for no reason. The vision makes my skin crawl even more.

"You know it as well as I do, Miss Bell," Agent Scarlett continues. "Civvies have summer camp and after-school activities to keep them out of trouble. Supers have LOS. LOS keeps Civvies safe from Supers, and Supers safe from themselves."

Hitori laughs. It's an ugly sound, and Agent Scarlett's face flashes with anger. "Is that how you're justifying it to yourself, Joanna? Pathetic, as usual."

"I'm not the one standing in prison, Hitori."

"You're not the one who put me here. Never one to get your hands dirty, huh? Always the coward, hiding behind others."

"I am a respected Agent. You're just a washed-up celebrity. I work every day to protect the citizens of this city *and of the world*. I don't have to take this from you."

"Don't pretend to be honourable. You're doing this for your own selfish gain!"

"You're wrong, Hitori. The world needs organizations like LOS. We are safeguarding everyone."

"Safeguarding? Don't make me laugh! Your kind killed Charley!"

There's a moment of loaded silence. Then Agent Scarlett makes a snorting sound. It takes me a while to realize she's holding back laughter. The sound makes me feel grimy inside.

"So this is what it's about, huh, Hitori? Your old friend? Your *only* friend?" Agent Scarlett sighs deeply. Her face goes sympathetic. Somehow, it's even more terrifying than her steely cold expression. "You know as well as we do that he was a danger to everyone. He had to go."

"You didn't help him."

"We *couldn't* help him."

"Maybe, but you didn't have to make it into a spectacle."

"I prefer to call it an efficiency. Neutralize a danger while gaining public support. Do you know how many companies pledged us money that night?"

"No amount of money is worth someone's life," Hitori retorts.

"So naïve." Agent Scarlett sneers. "Everything has its price. It's just a matter of numbers."

I shrink back. Their voices echo in the chamber. It sounds as though a dozen people are yelling at once. My stomach flip-flops. Agent Scarlett killed someone? *Charley.* The name sounds familiar.

Click. Of course. I've seen the name in the collection of Super cards under my bed. Charley X. Beamsman. But it wasn't Agent Scarlett who killed him, it was Hitori. Hitori dropped two oil tankers on him. *The explosion could be heard five kilometres away.* Unless—

I groan out loud. Unless the entire thing was also a sham. Unless Agent Scarlett has been manipulating this for decades. Unless she orchestrated the entire thing from the shadows, like a dark puppet master. I remember the odd feint Beamsman made in his last few moments. Why would he feint at someone when he could shoot lasers from his eyes? What good would a physical feint do? Now that I think of it, it was more like an involuntary movement. Like a flinch. As though he were punched.

Or shot, my mind hisses.

"Miss Bell, are you all right?" Hitori touches me lightly on the shoulder. He's suddenly a teacher again. "Do you need to sit down? Are you going to be sick?"

Agent Scarlett stands tall and takes a deep breath. Her nostrils pinch. She lets it out slowly. Her cheeks slowly return to their regular pallor.

"Well, this has been a pleasant reunion, Hitori, but I tire of talking." Agent Scarlett's voice is conversational, but her face is full of steel. "The world is oh so intrigued by where you've been all this time. The disappeared Super. What could be the reason?" She grins and spreads her arms out as though embracing the sky. "Imagine their shock, imagine their horror, when they realize their adored hero has turned against them. Hitori Yuuma, leader of the Counter-League. What a sensation!"

She giggles. It's a sharp, mad sound. A shiver runs up my spine.

"I won't cooperate," says Hitori resolutely.

"Of course you will." Agent Scarlett waves a hand in dismissal. "Deny it as you will, you're still a hero inside. You won't allow others to come to harm because of your obstinacy."

"You're trying to blackmail me. It won't work. There's no one you can use against me."

"Let me remind you, Mr. *Uzune*, in case you've been away too long. Super battles can get rather *fiery*. What a shame it would be if one of your students were to get in the way, like, say, clever Miss Bell here?"

Her eyes meet mine for a split second, and I feel the implication fall into place. My body takes a step back. Instinct.

"You wouldn't dare," says Hitori, but his face is pale.

"You know I would," says Agent Scarlett, her eyes blazing. "I have worked long and hard for this position, Hitori, longer and harder than any Super in this organization. I have risen through the ranks on my skill and *effort*. I will do what it takes to maintain LOS's standing in the world as well as my position within it. You think we don't know about your sorry entourage and lowly Supers, attempting to foil my plans along the way? Who would notice if they disappeared too? A couple of confused associates who can be easily swayed by media and money? You underestimate me, Hitori."

For once, Hitori doesn't speak. He just looks outraged. I can barely breathe.

Agent Scarlett waves a hand. "Prepare for your first broadcast as leader of the Counter-League, Hitori. You should be happy. You can join Charley as a traitor against LOS, since you're so loyal to him. Another hero fallen to the darkness. Unless, of course, you *really* don't want to."

She looks at him pointedly, then smiles down at me. My gut twists, and I want nothing more than to hide. From the corner of my eye, I see Hitori open his mouth and close it stubbornly. He shakes but says nothing. Agent Scarlett beams.

"Beata Bell, daughter of Phil and Tessa Bell, great-granddaughter of the prestigious Original Super, Frances E. Shaw. We have been watching you since your birth." Her voice softens. "I do apologize for your unfortunate kidnapping. If it were up to me, you wouldn't be in here at all, but once you figured out Alexander's identity, we couldn't let you roam free, see? Too risky."

"Why would you bother watching *me*?" I ask. "I'm nobody."

My heart beats so hard I wonder if everyone in the room can hear it.

"Your genes have greatness in them. You could have been a *Super* star."

"Well, I'm not." I start to feel hot.

"Well, now you have the chance."

My blood races. I'm filled with suspicion—and anticipation.

"I know how you feel, Miss Bell," says Agent Scarlett. "Always in the shadows, pining away. If only you could be more useful. If only you had power. You want to change things, don't you? I understand. I'm like you. I was left in the shadows, too."

Agent Scarlett's words cut through me. They resonate somewhere deep inside.

"Joanna," starts Hitori.

"It's *Agent Scarlett* to you," she snaps. Then her eyes move back to me, and her tone is like lava cake. "I was tired of being a lesser citizen. I was tired of all these *Supers*, blessed by some mysterious force, some sort of biology, some innate predisposition, become *better* than the rest of us. So I did the smart thing. I joined LOS. You're a smart child too. Ambitious. I see a little bit of myself in you. Why don't you join me? Become an Agent. If you can't beat them, rise above."

Agent Scarlett's voice goes even softer, and I strain forward to hear her.

"Look at me," she says, "holding the strings. I might not have fame, but I have power. I can't shoot lasers, but that's just fine. My power is greater. Do you know how many powers I control through my clients? I yell *charge*, and my clients attack. I yell *stop*, and they stop. I pick and choose the best Supers and mould them into perfect heroes. I give them fame and fortune."

Despite myself, a shiver of fascination passes through me. Agent Scarlett is like an oncoming summer storm: icy calm and threatening all at once. She makes me nervous. I can't read her at all, or predict her movements, or understand what she's thinking, but she's offering a way in, a step towards a future where I might be able to make something of myself. A future where being a Dud isn't such a big deal. I tell myself she's bad, that the future she offers is dark, but I can't stop listening.

Or wondering.

"How many times have you wished to be something greater?" asks Agent Scarlett.

"Many," I answer softly.

"*Joanna*," interrupts Hitori with a voice like ice. "Leave my student alone."

"I make and break heroes," Agent Scarlett adds triumphantly. "The only difference between a hero and a villain is perspective. Isn't that right, *Hitori*? Who's on top now?"

Hitori keeps his expression even, but his shoulders are tense.

"My offer still stands, Miss Bell," says Agent Scarlett, her eyes blazing. "Work with LOS. There's no reason a Civvie can't excel. Agree to work with us, and we'll put this unfortunate business behind us."

Agent Scarlett's smile is sympathetic.

"I don't want to be a burden anymore," I say quietly.

"I know," she says. "Bear with this for a while longer, and

I promise you more power than you've ever had. That'll be my apology for my foolish, metal-manipulating client's behaviour. For now, sit tight. If you join LOS, this will be the last time you feel helpless."

Her words ring in my head like a chime.

I step forward, craning my neck to maintain eye contact. "If you want to apologize, let me out of this cell."

"Oh, but that's not possible," says Agent Scarlett with a little giggle. "Not with the media whipping up such a frenzy about you. Not that I don't trust you, Miss Bell. I know you're a good girl who understands it's bad to blab about things you don't fully understand. But it's too much of a risk, you see. So you'll have to stay here, at least until things calm down."

"You mean until you can figure out a good story to go along with her release," counters Hitori.

"*Be. Quiet. Hitori,*" Agent Scarlett emphasizes with such vehemence that I jump.

Hitori bites his lip. Agent Scarlett's face goes smooth again.

"Kidnapping me is kind of a strange way of hiring me, isn't it?" I ask. "Don't most employers just send an email or something?"

Agent Scarlett laughs again. "You're a funny one. That's good. I like humour."

She winks as though we share a secret, but she doesn't say anything else.

Then the ceiling begins to spin closed, and Agent Scarlett flashes a triumphant grin. "No pressure, Miss Bell. I know you'll choose the reasonable path."

As she strides away, the metal ceiling clicks together, and

we're once again in darkness. Hitori sits back down with a deep sigh, moving as though he's aged ten years in ten minutes. I stand in the middle of the room, staring at the spot Agent Scarlett disappeared. My head is reeling. Join LOS. Become an Agent.

Maybe it's not such a bad idea, a small voice whispers in my head.

I reach into my pocket and touch the sharp outline of her business card.

It might be the best offer you've ever had.

Chapter 18
Supers of Days Past

Click, click, click. I rotate an imaginary Rubik's Cube.

Join LOS. Become an Agent. Become a part of the grand scheme. My head is spinning. LOS isn't what I believed it to be. It's all a ruse. All a front. The world is so safe its greatest threat is Supers themselves.

Join LOS. Never be helpless again.

Join LOS.

Rise above.

Frances, what would you do? I look up to the dark ceiling. No answer. The cell is so silent that the flow of blood through my ears sounds like a river. I scoff and shake my head. Frances E. Shaw wouldn't know what to do because she was never in my position. She was too famous and beautiful and important to feel what I feel. She wasn't a Dud.

I'm the only one who can decide what to do for myself. It's a mistake to draw inspiration from her. We were never the same, and never will be. A mouse doesn't ask a cat what to do. A mouse does its own thing. I imagine Frances drawing away, her face becoming smaller and smaller until the darkness blurs her features.

My thoughts are jumbled. I need a distraction, a way out of my own mind.

"Beamsman," I say into the darkness. "Charley. What happened to him?"

Hitori sounds weary when he speaks. He sounds defeated. "What do you know?"

"The same as everyone else. That he went rogue and tore up a neighbourhood. LOS sent you in, and you dropped two oil tankers on him. I saw the footage—though now I'm not exactly sure what to believe."

"He tore up a neighbourhood all right, but he didn't go rogue."

"We have time. Tell me your side of the story."

Silence. I can almost hear the gears revolving in Hitori's mind. I can barely see him in the darkness, but I don't need to see him to understand how difficult it is to rehash a hard past. I think about Agent Scarlett's words. It pains me to know she's right. Civvies don't achieve greatness these days. It's all Supers, Supers, Supers. How long have I wanted to touch even a fragment of Gwen's glory? Do all Agents know the truth? They must. A part of me is disgusted that I would even consider her offer, but another part of me urges me on. A lengthy pro and con list jousts in my head. Voices upon voices.

If I can't be onscreen, I can at least work behind the scenes. Dad always said there was no shame in being behind the action. This could be my way of leaving my own legacy. And at least, if I became an Agent, I would be involved in a small aspect of the Super world. All good movies need a producer, right?

It's better than being a Dud.

"Do you believe all powers are good?" Hitori asks at last.

"I guess it depends," I answer. "Some are better than others."

"Supers are immune to their own powers," Hitori continues. I remember Gwen saying something similar once. "But that doesn't mean the powers don't have side effects. I had terrible migraines as a Super. Sometimes, when they needed me on a *mission*—" He gives a short snort."—I would suck it up for an hour and go about my business. Then I would come back and vomit. Sometimes, I barely made it back to the LOS car. Joanna made it very clear that I was never to show weakness in public. *Heroes don't falter*, she said."

This is the first time I've ever heard of side effects. I wonder whether Gwen has any. If she does, she conceals them well.

"There's a lot LOS hides from the public. They're all about image, and there's a lot of ugliness to hide." Hitori sighs deeply. "Charley had one of the rarest powers in the world."

"Lasers." I always wanted lasers.

"Yes. It's also one of the hardest to control. He told me once that using his powers was like being burned from the inside. Like fire snaking up his arms and pouring from his hands. He trained, but the harder he trained, the more his body suffered, so he wasn't able to maintain a regimen like the rest of us. Even painkillers didn't help."

Hitori pauses. When he starts again, he sounds like he's speaking from far away.

"He was dangerous. Charley never meant to hurt anyone, but accidents happen. We tried to figure out what set off his lasers—arm gestures, facial expressions, thoughts, emotions—but as soon as we thought we had the trigger, he would prove us wrong. He would be fine one moment and pouring lasers from his eyes the next. LOS had special rooms built for him. More cells than anything. Glass, metal, concrete, rock. He could melt through them all given enough time."

I think about Frances E. Shaw. In all the old photographs I've seen of her, she looks perfectly composed and together. Then I remember the picture of her burning through tanks, an absolute powerhouse of strength. Her firepower overwhelmed battleships, planes, and entire battalions. No one ever mentioned if it hurt her to be so strong. I don't think anyone ever asked.

"Charley was afraid," continues Hitori. "No one wanted to be around him, and he didn't want to be around anyone. Not even other Supers were safe around him. The first time he fired an accidental laser, five kids were sent to the hospital."

I wince. "Lasers eat through everything, I know."

"So LOS assigned me to watch over him. As someone with another rare and powerful ability, I was the only one capable of checking Charley without risking terrible injury. I couldn't stop his power, but I could divert it. Every time he had an accident, I could pull something—anything—from nearby and deflect it, or at the very least, push others out of his way. Once, I even threw him into Lake Ontario so the water would muffle his damage. He wasn't very happy about that one. Charley always hated water—"

There's a warmth in Hitori's voice that makes my chest tighten. Then I hear him sigh.

"Point being, I was versatile enough to contain the damage until he got himself under control."

I swallow hard. I'm beginning to see where this is going.

"Charley ran away repeatedly. He didn't want to be in the city, where he could hurt more people, but LOS wouldn't let him leave. He would sneak out, and LOS would send me after him. Back then, I genuinely thought I was doing him a favour. I couldn't imagine a Super who *didn't* want to be with LOS.

They had helped me gain control over my own powers, after all. I was angry with him for not understanding. LOS was his home. He grew angry with me too, saying I didn't understand, that if I were a true friend, I would let him go. I didn't learn until later that Joanna had recorded all our exchanges and made Charley look like a villain, intent on raiding the city and causing damage."

Click. "The night he went on rampage, he was running away."

Hitori nods wearily.

"But you fought him."

"We argued. I called him irresponsible, and an idiot. Would running away help him control his powers? I told him if he was ready to give up, he could just throw himself off a cliff. No one was stopping him. I wouldn't stop him."

"You dropped two oil tankers on him."

"No," says Hitori. His voice is thick with anger. "I *threatened* to drop two oil tankers on him, to make it easy for him. I was so tired of being his caretaker. But I was angry, and bluffing. Someone else did it for me."

Click.

"Someone from LOS."

"They had a weapon trained on Charley the entire time. They shot him right in front of me. He didn't have a Supersuit on. I didn't drop those oil tankers on purpose. I dropped them because I was shocked." Hitori sighs deeply, with a weariness that shakes me. "I was the distraction while they set up their snipers."

Suddenly, I'm filled with emotion. I can't even imagine seeing Ling or Nuha or Gwen get hurt in front of me without shuddering. I also can't imagine making such a difficult call.

If someone I knew was rampaging through a neighbourhood—*Gwen*, I imagine—could I make the decision to take them down? I'm not sure.

"It crossed my mind that night," admits Hitori sadly, "that I could just go crazy. I was one of the world's only telekinetics. If I could stop Charley, who could possibly stop me? I could blow stuff up with my mind. I could swipe helicopters from the sky and throw them around like toys. I could get *revenge*. But I'm not that brave, Miss Bell. I wasn't ready to die. So I went into hiding instead. I withdrew my funds and ran away. LOS hunted me like a rabbit. They weren't going to let their star player disappear. For years, I jumped countries, assumed different identities, all to dodge them. Then over time, my powers faded, and LOS lost interest. I lived a few years in relative peace, but it never felt right. Every time I watched an LOS broadcast, I wondered what's being fabricated and what was true.

"It took me years to convince myself to return. I'm a coward, not a hero. People need to know what's happening. LOS isn't what they think it is. They need to know before sending their children for training. All this"—he waves a hand—"is a farce."

Quiet falls around us. I rub my knees.

"Escape then," I say, squinting into the darkness at Hitori's outline. "Get the truth out."

"I've been trying for ten years to get the truth out without giving myself away," says Hitori, sounding tired. "Me and those who believe me—we're small. But LOS is a giant."

We sit in silence afterwards and watch the light darken.

I have a feeling Hitori isn't going to do any more talking tonight, so I do some deep thinking instead.

Agent Scarlett is right. Becoming an Agent would give me everything I've ever wanted. Power, and fame, and influence. As a bonus, I would be able to work with Gwen.

Or be her boss. But more than anything, I want to make my family proud.

I don't think my mom and dad would approve of their only daughter becoming a manipulative Agent for LOS. My mom would probably yell at me. My dad would be sad. It bothers me to imagine them angry and sad.

Then again, they wouldn't have to know. All they would need to know is that I've ensured myself a healthy and respectable career. They don't know the truth. Yet.

And they never have to, my mind reminds me. It can be my little secret. I can tell them once I'm famous and important.

Hitori is watching me carefully, probably wondering about my thoughts, but I ignore him. I need more time to myself. When dinner slides through the food hatch, I munch my stale bun in silence.

Chapter 19

Jailbreak

"You should accept her offer."

I jerk awake. I didn't even realize I had fallen asleep.

"Whuu?" I groan inelegantly. One of my legs is numb. I shake it weakly and bite my lip when I get pins and needles.

"Tell Joanna you'll do it. Then at least you'll be on the outside." My eyes have adjusted somewhat to the darkness, and I can see Hitori across the room. He looks strange. He isn't wearing his brown jacket anymore. I realize blearily that it's draped over me like a blanket.

"You can live a good life as an Agent. I've seen the car Joanna drives."

"Why do you call her Joanna?" I ask, curiosity rising through my grogginess. "Everyone calls her Agent Scarlett."

"Because before she was Agent Scarlett, she was Joanna," Hitori says with a shrug. "We've known each other for a long time. She was fresh out of university when we first met. There was a time when she wasn't so—*mean*. I want to remind her of that."

"It just makes her mad, you know."

"Yeah," says Hitori, smiling sheepishly. "It does, doesn't it?"

He seems proud of himself. I have a feeling he's just causing trouble for the sake of causing trouble. *Trolling*, as the Internet would say. I study him carefully. I had no idea he had a roguish side.

"If I accept, what happens to you?" I ask. I hate the idea of leaving him behind. A small part of me still feels bad for blowing his cover.

"It's over for me anyways," he says with a sigh. "I had a good run. I thought maybe if I gathered enough followers, I would have enough to convince the world of LOS's true nature. But I was wrong. I was cursed the moment I rejected them. I tried my best."

"You're giving up?"

"You're a good kid, Miss Bell. Maybe you can be patient. Maybe you can change LOS from the inside out. It's certainly not going to change from the outside in."

"It sounds like a lot of work," I say truthfully. "I'm not smart, or very ambitious. I don't think I can handle the pressure."

Or the deception.

"Joanna is a scary woman," says Hitori, "but you don't have to be like her to survive."

There's a rumble in the distance. My ears perk up.

"Did you hear that?"

Hitori stands and nods.

"What is it?"

"I'm not sure." He motions for me to come closer. I do.

There's another vibration. It's close. Metal groans around us.

"Stay close," Hitori says, placing a hand on my shoulder. I clutch his coat as though it's a shield.

Bright blue sparks dance across the cell wall, growing brighter and more frenzied by the second. Another rumble shakes the ground, and Hitori and I shuffle to the middle of the room. My stomach jumps. I recognize the sparks—spidery lightning bolts, leaping in a stormy sky. My breath hitches.

"Gwen," I breathe a second before a portion of the wall warps and melts into a puddle of silvery goo. A cascade of sparks nearly blinds me, and I squint into the light. For a second, I'm filled with panic. What if she's still angry with me? What if it's awkward?

What if I don't want to leave yet?

Hitori and I are frozen, disbelieving, as Gwen steps through the hole. Her hair fans around her. Her nostrils flare. She gazes around, imperiously.

Then she spots me.

"Beata," says Gwen. Her face thaws. She rushes in and throws her arms around my neck. I almost choke. "You have no idea how hard I looked for you."

I think about the headlines. *Acting rashly. Defying orders.* A swath of destruction falls behind her like a shadow. She has busted through wall after wall to get to our cell, leaving broken pipes and crumbling plaster in her wake. The hallways are flashing red in alarm. The blare of a siren echoes amidst the chaos.

"Actually," I say weakly as she releases me from her grip, "I think I do. What have you done, Gwen? You have no idea what you just walked into!"

"I don't have to understand everything to know I need to rescue my friend," says Gwen. "They will face my full fury for kidnapping you, Bea. I promised to protect you, and I will. I keep my word."

"I don't think you can take on this enemy, Gwen."

Her eyes harden.

"We'll see about that," she says. "Right now, we need to get you out of here." Her eyes flick to Hitori. "And Mr. Uzune too. Good evening, sir. Fancy seeing you here."

"Oh," says Hitori, stunned.

I almost smile. Gwen has that effect on people.

My smile doesn't last long. Figures rush into the hallway behind Gwen. LOS security in dark suits, guns drawn. They race down the hall, their faces masks of silent determination.

"Gwen," I say, but she doesn't seem flustered. Quite the opposite. She rolls her eyes, strides back to the broken metal wall, and makes a swiping motion. The wall reforms. The sirens cut off.

Gwen sighs deeply in the quiet. She places three fingers on her brow. "What a mess," she says. "It's been a long couple of days."

"Gwen," I say. "Agent Scarlett. LOS. I think—"

"I know," she says solemnly, and I'm taken aback.

"You know? How do you know? How did you *find* me?"

Gwen fixes me with a steady gaze. "Your app works, Beata. Imagine my surprise when Nuha called me in the middle of the afternoon, sounding like hell just opened up before her eyes, blabbering something about a kidnapping and how you're in grave danger. She opened the Super Tracker app, typed in your name, and lo and behold, all your photos of the city popped up. Nuha superimposed them over some city maps, and they led us right to LOS headquarters."

There's a soft, airy sound, and the ceiling above us begins to open. Gwen narrows her eyes.

"Let's not dawdle," says Hitori. He points at the food hatch in the wall. "The wall's thinner here."

Gwen strides over. Her control is amazing. Only a small twitch in her cheek betrays her stress. She brushes her fingers over the metal with hurried grace, and the wall liquefies under her touch, revealing an empty kitchen. It looks recently abandoned, greasy plates still stacked by a sink full of bubbly water, cutlery strewn haphazardly across the counters. I see a discarded apron by the door, crumpled as though thrown. Plates of leftovers are piled in one corner.

That would explain the quality of our food.

The ceiling opens further, and curtains of light fall through the darkness. We don't wait to see who is waiting beyond. Hitori ushers Gwen and me through the hole in the wall, and I allow myself to be swept into the kitchen, feeling numb. Everything is happening so fast! Gwen touches the wall again, and the hole seals, leaving us in the cluttered kitchen.

"Let's go," commands Gwen. Her breathing is shallow and even. She strides through the evacuated room like a queen. At the doors, I see flashing lights.

"Code Red. Code Red. This is not a drill. Evacuate the building immediately. Code Red."

A Code Red hasn't been called in LOS since Beamsman attempted his last escape from LOS. I ball my hands into fists to stop them from shaking. I expect burly LOS security to barrel through the hallways, weapons drawn, but the hallway remains blessedly empty.

"I've never been in this part of the building before," Gwen says, "but I'm sure it won't be a problem." She flexes her fingers. The red light casts dark shadows over her face. They reflect in her eyes, making them dark and murky. It's clear she plans to exit as she came—forcefully.

"This way," Hitori pipes up before she can act, pointing towards the right.

Gwen throws him an odd look.

"Trust him," I say. "He knows."

Gwen studies Hitori for a moment, her brows furrowed, before acknowledging him with a quick jerk of her head. "All right," she says, "but stay behind me."

We move quickly. I try to keep my footsteps light. *This is like a horror movie*, my mind chimes, unhelpfully. The pulsing red lights, the eerily empty halls, the drone of the siren. Looking down the hallways, I can imagine zombies crashing through the doors, or axe murderers leaping from the shadows. Gwen moves as though she's in heels, even though she's wearing flats, all elegant and on her toes. She's in black sweatpants and a T-shirt as though she just leapt off her couch. No Supersuit.

Hitori leads us through the halls, occasionally asking Gwen to melt through locked doors, which she does silently and effortlessly. Finally, we arrive at a metal staircase, spiralling up.

"Be careful," says Hitori, "this leads upwards. The basements are evacuated, but there's no guarantee the ground floor has been."

"Proceed with caution," Gwen says. "Noted."

We take the stairs one at a time until we arrive at a door. The red alarm lights make familiar sights seem foreign and cold. We exchange silent glances before Gwen pushes the door open and steps onto the landing. I follow her, and Hitori takes up the rear. We're standing at the entrance of what appears to be a massive maintenance room filled with pipes, knobs, humming machinery, and electrical gauges.

I barely take two breaths before a voice rings out.

"Well, isn't this an interesting development."

I freeze.

Agent Scarlett stands in the middle of the room. Around

her stand half a dozen Supers all dressed up in their LOS outfits. I swallow as I see Gwen's team. Steeple, Khevan, Terrell, and Laire.

Beside me, Gwen tenses.

"Gweneira," says Agent Scarlett, sounding calm. "You've broken into LOS headquarters, caused inexcusable property damage, and put the building on lockdown. I asked you to stay calm about this situation, yet you charge off on your own. Please explain yourself."

Gwen falters. An inkling of doubt crosses her face. Then she straightens up and takes a deep breath. Calm falls over her, the same confident calm that Agent Scarlett wears.

"No, Agent," she says firmly. "I believe it's you who has some explaining to do. Why is LOS holding an innocent citizen in its cells? What has Beata Bell done to deserve this injustice? I was told the Counter-League had taken Beata Bell hostage, yet I find her locked up in LOS's basement. Just what is going on here?"

"Beata Bell was caught fraternizing with a suspected senior member of the Counter-League."

"Beata would never do something so despicable!" snaps Gwen. For a second, fury slips through her mask. Her lips curl into a snarl, but almost before I can blink, she suppresses it. "And if that were true, suspicions are not enough grounds to detain a citizen of the city. I advise you to tell the truth, Agent."

Agent Scarlett's face goes dark. Her voice is low and dangerous when she speaks again. "Are you threatening me, Miss Kendricks?"

A pause.

"I suppose I am," answers Gwen, sounding equally dangerous. A series of gasps arise from her teammates.

"Gwen," pipes Khevan, "threatening an LOS Agent is a serious offense!"

"I don't like this any more than you," says Gwen. The doorframe shakes slightly. The landing shakes too. I glance at Gwen. Her fist is balled so tight a thin trickle of blood dribbles from her hand. Every time a drop hits the metal, vibrations slither up my knees.

"Your control is slipping, Miss Kendricks," says Agent Scarlett. "You're losing your touch. Control is the most important aspect of a Super's training."

Terrell and Steeple step in front of Agent Scarlett. Khevan bites his nails at her side. Laire backs off. She's their information specialist, a precog who can see "echoes" into the future. I wonder what she can see now and whether her step back means worse is yet to come.

I think of Charley.

Control.

Bad things happen to Supers who lose control. I think of the Payton incident and how scary Gwen is when she's angry.

"Lesson's over, Agent," says Gwen. "Now is the time for action. I ask you once more. Will you explain yourself?"

This time, it's Agent Scarlett who falters. Her confidence slips for a split second, and I see fear in her eyes. She moves a hand to her hip. "I believe there is nothing to explain," she says. "If you can't be reasoned with, you must be stopped."

I suck in a quick breath. Is there enough room for snipers in the LOS building? I scan the perimeter, but don't spot anything out of place. There's no extra room in the tangle of ducts, pipelines, and gauges.

Gwen snorts softly.

"So you sent my old teammates after me." She nods towards Steeple. "Hey, Steeps. You always wanted to be top dog, didn't you? Does it not bother you that LOS detained a twelve-year-old schoolgirl? Or is your head too full of ambition to care? You must have leapt so high at the opportunity to take me down."

Steeple blushes high and pink.

"I don't have to take this abuse from a traitor!" she spits.

"Is that what they're calling me now?" Gwen puffs out her chest. She's not as tall as Steeple, but she has an aura of power that dwarfs her teammates. "You don't want to fight me. Any of you."

"No, we don't." Terrell steps forward, hands out. He's a gentle-looking fellow with droopy eyes. "So everybody just settle down. We can end this peacefully. I'm sure you have your reasons, Gwen. Just tell LOS your side of the story, and no one needs to get hurt."

"That's sweet talk for letting them detain me," says Gwen. "I'm not stupid." She turns to Agent Scarlett, rage in her eyes. "You made a big mistake targeting my friend. I don't know the whole story, but I know enough. Kidnapping children is wrong, and under the LOS Code of Justice, all wrongdoers must be stopped."

Then several things happen at once. Gwen takes a step forward. Agent Scarlett leaps back. Her hand moves from her hip. She draws a gun from a hidden holster at her side. Gwen hisses and leaps to the side. Her hand flies out and brushes a nearby pipe.

There's a flash of blue. Steam pours into the room. It gushes over the tiles, spewing heat in all directions. Hitori grabs my shoulder and drags me backwards. I hear shouts of surprise and a firearm discharging as steam crowds the room, turning everything white.

Chapter 20

Retreat

"Gwen!" I scream. "Gwen!"

Arms wrap around my waist and drag me away. Steam brushes against my bare skin. It hurts, but it isn't enough to burn. The vapour makes it hard to see. In the mist, I can barely make out moving shapes and flashing lights. A sparking ball slams into the wall just metres from my head. It crackles. The smell of burning metal reaches my nose. The arm around me gives a tug, and I'm hauled into a hallway, away from the chaos and noise. The very walls shake.

"I can't just leave her!"

"She'll be fine!"

"No!" I pull at the arm. "Let me go!"

"It's too dangerous."

I kick and scratch. What sounds like an explosion rocks the halls. Steam billows into the halls. A stream of hot water trickles after us. Hitori carries me down the hallway and deposits me around a corner. The building rumbles. As soon as my feet touch the ground, I make a run back towards Gwen, but Hitori grabs my arm before I can get far.

"Don't be foolish! That's a Super battle—"

As though to emphasize his words, there's a roaring noise. The walls groan.

"You're not a Super, Beata. You'll be killed!"

"Gwen is in there!" My voice hiccups. My bangs stick to

my forehead, and I wipe them aside angrily. Everything is damp with steam. "She came to rescue me and now she's in trouble! What if she gets hurt? Or worse?"

I haven't even apologized to her.

"Gwen can handle herself." Hitori kneels to bring himself down to my level. Water seeps into his pants, but he ignores it. "You need to calm down. Just—just come with me, ok? Breathe. Follow my lead. Deep breaths."

I don't realize I am hyperventilating until oxygen floods my lungs. My ears ring and my head feels full of static. Sparks of light encroach on my vision. The hall spins, and Hitori keeps a hand under my elbow to keep me standing. I can barely hear his voice over the sounds of battle. He makes breathing motions with his free hand. *In, out. Good.* I take in air until the room stops reeling. Another crash, and the howl of someone echoes from afar. It's not Gwen.

Hitori motions for me to move. He doesn't let go of my arm as we navigate our way into the lower levels of the building. Hitori moves as though he has a mini-map in his head. We half run, half stumble until the sounds of battle fade into the distance. Only then does Hitori weaken his grip. I yank my arm away and rub it, glaring at him.

"Sorry," he says, sounding forlorn and uncomfortable, and suddenly, all I see is my homeroom teacher. "Sorry if I was rough, but we need to find an exit, and *fast*."

"I can't just run away," I say weakly. "I can't—"

My words choke away. I see an Agent in green swing around the corner. Driven by instinct, I dive past Hitori without a second thought and catch the Agent across the knees with a muffled *umph*. The impact drives the breath from my lungs, and we tumble to the ground. Strong fingers grab my hair and tug. I choke back a cry. Tears spring to my eyes. Through my blurred vision, I see the Agent yelling into a headset. I grab at it. I can't let him contact his friends!

Hitori's foot smashes into the Agent's arm. The Agent yowls in pain. The grip on my hair weakens, and I struggle out of it. Strands of my hair rip from my head. It feels like my entire scalp is coming off. I roll away and cough. Drops of blood land on the floor. My nose. I must have smashed it when I tackled the Agent. Behind me, Hitori locks the Agent in a sleeper hold until he goes limp.

Then he hurries to my side.

I wave my free hand. The other is pressed to my nose. *I'm ok.*

"That was quick thinking, Miss Bell. You saved us both there."

A gun dangles from his hand. I glance at the unconscious Agent with cold horror. Would he have shot us? Hitori checks the gun with a look of disgust. He unlocks the cartridge and lets the bullets slide to the ground. They scatter at his feet.

"Waid!" I gasp through my bloodied nose. "Dat can come in handy!"

"This is a potentially lethal weapon, Miss Bell."

So were you, once, I think, but I let it slide.

I hear footsteps and glance at Hitori in panic. His face is grim. It sounds like five or six people. I wipe the blood from my face and pinch my nose. My mouth tastes like iron.

"Wud do 'e do?" I ask.

A Super fight raging in the back. Agents and security personnel approaching from the front. Talk about being stuck between a rock and a hard place. Hitori shakes his head.

"Prepare for a fight, Miss Bell. We at least have surprise on our side."

I struggle to my feet and fall into a fighter's stance, drawing from kung-fu movies and video games. I once attended a self-defence class in elementary school where they taught us how to get away from would-be attackers. I hope it's enough. The footsteps draw closer. I can hear shouting too.

Then—

"*Psst*, over here!"

I turn and find myself looking at a familiar pair of round glasses.

Nuha is suddenly standing in the hallway, a thin screwdriver tucked behind her ear. She clutches a vent cover in her hands. Her eyes are so wide they're almost circles.

"Nuha?" I gasp.

"Miss Bahar?" Hitori gasps, just as surprised.

"*Hurry!*" She bobs her head frantically and points at an open vent near the ceiling. Footsteps echo relentlessly.

I snap out of my daze.

"How did you get in here?" I ask Nuha as Hitori gives me a boost from below. I make a few failed grabs at the opening before Hitori gives an extra hard shove from below, almost throwing me in. I land awkwardly, nearly popping my shoulders out of their sockets. Emergency situations require emergency force. I slide into the vent with a dreadful *clang*. The darkness is claustrophobic, but it's a better than being in the open, waiting for Agents to jump us. Hitori scrambles in, and helps pull Nuha up.

Every sound we make in the vent is amplified. Nuha pulls the grate back and screws it in deftly. She crawls backwards, shoving all of us further into the darkness. Then she makes a shushing motion. We all drop low and hold our breath. I wipe my nose discreetly, and my fingers come away wet. I'm still bleeding.

Security officers flood the hall. Through the vent, I see the tops of their heads bob as they pass by. There's a shout as they find the unconscious Agent, then increased sounds of shuffling as they check his vital signs.

Suddenly, there's a *whir*, and the ventilation shaft vibrates to life. Air rushes from the back and blasts past us. A layer of dust crests over us as the AC kicks in. My hair tickles my cheeks and forehead. A puff of dust flies into my mouth. I can't help it. There's no time to suppress it.

I sneeze.

Nuha and Hitori stare at me, eyes wide. I hold my mouth, heart thundering. Security pauses outside. A gruff voice speaks.

"Did you hear something?"

"I think I did."

"Spread out!"

I almost whimper. I've done it now. I've given us away. There's no way Nuha and Hitori and I can take on armed security, especially not while crammed in a dusty vent. A forehead approaches, and I brace myself.

Then a shattering rumble shakes the ducts. Shouts and swears sound in the hallway. An energy ball flies through, lighting up the walls. The security officers leap out of the way. The Super battle has caught up with us.

"Retreat!" one yells as the air sizzles. Another energy ball crashes through the hall, burning the ceiling. Lights flicker madly. The officers beat a hasty retreat. I hear something being dragged along the ground. The unconscious Agent.

Nuha gives me an urgent nudge with her toe. I start crawling down the shaft, my sweaty palms picking up dust. It's like sliding down a throat. I imagine huge fans waiting for me, unseen, big blades that could slice off my foot, or worse. The cold wind brushes against me. Goosebumps rise on my arms.

"They almost had us there," hisses Nuha. "Lucky break."

It's strenuous work, squirming our way through the vents, pausing every time one of us smacks an elbow or lands a little too hard. Perspiration gathers on my forehead. I have to stop twice to muffle coughing fits. We hit an intersection.

"Left," says Nuha.

I take the left.

Tension is high. I imagine energy beams or fireballs busting through the metal. Surely, everyone is looking for us now. I wonder how deep Agent Scarlett's influence stretches, whether all of LOS has her mindset, or whether it's a personal philosophy.

We crawl for what seems like hours. Finally, Nuha calls for us to stop. She squeezes past Hitori and me, and towards a grille. I peek over. We're in the ceiling of what looks like a warehouse. There are at least ten metres of open air between us and the floor. A new wave of sweat breaks over me. Nuha makes quick work of the screws and tugs the grille out with a small *umph*. She shoves it away, sticks her head out, and whistles, short and quick.

A shape flies towards us. I blink, mistrusting my eyes.

"*Dieter?*"

"Hey, Bell," he says. He tries to look nonchalant but fails horribly. His eyes dart every which way, and his face is damp with sweat. He stretches out his arms, and Nuha jumps into them without a pause. He grunts and floats her down, then shoots back up and looks at me expectantly.

I stare at him.

He stares back, two spots of pink on his cheeks. "Well? Hurry up!"

I grab his hands. He grunts again as he lifts me—I'm heavier than Nuha—and flies me down as well. The open space is both a relief and a burden. After the cramped vent, it feels like a breath of fresh air, but I am also on high alert for more Agents. As soon as my feet touch the ground, I dart towards the shadows. Only then do I allow myself to examine my surroundings.

We're in a hangar. It's about the size of a football field and more than three stories tall. Like our prison cell, the ground is smooth metal. There are no windows and, as far as I can see, no doors either. In the middle stands what appears to be a large cannon. Along the walls—

If I had doubts about whose story is true, what I see along the walls ends them.

There are two rows of robot octopods, slumped against the walls, legs tucked under them as though sleeping. I count at least two dozen of them. In the dim light, they shine like bowling balls. Up close, I can see that each one has a hatch on its underbelly. It must open up for a driver. Right at the end, there are three empty spots—the three robots used in attacks against the city.

False attacks, my mind reminds me. *Attention grabs.*

I swallow hard.

How many people were injured in the attacks? How many homes and offices destroyed? All for entertainment?

Not as many as there could have been, my traitorous mind reasons. Had the Counter-League been real, the robot octopods would have caused much more damage. I shake away my cynical thoughts. If LOS hadn't launched the robots at all, no one would have been hurt. *And that's a fact*, I think sternly. All other thoughts fade reluctantly into the background.

Dieter lands Hitori, who claps him heartily on the back. Dieter almost collapses to the floor on contact, huffing like a marathon runner. Hitori brushes the dust off his head and shoulders. "Well done, Mr. Jaeger!"

"The ventilation shafts lead almost everywhere," Nuha says quietly once we've calmed our pounding hearts. "They won't be expecting you two to pop out in the hangars. This is a hidden room. I'm not even sure if most of the LOS employees know about this place. We should be relatively safe here."

"I'm glad to see you, Nu," I say. I can't help it. I hug her. She squeaks on impact. It feels good to be with someone familiar and comforting, even if the situation is less than perfect. "And I'm glad you're a passive Super. I mean it."

"We can't relax yet," warns Nuha. She pulls out her phone, the beta Super Tracker app running. My chest swells with pride.

"When you said you snuck into LOS headquarters, I didn't think you crawled its underbelly too," I say, impressed. Nuha actually blushes a little. I look at her in a new light. Quiet, serious Nuha. Who would have thought she was a daredevil?

"To be honest, I wasn't a hundred percent sure it would work." Nuha becomes solemn again. "I was paranoid there would be sensors, or a Super who could see through my passive skill. But so far, so good."

Hitori lays a hand against a robot's side, expression stern. "Now all that remains is to is escape."

"With Gwen tearing up the corridors, we're going to need to break out on our own." Nuha furrows her brows in worry. "I told her *not* to charge off on her own, but she's so pig-headed sometimes." She glances at me. "No offense, Beata. I know you can get pretty defensive about her."

"Gwen can be pretty persistent," I admit with a hitch of my breath. In our escape from the Agents, I had almost forgotten about Gwen. Guilt settles in my gut like a lead ball.

"This was supposed to be an extraction mission, but I don't think Gwen knows how to do discreet," continues Nuha. "Our original plan was to have her dissolve the hatch there." She points at the area above the cannon. If I squint, I can see a long rectangular entrance. "And have Dieter fly us all out. Now we need another plan. Any ideas? Dieter? Hitori?"

I stare at the hatch. "That hatch can still open, can't it?"

"Duh," gasps Dieter, still out of breath.

I roll my eyes. Some people never change.

"So we just need to figure out how to open it." My eyes fall back on the robot octopods. I remember the way they flew, the way they whistled through the air before slamming into the ground. "When the robots attack the city, I think they're shot out of the cannon." I point towards the massive instrument. "Except I don't see a control panel anywhere. I would say the cannon is controlled remotely, but I don't see a control room either. So I think it's operated from within the robot octopods themselves. It would have to be. Otherwise, how do the robots get out?"

"So the only way to get out is to get *into* one of those things?" Dieter asks, aghast.

"They're locked," says Nuha. "We tried earlier. There's a slit on the side that acts as a card reader, but we'll need either official LOS identification or some sort of key."

I bite my lip. So close, yet so far.

"Maybe you should check it again," says Hitori.

Nuha turns to him. "With all due respect, Hitori, I was very thorough—"

There's a jingle.

Hitori dangles a set of keys from his finger. I recognize the face of the LOS Agent I tackled in the hallway on the ID card. *Agent Olive*, the card says, complete with barcode and signature. Hitori's face is a mask of pure innocence.

"Would these help?"

I can't help but grin.

Chapter 21

Super Wild Ride

After resisting the urge to lock Hitori in a tight hug, I take the keys almost in reverence.

"I thought it prudent to liberate them from their original owner," says Hitori with the slightest smile.

"Hitori, you wonderful criminal," I breath, half-awed, half-tickled.

"I thought they could unlock some doors for us. I didn't think we'd be stealing a robot."

I shake with nervous energy. The keys quiver in my hand. I isolate the Agent's ID card, perch on one of the inert legs of a robot octopod, and swallow hard. One chance. I'm sure I'll trigger more alarms if I get it wrong. There's no way they would allow just any regular joe into one of these machines. Up close, the metal radiates cold, all dark and still. I'm almost afraid to touch it.

I swipe the ID card real quick. In and out. There's a light buzzing noise, then silence.

"Did it work?" squeaks Nuha, hands on her mouth.

"I don't know," I say, turning the card over in my hand. "Maybe I have to insert it the other way—"

TSZZZ—

I nearly fall off my perch as the robot octopod expels a breath of gas and the door slowly opens like the maw of a giant animal. On the inside, the robot octopod is lush and lit with soothing blue lights. The controls are sleek and modern. LED screens flicker to life. I can see touch controls for many of the functions. There is one seat inside, and it's lined with cushy padding, like a race car. My mouth falls open in awe.

"Welcome, Agent Olive," purrs a soothing, female voice.

It's a glorious machine. Nuha's expression mirrors mine. We glance at each other, faces filled with hunger. Talk about a technological wonder! I know she's itching to examine one of these machines. It's too bad we're on the run.

I rip my gaze from the robot's interior and glance back at Hitori and Dieter. "Looks like a tight squeeze. Who wants to drive?"

Hitori sighs. "Well, I *am* the only one with a license."

He puts a hand on Dieter's shoulder.

"As soon as the hatch opens, fly the girls out of here. Get as far away as you can and hide out somewhere until the heat cools." He meets Dieter's eye. "Can I trust you with that?"

Dieter bites his lip. "I-I'm not sure I can fly both of them out before the door closes. I mean, I only got into LOS this year. I'm not really that good at flying yet."

"He's right," I interject. "He's not that good."

Hitori looks grave. "We can't risk leaving anyone behind."

"We're not sure how quick the hatch will close," I retort. "What if one of us gets trapped inside? That's even worse."

"Hmm, I hadn't considered that. Good point, Miss Bell."

"I'll go with you," I volunteer suddenly. "Dieter can get Nuha out of here. She's lighter and easier to carry."

Hitori turns towards me. His eyes are kind. "Miss Bell, you realize that our chances of escaping, even in a weapon like this, are very slim. You're young. You have a bright future. You shouldn't dig yourself any deeper than you already are. If we're caught—"

"How heroic of you," I say with a scowl. "Sacrificing yourself to save the children. You know, I've always found that attitude a little annoying." I cross my arms and stare at him resolutely. "We're in this together, so we should get out of it together. Plus, LOS already knows we're co-conspirators since we escaped together. If I go with you—if I'm caught with you—Dieter and Nuha can still escape blame-free. No one will ever know they had anything to do with our jail-break."

"Nevertheless, I can't—"

"This is the best chance for all of us to escape. We can't all fit in there, and Dieter can't carry both me and Nu at once. If that hatch closes before we can all escape, it's over for whoever's stuck inside. It's better we split two-two. You know it." I breathe deeply. "It's not a matter of pride. It's statistics."

I know I've won by the way Hitori's mouth turns downwards.

"I've always hated numbers," he admits. "It's why I became a history teacher and not a math teacher. What are numbers anyway? Sometimes, what's right isn't what's optimal. I suppose I'm just not as logical as some folks." He gives a jerk of his head. "All right, then. Come on."

I can't help but grin as I scramble into the heart of the robot octopod, even though the idea of being shot through a cannon makes my blood run cold. *Think of it as an amusement park ride*, I tell myself. People have survived robot octopod launches before, so why shouldn't I?

It's a tight squeeze with two people. With just enough room for one, I end up sitting on Hitori's legs.

"Sorry," I mutter. It's weird being so close to your teacher.

Even weirder being so close to a once hero. I hope I'm not cutting off blood flow to his feet.

"Don't worry, you're not heavy." He straps the seat belt around both of us.

I look towards Nuha and Dieter and give what I hope is a cheerful salute. "See you both on the outside."

"Meet up at Ling's place," says Nuha. "We'll be waiting."

Dieter imitates a military salute. Then the door slides closed, and we're back in the darkness with only buttons and LED lights to keep us company.

"I'm sure there's a way to get an outside view," says Hitori, shifting. I hear him searching for buttons and latches.

"Computer," I say. "External view."

I don't expect it to work, but it does. I watch in wonder as screens flicker around me, reflecting the hangar and its fleet of robot octopods. My breath catches in my throat. This is serious, voice-control technology. I try to imagine the coding that goes into something so complex. It must be incredible. Below us, Nuha and Dieter back away as the robot hums to life.

Hitori grunts. "Good job, Miss Bell. Let's see how easily this lump of metal moves. Computer, start engines, please."

"Engaging," says the computer, monotone.

A thrum ripples through the robot as its eight legs uncurl. Even though I'm scared, I still feel a flash of delight. LED screens blink to life beside Hitori's hands. He places his fingers on them tentatively. The robot rises to its feet, trembling, awaiting instruction. Hitori moves his hands forward. The robot takes one step forward. He moves his hands in opposite directions. The robot begins to turn.

"Well, it doesn't seem too hard," Hitori says lightly. A

nervous laugh hangs off his words. His brows furrow as he directs the robot towards the cannon. The octopod takes a few lumbering steps forward, then jerks to a stop.

"My bad," breathes Hitori. "I was never good at this motor control thing. That was one perk of being a telekinetic. No need to move anything physically." He tries again, pushing his fingers forward on the screens.

The robot leaps towards the cannon. I bash the back of my head against Hitori's chin. Stars explode in my vision.

"*Sonuva*—" yelps Hitori.

"Sorry!" My head throbs. "Ow! Sorry!"

"Never mind. It's not your fault." Hitori touches the screens again, lighter this time. He twists the robot around and pushes forward. The octopod takes one step forward, then, after a few seconds, another one. It's excruciatingly slow. "Computer, engage—stabilizers?"

"Unrecognized command."

"Oh. Well, it was worth a try. I guess we continue."

We lumber towards the cannon—and overshoot it. We turn around and try again—and overshoot it. The screen shows Nuha and Dieter, looking befuddled at our lack of progress. I feel Hitori's annoyance growing as time goes by. He begins to mutter under his breath. Something about darn newfangled contraptions and unfathomable technological advances. Despite myself, I find myself captivated. The touch screens. The holographic images. It's like being in a sci-fi spaceship. If the situation weren't so tense, I would be enjoying myself. The robot octopod makes another jerky turn, and I almost bite my tongue. The controllers remind me of the new PlayStation 7x Pro's immersive 360-degree play system.

Like the one at Nuha's place.

"Hitori, could I have a try at the controls?" I ask after the third pass by. I hear and feel Hitori sigh.

"It's usually against my policy to let a twelve-year-old take the wheel, but desperate times call for desperate measures. Go ahead. Give it a whirl."

I take the screens and relax. Right hand forward, left hand back. Left turn. I turn the robot around until it's facing the cannon. I slide my fingers forward, lightly, as though flipping pages on an eReader. The robot glides toward, its legs shuffling. I apply more pressure to the front of the screens, and the robot moves faster. In moments, I have the robot pointed at the cannon.

"It's just like a video game," I mutter to myself. I give the screens a tap. The robot jerks up in a smooth leap. It nestles into the open cannon and slides into its shaft. Darkness engulfs us once more. My blood quickens.

"Good job!" breathes Hitori. "I guess it serves me right for being technologically challenged."

"Now what?" I ask. He hasn't tried to take the controls back.

"Let's get out of here."

"Where?"

"I'll leave that to you," says Hitori, "but be warned, as soon as we break free, we'll be announcing our location to every Agent in LOS. They'll send people after us. Supers too. The further away we get, the safer we'll be."

I imagine being assaulted by a dozen Super teams. If any of them are even half as powerful as Gwen—I shudder.

"Computer, prepare to launch," I command. The screen flickers. Various dots appear, marking parks, abandoned lots, dumps, and construction sites, all within a forty kilometres of LOS headquarters. The cannon's limit.

"Enter landing coordinates," prompts the computer. I can feel the machine adjusting around us, readying for launch, humming.

"Well, that would explain why robot octopod attacks only seemed to happen close to the lakeshore and never in the suburbs," says Hitori.

I enter a postal code. My own. Then I erase it. I don't want to crash into my own backyard. I don't trust the robot enough not to do serious damage. I lick my lips and type in another code. Nuha's. Her yard is large enough to allow for a safe landing, but landing there would cause lots of property damage. Their beautiful lawns would be ruined. It would bring her family into the fray. No. I erase her code. I flip through the prelisted choices. I need a public area. An open area.

"Queen's Park," I say. "Can we land there safely?"

"Should be a big enough space," says Hitori with a slight hitch to his voice. I glance up and realize he's as nervous as I am about being shot out of a cannon. I always thought Supers were fearless, but I suppose being shot out of a cannon isn't an everyday experience, even for a Super. "Right into the heart of government. That should give the media bloodhounds something juicy to chew on."

I punch it in.

"Landing site selected: Queen's Park," chimes the computer. Outside, the hatch above us begins to slide open, revealing a starry night sky. It takes about thirty seconds to fully open, which means it takes about the same amount of time to close. I hope it's enough time for Dieter and Nuha to escape.

Inside the robot, the screens flicker green. A big holographic button appears on the screen in front of me. I stare at it. LAUNCH, it says in bold letters. I pause. The butterflies in my stomach stir up a frenzy. My blood rushes through my ears, loud, like waves crashing against shore. My hand shakes. The robot octopod trembles around me as though in anticipation. My breathing is the loudest sound in the capsule.

"Are you ready?" I ask Hitori, stalling.

Instead of answering, he punches the launch button.

It feels like someone's stomped on my chest. We shoot from the dark pipe so quickly we're in the air before I can scream. The LOS building tumbles away, and the night sky opens up before us. I find myself facing the moon, large, semi-shaded, and the colour of bleached copper. Sparse clouds smear across the sky, bronzed by light pollution. We sail through the air, arcing over Lake Ontario, over the docks of Harbourfront, over the criss-crossed streets of downtown Toronto. For a moment, I'm mesmerized by the immensity and beauty of the nightscape, all the tall office buildings, the coloured lights, and the CN Tower rushing past us, a rod of green-red LEDs. I see Nathan Phillips Square zip beneath us. From above, Toronto City Hall looks like an eye gazing into the sky.

Then we begin to descend. The landscape rushes up to meet us. An uncomfortable thought occurs to me.

"How do we land this thing?" I break into a cold sweat.

"Um," says Hitori.

We pick up speed, and my stomach does a backflip. *No, no, nooooo!*

Impact in ten, counts the computer.

"Computer!" I shriek. "Auto-land!"

"Unrecognized command."

"Then engage landing *gear*!"

"Landing sequence initialized. Warning: Inadequate time to deploy. Manual override?"

"Yes!" Hitori and I yell simultaneously.

"Authorization requ—"

I swipe Agent Olive's card.

The robot shifts around us. I squeeze my eyes shut and brace myself. I pray it's not too late, that we don't crash and break up.

"Impact in five."

Our descent accelerates. The robot continues to shift. My stomach drops out from under me. I hold my breath, but can't help but make a whimpering noise anyway.

"Impact in three. Two. One."

We slam into the ground so hard I can feel trees snapping and dirt rippling around us. The impact shakes me to the bone. For a second, I can't breathe. I'm thrown to and fro. Only the seat belt stops me from being knocked unconscious. My teeth clatter, and I clench my jaw to stop from biting my tongue. I'm disoriented. I feel like a huge bruise. I gasp, hugging my limbs close. The entire robot vibrates as we slide to a stop.

Then—

Silence.

I lift my hand to my head, wriggle my fingers and toes. Still there. Still responsive. Still in one piece. I open my eyes to the glow of the computer's screens. The input signal blinks back at me, waiting. I groan. We're sideways, tilted at a forty-five degree angle. I can see broken boughs all around us.

"Everything ok?" asks Hitori, sounding just as rough.

"I'm good, I think."

"Good."

I wave at the screen to bring back the robot's controls. With a few laboured movements, I jerk the robot back onto its feet. Everything rights itself. I raise my palm to my forehead. My brain feels scrambled.

Free, it whispers. We've done the impossible. We escaped from LOS headquarters. I hope Dieter and Nuha are ok. I wonder if they got out safely too. *You stole a robot octopod.* Despite myself, I giggle. I'm a criminal now. A real criminal.

"Computer," I say in a spurt of curiosity. "Show networks."

"WIFI located." A list of networks appears onscreen. I connect to the closest unprotected one. Within seconds, I bring the holographic keyboard back onscreen and access Tweeter. I've lost two full days, locked in a cell. With so little access to the online world, I feel years behind. The incident at LOS headlines every major news outlet. Social media has whipped itself up into a flurry.

BREAKING NEWS: Gweneira Kendricks indoctrinated by the Counter-League? #CBC

LIVE: Cameras outside LOS HQ! Chaos inside the basement? Tune in for play-by-play updates! #CP24 #GwenKendricks

Code RED at LOS HQ! #GwenKendricks vs the world! Who will be the victor?! #PlaceYourBets #BetsBetsBets

Agent Scarlett to make a statement on Gweneira Kendricks's shocking defection! Click Here to tune in. #TheSun

I play the clip. "We have her corralled in the basement," says Agent Scarlett's voice. "LOS headquarters is built from concrete and steel. As long as she is trapped under concrete, we will restrain her eventually. Gweneira Kendricks is a strong metal manipulator, but she's no Charley Beamsman."

A clamour of voices.

"No, I do not know why she chose this time to defect. I want answers as much as you. I believe she may be unstable, yes."

The personal tweets are not much better. The crowd is divided between disbelief and condemnation. The elation of surviving our descent disappears. I bristle at the users calling Gwen a traitor and a coward. After years of loving her, how could they turn their backs on her so quickly?

BREAKING NEWS: Mysterious object seen flying over Toronto! Impact at Queen's Park! #CTV #RobotOctopod4

Hitori shifts in the seat and fumbles with our seat belt. It takes him two tries to get it undone. "That's our cue to vamoose. If we're careful, we can sneak out of here and take cover before any of the authorities arrive," he says. "Let's head for the trees. Once a crowd forms, we can slip into it unnoticed."

I don't take my hands off the screens. I stare at the blinking input signal in the robot octopod's command board. *Blink, blink, blink.*

I make a decision.

"I've done discreet all my life," I say, feeling a rush of energy. "Maybe it's time to do something bold."

I twist the controls. The robot stands, crushing a park bench in the process. It rears towards the sky. An eerie calm falls over me. This is right. This is what I have to do.

"Miss Bell?" asks Hitori, brow furrowed.

"Sorry about this," I say. "You're a great teacher, Mr. Uzune, and it was really nice meeting you, Hitori. I always admired you, you know."

I punch in a command. The door of the robot octopod opens, and a breath of cool autumn air floods the pod. I give Hitori a slight shove. He's balanced so precariously that he tumbles out without much fanfare. I punch in another command. Confusion flickers through Hitori's eyes as the door shuts in his face.

With the pod emptied, I settle back into the commander's seat and buckle myself in. I bring up the control screens and make myself comfortable.

Wait for me, Gwen.

I turn the robot back towards LOS headquarters.

Part 4

Chapter 22

Hurry

This is right.

This is what I can do.

My mind is abuzz. I can't think properly. I am breaking almost every major bylaw in Toronto. I have stolen a weapon. I have destroyed property. I am defying Toronto's greatest organization of justice and righteousness. The charges can't get much worse, unless I murder someone. *The night is young yet*, I think grimly. Plenty of time to add to my roster.

Buildings and trees blur past as I push the robot down Yonge Street, Toronto's longest road. Citizens leap out of the way, limbs flailing. I feel mild regret as they pump their tiny legs, faces white, but the feeling doesn't last. The real world seems distant when you're nestled in a giant robot. The machine is faster than I expected. I keep pressure on the controls. It scuttles down the street, legs a blur.

Just like playing CrashDasher.

Except this isn't a simulation.

I'm almost at the lake when I see the first Supers. A flying formation, up above, dressed in full Super gear. Their uniforms sparkle in the starlight.

I'm ready. I've seen enough sci-fi movies to know how this works, and if the robot octopod really is built like a PlayStation system—easy to use and easy to understand—then I've been training to drive one all my life.

"Computer!" I yell. "List weaponry!"

The screen flickers. A list of options appears before me. I scan them quickly. None are lethal. I guess LOS Agents didn't want their Supers actually getting killed. After all, they just want a good show. I see explosives, flares, and plasma shots.

"Computer, engage plasma guns."

"Engaging."

I hear a *whirr* and *click*. The Super formation breaks. Six flying Supers shoot towards me. I wonder what they're going to do. Fly me into surrender? Yeah, right.

I giggle to myself again and wonder what's wrong with me. It must be the tension. I'm not usually this reckless.

A new screen appears. I spin the robot around and veer off course just as a bolt of lightning streaks towards me. *Oh.* I brush my hands onto the new screen. Crosshairs appear in my vision. I rotate the plasma gun until it is aimed in the general direction of the Supers.

"Fire!"

The robot recoils slightly as a ball of plasma explodes from its system.

"Plasma guns discharged. Energy levels at ninety percent."

So plasma guns eat a lot of power. Of course they do. It makes sense. The robot octopods aren't meant to last long just in case unsavoury individuals steal them. *Like me.* I grit my teeth and spin the robot back towards LOS headquarters.

The entire building is swathed in red. Its floodlights, which usually light the sky with streaks of soft white, are bloody crimson. They swirl, more frantic than usual, drawing desperate figure eights across the heavens. I guide the robot towards the lake and perch at the edge of the bridge. From within the robot octopod, the LOS bridge seems tiny and fragile. I put a leg on it tentatively.

More lightning bolts.

My vision flashes white for a second as they strike the robot. The *BOOM* is almost enough to deafen me. The robot gives a jerk. I let out a little shriek before I can control myself.

"Experiencing electrical surge," offers the computer, as the lights flicker around me. "Stabilizing power in three…two…one."

"Distract them with flares!"

"Command not recogniz—"

"*Engage* flares, then!"

"Engaging flares."

"Putt, putt, putt," sound the flares. I watch them streak into the distance and close my eyes as they explode. The night sky erupts in a conflagration of white, yellow, and green. I see one flying Super drop out of the sky, surprised by the fireworks. I test the bridge once more, lean the robot's weight onto it. The concrete cracks. I bite my cheek. *Ok*, I tell myself. *Do it fast*. Like ripping off a bandage.

I slam both hands down. The robot octopod rushes forward. I feel—rather than see—the bridge crumbling under its feet. Waves ripple across the lake as concrete tumbles into the water. I bite my lip so hard it hurts. I don't let up.

The robot octopod takes another lightning hit. I yelp and blink the afterglow from my eyes but don't let up. Within a minute, I'm at LOS headquarters again.

If the robot octopod can handle a hard landing *and* lightning impacts, I tell myself, it will be fine. LOS headquarters looms above like a silent, watchman. Its imposing form glows. I don't let up.

The walls grow close. I am breathing so hard the air rushing into my lungs burns past my nose and throat, but I'm determined.

"Impact in three," warns the computer.

Still, I don't let up.

I scream as the robot octopod slams into the wall. Metal thunders into concrete, and I'm thrown back in my seat. The wall cracks upon impact. A shower of glass crashes over the robot octopod. I taste blood. I've bitten something—a cheek, or lip, or knocked out a tooth. I'm not sure, and there's too much adrenaline rushing through my veins for me to stop.

"Computer!" I shout. "Engage plasma guns!"

I aim the guns at the wall and unload all the robot's remaining energy into it. I get only three shots in, but it's enough. The first two shots chew into the building itself. The third shot sails through the expensive LOS lobby, burning desks and plants. The room is already evacuated. Only red lights occupy the space, throbbing like a pulsar.

My breath escapes in shaky huffs. I can't believe what I just did. I need to check the news one more time. "Computer," I gasp, "show networks. Show Tweeter."

LIVE: Fourth robot octopod slams into LOS HQ! Emergency in the city! #CP24

Omg, what's happening in our city? #Scared #GwenKendricks #RoboOcto4

SHOULD WE EVACUATE THE CITY? #CodeRed

Dun worry, guys, LOS'll protect us. Believe in LOS. #BelieveinLOS

I use the last bit of the robot octopod's electricity to open the doors and slip out. I'm so shaken I sink to my knees. *Come on, Beata, get up, get up, GET UP*. I force my legs to work and stumble for the empty lobby, where I duck behind the nearest couch. It's a weak shield compared to the metal body of the robot octopod, but it offers me some psychological quiet. I watch as the flying Supers land all around, moving cautiously. They have their hands out as though approaching a volatile animal. As they're distracted, I dash for the receptionist's desk. With a few quick commands, I access the directory and a rough map of LOS headquarters.

There's a quiet rumble. The fight below. I pray Gwen is still ok.

Keeping quiet, I swipe Agent Olive's card in the administrator's computer. The Supers outside are still circling the prone robot. One kicks its hull, then howls and clutches his foot.

The computer powers up.

WARNING, say large white letters on a red screen. *CODE RED IN PROGRESS. MAKE YOUR WAY TO THE CLOSEST EVACUATION SHUTTLE*. A map of the floor appears. A white symbol in the shape of a bus blinks along the perimeter.

I brush past the warning, pull up a list of programs, and access the building's LiveMaps system. It monitors the building room-by-room, shows where all the doors are, which rooms are locked, and which functions, like lights, ventilation, and piping, are in need of repair. I check the rooms for signs of damage.

Outside, the Supers peek into the robot octopod's interior. Finding it empty, they float further up, scanning the nearby grounds for an escapee. I wait until they're out of sight before I cycle through the maps.

LOS is a massive compound with multiple buildings and training fields. I spot the swath of destruction Gwen made on her way to rescue me, a beeline across LOS's basement rooms like an unstoppable war machine. I can tell by the number of red marks on the map where walls have been breached. Several appear pierced straight through. Gwen must have melted through no fewer than twenty rooms to get me out. I feel a swell of emotion. Not jealousy this time. Gratitude.

The information is incredible. My mind swells with pictures and data. I slow down, and remind myself that digesting data takes time. I breathe.

One...two...three...

The Supers outside float elsewhere. Still, I crouch behind the terminal, shivering.

If I layer the information carefully—which pipes are broken, which lights have gone out, which walls have been breached—I can recreate the battle taking place in LOS. I can see it flow. As I watch, more pipes go down, almost directly underneath the lobby. I shiver. The Super fight is right under me.

As though to prove it, the floor trembles. Agent Scarlett is right. Gwen can melt through metal, but thick layers of concrete separate the floors. The best she can do is collapse them—if she can get at the I-beams buried within.

I know what I have to do.

My fingers fly across the keyboard. I pull up the control panel, and search the system's hidden folders.

"Administrative rights required," says the computer.

I swipe Agent Olive's card. My eyes fly through the lists that scroll across the screen.

I find the program controlling the doors. With the building

on lockdown, only a select few are allowed to open. Gwen may not be able to bust through concrete, I think, but I can create some exits. I manually begin opening doors, swiping Agent Olive's card each time.

The flying Supers pass by again, and I dive under the desk as a precaution, but they don't notice me. I can hear their voices, loudly wondering what they're supposed to do now that the robot octopod is down. One wonders if they'll get points for completing their mission. Their body language is unassuming, as though it's a regular night and they're on a regular patrol.

A glimmer catches my eye. A headset.

I grab it, turn it on, and slip it over my head. A crackle of static greets me.

I poke my head out from under the table to check on the Supers. Aimless now, they drift over Lake Ontario, unsure of what to do. *Leave*, I think. *Go on, go away.* I wait, heart in my mouth, until their leader motions to the distance, and they zoom away over the water.

Free to complete my plan, I check that all the doors are unlocked. LiveMaps tells me the lights have gone out in yet another room in the basement. I give myself a moment to psych up. There's no telling who's in the building, and making an announcement is like drawing a giant target on my head. When I feel ready, I press the intercom button.

"Gwen, it's me. It's Bea. You need to listen to me. You need to trust me. You need to fly right. Take the right door." My voice booms back at me, relayed through the PA system. I swallow hard. There's no way to be discreet now. It's only a matter of time before someone discovers me.

I scan LiveMaps as I speak to determine the quickest escape route. There's no telling whether Gwen hears me over the sounds of her battle.

"I've unlocked the door. You have to escape! Go right!"

There's an excruciatingly long wait.

Then the LiveMaps show damage to the room to the right. I almost pump my fist into the air. Glee courses through me. *She hears.*

I shout over the intercom, leaping with excitement. I've never felt so energized. My fingers tremble. My entire body seems to vibrate.

"Go right again! Take the stairs! Go left! *No*, go *left*. Good, now straight ahead. That's right, fly straight ahead."

My heart thunders.

We're a team.

It's what I always wanted.

But I never imagined it would be like this.

"Keep going! See the hatch? Go through it! It'll take you to some more stairs. Fly up! That's right, up!"

There's a mighty crash. I dive under the desk once more. A door skids across the room, screeching against the floor. The desk shakes loose pens, and papers rain to the ground. Overhead, five dark shapes zoom into the lobby. One has hair so golden it could have been woven from sunlight. A cloud of metal chases after her, clinging to her arms and fingers, half-formed chains and swords.

"Gwen!" I scream.

I don't think she hears me. She swings around to face her pursuers. None are members of her team. All are flying. I wonder, briefly, whether Steeple, Terrell, Khevan, and Laire are still alive.

"Ceiling! Look to the ceiling!" I scream. I order LiveMaps

to open the sunroof. Cold night air spirals in.

Gwen slams a metal sheet into one of her pursuers, flinging him into the wall like a wet rag. Her head swivels, and she spots the opening in the ceiling. She shoots straight through it so fast,she's almost a blur. As she breaks free of the LOS building, my hopes soar with her. I watch her disappear into the distance, her three pursuers lagging behind. As she flies, other flying Supers join in the chase. They become dots in the distance before fading into the night.

The LOS building is silent once more, except for the incessant groan of the alarms. I stand behind the receptionist's desk, panting. I can hear echoes of my shouts reverberating in my skull, but I'm lightheaded, and overjoyed, like I might explode.

I force myself to calm down. This is no time to celebrate. Although no longer trapped, Gwen's still in trouble. She'll have a greater fighting chance in the open sky than caged in a basement, but she's not out of danger yet.

Neither am I.

I have to get out of here.

I scamper over to the fallen Super and check his vitals. He's ok, even though he has an ugly gash across his forehead. I fold him up into a more comfortable position against the wall. He doesn't look any older than me, and I feel a little sorry for him.

Evacuation shuttles.

My job here is done.

"Sorry, guy," I mutter at the unconscious Super. Then I dash for the buses and pray they're still running.

I sprint across LOS's well-groomed lawn. The green grass looks black in the dark. The LOS building pulsates red in the background, like an angry star. It's cold at night. My breath escapes in puffs of white.

I run until I see a group of people gathered by a metal wall, huddled together. They're LOS employees, dressed in uniforms and suits, clearly shaken. Nearby, a LOS shuttle bus idles. I spot the receptionist from the day I visited with Alexander's photo. I want to feel amusement at his discomfort, but I'm too tired to summon up any emotion stronger than mild dislike.

"Hey!"

I snap out of my daze, but I've already been spotted. I take a step back as one of the employees rushes towards me.

"Little girl, did you miss the civilian shuttle?" the woman asks, wringing her hands. Her fingers are bloodless with cold. "They left over an hour ago! Quick, get out of the open. Come here. There are Supers about. You're lucky. This is one of the last shuttles off the island, but someone's collapsed the bridge to the mainland, so we're stuck waiting. LOS is sending a ferry now. Come under the building so you get some protection. There might be another robot octopod somewhere!"

She doesn't know about the conspiracy, I realize with a burst of relief. At least the regular employees are innocent. LOS's corruption doesn't reach its lower tiers.

"Oh, sweetie," says another woman. "What happened? Did you hurt yourself?"

She gestures at my face, and my hand goes to my nose. It feels sore, like it's a big bruise. I must have a bit of blood left on my face.

"I tripped," I lie. "I got separated from my family." I sniff loudly and put on my best puppy-dog eyes. "I'm scared."

"Oh," she coos. "Oh dear."

They don't recognize me, I realize with a jolt. I put on my best little girl face. It's not hard. Adrenaline makes my knees buckle. I let the woman lead me into the group. As I pass the stern receptionist, I turn my face so he can't see my features. There's only a slim chance he remembers me, but I don't want to take any more chances tonight.

Together, we wait in the darkness, listening to the slop of water against the shore, and the fearful silence of the night. No one speaks. It's as though we're afraid our voices it might draw unwanted attention. Someone hands me a wet wipe, which I use to clean my nose. When the ferry finally arrives, I pile onto with the others, and we chug towards the main-land, away from the LOS building and its cold, flashing alarms.

Chapter 23

Home at Last

It takes me a long time to find a working pay phone. These days, with most people carrying cellphones, pay phones are considered redundant. The only ones left are in hotel lobbies and subway stops. I wander up Bathurst Street until I spot one at a gas station. The receiver feels foreign in my palm. Halfway off the island, it started to drizzle. Now, the cool, damp air clings to my clothes. I tuck my free hand into my pocket, but it doesn't help. The handle of the pay phone is smooth as ice. I listen to it ring with bated breath.

Finally, there's a *click*.

"Hello?"

Hearing Ling's voice is like listening to birdsong after a long rainstorm. I grin into the speaker.

"Ling, it's me."

"Who?"

"It's me, Beata."

There's a pause.

"Oh. My. God. Oh my God. Ohmygod, *it's Beata, everyone*. She got out. *She's ok*." A scramble of voices washes over the phone. I hold the receiver a little away from my ear to prevent Ling's squeals from deafening me. "Everyone thought you were *dead*. Nu called us. She said she found you, but we never heard from you after that! She's on her way over. Never, *ever* do that to us again."

A surge of relief warms me. "Nu got out?"

"Of course she got out. She's Nuha Bahar."

"Of course," I parrot, leaning against the phone booth walls for support.

"Where *are* you?"

"I'm at the corner of Bathurst and King. At the Petro-Canada. Could someone come get me?"

"We're coming right away!" squawks Ling. I can imagine her, flapping her hands, jumping from toe to toe. "Just hang tight, ok? We're leaving *right now*. RIGHT. NOW." Her voice draws farther away, and I know she's holding her phone away from her ear. "Someone alert the Chief! We found Beata!"

"Wait!" I bark into the receiver. Agent Scarlett's face appears in my mind. There's a small chance Agent Scarlett hasn't found out about my escape yet, and if she has, she doesn't know where I've run off to. The police and LOS work together. If the police find out where I am, then news will definitely make its way back to Agent Scarlett. I don't want Alexander descending on Ling's place, putting everyone in danger. "Don't tell the police anything yet!"

"Why?" Ling sounds confused. "They'll want to ask you questions."

"No, Ling. Listen to me." I make my voice quiet and serious. "This is important. I stumbled on something. Something big. I don't want anyone knowing yet. Are the police at your house still?"

"No, but they left their number—"

"Can you guys come get me? Personally?"

The sound of scuffling. Then a familiar voice.

"Bea? Is that you?"

"Hi, Dad," I say, tired and half-frozen.

"Are you all right? You're not hurt?"

"I'm ok," I reassure, even as my stitches give a stab of protest. A pause. Then quieter, "I stole a robot octopod."

"What? How? Where? *What was it like?*" he says, sounding proud. I'm not sure whether to laugh or cry. Everything is so surreal. He clears his throat. "But stealing is wrong, and you know it. We'll talk about your punishment later."

I laugh. It's so good just to hear him. My voice echoes.

"What's this about not telling the police?" Dad's voice is softer now, like we're sharing a secret. "Are you in trouble?"

"No, I don't think so." From the silence on the other end, I know he's not entirely convinced. I take a shaky breath. "Dad, do you trust me?"

"Of course. You're my daughter."

"Ok," I say, nodding to myself. "Then I'll explain everything. I promise."

"Ok," mirrors my dad, sounding a bit faint.

Then a mess of noises, and another voice.

"Beata?"

I seize up despite myself and brace for a firestorm of chastisement. "Hi, Mom."

A pause.

"My girl," she gasps instead. "Thank goodness you're safe!"

Tears spring to my eyes.

"I'm coming home, Mom."

She makes a little hiccupping noise—a sob. There's more noise on the line. Then a short pause.

"I love you, Bea," Dad's voice says, softer now.

There's a lump in my throat. "I love you too."

"See you soon, ok?"

"Ok."

"I'm going to hang up now."

"Ok. Bye, Dad."

Click. The phone goes silent. I hang it back on its hook with reluctance. Exhaustion sweeps over me. I exit the booth, flop down on the edge of the sidewalk, and watch the night breeze stir leaves across the empty streets. Wetness settles in my hair, but I'm too tired to move. Up above, red lights of LOS skirt along the clouds. I can hear the mechanical *whump-whump* of helicopters as they traverse the skies. Their searchlights scour the ground. Once in a while, I see a Super formation, gliding like hawks. It's like I'm stuck in a dystopian society. I've never seen Toronto streets so empty. A pop can rattles along the concrete and comes to rest against my foot. I don't even have the energy to nudge it away.

After my close encounter with LOS, the city is a stranger. A big billboard nearby promotes *COKE-COLA: The #1 drink of your local Supers!* Everywhere I look, Supers stare back at me, from the front of gossip magazines, plastered on product endorsements, staring out from advertisements. Their faces are cheerful, broadcasted on sparkling backdrops. They make statements in bold font. *CRIMSON BULL MAKES YOU LEVITATE*, and *IMAX, THINK SUPER*. Before, I would have admired these kids. I would have wanted to be like them. Now, all I can wonder is how much money the advertisers paid to have a Super face appear beside their product.

I also wonder where all the money will go. To sponsor another empty challenge, perhaps. To entertain the masses. The ads are suddenly garish and exaggerated. The LOS helicopters menacing, like buzzards circling for carrion. The abandoned streets dark and ominous.

CODE RED: HAVE YOU SEEN THIS SUPER? declares a nearby jumbo screen. Beneath it, a picture of Gwen's face. It begins to rain in earnest, so I force myself up and head to a nearby bus shelter, to stay hidden and dry. Every time a LOS helicopter flies overhead, I wince.

When my dad's Prius pulls up, my heart jumps into my throat. Ling tumbles out of the car when the doors open. My dad follows not far behind, leaving the engine running. My heart squeezes when I see him. Has he always looked so pale and tired?

"*Beata*," Ling ululates, scrambling for footing.

"Yo," I say, drained. I'm hungry and cold. I miss my bed, my programming, and my parents' delicious mac and cheese. Ling collides with me in a bear hug. I nearly choke.

"You must tell me everything—*everything*—don't leave out a single detail!" Ling blabbers. "We called everyone and they're all at my place now. A Code Red, Beata! Can you imagine? LOS hasn't called a Code Red since Beamsman went on the rampage ten years ago! It's scary but exciting! I didn't think I would ever experience another one!"

She moves aside, shaking with nervous energy. It's my dad's turn to engulf me in a hug. I let myself sink into him. It's the warmest I've felt in a long time.

"My little girl," he says, a tremble in his voice. "What an ordeal you went through. It must have been so, *so* scary."

I nod into his jacket. My chest feels tight, and I don't trust myself to talk. I might cry instead.

"You're ok now. You're safe."

I nod again. I think, Agent Scarlett could be ordering a team of Supers to track me down. Alexander could drop from the sky any moment. Robot octopods could crash down all over Toronto. But just for now, I let myself feel safe.

We pile into the car. Ling's warm presence and excited chatter are comforting.

Then with a purr of the engines, we're on our way into the night.

It's chaos when I get to Ling's house. Ling ushers everyone into the basement with quick motions. She's not kidding when she says *everyone* has gathered there. Nuha's parents are overseas on a business trip, but Nuha's caretaker, an elderly woman with warm, crinkled eyes, is there instead. Ling's parents are fiddling with a television in the corner. Her younger sister, Yue, waits with a blanket in her hands. To my surprise, I see Gwen's parents too, Victorique and Oswald Kendricks, perched on a couple of plastic-wrapped couches, looking uncomfortable and unsure of themselves.

When I spot my mom, time slows. Her eyes light up.

"Here she is," announces my dad. "Here's our Beata."

Suddenly, I'm surrounded by people. Mom edges in for a hug of her own, her large eyes shining with tears. Questions fly at me. Where have I been? How have I been? What happened? How did I ever get away from the Counter-League? They amass around me like bees.

"Come on, guys, give her some space," comes Ling's voice. "Everyone back off for a sec. Beata needs some room to breathe!"

Someone tucks a warm hot chocolate into my hands. Someone else pats my back. My dad puts a hand on my shoulder and guides me to a nearby couch. He seems reluctant to break contact with me, as though afraid I might disappear if he lets go. Someone throws a towel over me and attempts to dry my hair. Mindlessly, I take a sip of hot chocolate. Its sweetness on my tongue brings forth a round of tears. It's so good. Finally, the crowd subsides.

"Are you cold?" asks my dad. "Hungry?"

I shake my head. "Not really."

"Someone bring her some cookies, please."

"I'm ok, really."

Victorique pats her eyes. She has long, straight blonde hair and Gwen's green eyes. My mom sits beside her and strokes her back calmly. They've been best friends since their LOS days.

"What's happening in LOS headquarters?" Victorique asks, helplessly. "The media says Gwen betrayed the organization, but that doesn't sound like her at all. LOS is her home. What do you know, Beata?"

I look around the room at the expectant faces, the tears and fear. They gather around me, hungry for information. Craving it. I can see them holding back for courtesy's sake, allowing me space to think. Ling's mother places a plate of biscuits in front of me. I take a deep breath. Where should I begin? What do people know? Very little, or nothing at all, I conclude.

"I think everyone should take a seat. It's a long story."

I take one more sip of hot chocolate, lick my lips, and begin to speak.

I start at the beginning. I talk about meeting Alexander. I tell them about my visit to LOS headquarters. I tell them about Ling's photo. They're a good audience. They gasp when I tell them about my kidnapping. They lean in when I tell them about my prison cell.

I speak until my throat is scratchy and my tongue feels like a slab of drywall in my mouth. I speak until my hot chocolate is an empty mug of cocoa residue. Someone places a Coke-Cola beside me. I guzzle it so fast the bubbles shoot up my nose. Someone else pats my back as I cough. It seems I speak for hours. Eyes stare back at me, rapt. Mouths hang open. I finally finish my story with my escape and Gwen's flight into the night. The silence in the room is deafening.

"I know it's hard to believe," I say, suddenly abashed. I'm not used to public speaking. Their eyes bore into me. "You *have* to believe me."

Still, they stare at me.

"Mr. Uzune is Hitori Yuuma?" bursts my dad, his voice an octave higher than normal. "Oh my God! What is he like in person?"

"Seriously, Phil," chastises my mom, "*that's* what you took away from the story?"

"I'm sorry, Beata," says Victorique. Her voice is soft, like dandelion fluff. She brushes a strand of golden hair behind her ear. "It's not that I don't believe you, but it's a lot to take in."

"I don't think I would have believed it myself if I didn't live it," I admit.

"If you told us this in any other situation, I would be inclined to think you're making it up," says Oswald. Unlike Victorique, his voice is firm and cool. He holds himself upright, hands behind his back, nose slightly in the air. The only sign of his nerves is the slight twitch in his right hand. "But Gwen wouldn't turn against LOS for no reason. She's just not that sort of girl." His mouth purses into a thin line. "She's a good person."

"I never really liked that Agent Scarlett," adds Victorique with a nod. "Something about her always rubbed me wrong. She's so pushy."

"I think it makes sense," says my dad. He looks around with his chin up as though challenging people to defy him. "The oddly coincidental attacks. Why my daughter ended up in a LOS cell right under our noses. Why LOS is trying to make Gwen seem like a traitor. They don't want to lose face. They don't want to lose power. They're trying to get rid of anyone who knows their dirty secret."

"It does make sense if you're into conspiracy theories," says Oswald. "The simpler explanation would be that there really is a Counter-League out there and they have, beyond all odds, somehow managed to infiltrate LOS headquarters and are now persecuting my daughter as a criminal. Why? I don't know. Maybe because she's LOS's top star. Maybe because she's too powerful to leave alone."

"I *spoke* with Agent Scarlett," I say, staring him in the eye. "She told me outright the entire thing was a ruse. They're *using* Supers, Mr. Kendricks. They're using Gwen!"

He stares back at me. I can see a debate happening in his head. I don't break eye contact.

"I see now why you didn't want us to tell the police right away," interjects my dad. "LOS is a farce. LOS kidnapped Beata. LOS is playing us all like fools. And all the evidence we have is the words of a child. It's a hard pill to swallow, even for some people in this room."

He gazes pointedly at Oswald, who frowns in return.

"Don't be difficult, Oswald," groans Victorique. She looks

like she might be sick. "For once, just don't."

Oswald's chin trembles.

"All I want is my daughter back," he says at last.

"Then let's get to work," my dad replies, gripping Oswald's shoulder in a gesture of camaraderie.

"We've been keeping track of the stories," says Ling. "You won't believe what they're saying." She opens her laptop. On her screen are numerous social media networks, all in chaos, moving fast. Condemnation flies as quickly as doubt, but it looks like more and more people are believing LOS. Tips fly in from every corner of Toronto.

And why wouldn't they? asks my mind bitterly; they're a well-respected, long-established organization. *And you— you're just a kid.*

"They're saying she's a traitor," I read grimly. "It's all lies. Gwen didn't betray LOS. She—" I choke a little. "She came to rescue me."

"LOS has her on a wanted list," says Ling, looking more serious than I've ever seen her. "Reward money for whoever brings her in. Alive, luckily. It's at ten thousand so far, but I wouldn't be surprised if it goes higher. Two thousand to any-one who gives a clue that leads to her arrest. Beata, she's in *big* trouble. There are Super teams out there right now look-ing for her. Gwen's an A-rank Super, but she can't fight an entire army."

"We need to help her," I say immediately. "She's helped all of us, so we need to help her."

"Agreed," says my dad. "Everywhere she goes, people relay her location to LOS. There's no place to hide." He purses his mouth. "If I were twenty years younger," he sighs so hard his shoulders heave, "I would be able to hack into all these accounts and mess things up. Feed misinformation. Buy Gwen time to shake her pursuers."

"We can still do that," I protest. "Hack networks manually, I mean."

Ling fixes me with a look. *You think we haven't already tried?*

"I'll write out some press releases and see if any news stations are willing to run your version of the story," she says. Her mouth flattens into a line. "But I doubt it."

"Right now, the most important thing is helping Gwen escape," my mom says, nodding. "Then we can worry about proving LOS's conspiracy."

"So let's buy her time," I say fiercely. "Let's—I don't know—*blind* people or something."

"Even with everyone feeding false information, there are too many people tracking Gwen for us to make an impact," Ling continues. "No one pays us any attention, or we're dismissed as rumour-mongers. The biggest flux in media patterns was when that robot octopod crashed into LOS headquarters and started blasting."

I bite my lip. Another robot octopod would not be unwelcome right now. If I had one, I could even charge into the field and help fight off Supers with Gwen. As though reading my thoughts, my dad shoots me a stern look and shakes his head.

Ling's cellphone buzzes. She swipes it to look at the number. Then she lets out a little squeal and rushes to the door. She throws it open, revealing three soggy figures.

"Look who we found cursing the sky at Queen's Park," says Nuha with a hint of amusement. Her thick hair is frazzled from the long flight, and her clothes are soaked. Her glasses fog up as she steps into the warm room. She moves with familiarity, grabs a towel, and starts drying her hair. "I've never heard such aggressive Japanese."

Dieter follows her in, equally waterlogged. And behind him is Hitori, looking just as frazzled—or more frazzled than before.

Click. A puzzle piece falls into place.

"We need a distraction," I say. "We need to buy Gwen time to get away. She won't be able to do that if everyone's looking for her, so let's take their eyes off her. We need to fight media with media. We need a bigger story."

"It's hard to get much bigger than an LOS superstar turning sour," says Ling glumly. "Everyone loves a fallen from grace drama. How are we even supposed to compete?"

"It'll be difficult," I say. "But I think I have an idea."

I look towards Hitori.

Chapter 24

War of Words

HEAD OF THE COUNTER-LEAGUE REVEALED: LONG-LOST SUPER HITORI YUUMA'S SHOCKING RETURN.

"I have to give it to her," says Ling appreciatively. "Agent Scarlett comes up with some fascinating ideas. Evil, of course, but fascinating."

She has a professional camera balanced on her shoulder. It's so big I'm surprised it doesn't crush her. The lens is like a bulbous fish eye. She fiddles with the buttons and gives us a thumbs-up. "Ok, we're ready to roll. Hitori, are you ready to play Big Bad?"

Hitori stands in front of a green bedsheet, provided by Ling's little sister, Yue. It's the closest thing we have to a green screen.

"Do I really need to wear this?" asks Hitori, looking abashed. He has a long Dracula cape on. Ling has made up his face with dark eye shadow and light powder to give him a pasty, sickly appearance.

"Yes," insists Ling. "It gives you street cred."

She leans over and addresses the rest of us.

"Have we sent out the press releases?"

"Done," a chorus of voices answer her. In the past hour, we whipped up dozens of press releases and emailed them to all known news outlets, big and small, using new email addresses and anonymous IP addresses each time. Even if no legitimate news station will pay attention, the small gossip stations might.

Ling nods solemnly. "Patch us through to as many channels as you can, Mr. Bell."

My dad sits in a tangle of wires. He has so many laptops piled around him he's nearly buried by them. "I can only get a few."

"That'll have to be enough."

"Hitori," I interrupt. "Are you sure about doing this? If you reveal yourself, you won't be able to hide anymore."

Hitori shrugs. "I've already been busted. Joanna knows I'm back. She'll get it out eventually. I at least want to reveal myself on my terms, doing something useful."

Ling counts down with her fingers. *Three...two...one...* .She motions at Hitori with a finger.

"Good evening, citizens of Toronto," Hitori says in his best announcer's voice. I'm surprised how composed he sounds, but then I remember how composed Gwen usually sounds. With all the LOS training he's received, it must be second nature to him. "Having a chaotic night, are we? Looks like your defenders of justice are having a hard time with my precious Counter-League hellraisers. But why are you going after innocent Miss Kendricks? I assure you, we're not associates. Maybe LOS is getting senile and unreliable, but what else is new? Ah, but you're wondering who I am. Who would go against LOS? And why? I'll tell you why. LOS isn't as grand as it makes itself out to be. Trust me. I've been there. I've lived it. Many of you knew me as the world's most powerful telekinetic! My name is Hitori Yuuma, and I'm going to blow your minds!"

I monitor my screen. It's our goal to keep pumping false

information on as many social media sites as possible while Hitori postures on television. There are so many laptops open in the basement that we have opened all the windows to let the heat out. My palms feel sweaty as I type.

> Hitori Yuuma's shocking return?! #HitoriYuuma #Live
>
> A former hero gone bad! Is it jealousy, or something else? #HitoriYuuma #CounterLeague

I feel bad sullying Hitori's reputation, but I remind myself it's for Gwen's safety. My screen lights up.

"I got a few retweets," I say.

Ling lifts her head and gives me a thumbs-up. "Good, keep going!"

The sound of keys clattering fill the room as both adults and children get to work. Even Yue, who is no more than seven, works on reposting one of Ling's pre-written statements. I keep posting too. My fingers slip as I type. I suppose a few spelling errors could be forgiven at a time of crisis.

I scan the Internet. "People are starting to pay attention."

Hitori launches into a passionate speech about corruption and deception, about rising up against the oppressors and living as free people, out of the shadow of LOS. He's a dramatic speaker, and I find myself straying from my task more than once. He uses lots of arm gestures.

Then, the television flickers. LOS's emblem blazes on-screen with a crash of fanfare and colours. A suited Agent stands before us, wearing a calm, patronizing smile.

"As many of you may be aware, there is a disturbed individual attempting to besmirch Hitori Yuuma's good name.

Rest assured that this man is an imposter, and pay him no need. The real Hitori Yuuma is an honourable citizen. LOS is working on locating this imposter and ending his slander."

"A retort, and so fast!" says Ling. She shoots me a meaningful look.

"People are getting nervous. LOS doesn't want chaos in the streets." Nuha's voice is calm. "They want a good story, but they don't want actual riots. It's a fine balance between sensation and reassurance, but it means they're paying attention to us."

I smile grimly. "Good. The more attention we can tear away from Gwen, the better."

Ling's father flips through the television stations quickly. None of the major ones have picked up our story so far, but CP24 has a scrolling blurb on the bottom of their screen that says, *HITORI YUUMA CLAIMS TO BE COUNTER-LEAGUE LEADER. IS HE THE REAL DEAL?* More often, though, I see blurry security camera images of Gwen racing down the streets.

It's a battle for the eyes and minds of the people. Despite myself, I feel a thrum of excitement.

Hitori glances over. Despite his solemn expression, I can see a glimmer of mischief in his eyes. "You think I'm an imposter, but I'm not. Let me tell you why none of you have heard from your beloved telekinetic for so many years. I was in retirement, they tell you, but I was not! I was on the run, away from LOS and their craven ways. I fled for a decade, ten whole years. LOS did not find me then, so I challenge LOS to find me now. If I am not the true Hitori Yuuma, then where is he?"

"Can't they track us?" Oswald murmurs, eyes fixed on a

monitor.

"They'll have to descramble what I've put up," my dad reassures. "It'll buy us time."

I scan the Internet again. There are still significantly more posts about Gwen's location than there are about Hitori's return. I bite my lip. We need to buy more time. Every second gives Gwen more time to get away. Every distracted user means one less person with their eyes on the sky.

> Think I spotted #GwenKendricks in the suburbs. Flying east!
>
> Hitori is my hero. He'd never threaten LOS! #Hatersgonnahate
>
> Omgomg, #GwenKendricks just went ovr my house! #Scared

My eyes fall on one photo of Gwen. It's clearer than the rest and taken by what appears to be a high-speed camera. She looks rough. She's missing a shoe. Rips decorate her dark clothing. Her hair is a tumbleweed, and a swarm of metal travels with her. Through her makeshift shield, I can see a stain on her side. *Blood.*

The words *witch hunt* whisper through my mind.

"We need to push it, guys," I say, a tremble in my voice. "Gwen doesn't have much time."

In the photo, I can see a flock of flying Supers in the distance, trailing her, guided by user input and hearsay.

"We need to send those Supers on a wild goose chase." I'm starting to sound panicked. My fingers tremble over the keyboard. I type in a few quick lines. Gwen's been spotted in the west end of town. Gwen's heading up north. Gwen's holing up in the Rogers Centre. Anything to get them off her trail.

"Why don't you make a statement, Bea?" asks my dad. "Tell everyone to back off. You're the one who was kidnapped, right?"

"I'm not sure that's a good idea," Dieter interrupts. It's the first thing he's said since he got here.

I jump to my feet. "It's worth a try, right?"

He shrugs. "It won't work. You'll see. LOS will just say you're also a traitor, since you're Gwen's friend. Either that or they'll say you're being forced to make a statement by the Counter-League. As far as anyone knows, you're still in their grip."

I grind my teeth. Dieter tilts his head and shoots me a look that says, *Don't hate the player, hate the game.* I can't help but admit he's right. Annoyingly so. I return to my screen and sit down with a sigh.

"LOS is big. We're small. We have no credibility," says Ling's father, a hand to his chin. "We need credibility or no one will believe us no matter how much we yell."

"If we're talking evidence," says Ling, "nothing beats a live broadcast."

Even she sounds grim. How many hours has it been since I helped Gwen escape? Two? How much damage has she already taken? On the couch, Victorique makes a little sound, like that of an injured animal, and buries her head into her hands.

"A live broadcast would be amazing, but we can't just waltz in and demand a confession," says Nuha. "We don't even know where they are. LOS headquarters is evacuated, right?"

An idea pops into my head. My hand flies to my pocket,

to the crumpled piece of paper within.

I have Agent Scarlett's business card. I have all her information. My mind flashes back to the invitation she extended back in the cell. Was it really only a few hours ago? Everything is so surreal. I bite my lip until it hurts. Agent Scarlett could be my way in. If I can meet with her, then—

I nod. Yes.

"Everyone," I declare, "I think I can get something live!"

Heads swivel in my direction.

"I can go in with my app," I say. "All we have to do is make some small preparations."

"Let's hear what you have," says Victorique quietly. Her eyes are puffy. Oswald rubs comforting circles into her back.

I tell them my plan. Once I'm in her office I'll call Agent Scarlett to arrange a meeting, pretending to be interested in joining LOS. I'll use my Sound Isolator app to record and relay the live conversation to everyone else who has my app installed. They can broadcast it over as many channels as they can. Once LOS's schemes are revealed, once the chase is shown to be a falsehood, once Gwen's name is cleared of wrongdoing, everything will end.

My dad stands.

"No," he says. "No, absolutely not."

I wince at the hardness in his voice. "But, Dad, this is our best chance! If we wait any longer, Gwen could get hurt, or worse! You know what they'd do to get a good story! Dad, Gwen could *die*."

"You don't know how hard this has been on us—on me, Beata. All the waiting. The media reporting that you were kidnapped by the Counter-League! Ling and Nuha telling us you were snatched in broad daylight, right from a public park!"

"Dad, I could really help! Agent Scarlett asked me directly if I wanted to—"

"You're not walking back into their hands."

"But, Dad—"

"No, Beata!" he snaps. I shrink back. Dad almost never yells. "Just no. You are not allowed—no, you are *forbidden* from leaving this house!"

I take a shaky breath.

"I know you want to help," says Dad, a little bit calmer, although his nostrils are still flaring. "But—just let us handle this, ok? Let the adults be adults."

"Ok," I breathe, backing away, feeling thunderstruck. "Ok, sure."

I sit back down and wait.

Later that night, I do something rash.

I've been to Ling's enough times to know all the secrets to her house. I excuse myself to go to the bathroom and swipe Ling's cellphone along the way. I can hear the blaring of news reports, guessing at Gwen's location. Live citizens tracking her.

"I saw her at Yonge and Dundas."

"She's hiding out in a Walmart, that's for sure."

"I think she's in the Don Valley area."

"I swear she threatened my life if I spoke out, but—justice must prevail!"

Some guessed at her status.

"Last I heard she was dead!"

No, I think. Unacceptable. If I can steal a robot octopod, I can do this. Adults are capable, but adults can be slow. Cautious. Gwen can't afford slow or cautious right now.

I stand on tiptoe on the toilet's water tank and jiggle the bathroom window. It pops out with a small creak, which I cover by dropping the toilet seat. *Thunk.* I scramble down to place the window cover on the counter. Then I open the tap and lock the door. If anyone comes knocking, it will sound like I'm washing my hands. Maybe it'll buy me some time.

I lift myself up and squeeze through the window. It's tough without someone to give me a boost or pull me up from the outside. My muscles shake with exertion. I wriggle my shoulders through, brace my palms against the grass, and pull myself all the way. I slide onto Ling's lawn like an eel.

I check that Ling's cellphone is still with me.

Then I scamper into the rain.

Chapter 25

Fishing for Confessions

A body can take a lot of punishment, I conclude, as I half-jog, half-stumble down the empty streets. I'm exhausted. My side aches. My face hurts. My limbs are made of putty. Still, I run. Code Red is in full effect. No buses rumble down the streets. No taxis either. I take care to stick to the shadows in case patrolling Supers fly overhead. Only after a few big blocks do I feel far away enough to execute my plan.

I remove Agent Scarlett's business card from my pocket—I'm glad to see it's still there—and dial the number. I try to breathe normally as the phone rings. I rehearse my speech in my head. I don't want to sound afraid. Still, I hold my breath.

Brrrrnnnnng—

Brrrrrnnnng—

Then a click.

"Agent Scarlett here. Who is this?" She sounds slightly confused but nevertheless, smooth and calm. For a second I let myself hate her. All the chaos she's caused. All the fear she's instilled. I imagine her predatory smile and shudder. The city is in lockdown because of her schemes. How dare she sound so unaffected?

"Er," I say, all semblance of speech fleeing my tongue. My mind goes blank.

"Hello?" she asks.

"It's me. It's Beata Bell."

"Oh," Agent Scarlett pauses for just a moment. Then she sounds delighted. "Miss Bell, you sure caused some trouble escaping from our headquarters. I can't say I'm surprised. Nothing less from the descendent of the great Frances E. Shaw."

"Sorry about that, the escape, I mean." I shiver and huddle closer to a wall. The rain is coming down harder now. I picture Agent Scarlett's face, her hair in a prim bun, her glasses flashing. "I didn't want to leave, you see. It was Hitori; he forced me away."

I apologize silently to Hitori. I'm once again dirtying his name.

"Saving the children. How typical of him." I can hear the sneer in Agent Scarlett's voice now. "I suppose you fought tooth and nail to get away from him?"

It's a trap. I steady myself. "Well, no, but in my defence, I was in a prison cell. It's not the most comfortable rooming arrangement. I kind of wanted to get out."

"Hmm, and I'm sure it was much more convenient for you to leave the premises than come to me directly."

I assume an offended tone. "There was a Super battle going on! I wasn't even sure you were still *alive.* So I got away and waited for things to calm down. I'm contacting you now, aren't I?"

Agent Scarlett giggles. "All right, no need to get your panties in a knot, Miss Bell. I take it you've considered my offer?"

I take a deep breath.

"I have, and my answer is affirmative. I want to join LOS and become an Agent. I'm tired of being a nobody."

"Any reasonable girl would come to the same conclusion,"

says Agent Scarlett, sounding compassionate. "Where are you now?"

I know what she's doing. I've seen enough espionage films to know when someone's fishing for information. I'm glad I removed myself from Ling's house before calling. She might be tracing my call—somehow.

"On the street," I answer. "I managed to get away from Hitori. I'm at Yonge and Bloor right now."

"In the rain?"

"In the rain."

"You poor thing," coos Agent Scarlett. "Just sit tight. I'll send Alexander over."

Alexander. I'm seized by fear before I remember he's not the true supervillain. He's an unfortunate spectator, caught up in the storm. The true supervillain is on the phone. I steady myself.

"I'll be waiting," I say, and punch the off button. As soon as the phone darkens, my legs feel like rubber.

I sink to the steps of the Royal Bank building and wait. The damp soaks into my pants, but I no longer notice. As I wait, I make preparations. I put Ling's phone on silent so there won't be any distractions. I save a draft text to Nuha, ready to send at the press of a button. I prepare the Sound Isolator app. I test it on the water pouring from a nearby drain. It's not ideal. The playback is blurry, but it's not too bad. A bit of roughness gives authenticity. Live broadcasts are never perfect, after all, and I don't want it to sound too doctored.

Frances, I think to the sky. *Am I being stupid?* I imagine her face in the darkness, her eternal calm. *Were you ever scared before a big battle?*

Raindrops fall on my forehead and slide down my nose. The answer comes easily to me. Of course she was scared. She wasn't that much older than me when she faced the German air force in the Battle of Britain. I let out a small laugh. She was the Original Super, but she was also human.

I cross my fingers and hope for the best.

It doesn't take long for a black LOS car to pull up at the corner. I stand cautiously as the door pops open and Alexander gets out. He's dressed almost like a butler, with a white dress shirt and a pinstripe vest.

"Hello again, Miss Bell," he says, formal, as usual. There's confusion in his eyes. For a second, his face falters. "I hope you know what you're doing."

I raise my chin. Maybe I haven't completely forgiven him for kidnapping me in the first place. "Trust me. I do."

He shrugs. "It's your life," he says.

"It is," I confirm.

"Are you planning on doing something stupid? I'm obligated to stop you if your actions endanger the Agent, myself, or someone I care about."

"I'm planning on doing the smartest thing I've done all my life," I retort. I stare him in the eye. I hear this is what dogs do when establishing dominance. He doesn't look away, but he doesn't challenge me either. He only shrugs and makes a smooth, welcoming bow and motions towards the open door.

I crawl in and take in my surroundings. I've never been in an LOS vehicle before. The comfortable leather seats, the dim lighting, the silence, make me think of a whale's belly. Alexander gets in beside me, looking stiff and uncomfortable.

He hands me a towel, which I sniff cautiously before using it—just in case.

"I hear you and Agent Scarlett are close," I say after I've patted myself dry.

"Not particularly. Think of us more as business associates."

"Funny, that's what she said. So you're not on friendly terms? Say she were to suddenly disappear from the equation. Would you be sad?"

Alexander regards me out of the corner of his eye. For a heartbeat, he doesn't say anything, only waves his hand for the driver to move. The car hums to life.

"I don't know what you're playing at," he says at last. I think he's going to threaten me or give a word of caution. Instead, he says, very quietly, "But good luck."

I rein in my surprise. Of everything I expected him to say, good luck was not on my radar. I remember how reluctant he sounded on the phone when Dieter and I followed him that one day. It warms me to know he's not too enthusiastic about kidnapping schoolchildren. Maybe, just maybe, he has some morals.

We make the rest of the ride in silence. Being inside the LOS car is like being in a bubble. The chaos of the outside world falls away. The walls are soundproof, and the car glides down the streets without a hitch. The windows are tinted, so I can barely make out the flashing lights of the Code Red.

My fingers want to stray to Ling's phone for comfort, but I force my hands to stay still. No use coming this far only to give myself away with a nervous tick. I count my breaths instead and imagine pressing down my nerves until they're squished into a harmless puddle.

We don't make our way to LOS headquarters. Instead, we

head to a tall skyscraper by Harbourfront. SCOTIA-ROGERS TOWER, declares the building in a shiny silver font. Its shadow falls over us as we pull into its drop-off loop. It seems like the sort of building that usually has a valet, with a spacious unloading zone and tall revolving door. *Right by the CN Tower*, I memorize. Close enough to bathe in the glow of its angry LED lights.

Alexander leads me out with the same stiff formality that he greeted me with.

As we cross into the brightly lit lobby of the skyscraper, I ask, maybe a little snidely, "So what are you supposed to be this time? My bodyguard or prison guard?"

"I suppose that's all a matter of perspective," he says in that infuriatingly vague way of his. "Either way, you're stuck with me until we get to the Agent."

"Hitori tried to talk you out of doing her dirty business," I say. The building, if possible, is even colder than the rainy night. It's air conditioned to the max. Like walking into a freezer—a well-furnished freezer with mahogany desks and gold chandeliers. "You should have listened to him. You didn't have to dive into the dark side."

"Hitori Yuuma is a fool," Alexander says with more vehemence than I expected, "but I expect it's too much for a kid like you to understand."

Kid. I snort.

"Even kids know not to root for the bad guys."

"My parents died when my sister and I were young," Alexander offers, almost robotically. "I don't suppose you know why. I'll give you a hint. It had something to do with a certain laser-shooting maniac and his incompetent psychic keeper."

My blood runs cold. The image of Frances E. Shaw cutting through metal flicks through my mind. I do the math. Alexander is a few years older than me. Maybe sixteen. Eleven years ago, he would have been five. Young. If his sister is close to my age, she's twelve now, which made her a baby when Beamsman ripped through a peaceful suburban neighbourhood. She wouldn't even have been old enough to remember their parents' faces. I think of Mom and Dad. I imagine not ever knowing them. It's hard. I knew people died in the Beamsman incident. I just didn't know who.

I want to touch Alexander's arm, but I refrain. He walks as though stiff, jaw clenched, eyes on the pattering rain.

"I'm sorry," I say slowly, "but if you know the truth, you also know that Hitori did his best to stop Charley."

"How reassuring."

"I'm sorry. Really."

Alexander purses his lips but doesn't say anything. I can feel frustration emanating off him like heat. He leads me into the elevator and punches the highest floor. My stomach drops as the elevator shoots skyward.

Ding. The doors open to a long hallway with windows that stretch from floor to ceiling. The carpet is an arabesque pattern of steel grey and black. There is a series of offices, but we pass all of them. We head towards the double doors at the end of the hallway. My stomach grumbles, and I set a hand on it to calm it down. My nerves flit like hummingbirds.

Be strong, I urge myself.

Alexander pauses before the door, lifts a hand, and taps it twice in quick succession. An intercom buzzes beside us.

"Yes?" sounds Agent Scarlett's voice.

"It's me. I have Miss Bell."

"Have you performed the necessary security measures?"

Alexander looks at me. His gaze pierces like nails, but he doesn't move.

"Yes," he says.

"Thank you."

Click.

Alexander gestures at the doors. It takes me a moment to realize he doesn't intend to come in with me. I place my hands on the double doors and lean my weight into them. The movement send a stab of pain through my side. I suck in a breath and clench my jaw. *Show no weakness.* I push through the doors and walk into the light.

In the movies, rich villains have well-furnished and luxurious offices to show off their power and prosperity. This is not the case for Agent Scarlett's offices. This one is as neat and monochromatic as the one she has in the LOS building. Her desk is a slab of metal. Her filing cabinets are arranged against a white, unblemished wall. Her ergonomic chairs are adjusted to nurture a straight spine. Soothing classical music permeates the room. The same large motivational poster hangs off her wall. *Look past the exterior, and see that there is so much more within.* Somehow, the austere room suits Agent Scarlett perfectly. I wonder, for a moment, whether this is her backup or primary office. Agent Scarlett herself signs papers with nonchalance, somehow finding room for work even during a Code Red crisis.

She doesn't look up when I enter, or invite me in. I know what she's doing. She's making me wait. She's establishing her power over me. I fight the urge to grind my molars. How infuriating! It's almost enough to overwhelm my nerves—almost.

Fine, two can play at this game. *Hubris*, I remember Mr. Uzune saying, during a lesson about Shakespeare, *is a villain's greatest enemy.* Let her be comfortable in her power. I shrink into myself and fidget, brush my hair back from my face and bite my nails. I make myself seem awkward and unsure.

Once ready, she looks over her glasses at me.

"Ah, Miss Beata Bell, do make yourself comfortable. We have much to talk about." She waves a hand at the chairs lining her office, as though presenting them on *The Price Is Right.*

My first instinct is to stand, to be ready to fight or fly at a moment's notice, but I force myself into a chair, where I perch like a pigeon on a wire. Agent Scarlett gives me a once-over and smiles.

"Come, come, Miss Bell. Relax. We're just going to have a chat. A nice girl talk."

I nod and force myself to slump.

"I'm glad you called. I suppose I should commend you for driving that robot octopod into the side of our expensive headquarters," says Agent Scarlett with a grin. "Not bad for a first try."

"You knew?" My spine straightens again.

Agent Scarlett rolls her eyes and waves me back down. "Agent Olive reported being jumped by a schoolgirl and a frumpy Japanese man. One of our robot octopods launched soon afterwards. It doesn't take a genius to put two and two together. Of course it could only have been you."

"Could have been Hitori."

Agent Scarlett laughs. It sounds like a bark. "Hitori is an

idiot. He's like all good Supers, idealistic and simple, and much too used to relying on powers to learn anything new. But don't worry. I forgive you. Not every little girl knows how to pilot a highly advanced piece of technology, and not everyone has the gusto to ram it into LOS headquarters. What a thrill that was! What a wonderful headline."

I blink carefully, not wanting to take my eyes off her for a single moment.

"You and Gwen," Agent Scarlett breathes, "must be *excellent* friends. You did it to try to rescue her, no? I couldn't figure out for the life of me why you would come back, and so violently too! But then I remembered,"—her nose wrinkles—"the power of friendship. It's so sweet it's almost sickening. Oh, I wonder what it's like to have a friend like that, but alas, friends are the luxury of leisurely people."

She looks tickled. I wonder if everything in the world amuses her. Does she see everything as a game? Are people just chess pieces to her? Pawns? I wonder, suddenly, whether she has any friends at all.

"So." She crosses her arms and stares at me sharply. "Let's talk business."

Do it now. I press the send button on Ling's phone. My text spirals into empty space. The Sound Isolator app loads. My throat suddenly feels dry.

You can do this. Game on.

"I've been thinking," I say, keeping my eyes low, my expression meek, "about everything you told me. About LOS and the truth of the world. About how I don't have to be helpless anymore."

Agent Scarlett nods, anticipation making her gaze sharp. "Yes, continue."

"I think it's clear by now that I'm not going to develop powers of my own." I let out a sad laugh. "I'm twelve, almost thirteen. Look at the stats. What are my chances of getting them now? Basically none."

"You're a logical one, Miss Bell. I appreciate that. Too many people operate on emotion rather than logic these days."

"I want power too," I say vehemently. "I'm tired of being in the shadows, not getting a good spot in the cafeteria, getting stepped on by everyone. I'm tired of getting tormented in the playground and having my friends abandon me when they become Supers. I'm tired of watching everyone else hog the spotlight. I'm tired of waiting."

As I speak, I find myself sinking into my words. What's true and what's false? I do want power, yes. I am tired of being treated like I'm lesser. Being a Super is the only way to be anyone these days. I want glory for the little guy. For people like me.

But I don't want anyone else to suffer so I can get my fifteen minutes of fame.

Stoke her anger, my mind whispers.

"You and I, we're just as important as Supers, aren't we?" I ask plaintively.

"Of course we're just as important!" says Agent Scarlett, eyes glittering. "Why should we be repressed and tormented by people who are born with a certain affinity for bursting into flames? Being a Super is no different than being a blonde. Or a redhead. Do we submit to those who are born with blue eyes rather than green? No. There needs to be an equalizing factor."

"LOS is that factor," I say.

"Yes, we both train and police Supers. We act as their guardians and their supervisors. They are like our children. We make sure they are well controlled, both as individuals and as a group. You've seen what can happen when even one Super goes bad. Look outside. An entire city under lockdown because one of my own decided to betray me."

I'm surprised. Gwen didn't betray LOS. If anything, LOS and Agent Scarlett betrayed Gwen. I take a close look at Agent Scarlett's face. Yes. She believes that Gweneira betrayed her. Never mind that she did so to rescue me, her closest and best friend. There's something behind Agent Scarlett's eyes. Something like hurt. Something like fear.

A short silence descends.

"Some people will say things like, oh, that sort of deception is unethical. Or, oh, it's unjust, but ethics and justice are subjective concepts." Agent Scarlett leans forward, places her chin on her fingers, and studies me carefully. I stare back, unwavering. This is another test. *Stay calm.* If I can get through Agent Ecru's daunting Super test, I can speak to Agent Scarlett without being cowed. "One can argue they are both human constructions. Fallible. Do you know what that means, Miss Bell?"

"Those are some pretty big words, Agent Scarlett," I admit, "but I think I understand. What's right to one person isn't always right to another—right?"

Agent Scarlett nods slowly. "Whenever something good happens to me, it means it's not happening to another person. When I became an Agent, someone else was left in the cold. When I get a raise, someone else fails to get the same raise. The world at its core is a series of trade-offs. Cost-benefit analyses. And I determine that the benefit of controlling

Supers and deceiving the world far outweighs the cost of not doing so. Do you understand?"

She's still staring at me. I begin to sweat. She doesn't seem to blink. Ling's cellphone sits like a rock in my pocket.

"I think so," I answer truthfully. "Although it's a little bit confusing for me. I'm not really smart, so these things take a while to sink in. But my dad always said the world isn't always what it seems to be. I don't really think I understood him until now. Sometimes, deception is necessary, right?"

Apparently I strike just the right balance of sympathy and insecurity, because Agent Scarlett nods and sits back. Her ergonomic chair gives a little squeak. It feels like a great pressure has been lifted.

"Your father is a smart man." Agent Scarlett smiles.

Stroke her ego, my mind hints. *Let her dig her own hole.*

"Not as smart as you," I continue. "He always said the Civvies hold the Super world together, but he never made anything of it. It's one thing to say something and another to actually do it. Without people like you, the Super world would fall apart."

"Ultimately, it's the low downs, the peasants of the world, who hold everything up." Agent Scarlett nods. Her eyes sparkle with pleasure. "There can be no pyramids without slaves. No movie without extras. No fame without an audience."

"Civvies make the Supers," I blurt as though coming to a sudden epiphany.

"Not so normal now, are we?" Agent Scarlett hisses, smiling.

"My dad also said," I continue in a more businesslike tone, "that I should never sign a contract without reading the small print. If I become an Agent, what sort of power do I get?

'Cause if it's not worth the work, then I don't see why I should become your apprentice. Cost-benefit analysis, right?"

Agent Scarlett nods. Approval flashes across her face. "You get responsibility over Supers, naturally, their schedules, their missions, even small things like the breakfasts they eat at LOS. Of course, no Agent begins with such influence. We all work our way up."

"What if I can't handle it? I'm not as great as you. You have a nice car and *two* nice offices. Scotia-Rogers Tower is prime office space. Right on Harbourfront, by the CN Tower too! I bet you have a nice house. Probably in a gated community. What if I can't be as successful? I don't want to be a disappointment *again*."

"It is a lot, isn't it?" preens Agent Scarlett. "I might be great now, but I grew into it, as you will. Your only responsibility as an entrance level Agent—other than your administrative duties—is to bear the burden of the truth that—"

"Supers are the world's greatest threat," I finish, feeding into her paranoia. "I know. I got twenty-four stitches because a *certain* Super wasn't watching where she threw an I-beam."

"Attack dogs need to be kept on a leash," Agent Scarlett says with a definitive nod. Suddenly, I see where Gwen gets all her one-liners. "Give them an inch, and they'll rip up everything. That's human nature. Those with power will abuse it, and those without will suffer."

The irony of her words doesn't seem to reach her.

I think about Dieter, about cold noodles sliding down my back. I remember my mortification and anger, and how much I wanted to strike back, but I also remember how he stood up for us against Alexander, a Super who was obviously stronger and better trained.

"I always wondered how people became Agents," I admit. "They don't teach you in school, and there isn't an online application process."

"Agents are appointed," says Agent Scarlett with a wave of her hand. "Chosen. Not everyone can become an Agent. An Agent must see the bigger truths of the world. An Agent is special."

"When I become a real Agent, do I get to engineer battles and make up enemies too?" I ask, sitting at the edge of my seat. I let a glimmer enter my eye, like I'm excited. *Bury her deeper*, my mind hisses. *Engage public outrage.*

"Oh, the enemies are real," says Agent Scarlett with a wild glint in her eye, and for a second, I wonder about her sanity. "The enemy is chaos. Forget Supers, even Civvies fight against chaos. What do you think organized sports are for? Teenagers love games. False rivalries keep the mind occupied. Controlled outlets for violence and aggression."

"But some people *do* get hurt," I say, thinking of all the times Supers have broken bones, gotten burns, and ended up with concussions. I think of Gwen with her broken ribs. I remember my own stitches.

"If some people are hurt in the process of protecting the masses, don't you think it's worth it?" Agent Scarlett frowns. I keep my expression neutral and placate her with a nod. "Besides, we pay our people well."

"The Payton lawsuit?"

Agent Scarlett's smile goes mean. "Payton is a greedy fool. We paid him his weight in money for that little stunt. A bank robbery! Ha! Who robs a bank these days? Who dares? He signed a liability form. He knew there was a chance he would get hurt, and now he wants to be compensated further. He won't have it!"

"It sounds complicated."

Change it from the inside, Hitori's voice echoes.

"Don't you worry," says Agent Scarlett, "I'll take you under my wing personally. I am one of the most influential Agents in LOS. You should be honoured."

"I am," I say as humbly as I can. "Thank you."

"The mentor of the descendent of Frances E. Shaw," Agent Scarlett murmurs to herself. Her eyes go glassy for a moment. A small smile twitches at the edge of her lips. "I'll be remembered forever. I'll shape you into something great, Miss Bell. Just wait and see."

She sighs and leans back as though she just finished a marathon. The tinkling of piano keys fills the room.

"I wonder," I say cautiously, trying to sound airheaded and distracted, "if there are other ways of keeping Supers in line other than deception."

"Like asking them nicely?" Agent Scarlett snorts in derision. "What an innocent, foolish notion."

Her eyes go distant, and I wonder whether she's tried asking nicely before and whether it failed. She must have been a regular girl before she became an Agent. I wonder if she was bullied in the past. *Joanna*, Hitori called her. I try to see Joanna in Agent Scarlett, but I can't.

"What you told me makes a lot of sense," I say. "I think people would understand if you just explained it to them."

Agent Scarlett looks at me. She looks at me for a long moment. I begin to sweat. Did I go too far? Then she laughs.

"You're cute, Bell, and you're young. Once you're older, you'll realize the silliness of your words. There are good kids, yes, but the majority are bad. Give them leeway, and *they'll* be the criminals. Super criminals. Unstoppable. They need to be collared and leashed and trained. The earlier the better."

She leans over the desk. When she speaks again, her voice is quiet and deadly. "Do you understand, Miss Bell, how important LOS is? For this city. For the *world*?"

I nod.

"Do you really?"

I nod.

Agent Scarlett leans back and sighs. She opens her desk and pulls something out. It jangles. She looks at me.

"Then what's that in your pocket?"

It's like someone dumped a bucket of ice water over my head. I seize up. My body goes cold. I glance down. Ling's phone is glowing through my shirt. I swallow thickly.

"My cellphone," I say weakly. "I must be getting a call. Excuse me."

I reach into my pocket, but Agent Scarlett dives at me. She leaps right over her desk like a rabid animal.

"*Give it to me.*"

"No!" I push my chair backwards and topple over it. I crash to the floor, knocking the breath from my lungs. I clutch the cellphone to my chest and roll away. Agent Scarlett is on top of me, snarling. Her face is twisted in rage. I yell as her fingernails dig into my arm.

"Give it to me, you little brat." She claws at me. "What is it? A recording? Eavesdroppers?"

"*Get off me!*" I shriek. I kick at her. My toe makes contact. Agent Scarlett lets out an *ouf* and rolls to the side. I scramble to my feet and rush for the double doors. Something hooks my leg. I crash to the floor again. The cellphone bounces from my hands and comes to a rest several metres away. I reach for it, but Agent Scarlett drags me back. The carpet scratches against my skin. I kick again but hit nothing. Agent Scarlett lets out an enraged cry.

"Liar! You don't understand," she snarls. "No one understands! This is why I hate children. They lie, cheat, and steal. They think they know everything when they know nothing. Children need to sit down, shut up, and obey their elders!"

She brandishes the object she pulled from her desk. A pair of handcuffs. I wriggle as she tries to clamp one around my arm. She tries to pin me by leaning on my back, but I jerk my head back and knock her in the chin. She howls. I see stars.

"You're wrong!" I choke. "I do understand. I just don't agree with you."

My ears ring.

"LOS is important," Agent Scarlett roars. "You don't know what you're doing!"

My lungs are compressed. I can't breathe. I feel myself being dragged across the room. My eyes are on Ling's phone. I can see the number on its screen. Dad's number. I heave a dry laugh. He must be so worried. My bangs stick to my face.

"You foul child!" Agent Scarlett dives for my arm once again.

"No!" I shout, twisting away.

I'm not fast enough, and a cuff clicks closed around my wrist. I yank at it. It digs into my skin but doesn't give. She's chained me to her desk.

Agent Scarlett heaves a huge sigh and stands. She brushes off her jacket, fixes her hair, and rights her glasses. It takes her several moments to regain her composure. For a minute, all that sounds is our laboured breath, and the smatter of piano music.

"Well," she says breathlessly. "Aren't we *bad*? Aren't we sneaky? Sneaky children deserve to be punished!"

She walks over and picks up Ling's phone. The Sound Isolator app is open on the front screen. Agent Scarlett's nose wrinkles as though she smells something rotten. Without another word, she marches to her window and pops it open. The roar of wind overpowers the soothing classical music as she drops the phone out the window.

"No," I breathe as the phone spins away.

"What a pity," says Agent Scarlett. I can see her anger lurking just under her skin, in the too white gleam of her eyes and the thin line of her lips. "I liked you, Miss Bell. I saw a bit of me in you. You could have been great. Perhaps I was too sentimental. Too impatient for an heir, for someone to carry on my greatest work." Her face twists once more as she struggles for calm. "But I see now that I was mistaken. You're not special. You're nobody. You will never be anybody important."

She leans over her desk, looking weary. Then she opens her desk once more and removes a pistol. I stare at it, breathing hard. *Game over, Beata. No lives left.* I wonder how much it'll hurt, but she only strokes it like a cat. The motion seems to soothe her. Finally, she gives me a penetrating stare and marches out the room.

I'm left in the empty room, with only soothing classical music to accompany me. I want to curl up, but what good will it do? I messed up. It's all over now. *Forgive me*, I think. I imagine my mom and dad, their devastated faces when they realize I'm gone. *I tried.*

Tears crowd my vision. I slump against the desk. I stare at the double doors and await my fate.

Chapter 26

The Final Showdown

When the double doors open, Agent Scarlett walks in, followed by Alexander.

"Alexander," I say glumly. "We meet again."

"Finish her off, Alexander," orders Agent Scarlett, waving her hand at me as though I were a piece of garbage. "I suppose the headline will be more sensational this way, anyhow. Poor Miss Bell, the last of her bloodline. Only child. Great-granddaughter of the Original Super. Fallen to a new and vicious organization of anarchists bent on destroying justice."

People are funny, I think grimly. It would be so easy to give up, to write it all off as an adventure gone wrong and accept my failures. My body is ready for rest, but my mind rears up and roars. *Fight*, it commands. *Don't give up.*

"Don't do it, Alexander," I retort. "What would your sister say?"

"Yes, *think* about Amie," Agent Scarlett counters. "She's very sick, isn't she? Who else will manage her recovery? Who else has the expertise? A sick Super. Can you imagine? Only LOS has the equipment available to deal with her!"

"It's wrong!" I snap. "She's wrong! LOS is wrong!"

"It's not about right or wrong." Agent Scarlett circles around Alexander. "It's about numbers. Risk assessment. Which girl is worth more to you? Which one is worth sacrificing? Some snot-nosed kid or your last remaining family member?"

"There doesn't have to be a sacrifice," I argue, growing desperate. "*Please*, Alexander."

"Please, Alexander," mirrors Agent Scarlett, albeit much more calmly. She fixes him with a pointed look and pats him on the shoulder. "Being a hero means making difficult decisions. Choosing whom to save. Picking where to protect. You know what to do."

He's a polypower. I imagine his powers turned against me, and a wave of panic washes over me. I don't stand a chance. I can't imagine a better time than this to develop powers of my own. *Anything*, I beg the universe. It doesn't have to be fancy. I don't need to throw lightning, or even fly. Just something small. A passive power, maybe. Something to give me a fighting chance. But the universe is as cold and unmerciful as ever. I tug at my handcuffs, but all they do is jangle. So much for appearing brave.

"She's just a kid," Alexander mutters. His gaze stays on me. I'm not sure who his words are meant for.

"How many children do you think die for less than this?" Agent Scarlett says with a sniff. "Do it quickly. You're skilled enough to make it painless."

Alexander turns towards Agent Scarlett. "You never asked me to do anything like this before." His eyes dart to and fro, searching for something on her face. There's hesitation in his movements. "You told me she wouldn't be harmed."

"Circumstances have changed," Agent Scarlett says shortly.

Alexander stands there, looking unhappy.

"Don't worry. It won't go on your record. In fact, it'll be a great help to LOS. Espionage is an offence, you know. Miss Bell is a spy. A criminal. Do it nice and quick, just like ripping off a bandage. I'll take care of the rest."

Alexander's face falls. *He's hesitating.* I take a shaky breath and push my advantage.

"I know you, Alexander. You're a good person. Remember that one time you defended me from bullies? I really looked up to you then. I don't have a big brother, but if I did, I'd want him to be like you—"

"*Be quiet*," Agent Scarlett snaps. She waves the gun at me, and I clamp my mouth shut. Her face is livid. Hot spots of red colour her cheeks. "Alexander, think of who will suffer if you don't comply. I asked if you performed the necessary security measures. You said yes, but if that was true, why did I find a cellphone on her? You *lied* to me, *boy*." Agent Scarlett's face twists into a monstrous mass, but almost as quickly, her expression calms. Her voice becomes creamy. "But I'm a forgiving person. This is your chance to make it right."

I want to say more. Words brim in my throat, but I'm afraid. Agent Scarlett's gun is steady. She seems the sort of woman who knows how to use one. I stare at Alexander. Something hard enters his eyes. He steps away from Agent Scarlett and strides to her desk. He brushes his hand over it. I notice he doesn't wear gloves like Gwen does.

A strip of metal peels from the desk. He shapes it into a long, thin sabre. It gleams in the light.

"Close your eyes, Beata," he says, not looking at me.

I shake my head.

"Please." His voice is plaintive.

I bite back a sob and do as he says.

"Count to ten."

I clamp my eyes shut and begin to count, like I've done a million times before.

One…two…three…

I wonder when he'll strike. Will he wait the full ten seconds, or will he surprise me? Would it be faster if he surprised me?

Four…five…

A shift of air. Something moving. The scuffle of footsteps.

Six…seven…

It must be close now. I can still see the sabre's deadly point in my mind's eye. A shout interrupts my thoughts. It sounds like Agent Scarlett.

Eight…nine…

Silence.

Then—

A resounding *CRASH*. Glass breaking, falling to the floor. The room vibrates. My eyes snap open. The roar of wind fills the room. Cold air and damp blasts in, soaking the floor and walls. The windows have shattered, and everything is chaos. The lights blink furiously, then go out. Dark shapes bound to and fro. I spot Agent Scarlett's red hair, flashes of metal, a blur of gold. Frenzied clinks echo. A gun flies across the room.

"You *dare*," sounds a familiar voice. "*You dare.*"

A body hits the desk beside me. There's a flash of red. The desk shudders as a wall of metal sheaths us both.

The shield doesn't last long. A spark of blue weaves across its surface like lightning, and a strip of metal tears away from it. Beyond it floats a lithe form with hair like sunlight and shining emerald eyes.

"You dare threaten my friend!" roars Gweneira Kendricks. She looks like she flew through a tornado. Her lip is split, and her face is a marble mask of wrath. She gestures wildly, and the metal around her snaps into two long swords. She swings them over my head.

The body beside me ducks and swears. Alexander. I spot Agent Scarlett in the background, cowering by the double doors.

Gwen's metal swords smash through the desk above me, slicing it clean in half. Papers explode into the air. My handcuffs snap off with a defeated *clink*, and I roll wildly to get out of the way.

"Gwen!" I shout, but I don't think she hears me.

She steps after Alexander, her hands working into a frenzy. Alexander draws himself up. They crash into each other.

I've never seen two polypowers fight up close.

It's terrifying.

Flashes of red and blue dance across my vision. Silhouettes bound between the walls. Gwen levitates. She smashes through the fragile ceiling panels with her fist. Pipes spear downwards, piercing the floor. Alexander dances back, his initial surprise wearing off. He brushes each pipe with his fingertips as they pass. They melt around him. He moulds them into two sturdy shields.

Gwen sends a barrage of metal clippings his way. She floats through the room, metal streaming around her. She's not even creating shapes. Just lobs chunks of metal in Alexander's direction. They bounce off his shield, creating a ruckus so loud it hurts my head. With a frustrated sound, Alexander flings a shield towards her. Gwen tears through it like a tiger.

She charges forward and sinks her fingers into Alexander's remaining shield. It explode outwards, nothing but liquefied streams of silver. Alexander jumps back and grabs a filing cabinet. Records spill across the floor as the cabinet transforms into ropes of metal. They reach towards Gwen and wrap around her limbs. Gwen shoots him a withering look of disdain. In a flash of blue, the metal melts off her as though it's butter. She flexes. The molten mess erupts from her as a burst of spikes. Alexander dodges them.

Gwen chants something under her breath. I can barely hear her over the wind of the city. "Kill you," she whispers. "Kill you, kill you killyou*killyou*."

A gale rips at my hair and clothes, and I'm suddenly reminded that I'm in a skyscraper. Debris from the fight spills from the office and into open air. The room shakes with the effort of battle. I want to grab something, but everything around me is shifting, melting, changing—

Clinkclinkclinkclink, goes the shrapnel. Gwen runs off sheer anger. I've never seen her fight like this, all sharp angles and quick movements and vicious, hot fury. Her fingers and hands are in such motion they seem a blur. I realize, suddenly, that her television persona is always holding back, always looking elegant and beautiful for the cameras. Now she acts not for the cameras but from killer intent. It's all Alexander can do to fend her off.

I told him once that Gwen would hunt him down. I realize with horror that I was right. Till now, I doubted how she would fare against Alexander. A shimmer of shame bubbles up in me, then a spike of fear. Gwen looks wild, like a cornered animal. I scramble to my knees. A metal sheet flies above me, and I dive to the floor once more.

"Stop!" I scream into the chaos. "Gwen, stop! Alexander! Stop! You'll hurt each other!"

Gwen lets out a yell. It's more of a howl.

"*This is your fault.*" She spins metal around her, streams of it. "You and your Counter-League! LOS and its conspiracies! I'll destroy you all! You're all poisonous! If I'm going down, I'm taking you with me!"

She shoves the metal away from her, forming beams midair. She throws them like javelins. Alexander barely dodges one. He holds out his hands as though to defend himself. Another beam flies by him. He grabs it in mid-air and winces. I can see pain in his face. He spins it into another shield.

"Gwen," I plead. "Stop! You're going after the wrong person!"

Alexander was about to end you, my mind whispers poisonously. Why not let her take him down? Why not eliminate a threat?

Because it's wrong, another part of my mind, a clearer part, chimes. *Because it would destroy her too.*

A Super doesn't hurt others. A Super is supposed to stand for justice.

Gwen lifts the final filing cabinet like a hammer and shapes it into a solid beam. She swings down. It hits Alexander's shield with enough force to shake the room. Panels shake from the ceiling. I can hear glass shattering further down the building. I'm afraid the entire floor might collapse.

I get to my feet. A stinging pain erupts in my cheek. Shrapnel clatters around me. I cover my face and push forward. Pieces of metal fly by me. They tear into my shirt, my pants, my arms. I feel cuts open on my skin.

Gwen lifts her beam once more and brings it down with all her might. There's no finesse in her movement, only brute force. Alexander's shield dents and cracks. He lets it go and dives for cover, but Gwen is ready.

She kicks a panel at him. It bowls him over and smashes him into the wall.

I hear something crunch. Alexander grunts in pain and collapses onto his knees.

Gwen lifts her beam once more.

I leap for her legs.

I grab and squeeze just as she's about to bring her beam down. She wobbles in mid-air and drops it instead. It *clangs* to the floor with enough force to dent it. It misses Alexander by a hair. Her head swivels down, and for a moment, all I see is rage. Then a flicker of recognition.

"Bea?" she breathes.

"*Listen to me,*" I beg her. "Please, Gwen. You need to calm down!"

"Calm down?" She huffs a breath. "My life is upside-down, Beata. What have I worked for all this time? What have I stood for? My life is a sham! It's all a joke! I've been chased and attacked by my own people. I'm a traitor, apparently, to be hunted like a criminal! After all I've done, this is what I get?"

"It's not fair. I know!" I feel blood seep into my clothes. Gwen is covered in cuts. She must be working off pure adrenaline. "But, please, you have to stop."

"He's a villain," Gwen says, turning back to Alexander, who huddles by the wall, clutching his arm. A trickle of blood meanders from his temple. "He's nobody. If it weren't for his intervention, everything would be absolutely fine."

"Then you'd still be living in a lie, Gwen."

"Ignorance is bliss," Gwen whispers bitterly. "It's better than *this*. Let me have my revenge. Let me go, Bea!"

"If you want revenge, direct it at *her*." I let go of Gwen's legs and point at Agent Scarlett, whose mouth falls into a stunned O. She looks at us, then looks at the open window. Seeing no way out, she grabs a nearby paperweight. It's a futile and pitiful gesture. "She's the grand master. The orchestrator. She's the one who made LOS what it is. Leave Alexander alone! He doesn't want this any more than you."

Good luck, he said. Now I think I understand why. His hands were tied, but mine were free. He was asking something of me. Depending on me.

"Agent Scarlett," Gwen says. She lands. Shrapnel crunches under her feet and glass digs into her heels, but she doesn't seem to notice. "I trusted you."

Agent Scarlett arranges her face into one of compassion.

"You can still trust me," she says, silky smooth, opening her arms. Her suit is ruined, and so is her hair. It falls around her face in sprawling strands. "I can make it right, Gweneira. My star."

"You betrayed *me*," thunders Gwen. "You betrayed all of us! Every citizen. Every Super. Everyone who ever believed in you. LOS will never recover from this!"

"Gweneira," says Agent Scarlett, her voice like honey. "You poor girl, let—"

"Give me my years back," Gwen hisses. Agent Scarlett's eyes go wide.

"What?"

"Give me my years back." I can see tears in Gwen's eyes. "Give me my childhood. Give me my time. All those years I've worked for you, for the city, for everyone who lives in it. I sweated, and bled, and tried my best. Where is my happy ending, Agent? What was it all for?"

"The safety of the city," Agent Scarlett says.

"You still believe that?" Gwen asks, stony cold. "You sell us out to sponsors and make us fight like dogs. And you *still* believe that?"

She takes a step forward. Agent Scarlett shrinks back.

"Justify it all you want," Gwen continues. "Believe you're doing it for the greater good. But I know the truth. You don't care about anybody or anything other than yourself. You think the world is your playground, but let me tell you this, *Agent*. We are not your playthings. We are not entertainment! We are living, breathing *people*."

She raises a hand. Metal spins up her arm and shapes into a drill. She points it at Agent Scarlett. Her face goes blank.

"Goodbye, Agent. I wish I had never met you."

Icy dread rushes through me. I grab her arm. Gwen is stronger than I am. She barely budges.

"No," I hiss into her ear. "Gwen. You'll never recover if you go through with this. You'll never forgive yourself! A Super is supposed to protect the weak, right? Look at her, Gwen. She's weak. You're strong. You've *won*. It's over."

Gwen's cheeks are wet with tears. Still, she doesn't budge.

"And look at me," I continue. "I'm ok. You got to me in time. You're still a hero, Gwen. You're *my* hero."

"What was it all for, Beata?" Gwen whispers.

"Lower your arm."

A tremble runs through her. I know she must be tired. I'm tired too. I'm drained to the core. My legs are shaking, and my head is abuzz.

"Please." I rest my head in the crook of her shoulder. I can feel her heartbeat, wild and fast. I wrap my other arm around her shoulders. "Let's go to the Ice Cream Emporium together. They'll have a weird new flavour by now. We can chill and talk about nothing—the weather, the latest fashion, whatever. You know Ling will chat our ears off, but we'll listen anyways. The Sound Isolator app still needs tweaking. I need you to fly over the streets and do some test runs for me. Let's do all that together. Let's go home, Gwen."

Gwen trembles all over now. My legs are too weak. I'll fall over if I let go, so I don't. It's all I can do to stay conscious. *Please*, I think. Seconds go by. I don't bother to count them. I just hang on. *Please let go, Gwen.*

"I'm sorry I yelled at you before, at Nu's place," I say. "I wasn't being fair. I know how hard you work. I know you're watching out for me. Let me make it up to you. Let me treat you to ice cream. Come on, Gwen. Say ok. Say we'll hang out again."

Another shudder goes through her body. I'm sure she's as tired as me. Maybe even more.

"Gwen," I repeat. "Let me apologize properly."

For a moment, we're a scene frozen in time. Only the soft plash of rainwater sounds outside. The lonesome wind blows through the devastated office, rustling loose papers. My limbs begin to go numb. *Please, Gwen.*

Finally, she answers.

"Ok," she says. Her voice is smaller than I've ever heard it. She sounds young and scared—and overwhelmed. "Ok, Beata. Let's go home."

She lets the drill drop to the ground with a loud *clang*. It rolls haplessly to the side, a mere chunk of metal. I can't help it. I laugh breathlessly into her shoulder. It's over. It really is over. I sink to my knees, spent. Everything hurts. Even drawing breath hurts. I feel like a rag, wrung and spun and thrown to the ground.

Suddenly, the room floods with light. I muster the energy to shield my eyes. I squint against the brightness.

The sight that meets my eyes is almost too unbelievable to be real.

Floating outside the broken room, hoisting a floodlight, is Dieter. On his back, balanced precariously, is Ling. In her right hand is a large camera. A red light blinking in its corner tells me it's rolling live. In her left, she holds Nuha's cellphone. I can see the orange interface of the Sound Isolator app blinking in the night. Ling wears an expression of pure triumph.

"Breaking news," she declares. "Live from Toronto's Harbourfront."

Then behind Dieter and Ling, rise a half dozen news helicopters. More floodlights join Ling's. The wind whipped up by their blades tosses Gwen's hair back. As though by instinct, she throws back her shoulders—defiant. A Super to the very end. Camera flashes go off.

I feel Gwen's hand slip under my arm. She carefully pulls me to my feet. I fall against her, a deadweight. She braces against me. Propped against each other, we face the lights together.

Epilogue

It's a windless day. The pond is still. Trees stand naked against a piercing blue sky. In the distance, ducks leave little Vs as they glide through the water, quacking.

After the LOS debacle was revealed on air, the government launched an official inquiry into the organization. They declared a temporary suspension of LOS, with exception of a select few emergency divisions. Agent Scarlett is detained and awaiting trial. They are currently selecting her jury. Many of her associates, high-ranking Agents who perpetuated the Super farce, are also detained for questioning.

I spot a shock of golden hair, a figure seated on a bench near the pond. I approach.

"It's the new sauerkraut and ham ice cream," I say, holding out a cone. As always, the Ice Cream Emporium prides itself in its versatility.

"Thank you," says Gwen, taking it with the same grace and style that made her so beloved as a Super. It's been a month since LOS's downfall, and most of her cuts have healed. She still moves gingerly, however, as though she's aged. She takes a lick.

"How is it?"

"Odd," she says, and scoots over on the bench. "Sit."

I seat myself. The autumn wind shifts. A newspaper scuttles across the ground. I can read its headline. *LOS CONSPIRACY. THE SHOCKING TRUTH EMERGES.* On it, is a picture of Gwen and me, looking haggard against the light, two survivors in the broken room, and Agent Scarlett's white face, staring from a corner.

It took Ling and Nuha a good half hour to realize I was missing. It took Ling another half hour to realize her phone was gone. Soon afterwards, Nuha received my text. Two words:

Start broadcasting.

Nuha opened the Sound Isolator app and noticed I was streaming. They upped the volume and began streaming it live. Over the Internet. Over the airwaves. Stations began to take notice. Small stations picked it up. Then larger ones. Agent Scarlett's words rang over the city, revealing LOS's inner workings, spreading from broadcast to broadcast like ripples on a pond. Ling was right. There's nothing more powerful than a live broadcast. The world finally listened. It finally believed.

By the time Agent Scarlett found me out and discarded Ling's phone, Ling was already on the way to the Scotia-Rogers Tower. And so was Gwen. Having heard our conversation over the airwaves, she had cut a wide U-turn across the city and gunned straight for the office building. Ling and Dieter arrived first and had barely settled on the roof of a nearby building when Gwen stormed the scene. As such, Ling managed to grab a dark and shaky rendition of Gwen and Alexander's battle. The only one in existence.

There was an uproar as parents demanded their Super children be released from LOS's grip. Lawsuits sprang up right and left from former Supers who felt used. Big sponsors withdrew their support. Small sponsors left too. LOS is currently saddled with the class-action lawsuit of the century, and their popularity is at an all-time low.

Gwen pulls out something from her pocket. It gleams in the light. A gold pocket watch. On one side is the entire night sky, etched with fine precision, all the stars and constellations. On the other, a fine clock face. She holds it up to the light and turns it around carefully, so that the dying sun hits every facet.

"It looks good," I say.

After LOS's downfall, Gwen took a hiatus from Super work. With a slashed budget and many members under investigation, LOS runs on a skeleton crew of employees, many of whom were ignorant of the Agents' conspiracy, and continue to work despite severe pay cuts. "It might not be much," a representative had said during an interview, "but we're trying to make things right again." Many companies are opening their doors to jobless Supers, offering apprenticeships in construction, investigational work, and wildlife protection, just to name a few. As predicted by Agent Scarlett, some Supers went on crime sprees, but others also stepped in to stop them. Nothing's collapsed into chaos—at least not yet.

Gwen picked up work at a local watchmaker's, dealing in antiques and valuables. She says it helps her take her mind off things—and helps hone her gift. *It's one thing to make metal swords*, she told me. *It's another to make art.*

She's also taken up sculpting, photography, violin, Japanese, German, and Spanish. In her words, she needs the distractions.

"It's yours," Gwen says, dropping the watch into my hand. "Keep it. As a token of my thanks."

"You've thanked me enough, Gwen."

She really has. I don't think there has been a conversation where she didn't thank me.

"I can never thank you enough," she murmurs, casting her eyes over the pond. She gets a faraway look. She gets that look often now, like she's gazing at something in the distance. It's contemplative—and a little sad.

I don't know what to say to that, so I just sit beside her and breathe the crisp air. Sometimes, the silence already says everything.

LOS headquarters looks smaller without the floodlights. The building was badly damage during the Super battle, and much of the damage has yet to be repaired. The hole in the wall where I crashed the robot octopod is still open. Volunteers have covered it in tarp so the insides don't flood during rainstorms. Seeing it makes my cheeks burn with mortification—and also fills me with an odd sense of pride.

I visit Alexander.

The guard nods to me as I pass, almost in reverence. I've gained some fame after the LOS incident. Miss Beata Bell, descendent of the Original Super, downfall of LOS. I have to say I'm not enjoying the attention as much as I thought I would.

They built a cell especially for him. It's a cylindrical room of pure glass. There's no hint of metal anywhere. Even the intercom that allows us to communicate is made of plastic.

Today, he's leaned against the wall, staring into the distance, arm is wrapped in a cast. His diagnoses: a shattered humerus, a nasty concussion, a dozen stitches on his temple. He doesn't notice me when I walk in. I beep the intercom on the wall.

"Hey, Alexander."

At first he doesn't move.

Then—

"Hey, Miss Bell."

"How are you today?"

"As good as I'll ever get, I suppose."

After LOS's downfall, they arrested Alexander. He is to be detained until he is proven innocent of wrongdoing. Until his trial, he is stuck inside the cell and guarded day and night. I spot an armed soldier patrolling the perimeter.

"They have orders to take me out if I escape," says Alexander, noticing my gaze. "They'll turn me to Swiss cheese if I even try. They've been *very* clear on that front."

"How charming."

"Just so you know," he says. "I was never going to hurt you that night. I made a decision then, in that room, that I wouldn't follow Agent Scarlett's orders anymore, that if I had to make a sacrifice, I would sacrifice *her*. I didn't want you to see the mess, Beata. You're just a kid, after all."

"Thanks," I say, feeling awkward. It seems I never know what to say around him.

"I suppose I should be grateful," he says, turning towards me. "Without you, I would have never broken free. My sister and I—" He pauses. "After the broadcast, people came forward. Like you wouldn't believe, Miss Bell. Thousands of sympathizers, all trying to help. Amie's a special case. A girl who can knock people unconscious with her headaches isn't someone any old hospital can handle. I have regular people donating money for research. I have doctors from Germany and China offering their expertise. They could have been petty. They could have been vengeful. I caused a lot of trouble. But they chose to be kind."

I nod. "I'm glad."

I really mean it. My chest fills with emotion. I haven't met his sister, Amie, yet, but she sent me a card soon after LOS's downfall, thanking me for stopping Gwen. *It's thanks to you,* she wrote, *that I still have a big brother.* I want to meet her one day.

"When is your trial?" I ask.

"It's been postponed," he says. "They say it'll be in two weeks."

"I'll be there to testify," I say fiercely. "I'll make sure everyone knows you're not a bad guy."

"I don't know." Alexander grins. "I did kidnap you."

"And I stole a weapon of mass destruction and caused extraordinary property damage," I say, thinking of the robot octopod. "So why aren't I behind bars?"

"'Cause you're a hero," he says easily.

"Am I really, though?" I give him a pointed stare.

"Let's not argue semantics," he says, and I can't help but grin.

The guard pokes his head in and clears his throat apologetically. I wave at him. My time is up. I bid farewell to Alexander and promise to drop by again in a few days. My life is busy now that I'm famous. Reporters flock to my door. They want pictures and statements. They want me to sign their clipboards. I deal with them with tempered patience, all nods and appreciative glances and elegant movements. It's gratifying, and exhausting, work.

Sir Frederick Banting fired the entity known as Mr. Uzune upon learning he was a fraud. They tried to hire the great Hitori Yuuma in his stead. Imagine! One of the world's most famous Supers, working in their classrooms! But it was too late. He had already moved on to bigger things.

"I was contacted by government officials the other day. They want me to help rebuild LOS," Hitori tells me as we sit in a local café, sipping a black coffee and hot chocolate, respectively. "As the most famous name they have, they thought it appropriate to recruit me. They're practically throwing benefits at my feet. As much vacation time as I want. A staff all of my own choosing. Administrative freedom. A fat paycheque."

"That's great," I say. "Change it from the inside! You *are* taking the position, aren't you?"

Hitori shrugs, but I can see the excitement in his eyes. "As much as I've had enough of LOS, it seems I can't get away from it. Maybe it's fate."

"Maybe it's for the best."

Hitori lays a hand on my shoulder and squeezes warmly.

"When I get the position, what would you say to becoming my helper?" His eyes twinkle. "I know you're a little young, but in a few years, when you're legally able to work—"

"Say nothing more," I declare. "I'll do it. You know, that's the second time I've been asked to work at LOS."

"Hopefully, under happier circumstances?"

I grin. "Much happier circumstances."

We shake on it.

I'm grounded for a month for sneaking out and disobeying direct orders. I don't get access to any electronics, so the Sound Isolator and Super Tracker apps sit unfinished on my desk. I get letters from companies expressing their interest, both in helping me fine-tune the apps and in purchasing the rights to them. I politely decline them all. For now.

Despite being grounded, Mom and Dad cook my favourite mac and cheese every day until I'm sick of it.

Life goes back to normal, with a few small changes. I wake up in the morning, wash my face, eat my breakfast, and go to school. I hang out with Ling and Nuha during recess. We climb the jungle gyms. We play with programming. With talk about mundane subjects, like the weather, the latest movies, and homework. It's relaxing. It's good. Sometimes, I pass Dieter in the hallways. We'll nod to one another with newfound respect. We have a new teacher, Miss Ndiaye, who is young and bubbly. She's no Mr. Uzune, but I like her well enough.

Sometimes, I pick up the photo of Frances E. Shaw, the one where she's positioned with the Royal Air Force, looking young and small. Before, I could only see Frances Fantastic, the Original Super. Now, I see more. Beyond the fame, she was just a girl. Just like me. She felt pressure, and anxiety, and hurt, and love. I see parts of me in her, in the slant of her nose and the shape of her cheekbones. I gaze at it for some time, then place it carefully on my desk. I wonder if we would have gotten along. I wish I could speak to her. Maybe I'll never achieve her level of fame. Maybe I won't be as powerful. Maybe I'll never become a Super.

But Frances, I think, warmth flooding my chest, *somehow, I think I'm ok with that.*

Then I lie down and pick up my Rubik's Cube. *Click, click, click.* I watch the colours spin as the orange sun sets over the horizon.

Everything falls into place.